Praise for BITTERSWEET

"With finely tuned characters, Freddie Lee Johnson III effectively harmonizes the varied strains of an African American family and proves that, when it comes to the black male voice, he's got perfect pitch."

—CHRIS BENSON, author of *Special Interest*

"A tender, touching, sometimes achingly painful, and sometimes humorous testament to the power of love between black brothers and the women they love."

—*Detroit Free Press*

"[A] SASSY DEBUT—A TREATISE ON DIVORCE, TEMPTATION, AND FAITH . . . In alternating chapters that bear each brother's name, *Bittersweet* weaves true-life narrative that's written mano a mano, and is also highly entertaining."

—*Black Issues Book Review*

"A book to curl up with . . . An appealing tale of sibling rivalry and revelry from a man's perspective."

—*Essence*

Praise for A MAN FINDS HIS WAY

"Collins is an intelligent, well-drawn protagonist with believable strengths and flaws . . . a thoughtful take on some tough contemporary issues in job politics and race relations."

—*Publishers Weekly*

ALSO BY FREDDIE LEE JOHNSON III

Bittersweet

A Man Finds His Way

OTHER MEN'S
WIVES

OTHER MEN'S WIVES

A NOVEL

Freddie Lee Johnson III

One World
Ballantine Books • New York

A One World Books Trade Paperback Original

Copyright © 2005 by Freddie Lee Johnson III

*Published in the United States by One World Books,
an imprint of The Random House Publishing Group,
a division of Random House, Inc., New York.*

*One World is a registered trademark, and the
One World colophon is a trademark of Random House, Inc.*

Library of Congress Cataloging-in-Publication Data

Johnson, Freddie Lee.
Other men's wives : a novel / Freddie Lee Johnson
p. cm.
ISBN 0-345-44601-1
1. African American men—Fiction. 2. Married people—Fiction.
3. Adultery—Fiction. 4. Revenge—Fiction. I. Title.
PS3610.O34O87 2005
813'.6—dc22   2004063610

Printed in the United States of America

www.oneworldbooks.net

9 8 7 6 5 4 3 2 1

First Edition

Text design by Meryl Sussman Levavi

Dedicated to Freddie L. Johnson Jr.
My Father, the Undaunted One who
taught me life lessons anyway

"Let's make us medicine of our great revenge,
to cure this deadly grief."

SHAKESPEARE, *Macbeth*

"'Vengeance is mine; I will repay,'
says the Lord."

ROMANS 12:19

Acknowledgments

The joy of writing this book was enhanced by all the people who encouraged, guided, challenged, and laughed with me along the way. To my agent Peter Miller of PMA Literary & Film Management, Inc., I express many thanks for his unwavering support, direction, and efforts to help me and my writing always get better (Roars to you, Peter!). The friendship, sharp wit, formidable intelligence, and consistently accurate suggestions from Anita Diggs were of immeasurable value. I thank Pershail Young for valiantly enduring me through several drafts of this work. To my fellow historian, novelist, and colleague Dr. Albert Bell Jr., I send my deepest gratitude for his stellar example of fortitude, proving that it is indeed possible to love history and novel writing with equally great passion. To my fellow historians in the Hope College History Department, thanks for celebrating my works of fiction as enthusiastically as has been the celebration of my works of fact. Many warm thanks go to Peter Schakel and my colleagues in the Hope College English Department for their welcoming me into their midst as an "honorary member." A special thanks to Dr. Jennifer Young whose love of words, warm smile, and big heart encouraged a brother to come in from the cold. I am thoroughly grateful for the steady, guiding hand of my editor, Melody Guy, whose calm focus and gentle approach injected sanity into my frenetic moments. For Monica Harris Mindolovich I express admiration for her refusal to let me off the hook until the work was as good as it could get. To Rev. Dr. Ronald J. Fowler, Rev. Dr. Clifton Rhodes Jr., and my respective church families at Arlington Church of God in Akron, Ohio, and Messiah Missionary Baptist Church in Grand Rapids, Michigan, I offer my most heartfelt love and thanks for embracing me and my work, praying for my success, and reassuring me that the words I've written have had an impact. To Janice Noel, thanks for the awesome steadfastness you've shown, being a living miracle in my presence. Most of all and from the bottom of my soul, I thank God, Master of the Universe and the Great I Am, who has given me the privilege of helping to get His work done.

OTHER MEN'S WIVES

ONE

Today's Wednesday, and it's our wedding anniversary. It's been five years since Sierra Darcelle Montague agreed to marry me, Denmark Vesey Wheeler, a battle-hardened street warrior from one of Cleveland, Ohio's most dangerous neighborhoods. I'm still amazed that my beautiful uptown princess said "Yes!" she'd spend her life with me, but she did, and made me the happiest man in the world. So whenever our anniversary rolls around, I always do something extra special to show her how much I love and cherish her. That's why I got up this morning at 4:15 instead of my usual 5:00 to run three miles. I wanted to be back early enough to wash up and surprise Sierra with breakfast in bed.

I step back and admire my preparations. The tray's sitting on a large white marble-topped island in our kitchen. Along with a rose in the vase on the tray, there's a small bowl filled with cantaloupe, strawberries, grapes, and passion fruit; three strips of turkey bacon cooked to the exact crispness Sierra likes; a slice of wheat toast, both sides lightly buttered; Sierra's favorite blend of Colombian mocha decaf coffee (when Felipe at Café Nuevo told me that he'd run out, I got on the turnpike and drove like a madman for two and a half hours from Cleveland to get some from his other store in Pittsburgh); and a small bowl of raisin bran with a cup of soy milk on the side.

This breakfast wouldn't satisfy me. I'd prefer a big bowl of grits, three sizzling pieces of scrapple, scrambled eggs with cheese, and a big mug of caffeine-rich Maxwell House. But forget my tastes. This is the food that Sierra likes, and I'm glad to fix it for her.

I glance at the big green digital numbers on the stove's clock. 6:22 a.m. It's time to get moving.

"She's going to love this," I say softly to myself.

I've got a whole day of sweet surprises planned for my baby. I've even maxed out a credit card to make sure that this anniversary is one she *never* forgets.

I won't start tripping about how it seems just like yesterday when we said our vows, but my love for Sierra has only gotten stronger in the past five years. I'd dated lots of talented, beautiful, smart, and accomplished women, but *none* of them could compare with her. Like a ray of light splitting the darkness, she stepped into my life.

Some nights when Sierra's lying in my arms and snuggled up against my chest, I look at her and relish the peace she's brought me. No matter how deeply she's sleeping, she'll stir and snuggle closer.

I pick up the tray, step off briskly for our bedroom, and review the things I need to accomplish before this evening. Tonight when Sierra and I get together I don't want any work-related Speed Shift Auto Parts business distracting my thoughts from her. So I'm going to stop in at work and see how things are going.

After that, I need to double-check with the travel agent about the party I'm throwing for Sierra in a few days at the luxurious Vegas hotel where we had our first date. Coordinating to get her family and friends to arrive there before us took some doing, but it'll be worth the effort to see the smile on Sierra's lovely face. It'll be even better the morning after the party, when I tell her that we're flying to Hawaii. Sierra's visited some of the best vacation spots on earth, but she's never been to Oahu. For her, it'll be a thrill. For me, it's a miracle, especially after growing up in the Brownfield District.

My last task will be handled when I meet the guys—Harry Bancroft and Gordon Wilhite—for breakfast down at our favorite greasy spoon, the Hog Jowls restaurant. I haven't seen them for a while, so it'll be good to catch up. We'll also need to discuss finding a fourth person to run with us in the 4 × 100 relay in this year's Greater Cleveland Community Sports Challenge. It's only a few weeks away, so we'll have to find someone quick. Last year, Harry's dud brother-in-law ran with us, and he was a disaster. Another good friend of mine, Mason Booker, owner and operator of the Second Shadow Enterprises private detective agency, had been training with us but had to stop with apologies when he ended up with the good problem of having too much business.

I end my list as I step quietly through the living room on my way toward the stairs leading up to the bedroom and Sierra. The stonework in the fireplace catches my eye, and I once again admire the skill of the contractor who did the job. That part of the living room remodeling project was a hassle, mostly because Sierra kept changing her mind. She'd worn the contractor's nerves thin, and mine weren't much better, trying to deal with the stress of watching our budget hemorrhage with each modification. But I'd promised Sierra a remodeled living room and fireplace for her birthday and meant to see it through to the end.

The contractor saw things differently, which explains why the fifth time Sierra called him he said: "Not on your life, lady!

I've already wasted too much time on this fiasco. The plans stay the same!"

Sierra called me at work and had barely hung up before I was dialing that sucker. I appreciated his frustration, but he had to understand that I wasn't letting him disrespect my wife. When he got nasty with me, I knew we had to have a heart-to-heart talk. At dawn the next morning, when he pulled up to the trailer that was his office, I was waiting in the shadows. Twenty minutes later he was on the phone, trembling and talking through a bleeding lip as he apologized to my baby. He not only made the changes she wanted but did the work for *free*.

I ease quietly into our bedroom and stop, taking a moment to savor Sierra's loveliness as she lies on her side, sleeping like an ebony angel. Soft rays of bluish purple light cut through our partially open vertical blinds, stretching across Sierra, blending with her smooth, dark skin into a wonderful portrait. Her shoulder-length hair swirls over her head, the soft unruly strands melding into chaotic beauty. The peach-colored satin sheet clings to her, rising along the smooth arch of her hip and dipping back into the tight curve of her waist. The soft morning light, the peach linen, Sierra's dark skin, and her shiny hair combine into making my sweetheart look like a goddess.

I tiptoe over, set the tray on the nightstand, and sit quietly down on the edge of the bed beside Sierra. She stirs and rolls onto her back. I kiss her cheek, wrap my arms around her, and cradle her close, rubbing my nose against hers.

"Hey, sleepyhead," I say softly.

She smiles. I kiss her lips, eyes, forehead, and cheeks; the tip of her nose; and then her lips again. "I love you," I say.

Her eyes crease open. "I love you too."

"What right thing did I do to deserve you?" I ask, pulling her close and rubbing my cheek against hers.

She massages the back of my neck. "You loved me with all your heart and made me your one and only."

"I do love you, Sierra, with all my heart and strength." I kiss her neck and hug her tight. "And you'll always be my one and only."

She sighs sweetly. "I thank God for you."

God is one of those areas where Sierra and I struggle. For her, God is an omnipresent deity, possessing boundless love, power, and glory. For me, He's a lazy pot-smoking bum who's been laughing Himself silly while watching humanity stumble through a house that was on fire the day He created it.

I grew up in a household with a God-fearing mother and a Bible-thumping father. When crisis came, all their worship, prayers, and faith couldn't move God to act in our defense, so I ditched Him just like he'd done us.

"Happy fifth anniversary, darling wife," I say.

"And happy anniversary to you, darling husband."

I set the breakfast tray down in front of her. "Have some breakfast."

Sierra's eyes widen with delight. "Denmark, this looks fabulous," she says. She sniffs the rose and smiles. "Thank you, honey. Everything's just the way I like it."

I watch in satisfied silence as she closes her eyes, says a quick prayer, then tastes a spoonful of the fruit salad. "This is delicious."

I pull a lilac-scented card and envelope from my robe pocket and hand it to her. She swallows a bite of turkey bacon, cleans her fingers with a napkin, takes the card, and reads it. Her eyes mist over as she reads down each line.

She sets the tray off to the side and opens her arms wide. "Come here."

I lean over and into her embrace, wrapping my arms around her as she encircles me with hers. "You feel so good," I say.

I've never found the words to describe for Sierra the way electricity bolts through me every time I hold her. I don't know how to explain the heat that spreads through me, or the sudden dryness in my mouth. Every part of me wants to get close and love her in all the delicious ways I know how. But my baby's not an adventurous lover, preferring the tried-and-true, achingly predictable and prudish missionary style. At least she's never been stingy.

Sierra reaches inside my robe and rubs along the contours of my solid wide chest. I slip my forefinger beneath the spaghetti strap of her lavender silk gown, moving it out of the way as I kiss her shoulder. I lick along its roundness, kissing from her shoulder to her neck and back, moving my hand along her flat stomach up to her breasts. She sighs, lies back, and pulls me toward her. I stretch out beside her, kissing her tenderly and rubbing my hand back and forth along her thigh, caressing her behind, and then moving along her stomach and down to her lavender silk panties. She lifts up slightly, giving me room to pull them off, and then she helps undress me. I move over her and slowly lower myself into her passion, uniting us in the ancient ritual.

Sierra bites her lower lip and closes her eyes tight, her nostrils flaring with each inhaled breath. She wraps her legs tight around me, locking her ankles together behind my butt and pulling me deeper. I change up my movements, stroking her high then low, straight in and out, and then in deeply plunging circles, trying my best to add a little spice to our dry-as-dust routine.

Sierra moans and presses her thighs in on me, tightening her love crevasse. It feels good—*so very good*!—and the tingling in my stiffness builds into a riot of bliss.

"Oooh!" Sierra moans.

I grunt my agreement, my thoughts and speech muzzled by the thrill spreading through me. Sierra's eyes are still squeezed shut as she trembles beneath me.

We hold on to each other, exchanging light kisses and soft laughter. "You're a beast," Sierra whispers.

I answer with a playful growl, and we laugh. "I'm the beast you tamed," I say.

She looks deep into my eyes, strokes my cheek, and smiles softly. I stare back and am startled by a shadow that quickly passes over her face. We talk quietly a little longer, eventually releasing each other and straightening up. Sierra eats more of her breakfast, mostly the fruit salad and cereal, since everything else has gotten cold.

"So what are your plans for today?" I ask, standing in front of the mirror and brushing my hair.

Sierra sighs. "The first thing I'm going to do is stop by Amos's and see how my wild nephew's doing. It's only a few more weeks before his trial, and I want to be there."

I listen while keeping my tightened jaws shut. Amos is Sierra's brother, who, quite frankly, I can do without. Yarborough, his twenty-two-year-old crackhead son and my nephew by marriage, might end up doing hard time for stupidly attempting to rob a convenience store last month.

Sierra laughed it off when I first mentioned that Yarborough had a drug problem. But I'd seen enough junkies in the Brownfield District to know when somebody was strung out, and Yarborough was *way* out. He kept hitting up the family for money to score drugs, but he stayed clear of me. I was on to his game, so he knew there was no point in trying to scam me. The rest of his family was finally shocked out of their denial the evening his mug shot showed up on the six o'clock news.

Family wealth and connections got him out on bail, but he's up to his old tricks. He's already called twice asking for money. I answered both times, so it was a short conversation. I don't know if he's contacted Sierra, but if he has, and she's given in to him, we'll have to talk about that.

Sierra continues, saying, "Then I've got to give City Council a presentation on the costs of revitalizing Public Square, and see if I can generate some interest in the architect's conference I'm organizing."

"Why does Public Square need revitalizing? That's a Cleveland landmark and a main attraction."

"Yes, it is. But City Council wants it to have more of a high-tech look. That means redesigning the buildings to represent Cleveland's boldly stepping into the twenty-first century."

I sit down in the reading chair near Sierra and lean forward, elbows on knees. "Well, baby. Whatever it costs, your firm couldn't have found anyone more talented or capable to be the project's lead architect."

She smiles and extends her hand to me. I take it and kiss her palm. "You don't have to go in today."

She chuckles. "Of course I do. I told you that I have a presentation. Don't worry," she says, lowering her voice into a husky, sexier region. "I'll be home in plenty of time for us to finish celebrating."

I squeeze her hand. "I know you'll be home in time. I've got it all arranged."

Sierra frowns again, not just puzzled this time but concerned. "Denmark, what are you talking about?"

My smile gets bigger as I explain. "I called your firm *and* City Hall and explained to them both that today was your anniversary, and that your husband would be grateful if your presentation was moved to the end of next week. I next spoke with Brad Langley, and he said . . ."

"You spoke to my boss?"

"I sure did," I answer, nodding. "And he said it would be no problem. He also said that he'd been debating whether or not to push the meeting back a week so that everyone would have more time to prepare. He also said that he wished he'd been as diligent about remembering *his* anniversary."

Sierra laughs. "No kidding. Brad forgot his anniversary two months ago, and Courtney's still got him sleeping on the couch."

We laugh, and Sierra comes and sits in my lap, wrapping her arms around my neck. "You must've been pretty persuasive. Brad assigned me full duties to coordinate the conference, since he's so swamped with work."

I shrug indifferently. "But isn't that why he's paid the big bucks?"

"Yes. And it's also why he has the authority to dump his work onto me," she notes, frowning slightly.

"Forget Brad. Forget the firm. Forget the presentation and the conference," I gently order. "You've got the day off, but you're not going to spend it lying around here snoozing."

"And what will I be doing instead, dear sir?" Sierra asks, giggling.

I pull her close. "You're going to spend all day getting pampered and indulged and doing whatever you want," I say, punctuating each word with a kiss.

Sierra answers with a beautiful smile. I'd make love to her again, but a quick glance at the clock tells me there's not enough time. So I hug her and finish explaining. "At nine o'clock a limousine is going to pick you up and take you down to Salina's Spa and Boutique."

Sierra's eyes widen with delight. "Salina's! That new place that opened up last month down in the Galleria?"

"That's the one, baby. I've checked it out, and they're the real deal. Just like their advertisements promise, they cater to the delicate skin, body, and hair needs of gorgeous black women like *you*."

"And you've hired a limousine?"

"But of course!" I answer, faking indignation. "I'm not having my wife treated like a commoner on our anniversary."

Sierra laughs. "You're too much."

"No," I answer. "I'm in love."

She searches my face, her expression a strange mixture of wonder and happiness. She brushes my cheek with her palm, pulls me close, and kisses me, tenderly at first and then with building urgency. Sierra pulls me back to the bed and down to her. Moments later, I'm back inside her and loving the feel of her ankles pressed hard against my butt, urging me deeper into her sweetness. It's good, so very good. And it's plain, so very plain.

TWO

Sierra and I kiss quickly, then she breezes past the rigidly standing limo driver. He's decked out in a black stiff-billed cap, black suit, and shining black shoes, and he's holding the car door open for her. My baby gets into the car like a movie star, and certainly like someone who comes from a class and status where limos are the rule and not the exception. Over the years I've adjusted to Sierra's upper-class world, but I'm still a mere student of its ways and wonders. Sierra flows through it as one bred to its customs and privileges.

The driver closes Sierra's door, then gets into the car himself. Sierra rolls down her window and blows me a kiss as the limo backs out of the driveway. I cup my hands around my mouth and speak loudly. "Have fun!"

She waves as the limo glides down the street, rounds the corner, and disappears. I watch until it's gone, check my watch, and hurry into the house. We finished making love just in the nick of time before the limo pulled up.

I shower quickly and dry off, stopping for a moment to inspect myself in the mirror. My body's lean, tight, and hard. It's a pleasing result from all the hard hours of effort and sweat I expend every week down at the gym. At thirty-seven it's not so easy keeping off the fat anymore, but I refuse to be like some men I've seen in their late thirties. They look like they just woke up one morning and said, "I quit!" What really gets me are the guys with the big guts and boobs bigger than a woman's who insist that their wives, girlfriends, or significant others stay a size six. Sierra's kept herself slim and trim for me, and I'm going to keep myself toned and muscled for her. When we step out on the town, I want my baby to be proud of the man strutting beside her.

I turn to the side, run my hand along the six-pack of ridges in my stomach, and turn back to the front. At six feet two inches with a midsection like solid rock, a chiseled chest, and shoulders that have broadened further to give me that coveted upper body "V" shape, my physique is a testament of power. My narrow waist doesn't have the slightest trace of love handles, and there are a few barely visible gray hairs on my head. My face is smooth, and my skin is deep brown and offset by what Sierra calls my "sexy, light brown" eyes. All in all, the reflection I see in the mirror is pleasing. I finish my survey and get dressed in business casual attire.

This is going to be a short workday, and since I'm not passing through corporate headquarters, it'll be all right to be informal. This is one of the reasons I like being an inner city regional manager for the Speed Shift Auto Parts retail chain. I spend most of my time in the field checking the operations of "my" ten stores, and I'm mostly my own boss. So on days when I don't feel like wearing a suit and tie, I don't. But I still have to fight being imprisoned by my schedule, especially when it comes to meeting Harry and Gordon for our monthly breakfasts.

Sierra normally gets her hair done down at Our Hair, which is owned by my home-girl, Desiree Easton. I felt kind of guilty about steering one of Desiree's customers to someone else. But

Sierra's appointment at Salina's is just for today, so Desiree's not permanently losing a customer. Besides, Sierra truly likes what Desiree does with her hair.

"She's the only stylist who gets my hair to grow instead of fall out," she once praised.

About two years ago, Sierra mentioned that a new hair salon had opened near our Diamond Ridge Estates neighborhood and that everyone was raving about the service, skill, and affirming atmosphere of the place.

"And I hear that the owner once lived in the Brownfield District," she informed me. "You should come meet her. You two might know each other."

I had my doubts. Few made it out of Brownfield, and fewer still made it into business success. But my interest was piqued, so I went down to Our Hair with Sierra on one of her appointments. The instant I saw Desiree, it turned into a reunion. Her brother, Chub, and I had been part of the same wrecking crew. He was one of the first and few people who'd implored me to get out of Brownfield.

"Denmark, you're too smart for this dead end of a life," he'd encouraged. "You've gotta sky outa here!"

Oddly, Chub never took his own advice. I was puzzled by that but didn't let it hold me back. I got to thank him the night I saw Desiree in the street getting slapped around by a small-time thug named Odin Meers.

"Your punk brother owes me money!" he'd hollered. "He ain't paid, so you will."

He grabbed a breast. Desiree slammed her knee into his nuts. He grunted, then tore open her shirt. I attacked. Odin left the hospital two weeks later on crutches and wearing a neck brace.

I grab the keys to my Corvette, my cell phone, and my briefcase and hurry out to the garage. Moments later, I'm on the road and heading into town to meet Harry and Gordon down at the

Hog Jowls restaurant. The sun is out. The air is crisp. WCLV is spinning some classic Biggie Smalls. And today's my anniversary.

From the moment I saw Sierra, I knew that my days of ripping and running were over. I tore up my five little black books, told the crying honeys I was dumping that they needed to get a life, and got down to business making my baby happy. It all started six years ago on Continental Flight 5667, en route from Cleveland to Las Vegas.

I was on my way to a fun-filled week of gambling, booze, and entertainment, my reward for winning a lottery drawing at work. Sierra was going to meet some old college friends who were gathering to see a former classmate making his debut at the Gut Busting Comedy Club. I was sitting in first class (for once, *free* didn't mean second-rate), stretched out, and glad no one was sitting in the aisle seat next to me. Then the sweetest voice I'd ever heard said, "Excuse me."

I looked up and was slain. Whatever future dreams, plans, or schemes I had were over. Sierra's smile shone like ten suns. Her golden eyes were soft and contrasted wonderfully with her rich, dark skin. The sound of her voice was like a plucked harp string. Her hair was cut short and sassy. She was dressed in a simple white blouse that hugged a pair of big, full breasts crowned by large, erect nipples. And her snug Levi's held in their grip a tightly curvaceous rear end that demanded a first, second, and third lusty glance.

"The flight attendants told me I could sit here," she said, glancing down at the magazines I'd placed in the empty seat. "Can I sit down?"

I snatched up the magazines. "My pleasure," I said.

She sat down, buckled up, and exhaled in a huff. "Thanks. I just couldn't take it anymore."

"Couldn't take what?"

"That ignoramus sitting behind me."

"What was he doing?"

"It was a *she*. And it wasn't so much what she was doing, but saying." She adjusted the tightness of her seatbelt and kept talking. "This woman was bragging about having just quit her job, since her bosses had the nerve to . . . how did she put it?" Sierra thought for a second, then snapped her fingers. "Oh! For having promoted some 'f-in darkie,' over her."

I clenched my jaw. "Even at thirty-three thousand feet, a bigot still bubbles up from the slime."

"And a stupid bigot at that."

"What do you mean?"

Sierra chuckled. "Along with being narrow-minded, she's now unemployed. And I'll bet her 'darkie' supervisor isn't losing a wink of sleep."

"Good point," I said, nodding.

Sierra pulled a book out from her large purse.

"What's the title?" I asked.

"*Within These Hearts.*"

"By Phyllis Friedland?"

Her eyes flashed, and she nodded, smiling.

"That's a great book," I said. "It's one of the best histories out there on the role of black women during the Civil Rights movement."

Sierra's smile broadened. "You're well informed."

I sat taller. "I try."

"I'd love to read more," she lamented. "But with all of my work projects, it's all I can do to keep up with my professional reading."

"What do you do?"

"I'm an architect. And you?"

"I'm a marketing exec."

It was a fact, but not the truth. Sierra was confident, talented, and obviously educated. I hadn't gotten interested in education until I was well out of high school and had decided to redirect my energies into something that wouldn't get me killed,

addicted, or caged. I'd moved steadily up Speed Shift's management ladder and, by the time I met Sierra, had almost completed
a business degree night program at Kent State University. Once I
graduated, I intended to go straight for my MBA. But on that day
when Sierra sat down beside me, we were educational oceans
apart. When I didn't see a wedding ring on her finger, I grabbed
an oar and got busy rowing!

I extended my hand, and we shook. "I'm Denmark Wheeler."

"Sierra Montague," she said. "I'm a little rusty on my history,
but wasn't there a slave revolt leader named Denmark Vesey?"

I nodded proudly. "In 1822, he masterminded what would've
been one of the biggest revolts in North America."

"And you're named after him?"

"To put a fine point on it, *yes!*"

"As I recall, Vesey came to a pretty bad end, didn't he?"

"He was betrayed."

She sighed. "And the struggle continues."

We shared a bitter laugh and spent the rest of the flight talking, moving quickly from work hassles to sharing impressions of
our favorite movies, singers, books, and writers. The conversation gradually expanded to include talk of family, friends, professional experiences, and aspirations. We went far and wide,
always coming back to books that reminded us of some person,
place, or event.

"You've certainly read a lot!" Sierra commented as the plane
was landing. "What college did you graduate from?"

I glanced out the window, deciding whether or not to come
clean about my college situation. It was evident from Sierra's
speech, poise, and outlook that she was a black blueblood. She
was no stranger to hard work, but it was different from the hard
work I'd known. She had labored to get on the dean's list. I had
struggled to stay alive. She'd vacationed in Paris, Montreal, and
Rio. I'd gotten as far as Detroit. Some of her friends got invita-

tions to the White House. Some of mine were just getting out on parole.

But I was feeling close to her. If she rolled me for shallow credentials, she'd surely roll me for being an auto parts store manager—and the sooner I knew the better. So I said, "I'm finishing up a business degree right now at Kent State. A few years after high school, I started working at Speed Shift Auto Parts. The money got good, and I got promotions. I didn't get interested in college until just a few years ago." She didn't say a word or bat an eye, so I went on and said, "And my actual marketing exec duties are those of a store manager."

She looked into her lap, then at me. "Do you like what you're doing?"

"Yes. I do, very much."

"And is it paying you what you want?"

"More than I could've imagined."

"Then you're one of the lucky few working at a job they like, getting paid top dollar, and looking forward to Mondays."

The plane was taxiing toward the terminal, so we updated each other on our mostly uncommitted love lives, exchanged numbers, and discussed the possibility of getting together before leaving Vegas.

"Why don't you let me take you out for a late show when you're through with your friends at the comedy club?" I asked her.

"Why don't you come with us?"

I smiled and quickly agreed. The plane was pulling up to the jet-way. Time was running out, so I leaned close and went for broke. "Sierra, you're a captivating woman, and I'd like to see you again after this trip." I looked straight into her eyes. "As a matter of fact, I'm thinking that I'd like to keep seeing you after we get back to Cleveland."

Just over a year later, her highbrow family and friends ventured out from their gated enclaves to join me and my fellow working stiffs from the factory floor, construction sites, and alleys to celebrate our wedding. Harry and Gordon kidded me about getting lucky and marrying into money, but I shut them down quick.

I loved Sierra not only for her sweet, darling self but for the freshness she brought into my life. She was so different from *any* woman I'd known before, captivating me with stories of people she'd met, places she'd traveled, and events she'd experienced. Her world was more gentle, peaceful, and inspiring than what I'd endured in the Brownfield District, and I loved her for sharing it with me.

Harry and Gordon still couldn't believe the change in me. I was on a short leash and loving it. They bet big money that I'd be cheating before my first anniversary. I took Sierra on a week's Caribbean cruise with the money I collected from those clowns. Flirting women let me know that I could have them with a word, but I refused to hurt my wife. Sierra was the one I'd chosen to love and grow old with until the end, and that's how it's going to be.

THREE

'm on the way to Harry's house to pick him up. He called a few days ago to ask for a ride, explaining that as soon as we finished breakfast a salesman from a Harley-Davidson motorcycle dealership was stopping by to get him. "He's takin' me down to pick up my brand-new black-and-chrome Sportster," Harry had boasted. "I won't drive my car again till the first snowflake falls."

I punch the speed dial button on my cell phone for Harry's pre-programmed number and wait through two rings. He answers with a shout: "What!"

I flinch as his booming voice whacks my eardrum. "What's got you so pissed?" I ask. "You still couldn't get it up last night, even with the Viagra?"

The hostility seeping through the phone is fanned away by Harry's soft chuckle. "Man, don't be tryin' to make your problems mine," he quips. "My stuff springs stiff the moment I need it."

"And that deep groove in your palm says you need it a lot."

We laugh, and I say, "I'm heading your way."

"Good! Make it quick. Inez is gripin' about her biologic clock again."

"What's she saying?"

"What ain't she sayin'? She got up, got dressed for work, and started complainin'. It went downhill from there."

"Is she still at home?"

"She's too drunk to be anyplace else. That's the worst part. Whenever we have this argument, Inez grabs a bottle and turns into the classic mean drunk."

"You sound like you need to be rescued."

"I do! So *hurry*!"

We hang up, and I shake my head. I feel bad for Harry. Even before he married Inez three years ago, his life was complicated by doing contract carpentry work and running two rib shacks, a janitorial service, and his half-stake ownership in a bowling alley. Before the wedding he explained to Inez in clear, strong language that he absolutely *did not want children*. She seemed fine with that then, but she's changed her mind *now*. She's got a battle on her hands, since Harry's still smoldering about Claude, his son from his first marriage.

For almost ten years Harry poured money into a special insurance policy for Claude's college tuition. All the young man had to do was attend an Ohio college or university. Once he graduated from high school, the insurance company sent the check to Claude. And young, adventurous Claude, suddenly loaded with cash, flew off to Europe. Life was good till the money ran out. He's been bumming around the continent ever since. Harry hasn't heard from him for nearly a year, and he's worried sick. And then there's Inez.

"I don't care how much she complains!" Harry declared after their last "let's have a baby" argument. "I ain't settin' myself up for another eighteen years of sleepless nights and bankruptcy."

Both of them have explosive tempers, especially Inez. I've sometimes wondered if one day I'll drive over to their house and find a smoking crater and a hovering mushroom cloud.

Inez's parents aren't happy about Harry's refusal to give them more grandchildren. Her older brother thinks he's a self-centered jerk for squashing his baby sister's desires. And her younger sister says that that's what Inez gets for "marrying a re-tread."

Harry's hassles with Inez's family sometimes remind me of the troubles I've had with Sierra's people, especially her older brother, Amos. Except for Sierra's father, Theodoric, none of the Montagues were thrilled that she was bringing an urban pauper like me into their "royal" midst.

Gordon's the only one of our crew who doesn't have to deal with family hassles. Alice's family loves him to the point of being sickening. His being the celebrity host of the late-afternoon TV show, *Getting Down with Cleveland*, has probably deepened their "love"—but I'm not being fair. They truly adore him, especially Alice's father, who, after spending years in a house ruled by his wife and three daughters, considers Gordon to be the son he never had. It's a beautiful situation that Gordon keeps risking by fooling around with those airhead groupies who aren't interested in him but in his TV-manufactured personality.

When he's out of the public eye, Gordon's a great, down-to-earth, fun-to-be-around human being. But the moment a fan sees him, or reporters are sticking microphones in his face, or he's in front of a TV camera, he transforms into the king of superficially pretentious jerks. At those moments, he's nearly insufferable, and I have to remind myself that once the lights, microphones, and public adulation leave, the real Gordon will re-emerge.

I've known Harry and Gordon just a year or so longer than I've known Sierra. We met seven years ago down at Butler Park while training with other over-the-hill athletes for the Greater Cleveland Community Sports Challenge. During the sprint time trials, Harry, Gordon, and I clocked the fastest times, so we decided to team up for the 4 × 100 meter relay race to win the cash prize: fifteen hundred dollars for each of the victors. We started practicing together, found a decent running fourth person named Xavier Brown, and took first place.

On the way to victory, we became friends. Then Xavier's job transferred him to Memphis, so we had to find someone new for the next year's Challenge. It's been that way ever since. Before each Challenge, the guys and I scout around for someone who'll be fast enough to at least give us a shot at winning. Last year, Harry's brother-in-law, Lofton, ran with us. He was so slow that other teams were crossing the finish line by the time he handed me the baton. That's why it was such a loss when Mason Booker dropped out. Along with being a good-humored southerner, he's pretty fast, and Harry, Gordon, and I were each counting ourselves fifteen hundred dollars richer.

So it was through the Sports Challenge that the three of us started hanging out together. We went fishing, shot pool, risked our lives by cheering for the Browns when they played the Steelers *in* Pittsburgh, played golf, and talked about women, women, and more *women*! Those were hilarious conversations, especially when Harry and I tried to outdo each other's bizarre stories of recent dates. What was more bizarre was that Gordon had stories of his own recent dates, *and he was married*!

The year I met Sierra, things changed. I got promoted to inner city regional manager, married my baby, and was happily spending most of my time with her. Two years later, Harry met and married Inez. Then the TV execs, impressed by the popularity and exploding ratings of Gordon's late-afternoon show, moved him from three days to five days per week.

I was tending to home and career and loving it, but I missed the company of my friends. Harry and Gordon expressed similar feelings one day during a phone conference grump session. So I suggested, "Why don't we meet once a month for breakfast?"

It's been tough keeping our appointments, but that's not the case today, and I'm looking forward to having breakfast with my two crazy friends.

FOUR

I pull up in front of Harry's house and tap the horn a few times, but there's no answer. I knew he wouldn't be ready. I get out, hurry to the door, and knock hard. Harry had better hurry before his ride turns into a walk. I'm not letting anyone or anything upset my plans for celebrating with Sierra.

I knock again, and the door whips open. I'm about to get on Harry's case until I see that it's Inez. The thin silk bathrobe she's wearing contrasts with her made-up face, snazzy hairdo, sheer stockings, and burgundy high-heeled shoes. Except for the robe and her smelling like a distillery, she's ready for work.

"Where is he?" Inez demands to know, slurring her words and looking past me. "All he had to do was get Bubbles some dog food, and he's messing that up."

I hold my breath to avoid the choking blast of Inez's boozed breath. Yipping away and safely distanced from me, Bubbles the miniature poodle is carrying on like she's a snarling timber wolf. She's like those Brownfield District ghetto dogs that bark loud while running away.

"And good morning to you too, Inez," I say.

She clucks her tongue, rolls her eyes, and sways off into the living room. She grabs a drink off the coffee table and orders the dog upstairs. Inez has a great body, but I *refuse* to stare at her succulent round breasts, curvy hips, slender calves, soft shoulders, and firm half-moons of her quivering behind.

"I wish he'd hurry," Inez complains, finishing off her drink. "I told him almost an hour ago that Bubbles needed some dog food. The market's just around the corner, so he should've been back by now."

After a couple of wobbly tries she lights a cigarette, takes a drag, and blows a cloud of smoke. "What're you doing?" she asks, irritated, and looking at me still standing in the doorway. "Come inside. Bubbles won't bite."

Forget Bubbles! My concern is being in Harry's home with his juiced wife—*when he's not here*! It's the kind of situation that can have me staring down the wrong end of a pistol. Harry probably wouldn't suspect anything, but I also don't want to give him cause.

So I tell Inez, "That's okay. I'll wait in the car."

"Fine!" she snaps.

I turn away as she takes another drag of her cigarette and pounds the remainder into a large gray marble ashtray.

"I hate him!" she yells.

I turn in time to see her grab the ashtray and hurl it at the patio window.

"You're a selfish bastard, Harry!" she screams, her voice breaking with the shattering glass.

She plops onto the couch behind her, buries her face in her hands, and sobs. I close the door and rush over to Inez. "Inez, take it easy," I say, softly touching her shoulder.

I'd sit down beside her, but on second thought, *no*. I can hear just as well on my feet. She slaps my hand away and looks up at me with wet, red eyes.

"You're Harry's friend, Denmark," she says in a soggy voice. "Why is he so hostile about having children?"

I don't know what Inez expects me to say. Harry's repeatedly told her about his many frustrations with Claude. That's why I was shocked to learn that he hadn't gotten a vasectomy.

"I use rubbers," he explained. "I ain't lettin *nobody* slice *my* meat."

"He's making me pay for the past," Inez sobs. "He won't even give me a chance."

I feel bad for Inez, but she and Harry knew better. Harry told her how he felt, and Gordon told Harry that no matter how much Inez promised before the wedding, sooner or later she'd change her mind.

"I've done shows on this subject," Gordon had insisted. "There's too much proof to ignore the facts."

Inez springs to her feet and jabs her stiff index finger into my chest. "He's got a girlfriend, doesn't he?"

I've mellowed out since the Brownfield District, but the only person I allow to touch me so freely is Sierra. Inez is flying high right now, so I'm going to give her a pass, but she still needs to back off.

"Inez, please don't put your hands on me," I warn.

"You're all the same," she accuses, jabbing. "No good *men*! All of you!"

I firmly shove Inez away and head for the door. "Denmark, wait!" she implores. "I'm sorry. It's just that . . . I know he does."

I inhale deep and turn slowly back to Inez. "Inez, why do you think Harry's cheating on you?"

She walks across the living room and stares directly into my eyes. Big tear diamonds fall from hers. "He won't make love to me, Denmark," she says softly. "Not even with a condom. That's how I know."

I take a safe step back. "Maybe he's just being extra careful to make sure he doesn't get you pregnant."

She takes a bold step forward. "It's true that I want to eventually get pregnant," she confirms, edging closer. "But what I need right now is the *hard* feel of a man inside me."

I'm getting out of here. Still facing Inez, I reach back for the doorknob. She throws herself against me and hugs me tight. "Don't go!" she says desperately.

She grinds her pelvis against me, and a warm glow ignites in my crotch. I peel Inez off of me and shove her away. "No!" I declare. "This is wrong."

Her expression darkens with anger, and she hollers, "Go to hell!" as I'm slamming the door shut behind me.

FIVE

I'm sitting back in my Corvette a few minutes later when Harry pulls into his driveway, gets out, and waves to me. "I'll be right out," he says, smiling.

"Make it quick, H. I'm on a tight schedule."

"Trust me," he says loudly over his shoulder. "I wanna be gone more than you."

He lugs the dog food into the house and closes the door. Almost immediately I hear him and Inez arguing. I turn up the Corvette's special edition satellite radio and try to relax as love balladeer Faze-2 croons to his sweetheart. Moments later, the front door whooshes open, and Harry storms out.

I wonder if Inez said anything to him about our confrontation. We'll see in a moment. In a huff, he gets into the car but doesn't slam the door.

I watch him as he buckles up. "Are you all right?" I ask.

"Yes!" he snaps. "No! I mean, let's just go!"

I shift the car into reverse and back out the driveway. I cruise out the neighborhood and zip into traffic, and fuming Harry opens up.

"Man, do you know what that crazy woman did?"

"No, H. What happened?"

"She threw an ashtray through our patio window!" he blasts. "I shelled out twenty-three hundred dollars for that special high-tech Sun-Blocker Weather Warrior window."

"I thought I heard something break."

"It's all because of Inez's idiot cousin, Bernie," he grouses. "If he hadn't been gloatin' last night about finally havin' a daughter after makin' them five hardheaded boys, Inez wouldn't be buggin' me again about havin' a baby."

I grunt, not sure what to say.

"I've tried every which way from Tuesday tryin' to explain to Inez that *I don't want no more children!*" Harry rails.

He pounds his sledgehammer fist into his knee. Harry's hand represents him well. He's an average height, thick power cylinder of a man with slightly bowed legs, wide bricklayer's shoulders, bowling ball biceps, and hands that look like crushing tools.

"I wanna love just *her*," he emphasizes. "I want only Inez, and nobody but Inez!"

"I hear you, H. I feel the same about Sierra."

"That's what great about you'n Sierra. Ya'll's stuff is balanced. She's all her, and you're all you, but ya'll know that you couldn't even be pieces of yourselves without each other."

Sierra's beautiful face flashes before me, and I nod in slow agreement. "That's true, H. I didn't even know I was empty until Sierra made me whole."

"Empty is what I'd be if I ever shot that magic bullet into Inez."

"What do you mean?"

He exhales a loud sigh. "She's desperate to have a baby, Denmark. I mean, *really desperate*! The moment she's pregnant I won't be nothin' but a has-been sperm donor."

"C'mon, Harry, you don't really believe that, do you?"

"She'll forget me, man. She won't mean too, but she will. By the time it's all said and done, I'll be standin' in the corner next to her potted plant."

"Negro, get a grip," I chuckle. "Even if you are the plant, you'll still be the daddy."

"It ain't funny!" Harry snaps loudly. "It ain't fun lovin' somebody who thinks you're a problem. Somebody who wishes you'd get lost. Somebody who's always communicatin' that you're in the way."

I glance over and see Harry balling his bear paw hands into fists. In his mind, Inez's baby blues are really working him over. He fires off a series of curses, and his thunder rolls.

"I tried to be a good father," Harry bitterly recounts. "I swear to God, *I tried*! I did the Lamaze classes. I turned my home office into a nursery and painted the walls bright blue and yellow with smilin' moons and stars. I was there when the doc pulled Claude out. I was the one who stayed up nights with 'em when he had colic. I—*not Clarisse!*—saw 'em take his first step."

"Harry, I know you were a good father," I say quickly. "I was just saying that if you and Inez were to get . . ."

"Do you think I wanted people thinkin' I was jealous of my son?" Harry rails. "Do you think I enjoyed 'em makin' jokes about *me* bein' the baby instead'a Claude? How do you think I felt havin' to compete for *my own wife's* affections?"

"Look, H. I know it must've hurt, but . . ."

"Hurt!" he scoffs. "I could'a handled hurt. I could'a beat hurt down. But this was different! This sucked out my spirit. I was a walkin' dead man until Inez. And I ain't lettin' her go. I ain't losin' Inez to *nothin'* or *nobody*!"

Harry's jaw hardens, and he looks slowly over at me. Lightning bolts of anger arc across the hazy sky behind his sad eyes. "Inez is cheatin' on me, Denmark."

Inez's sobbing whisper echoes back: "*Harry's got a girlfriend, Denmark.*"

Later for this! One of them is lying. Maybe they both are. Either way, I'm not getting boxed into the middle of this chaos. I'll support Harry, but I'm not going to referee, and I'm definitely staying away from Inez.

So I proceed carefully. I reach into the glove box, pull out some tissues, and give them to Harry. "I'm sorry to hear that, H," I say softly. "I'm really and truly sorry."

"Not as sorry as Inez's boyfriend is gonna be," Harry growls, wiping his eyes. "I'm'a make 'em curse his momma for not killin' 'em at birth."

"Do you know who he is?"

"No, but you can bet the bank that I'm'a find out!"

I shake my head in dismay. "This sucks."

"I'm'a send that wife-screwin' toad to the deepest, hottest part of hell."

"Whoa, slow your roll," I caution. "Look, Harry. I know you love Inez, but the last thing we need is another brother behind bars. Are you *sure* Inez is cheating?"

His eyes cloud back over with tears as he looks straight into mine. "She won't let me touch her, Denmark. It's been weeks now. She says it's because she wants to get pregnant and I keep using condoms. But that's a lie! Another man's *hittin' my spot!*"

Inez's sobbing whisper echoes back: "*He won't make love to me, Denmark. Not even with a condom. That's how I know.*"

"It's gotta be somebody I know," Harry announces. "Them cop shows always say it's somebody you know."

I look hard at Harry. He looks hard back at me. His bear paw hands haven't moved, but I'm watching. "Denmark," he calls, sniffling, "you're the *only* one I trust."

My heart resumes beating. "H, are you saying that you don't trust Gordon."

"Absolutely not!" he declares. "Man, you know Gordon's a dog. He'd screw a mailbox if it was wearing a skirt." He clenches his jaw and stares morosely ahead, seeing but not seeing. "Them cop shows always say it's somebody you know. And from what I know of Gordon, he needs watchin'."

I'm tempted to ask Harry if he's also watching Inez, since the only way someone can cheat with her is if *she's* cheating with *them*, just like she tried with me! But Harry's not ready to deal with Inez's being another man's willing lover. Forcing him to confront that possibility is asking for trouble. He might get agitated and wonder why I'm trying to make him turn on his wife, so forget it.

Harry looks at me, his expression drawn and eyes forlorn. "Denmark, I'm guessing that there's probably not much you don't tell Sierra, but could you keep this . . ."

"There are *no* secrets between me and Sierra."

He purses his lips and nods sadly. "Will you at least think about keepin' this . . ." He slumps with wearied frustration. "Never mind," he groans. "I just remembered that you said Sierra goes to that Our Hair beauty salon where Inez gets her hair and nails done."

"Yes," I answer, nodding. "Sierra, and just about every sister I know on this side of Cleveland, goes to Our Hair."

Harry grimaces. "Then I guess it don't make no difference."

"What doesn't?"

"With the way Inez runs her mouth, always puttin' our business in the streets, Sierra will hear about it durin' her next visit."

That's another reason why I love and cherish my baby. She doesn't run all over town blabbing our secrets to family, friends, or co-workers. What happens in our marriage *stays* in our marriage.

"I swear, man," Harry grumbles. "I can't win for losin'."

I glance at my watch. Time's wasting, and I've got to get going. Harry's my good friend, but Sierra's my darling wife, and as bad as I feel for him, I'm not going to let him stymie my anniversary plans.

I turn into the Hog Jowls lot, park, and give him a soft punch to the shoulder. "Come on, H. Let's go inside and eat. You'll feel better."

We get out of the Corvette and head inside. Just as we get to the door, Harry grips my arm and stares hard into my eyes. "Denmark, I mean what I said," he rumbles. "You're the *only* one I trust."

SIX

arry and I stroll through the front door of the Hog Jowls restaurant, and the scent of frying bacon pulls us inside.

"Man, do you smell that?" Harry asks, inhaling with an appreciative moan. "Cleo knows how to work that skillet."

The place is humming with the noise of conversation, the myriad smells of cooking food, and a booming radio that's tuned to a station doing a '60s soul music tribute.

"I'll see ya'll in a bit," Harry says, hurrying toward the bathroom. "Nature's hollerin' 'Go now, or else!' "

I laugh and turn toward Cleo Exeter, the restaurant's owner and head cook. She looks up from the grill, sees me, smiles, and waves her spatula.

"Denmark! Get over here and gimme a hug wit'yo *fine* self," she says, talking over the popping bacon, din of conversation, and radio.

Several women look around to see whom Cleo's talking to. One woman who's scoping me looks away when the man beside her snarls a whisper into her ear. The rest of them, some alone, some not, take their time enjoying me. I let them have their fun and keep stepping. One of the gawkers is Vondie Hamilton.

Vondie works in Speed Shift's corporate procurement department, stands about five feet five, wears a close-cut natural, and has some of the smoothest, prettiest dark skin I've ever seen. A man could run his finger across her cheek and get back a thick drop of chocolate. She's also got some dynamite legs and loves to show them off. She and I were dating just before I met Sierra. It was nice and we had fun, but when Sierra showed up, Vondie was *out*!

Vondie's sitting at a table with a stylishly dresssed butterball of a guy who's running his mouth a mile a minute. She's probably not hearing a word he's saying, since she's so intensely focused on me. Butterball finally realizes that he's talking to himself, follows her gaze over to me, scowls, and looks back at Vondie. She's stirring her coffee like all is well.

Sierra and I would never disrespect each other like that. But I'm not naïve. I know my baby appreciates attractive men, just like she knows that I'm not blind to pretty women. The most important thing she knows is that no one is more beautiful to me than she.

I get over to the counter and wait for Cleo to finish fixing a plate before she comes to hug me. She's a wiry, honey-skinned woman with a glass eye and cigarette burns on her lower jaw. She got her wounds from the ogre she once called husband. But Cleo got even. One night after he'd passed out drunk she undressed him, tied his hands and feet to the bed, fixed a big pot of grits to throw on him, and got a bat. People still remember the blood-curdling scream and sight of the naked man who found the strength to break loose from his bonds, leaped from the second-floor window and tore down the street like slave catchers were on his case.

I slip between two bar stools, lean across the counter, and hug Cleo. "Hey beautiful," I say.

"Beautiful! Don't make me drag you in the back," Cleo threatens. "It's been a long time since I had some good loving, and I'd hate to wear out a fine man like you."

"Don't hurt me, Cleo," I beg playfully. "You know I'm delicate."

She shoves me back and waves me off. "Stop talking trash. How's you doing?"

"Good and getting better. Today's my anniversary."

"Well, that's just wonderful. Are you still in love?"

"Madly," I answer. "How are you doing?"

"I got up on the green side of grass, honey. It don't get much better than that."

"True word," I laugh. "Do you have some fresh coffee for me?"

Cleo rolls her eyes. "Everything in my establishment's fresh."

She pours me a cup, and I add cream and sugar. "Go on in the back and have a seat," Cleo directs. "Gordon's already in there with his sweet wife."

I glance into the private area that Cleo graciously sets aside for me and the guys when we meet for breakfast. Gordon's definitely in there, and so is Alice. They look like the world's happiest couple, sitting close, holding hands, whispering, and staring deep into each other's eyes. I should let them have their peace and sit in the main dining section with the other customers. But Harry won't care about disturbing their bliss, so I might as well take my regular seat.

"Somebody'll get ya'll's order in just a few," Cleo says.

Cleo's lying through her teeth. The service in this place is glacial, but the food's great, so it's worth the wait. I just hope that today it's not too long.

I wink my acknowledgment and start toward Gordon and Alice. They spot me, smile, and wave, and I wave back. Alice is one good-looking woman. When she's dressed in her Horizon Airlines flight attendant's uniform, she's absolutely stunning.

And she's so gentle. Sierra's gentle too, but Alice is almost too sweet to be human. It's too bad that she's married to a dog like Gordon. I sometimes want to shake her and yell "Wake up!"

But that's the kind of nonsense that can get a brother killed. Gordon has always respected my Brownfield District roots, but nothing stirs a man's courage faster than news of his woman's cheating. And Gordon owns a gun. For all that I learned while battling in the streets, *I never learned to outrun a bullet*.

Besides, Alice is free to walk any time she wants. If after all the gossip, catching Gordon in lie after lie, and not one but *two* court-ordered paternity tests (which cleared Gordon— but still), she continues to put up with him, nothing I could say would impress her enough to leave. He needs Alice far more than she needs him, and I keep telling him to be careful. If she ever bolts, Gordon will be like a blind zombie bumping into walls.

My stroll across the restaurant is slowed as I exchange greetings with Cleo's many regulars. From a nearby table, a soft female voice says, "Hello, Denmark."

I stop and look at fine Vondie Hamilton. "Hello, Vondie. How are you?"

"I'm doing okay. And you?"

"Things couldn't be better. Today's my anniversary."

She purses her lips, then gestures to her butterball companion. His scowl deepens. "Denmark, meet Lennox Foster," says Vondie. "Lennox, this is Denmark Wheeler."

We exchange a shabby handshake. Lennox's face is a contorted frown, but I can't blame him. If I were standing as deep in his shadow as he is in mine, I wouldn't be happy either.

"We're in the same investment club," Vondie quickly offers. "Lennox is the founder and has offered to help me learn how to best plug into the markets."

From the way Lennox's eyes are scoping Vondie's boobs, he's interested in "plugging" into more than the markets.

"I'm told that those clubs are pretty good," I respond. "Maybe I should join."

"Yes, you should," Vondie agrees. "It's a nice way to learn the ins and outs from someone like Lennox who really knows."

I look at him. "Is that your line of work?"

He starts to answer, but Vondie cuts him off. "Lennox is vice president of North Coast Bank & Trust," she proudly informs me.

I glance at Lennox. "That's some outfit. The financial news says that you guys are one of the fastest-growing banks in the Midwest."

Lennox starts to speak, but Vondie cuts him off again. "Lennox is masterminding their expansion into the Detroit and Chicago markets."

I nod approvingly. "That sounds like a nice little job."

"Little!" he snaps. "I'm the *vice president* of a bank. That's more than a little job."

"Don't get your back up," I chuckle. "It wasn't meant as an insult."

"Yes, Lennox," Vondie quickly adds. "Don't take it the wrong way. Denmark's *just* an inner city regional manager for Speed Shift Auto Parts, so *your* position carries a lot more power, prestige, and pay."

I fix my eyes on Vondie. She smiles back like the portrait of innocence.

Lennox twists his pursed lips into a smirk. "So you're an inner city regional manager, eh. Now *that* sounds like a little job."

He glances at Vondie, who's looking at him with unhinged adoration. Okay, I've had enough of this game. I once would've made this fool suffer twice, first for his insult and then for being stupid enough to let Vondie manipulate him into antagonizing me. But forget them. Today's my anniversary, and in a few short hours, I'm going to celebrate with my wife.

I look at Vondie, shake my head, and step off. I'm disappointed in her. I thought we'd buried our differences during that business trip to Orlando last year.

Once she, the chief financial officer, Porter Grant, and I had finished our day's work, we cruised back to the hotel, where we talked and laughed through dinner. After the meal, we moved to the bar and lounge for drinks. Porter wanted to call his very pregnant wife to see how she was doing, so I let him borrow my cell phone. He left the noisy lounge to make his call, and, for the first time since our breakup, Vondie and I discussed what had happened.

"You were a real *jerk*, Denmark," she said. "One day we were dating; the next there was nothing."

I sat back and sipped my rum and Coke. "What can I say? I met Sierra and fell in love. I didn't want to lead you on, so I ended it."

She pursed her lips. "You didn't have to be so mean."

She had a point. The day I took her to lunch to tell her it was over, I said: "Vondie, I've fallen in love with someone else. *It's over!*"

She gasped, threw her drink in my face, and stalked out of the restaurant.

That evening down in Orlando I asked her, "What would you have preferred?"

"I don't know!" she snapped. "You could've at least said 'I'm sorry' or *something!*"

The bar and lounge had gotten more crowded, noisy, and hot. Porter was still talking with his wife, so Vondie and I moved out by the pool. I told the bartender to send Porter our way when he got back, then ordered us a couple of potent Florida Hurricane drinks. The server brought them, and I listened quietly as Vondie unloaded more of her frustrations.

"Vondie, I'm sorry," I said when she finally finished.

"You should be."

She excused herself, got up, and started to leave. I stood quickly, blocked her path, and took hold of her hand. "Vondie, I really mean it," I stressed. "I'm truly sorry."

She smiled tightly and nodded, then went up to her room. When I told the guys what had happened, Harry insisted that Vondie had been trying to one-up me.

"Inez does that whenever we argue," he reasoned. "She has to either get in the last word or make sure I know that I've been a slug."

Gordon wanted to hear more about the alluring stranger who'd bought me a drink. "Forget Vondie!" he'd insisted. "Tell us why you turned down that honey who wanted to give you some poo-na-nay."

After Vondie went up to her room, I kept waiting for Porter to bring me back my cell phone. I'd nursed my Hurricane down to the last sip when a server brought me another.

"I didn't order this," I said.

"That's correct, sir," he agreed. Gesturing toward a gorgeous woman sitting on the other side of the pool, he said, "She did."

We made eye contact. She was breathtakingly beautiful, with a brick-house body that she proudly displayed in her skimpy two-piece swimsuit. Her bronze skin, large bright eyes, delicious lips, thickly flowing hair, and sweetly angular face betrayed centuries of finely blended African, European, and Amerindian bloodlines. Her eyes were lit bright with invitation, her smile was an assurance of her willingness, and her sexy posture was a foreshadowing of sweet satisfaction to come.

In another time as another person, I'd have escorted her to horizontal heaven in an eye-blink. But it wasn't that time, and I was no longer that person. I held up my left hand and wiggled my ring finger for her and the world to see. She frowned. I shrugged, picked up my new drink, told the barkeep where Porter could find me, and strolled down to the beach for a nice long walk—

away from her! Getting my cell phone from Porter was important, but not enough to stray into the crosshairs of temptation.

When I told the guys, they were appalled. "Man, you could'a smoked that booty and been gone before the sweat dried," Harry had teased.

"And if the candy was as fine as you say," Gordon chimed in, "you should've at least gotten a taste."

"I'd'a been hittin' that goodie like it wasn't no tomorrow," Harry boasted, slapping five with Gordon.

"You clowns ought to stop," I laughed. "The moment that fine woman said 'Hi!' you'd both have been tongue-tied."

They kept up their harassment until I said, "Look, you guys, there's a simple reason why I didn't do it."

"Why?" they asked together in equally incredulous tones.

I looked at Harry, then Gordon, and said, "*I love my wife.*" Harry frowned. "Is that *it*?"

"That's all there needs to be," I answered defiantly. "Sierra's the only woman I want. She's the only woman I'll ever need."

Gordon nodded thoughtfully. "That's admirable, Denmark. It's stupid, but admirable."

"Think what you want," I retorted. "But I'm not risking a romp with a babe who might heap all kinds of biological, psychological, and emotional poisons onto the good life I've got with Sierra."

And I meant it! I'd dealt with enough drama queens, nuts, she-wolves, and lowlifes to know that women like Sierra didn't come a dime a dozen. And they certainly didn't hook up with hood escapees like me. So no matter how much Harry and Gordon have pestered me about having a ring through my nose, or the vacant space where my balls used to be, I'm married and loving it, and I'm staying deep inside the safety zone.

SEVEN

Alice's eyes smile as I approach her and Gordon. His cheesy smile says that he's encountered some fans, so he's being his best on-camera self.

He gives me his best star smile and points his stiff index finger at me. "You're the one!" he says, his tone full of admiration.

Gordon doesn't have to go through this routine with me, but he does it with everybody, so it's just him being him. It's the same technique he uses with all his TV guests to make them feel like no one has ever been, or ever will be, more important to him. People get sucked in, then tell him their most intimate secrets. Harry and I once watched Gordon do a special on Cleveland's persisting segregated housing patterns, and we sat amazed as people of all types bared their bigoted souls about whom they didn't like and why.

"They're stupid for openly admitting this stuff on camera," Harry asserted.

"No," I corrected. "Gordon's a genius for getting them to do it."

He's used that same "genius" to feed Alice truckloads of crap about his womanizing, complaining that it's the price he pays for "their" success.

"Alice knows I'm only doing my job," he once lamely insisted. "I've told her time and again that TV's a tough racket. You can be a hit in the morning and scrubbing toilets by afternoon. If I'm going to stay a winner, I've got to do whatever it takes."

"How is bedding every babe who walks onto your set accomplishing that?" Harry pressed.

Gordon's brown skin reddened. "That question explains why you're in the audience, and I'm among the stars."

Gordon gestures vigorously for me to hurry and take a seat. "Get over here and let me soak up some of your power," he urges, pouring on the flattery.

He stands, and we shake and hug. I notice several women standing in the doorway, whispering excitedly and pointing at him. Gordon looks over at them, and I step aside so he can have the spotlight.

He winks at Alice. "Honey, I'll be right back. You know it's all for the show."

"I understand," Alice says softly.

Gordon gives her that "You're the one!" pointed finger, then looks at me. "She's the best, Denmark. She's the absolute best!"

He backs away, points again at her, then me. "You—two—are—*the*—best!" Then he scurries off. The starry-eyed women are joined by a few men. Gordon plunges into their midst like a fish returning to water.

"I just loved the show you did on staying young and fit," coos one woman. "It changed my life."

Gordon hugs her. Another woman shoos people away so she and Gordon can take a picture together. They stand close, her hugging him tight. He slips his arm around her waist so that his hand is just beneath her boob. He hugs her tighter, moving his hand slightly higher. She glances down at his hand, then up into his grinning face, smiles, and bats her eyes. After the picture, another woman pulls him close and whispers into his ear. Gordon glances at me and Alice, sees Alice rummaging in her purse, and quickly accepts the slip of paper the woman gives him. His eyes meet mine, and he grins.

"They really love him," says Alice, looking into a small mirror as she refreshes her lipstick.

"Yes. They certainly do."

"He loves them, too, each and every one of them. As often as he can."

I snap my eyes onto Alice. She's still looking into the small mirror while using her free hand to tame an uncooperative lock of hair.

"What do you mean, Alice?"

She puts the mirror away, glances at her watch, then looks at me. "How are things with you, Denmark?"

I study her for a moment. Her eyes tell me not to revisit the question she didn't answer. "Things are going great. Today's my anniversary."

"Congratulations!" she says, smiling large. "How many years does this make?"

"Five."

Her smile dims. "Gordon and I have been married for twelve."

"That's encouraging. It's good to know people whose marriages are working."

Harry squeezes his way through Gordon's thronging worshipers, nodding a stiff greeting to Gordon as he passes. Gordon smiles and gives him a "You're the one!" finger point. Harry rolls his eyes and hurries over to me and Alice.

"Hi, Alice," he greets, shaking her hand. He jerks a hooked thumb back at Gordon. "You're too good for that bum," he declares.

Alice laughs. "That's sweet of you, H. Good morning to you also."

Harry looks at me. "I'll be right back. Skinny Bumpers just walked in. He's agreed to sell me his barbecue joint and come work for me."

"H, Inez is going to brain you," I warn. "You don't have enough room on your plate for another venture."

"Man, get real," he retorts. "There's always room for makin' money. Besides, Inez is already brainin' me with her baby-makin' belly-achin'."

Then he's off. Gordon's still happily signing autographs and posing for pictures. "Gordon's told me about Harry and Inez's disagreements over children," Alice confides. "Is Harry really that opposed to the idea?"

"Harry's one thousand percent opposed," I confirm.

Alice shakes her head sadly. "Something like that could strain a marriage to the breaking point. Denmark, have you and Sierra ever discussed having kids?"

I nod. "We've talked about it a lot more these past couple of years. It's kind of exciting."

"I used to want kids," Alice calmly shares. "Not anymore."

Gordon once mentioned that in the first few years of their marriage, he and Alice had made definite plans for children. Then he got famous, the rumors started, and she changed her mind. He concluded that she was just going through a phase.

"But don't worry," he'd said, lecherously hiking his eyebrows up and down. "When she comes out of it, I'll be ready."

A collective groan rises from the gathering surrounding Gordon. "I'm sorry, folks," he announces, backing away with his hands raised in apology. "But I need to get back to my lovely wife."

"Oh, please," urges a pouting beauty. "Nobody will believe that I saw you unless I have your autograph."

She opens up her blouse, revealing her swelling breasts.

Gordon blinks wide-eyed. She hands him a marker, opens her blouse wider, and leans forward as he signs. She whispers in his ear. He whispers back, and she laughs as he finishes with a flourish.

I quickly look to Alice. She clenches her jaw. "God, please help me turn it off," she says.

"Turn what off?"

"My love."

Gordon finishes clowning, then hurries back and sits down, scooting close to Alice. "They were insatiable," he observes. "Sometimes being famous can be a pain."

"Give me a break," I reply. "You know you love it."

Gordon smirks slyly. "Okay, maybe just a little bit." He hugs Alice around her shoulders, pulling her close. "I'll do whatever it takes to keep this lovely lady living the lifestyle she deserves."

"Gordon, all I want is a loving marriage," Alice offers.

"And that's what we've got," he brags. "We're a great team, and that's why we're a success."

Alice answers with a brittle smile. He gestures to me. "Did she tell you, Denmark?"

"Tell me what?"

"Alice has new flight routes to Singapore and . . ."

"Not Singapore, Gordon," Alice gently corrects. "I'll be working the trips to . . ."

His cell phone rings, and he holds up a rigid finger. Alice quiets herself, and we both listen to Gordon. "Hello? Hey Leo, what's up?" He covers the phone and whispers, "It's Leo Myers, my producer," then keeps talking. "What's that you say? She did? That's great! Leo, you're the best!" He hangs up, his face ruled by a smile. "We did it!" he crows. "We've been trying for weeks, but we finally did it."

"Did what?" I ask.

"Valencia Burton has agreed to come on my show."

Alice and I shrug. "Who's that?" she asks.

Gordon's appalled. "You two have never heard of *Dr.* Valencia Burton? You ought to be ashamed," he jokes. "Dr. Burton belongs to a group called Doctors without Borders. She's been in the Sudan in Africa. The country's been ravaged for years by civil war, and the Khartoum government in the north has been terrorizing black Africans in the south, rampaging, murdering, and selling people into slavery. The village where she was working got raided, and she led about seventy men, women, and children across a wilderness into an area controlled by African Union peacekeepers."

"That's awful," Alice observes.

"And a great story," Gordon gushes. "It'll be great for ratings."

"What about the black Africans being sold into slavery?" I ask. "Aren't you concerned about them?"

"If they boost the numbers, I'll love them."

I stiffen and take a deep, calming breath. My namesake, Denmark Vesey, was executed in 1822 after being betrayed by someone like Gordon. Alice's eyes communicate her embarrassment to mine.

"Valencia barely escaped with her life," Gordon continues, oblivious. He punches numbers on his cell phone.

"Congratulations," says Alice. "That's a wonderful accomplishment."

"Yes, it is," I add. "Dr. Burton deserves all the recognition she gets."

Gordon frowns in puzzlement, then says, "Oh, yeah, right. Don't worry. I'll make sure she gets her due. She'll have my undivided attention. She'll get the red carpet treatment." He gets his connection and speaks into his cell phone. "Hey Ned, how's the newspaper business? I'm fine. Listen, tell your bosses at the *Plain Dealer* to stop the presses. Okay, here it is: Valencia Burton has agreed to come on my show." He laughs, gives me and Alice a thumbs-up sign, and keeps talking. "Wait, Ned. You're breaking up. Let me go to where there's better reception."

He gets up and hurries out, shaking hands and hugging fans on the way. Alice gathers up her belongings. "I need to leave."

"Are you okay?"

She smiles sadly. "No. But thanks for noticing and asking."

I sit silently. How can Gordon live with her and not see this? I stand with her as she gets up. "Try to hang in there, Alice. Everything's going to work out."

Her eyes harden, and her nostrils flare. "Will it, Denmark?" she snaps.

I purse my lips and look away. She takes hold of my hand and squeezes. "I'm sorry. Tell Gordon that I'll see him later. I know he's forgotten that I'll be gone for a few days."

"How could he forget something like *that*?"

"The same way he forgot that my new flight route is from Cleveland to Sydney, Australia, and not Singapore," she sighs. "It's no surprise that he got it wrong. I'm not part of his adoring public or a guest on his show. What I say doesn't matter."

"Alice, you're all the adoring public *any* man would need."

She smiles. "You're sweet, Denmark. I envy Sierra." She glances at her watch. "Well, I'd better go. My bosses have no sense of humor when it comes to being late."

"Take care, Alice."

She gives me a quick peck on the cheek, turns to leave, then faces me again. "I want to give you something," she says, pulling a business card from her purse. "This has all my updated contact information, including my voice mail. I always check my messages as soon as I get to the hotel where the flight crews stay." She looks hard into my eyes, again looking straight to the center of my mind. "Denmark, if you ever feel like being as good a friend to me as you are to Gordon, give me a call."

EIGHT

Harry and Gordon aren't yet at the table, so now's a good time to try and make sense of this morning's events. The wives of my two best friends are miserable. One threw herself at me, and the other practically asked me to bust on her husband's cheating action. At least Harry knows Inez isn't happy, but Gordon's unbelievable. The ice beneath his feet is so thin it's not a question of "if" but "when" it'll crack. And I wonder: is Sierra secreting some heartache, dissatisfaction, or resentment about me? She seems happy, but is she *really*? Let me stop being stupid. Sierra knows I love her with every molecule of my being.

I hear whistling, look up, and see Harry high-stepping in my direction. "It's been a good day for makin' money," he announces. "And it's not even noon."

I glance at my watch. It's ten after ten. If these guys don't hurry so we can eat breakfast, I'm leaving. I still need to stop in at work, take care of my business, and leave in time to prepare for my celebration with Sierra.

Gordon pokes his head from around the corner and swaggers in, grinning and gesturing back toward the main dining area.

"I saw Alice go, but I was still on the phone," he says, sitting down with me and Harry. "She's a good woman."

"Then how could you flirt like that in front of her?" I ask.

"Alice knows me," Gordon says, grinning. "I'd never disrespect her."

Harry sits back and crosses his arms over his chest. "Well, then, you're lucky she believes all them lies you feed her about other women."

Gordon's expression hardens. "You know, Harry, sometimes you can be a real pain!"

"You want pain? I'll show you some pain!" Harry challenges, his eyes narrowed.

Gordon flips him the bird. Harry reaches for Gordon's wrist. I grab Harry's shoulder and shove him back.

"Knock it off!" I order. "What's up with ya'll? We're supposed to be meeting for breakfast, not combat."

Gordon glares. Harry scowls. And then with the skill he's perfected into an art, Gordon defuses the crisis by slipping into his TV persona self. "Denmark's right, H," he says, forcing a hollow laugh. "I'll beat you down *after* I've had some grub."

"You wish you could beat me down," Harry growls.

Gordon's star smile dims. "Harry, are you really mad with me about something?"

"He's mad about Inez jamming a broom up his butt for getting on her nerves," I quickly interject. "You know the only thing that gets this clown pissed off is his checkbook not balancing."

"Or some sucker messin' around with *my wife*!" Harry adds, speaking low and threatening.

"Well, it's lucky for you that Gordon's too sad and trifling to interest a woman like Inez," I say.

I stare hard at Harry, narrowing my eyes slightly. It stinks that Gordon cheats on Alice with the regularity of a sunrise, but that doesn't mean he's doing Inez. I'm not letting Harry poison this friendship when all he's got is suspicion. If he gets proof, I'll help him drag Gordon out back and supervise the beating. Until then, he's going to follow *my* program.

"Denmark, who're you calling sad and trifling?" Gordon quips, chuckling. "You're an okay guy, but you'll never be as wonderful as me." He gestures to Harry. "Even hammer-hands Harry has more class than you."

Gordon's extended the olive branch, but Harry's not having it. I clench my jaw and mash Harry's foot with mine beneath the table. He glances at me, sits back, and finally loosens up.

"My balls have got more class than either of you two suckers," Harry responds.

"H, statements like that are proof that you're doing drugs," Gordon laughs.

This exchange of jibes is feeling better, and I'm glad Harry's getting with the program.

"Man, I know the service is slow in this joint, but this is ridiculous," Gordon comments, glancing at his watch.

"For real," I agree. "Somebody better come soon, or I'm gone. I've got things to do before tonight's celebration."

"What celebration?" Harry asks.

I roll my eyes. "C'mon Harry, I told you about my anniversary."

"That's right!" Gordon exclaims, smiling large. "Man, Sierra's going to be speechless."

Harry snaps his fingers. "Now I remember! You're taking Sierra to the Sapphire Spire, right?"

"Yes," I answer, nodding. "And that's just the first of my surprises." I lean forward and look hard at them both. "Sierra *will be* surprised, won't she?"

Gordon crosses his heart and gestures like he's zipping his lips. "My lips have been sealed," he assures me. "I haven't said a word."

"Me neither," Harry quickly adds. "Besides, if I'd said something, you'd'a heard about it from somebody who'd been jabberin' with Inez."

I sit back and relax. "Okay, you guys. Thanks for keeping it a secret."

"So how many years will this make for you and Sierra?" Gordon asks.

"Five," I proudly answer.

"I've been married to Alice for twelve, and it's been a ball," he crows.

"I've been married to Inez for three, and it seems like forever," Harry says glumly.

Gordon gestures to me. "Okay, Denmark. The Sapphire Spire restaurant's classy and expensive but get to the juicy stuff. What else are you planning to do?"

"It's already in motion," I answer. "Sierra's down at Salina's Spa and Boutique getting their top-of-the-line Encounter."

Harry and Gordon exhale slow, low whistles. "Life in the automotive retail business must be good," says Harry. "I've told Inez she better not drive within fifty miles of that place."

"What's good is my life with Sierra," I correct.

Harry purses his lips and looks down at the table. "It must be nice," he sighs.

I describe how the concierge and servers at the Sapphire Spire will treat Sierra like royalty, the special serenade I've ordered for her, and the diamond necklace I'll put around her neck at the end of the evening.

"And then there's Vegas," I continue. "You guys are still coming, aren't you?"

"I'll be there with bells," Harry answers.

Gordon nods enthusiastically. "I'm looking forward to it." He looks slightly glum and says, "Alice has to work." But then, quickly perking up, he adds, "but not to fear. I'll make sure to have enough excitement for her and me."

"I just bet you will," Harry quips.

Gordon scowls, and I speak quickly before he and Harry start sniping again. "The best part will be our trip to Hawaii afterward. Sierra's never been there, and I'm psyched about introducing her to something new. It's usually the other way around."

Harry shakes his head. "This must be costin' a bundle. I'm in love, but I ain't *that* in love. How'd you get it all hooked up?"

"It wasn't all that hard," I reply. "Phone, e-mail, and a travel agent made it easy."

"Speaking of getting things 'hooked up,' " Gordon re-directs, "we need to figure out who's going to be running in the number three spot this year." He looks at me. "You're still running the anchor leg—right, Denmark?"

I nod. Gordon knows I will. He and Harry are fast, but I'm faster. The anchor leg is the final portion of the 4 × 100 relay. It's the money segment. Each team puts its fastest person there to chew up the final hundred meters to make up for any slowness in the first three legs. The anchor is where the race is either won or lost.

"It's too bad Mason Booker had to drop out," Harry laments. "He was fast, and a pretty nice guy."

"You've got that right," I confirm. "Mason's old-style Southern gentleman. He believes in all that stuff about duty, loyalty, and honor."

"Does he also duel at sunrise?" Gordon asks, smirking.

Harry and I chuckle, but then I answer Gordon seriously. "No, he just believes in treating people right. His volunteer work as a community liaison with the Cleveland Police Department is one of the main reasons the cops are treating people from inner city hoods with more respect."

"I know he only practiced with us for a short while," Gordon soberly observes, "but he never mentioned any of this."

"That's Mason for you," I say. "He does what has to be done, and keeps on moving. He's not out for glory, just results."

Harry snaps his fingers. "There's a guy who lives over near Loudon Circle and works on my night janitor crew. He says Mason's the real deal, a straight, standup kind of brother."

Gordon frowns. "If he's so wonderful, I should've heard about him. He'd be great to have on the show."

"You'd better tell the people in your research department to get on their J-O-B," Harry gleefully chides.

Gordon nods in agreement, cheating Harry out of the joy of his attempted irritation. "Anyway," says Gordon, "we still need to find a fourth runner. Do you guys have any ideas? Got any names?"

"It's only three weeks away," Harry observes. "That's not much time."

We settle back and wait on our food while discussing how to best win the 4 × 100 relay a few weeks from now.

NINE

I pull into the parking lot of the revitalized Henderson Village strip mall, where Speed Shift Auto Parts' newest, most profitable store is located. Along with being a place of retail, it's my base of operations. I park, get out of the Corvette, and see a familiar, grubby sight. It's Burned-out Bobby, a medium-height, very round, scraggly white–bearded, homeless guy I've helped out from time to time.

Bobby's standing down on the corner at the far end of the parking lot. He spends most of his time there, but I've seen him other places around town, some pretty far from Henderson Village. I've always been slightly amazed that he gets around so far, so often.

He's dressed in his usual two layers of dingy clothing, which should leave him roasting in this heat, but he doesn't seem to mind. As usual, Bobby's holding a cardboard sign and pointing to its message whenever cars pass. I can't see what it says, but I'll bet it's good. Bobby's always got a different slogan that'll either get me laughing or leave me thinking. His last one read: "I used to be you!"

I can't resist seeing what his message is for today, so I hurry down to Bobby, pulling a twenty-dollar bill from my wallet on the way. "Hey Bobby," I greet him, getting close. "Where've you been?"

"Here and there," he answers in a wheezing voice. He keeps his eyes on the road, watching and waiting for the next car or group of cars.

"So what's the good word for today?"

He turns so I can read his sign. It says: "Live, laugh, love."

I'm fully alive, I'm very much in love, and Bobby's sign so accurately describes my happiness that it leaves me laughing. I hand him the twenty. "You take care of yourself, Bobby. Will you have a new sign tomorrow?"

"Guess so, maybe."

I tell Bobby good-bye and stride off briskly into work. I could almost envy the open-endedness of his responsibility-free life, but he's also dealing with some material hardships that I've gladly left behind. And then there's Sierra. My world may be cluttered with meetings, sales projection targets, employee disciplinary hassles, and a myriad of other management headaches, but Sierra's worth every pain, frustration, and challenge I have to endure.

I walk in to the store and see Keith Billings, the store manager. "What's up, KB?" I ask.

"You've got it."

"Talk to me about cash flow."

"The river is deep, wide, and rushing with federal green."

"Sounds like my kind of flood."

"And the water can't get too high."

"Say that, my brother."

We slap each other five and I quick-stride to the back of the store and up the few steps into my office. The phone's ringing, and I hurry to answer. "Speed Shift Auto Parts: Denmark Wheeler speaking."

"Ha, hey . . . Uncle Denmark," says Sierra's worthless crack-head nephew, Yarborough Montague. His speech is halting and strained.

I drop my briefcase onto the floor beside my desk and sit down. Yarborough must be desperate to be calling me "Uncle." He normally addresses me with the more generic and barely respectful "You."

"What do you want, Yarborough?"

"Well, ah, I was, you know, wondering if you could slide me a few . . ."

"No."

"C'mon, man," he whines, his voice taut with desperation. "I'll pay you back. I swear it!"

"No!"

He cusses me out and slams down the phone. I turn on my computer and quickly check my e-mails. I want to get out of here in time to get home, get rested, and be ready for when Sierra arrives.

There's an e-mail from the boss. Some representatives from the Forrester & Company advertising firm will be coming out to Henderson Village in a few days to shoot a commercial. That's great news. It's not only proof that this location's a moneymaker, but a clear sign that this part of Cleveland is bouncing back.

I see the Web address for Mason Booker's Second Shadow Enterprises private detective agency and quickly open the e-mail. He's been checking on a prospective new hire. If the guy's clean, he'll help out Keith and his high-performing, overworked employees.

Mason's message says that our potential new hire has been fired from his past three jobs for theft. Mason once more proves that he's worth his weight in gold. He's one of the most brutally honest people I know. Whenever I want the straight, unvarnished truth about something, Mason's usually my first stop.

I re-read Mason's e-mail and shake my head. Keith won't be

happy about this, but he'd be less happy about working with a thief.

There's a knock on my door. "Come in!" I say.

Keith sticks his head inside. "Denmark, you've got a FedEx delivery out here."

I frown, puzzled. "Why didn't you just sign for it?"

Keith shrugs. "I tried. The guy says his boss instructed him that only *you* were to sign for it."

It sounds dumb to me, but I'll figure it out later. "Okay, Keith. Tell him I'll be right out."

Keith nods and starts backing out the door until I say loudly, "Keith!"

"Yeah, boss. What's up?"

"That guy we interviewed, he's a no go."

Keith purses his lips and snorts. "I guess we're back to square one."

I nod and he leaves. I open a last e-mail, send a reply, and then hurry out to get my FedEx delivery. I glance at my watch and smile. It's 11:20 a.m. Sierra should be getting her misted mineral bath right about now. That's the second part of a five-step skin treatment process that, according to the spa's Experience coordinator, will leave her skin feeling more soft and smooth than a newborn's.

"They better treat her right," I say softly, getting up and hurrying out onto the retail floor.

"Hello, Denmark," greets a smiling older black woman.

It's Mrs. Hannah Randall. She's a sweetie who comes in daily to buy an air freshener for her car. She's also the events manager at the plush Lake Shore Gardens Hotel, where Sierra's organizing the architects' conference.

The day Sierra came home raving about the "wonderfully efficient" woman down at the Lake Shore Gardens who was making her job of planning the conference so easy, I knew exactly whom she was talking about. When I explained that Mrs. Randall stopped into the store every day, Sierra insisted that we invite her over for dinner. We did and got to know Mrs. Randall and her husband, and had a generally wonderful evening.

"Hi, Mrs. Randall," I say. "How are you?"

"Wonderful!" she answers, beaming. "And happy anniversary."

I look at her, puzzled. I haven't said anything to her about that. "How'd you know that today was my . . ."

"Sierra told me," she interrupts. "She's such a dear."

"Yes, she is," I agree, smiling softly.

"So how many years will this make?"

"Five."

"That's precious, Denmark," she says, purchasing her air freshener. "Tell Sierra I said hello and you two have a good celebration."

"I will. You take care."

Mrs. Randall and I wave good-bye to each other and I spot the FedEx guy off to the side, impatiently tapping his foot and glancing at his watch. He hurries over, his steps brisk and purposeful. "Mr. Wheeler?" he says.

"That's me."

"Sign here, please."

I sign the receipt slip on his clipboard and give it back to him. He hands me a sturdy 8½ × 11 cardboard envelope. I glance at the envelope and see that it's from

I Got Your Back, Inc.
P.O. Box 8920
Cleveland, Ohio 44645

"That's odd," I say to myself.

He shrugs and jets away. I hurry back into my office, tear

open the envelope, and pull out a DVD disk and a small note. It's today's date and reads: "*Happy anniversary and enjoy the video. It'll make great conversation at the Sapphire Spire.*"

I glance at the DVD, then the note. This has to be the work of Harry, Gordon, or both.

"For all their warts and weird ways, they're decent guys," I say, smiling.

I look at Sierra's picture on my desk. She looks so sexy standing in her rainbow sandals, bright flowered wraparound skirt, halter top, and floppy straw hat, with the bright Caribbean sun and cruise ship behind her.

I place the DVD into the disk tray of the computer processor sitting beside my desk, roll back to the door, and lock it as the media player activates. I hurry and scoot back to the desk, focus hard on the computer screen—and *choke*!

My lovely wife Sierra is naked and on her knees in front of a naked man, giving him an exquisitely tender blow job. His head and upper torso are blurred, and his voice is garbled, but Sierra's image is crystal clear.

Her lover slouches deep in a thick cushioned chair, spreading his legs wide so that Sierra has room to work.

"Yeah, baby," he gurgles. "That's the way I like it!"

He finger-combs her hair as his undulating pelvis matches the up-down motions of her attentive head. He reaches down for her, motions her to her feet, and turns her around until her back faces him. She glances over her shoulder and smiles, her gleaming white teeth gracing him with their brightness. And then slowly, oh so slowly, the light of my life lowers herself onto him. He wraps his arms tight around her waist as they move together, slowly at first and then faster. She places her hands over his as he massages her breasts, licking her lips and grinding hard, her butt muscles flexing with each downward thrust.

A filmy sheen of sweat makes their skin shine. He moans, and Sierra stands quickly. She turns and gives his blur a kiss.

"No, baby," she sweetly admonishes. "You have to make *me* come *first*!"

She places one foot on his upper thigh, smiles down at him, and guides his distorted face into her womanhood. He caresses her butt cheeks, and she closes her eyes tightly, sighing as he sends her riding a wave of pleasure.

Her breaths get deeper as he works his magic. "Like that!" she gasps. "Yes, baby. Do it like *that*!"

She grips his shoulders and moans like she's NEVER moaned for me. He holds her hips tight as she bucks gently against his blur and grabs handfuls of her beautiful long hair as rapture surges through her body. The high rise and low fall of her chest level off as her breathing returns to normal.

Her lover stands, takes her hand, and guides her over to a bed. They stand face to face for a moment, her head covered by the cloud of his blur when he leans in to kiss her. Sierra wraps her fingers around his excitement, stroking and squeezing. He gets into bed, pulls her down into his arms, and massages her majesty as they kiss.

Sierra opens her legs wide. "Now, baby!" she urges.

He moves over her, hovers for a moment, then slowly explores her yearning with his excitement. And my one and only Sierra, who detests vulgar jokes, and complains if my eyes linger on other women, and won't go to a violent movie, and screws her lover like a sex-starved freak—she urges her lover to keep doing what he's doing and make sure that he does it *right*!

The computer screen fades to black. Daggers of searing heat slice through me. The room's spinning. My lungs ache. The echoes of Sierra's lying words ring in my ears: "*Baby, you're the only man for me.*"

My face is hot, so painfully hot. Scalding tears blur my vision. Invisible hands squeeze my skull. I roar! I grab the computer monitor and hurl it across the office. Glass, plastic, and electronics splatter everywhere. I flip over my desk. Papers fly. The phone clatters onto the floor. Sierra's picture smiles up at me from the clutter. I smash it with an elephant stomp, twisting and grinding into it until her face is a mangled mass of paper.

I stagger back into a wall and slide down onto the floor, suppressing the sobs crowding my throat, but there're too many. They squeeze through my lips in mumbles and mutters.

Someone knocks. "Denmark! Are you all right?"

It's Keith Billings. I wipe my nose and eyes and try to speak. A dry blast of air comes out.

"*I'm fine!*" I finally manage to yell. "Get back to work!"

Keith grumbles and leaves. I struggle to my feet, shuffle over to my toppled desk, and pull open the bottom right drawer. I grab a bottle of Scotch and a still intact glass, pour myself a healthy drink, and down it. The Scotch burns its way through my chest and into my stomach. I pour myself another. The images play back in my mind, taunting me. I hurl the bottle into a large picture of me and Sierra, hugging on a carnival Ferris wheel.

I jam my hands hard up against my ears to muffle Sierra's echo: "*No, baby. You have to make me come first!*"

I hurry into my office bathroom, run some cold water, and grip the sides of the sink. The splashing water beckons my tears. I cover my mouth to muffle my sobs, close the bathroom door, and sit down on the toilet seat, sobbing and convulsing until the flood subsides. Slowly, gradually, it does.

I creak to my feet and look into the mirror. The reflection is mine, but someone else is staring back. His jaw is hard-set, nostrils flared, and cheeks sunken. His red, swollen eyes smolder with the focus of a predator. My fingertips burn. I ball my hands into fists and grit my teeth as my heart welcomes its new lover: RAGE!

TEN

The reflection staring back at me from the bathroom mirror says: "Why are you still standing here, stupid? *Go—make—her—pay!*"

I stride from the bathroom over to the computer processing unit and press the DVD player's eject button. I carefully lift out the disk and glance at my watch. Barely fifteen minutes have passed since I first saw Sierra blowing Mr. X. *Fifteen minutes.* Three minutes for each year of my marriage. But it wasn't a marriage. It was a circus where I was the ignorant dancing bear, grateful for the small, dry sugar lumps Sierra threw my way.

I've given her my all and my best while she's given Mr. X much heat and head. I've been devoted and faithful while she's sneaked and skulked. I've opened my heart and given her my love while she's opened her legs and given Mr. X her treasure. And she's been so smooth about it, so calm and cool, so two-faced and treacherous. But Sierra's not the only one who knows how to pull a scam.

I survived childhood in the Brownfield District by using my

wits. Just getting back and forth to school took smarts, skill, and courage. Between the crooked cops and thugs, junkies and con men, perverts and prostitutes, snitches and corner kingpins, and all the muggings, shakedowns, shootings, it's a wonder anyone made it out. But *I did*!

I was only fifteen when that junkie broke into our apartment and shot my father. I knew I had to leave. Mom's nervous breakdown left me and my baby sister Harriet high and dry. I refused to let those jackals from county social services separate us, so I started a hustle, made some quick cash, and paid the right people to be blind when I moved us across town into Lancaster Heights. My closest running partner, a hulking body-breaker named Blinker Hughes, felt sorry for me and decided to do me a favor.

Blinker had done time in the joint and had an enforcer on the inside. The enforcer agreed to cut the junkie's throat for a carton of cigarettes, some skin magazines, and a promise that Blinker would persuade the enforcer's ex-girlfriend that she wasn't in love with her new finacé after all.

I was angry that Blinker hadn't first talked with me, and worried that the cops might connect me with the crack-head's murder. But the crack-head was just another black man in jail, so no one was going to bust a sweat solving his case. They didn't, and I fled the Brownfield District.

Blinker's three older cousins, Stinker, Thinker, and Tinker, made doubly sure my trail was clean. They'd thugged their way through life until one day they realized they could do the same by becoming cops. So they joined the force, got their shields, and started thugging in uniform.

Before mom died in the nuthouse I got my G.E.D. and started working at Speed Shift Auto Parts. I put Harriet through Ohio State, gave her away at her wedding, and steadily climbed Speed Shift's management ladder. The only street skills I kept from the hood were the ones that helped me on my job. *It's time to resurrect the rest!*

I rummage through the mess on the floor and find the FedEx delivery envelope and the note that came with the DVD. "I Got Your Back, Inc.," knew exactly where to hit me hardest. And then there's the note: *"Happy anniversary and enjoy the video. It'll make great conversation at the Sapphire Spire."*

Only Harry Bancroft and Gordon Wilhite knew about my plans to take Sierra to the Sapphire Spire. One or both of them has set me up, and *I'm going to find out who*! As for Sierra, there's no doubt that it was *her* in that video. I'll surely deal with her, but first things first.

I grab the phone off the floor and call my old friend and former lawyer, Nelson Fox. When I started at Speed Shift, Nelson had just opened his private practice and needed clients. I needed a hungry, capable lawyer to make disappear some misdemeanors that had followed me into my new life. Nelson made them go away, so I gave him my business. He was my main source of legal advice, steering me to people who handled wills, insurance, and other matters not his specialty.

I tried to pay Nelson back with some business by recommending him to Blinker when his cousin Tinker was brought up on charges after an Internal Affairs investigation. Mason Booker, a cop at the time, had testified against Tinker, earning him the hatred of Blinker, Stinker, and Thinker. Nelson was swamped and had to decline the case, and now Tinker's doing time.

After I married Sierra I explained to Nelson that we'd decided to get a new lawyer. We were starting fresh and wanted someone whom we both trusted and whose allegiance wouldn't be to her, or me, but *us*! Nelson took it in stride and gave some recommendations. We went with the person suggested by Sierra's family lawyer. As of fifteen minutes ago, that was a big mistake.

Nelson's assistant answers on the first ring: "Fox and Associates, how can I help you?"

"I'd like to speak with Nelson Fox. This is Denmark Wheeler."

"Hello, Mr. Wheeler," she says. "Hold a moment, please."

And a moment later an energetic baritone voice says, "Hey thug! What's happening?"

Nelson's cheery greeting grates on my nerves, and I remind myself that Sierra's cheating isn't his fault. "Nelson, I need your help," I say grimly.

His cheeriness fades. "Okay. Talk to me."

"It's about me and Sierra. We're getting divorced."

Nelson's speechless, but not for long. "Sorry to hear that. But you know I'm not a divorce lawyer."

"I know. Can you recommend someone?"

"Hold on a sec. I think I've got just the person for you. Her name is Hilda Vaughan," says Nelson. He gives me the rest of her contact information, then says, "You can't do better than Hilda. She's smart. She's tough. She's thorough. She's a fighter."

"That's all wonderful and good to know, but will she *win*?"

Nelson snorts. "If I could predict that I'd give up law and spend more time at the track."

"Okay, that's fair. Thanks for the referral. I'll talk to you later."

"Hold up!" Nelson quickly replies. "Are you really serious about this?"

"I'm deadly serious."

Nelson sighs. "This sucks. You two were such a great couple."

"I thought so too. You and I were wrong."

Silence, and then: "Okay, Denmark. Call if you need me."

"You can count on it."

We hang up, and I dial Hilda Vaughan's number. I wait through four lazy rings, pacing back and forth beside my toppled desk. On the fifth ring, someone picks up the phone.

"Hello," answers a soft female voice. "This is attorney Hilda Vaughan's office."

I clear my throat and inject politeness into my voice. "Hello," I say. "I'd like to speak with Hilda Vaughan, please."

"This is she."

What? She answers her own phone? Even cheapskate Nelson has a receptionist. I hope this Hilda's not some shade-tree lawyer working out of her mother's garage at the Joe Blow School of Law.

I forge ahead and explain my business. "My name is Denmark Wheeler. Nelson Fox recommended that I give you a call."

"Oh, yes! How can I help you?"

"Look, let me put it on the table. I caught my wife cheating, and I want a divorce. What's required for this to happen ASAP?"

"Well, we should first have a face-to-face meeting. How soon are you available?"

"Ms. Vaughan, I'm available *now* if you are."

She laughs. It's light and gentle, and soothing. It's a kind, compassionate laugh, certainly not one I'd expect from a lawyer—*especially a divorce lawyer*!

"I know this is short notice," I say, "but it would be perfect if we could meet *today*."

"Hold on," she replies.

I listen as she speaks to the person who must be her assistant, the one who didn't answer the phone and will probably be reprimanded once we hang up.

"Lucille!" Hilda calls. "How tight is my afternoon schedule?"

A strong but elderly voice answers back with more insolence than should be allowed for office help. "Hilda, after you get back from that hospice, you don't have room to squeeze nothing else into today."

"Are you sure?" Hilda gently persists.

"You're so hardheaded. I don't even know why I waste my time trying to keep you from wearing yourself out."

This exchange is cute, interesting, and peculiar. But from

what I've heard of divorce court warfare, I don't need cute. I need sharp, highly skilled legal talent that'll take the sword of the law and hack Sierra into salad.

Hilda clears her throat and speaks low. "Lucille's my secretary, and she's right. I can't see you today, but I'm free late Saturday morning."

"But that's the weekend."

"Yes, I know. What's the problem?"

There's a sudden steeliness in Hilda's tone, and the crispness of her response reminds me of Nelson's saying that, among other things, "She's tough."

"There's no problem," I say. "I just thought that since it was Saturday you wouldn't be seeing . . ."

"Normally I wouldn't. But you sound urgent, so I'm making myself available."

We make the arrangements and hang up. I hunt for my briefcase amidst the chaos of my office, find it, and slip the jacketed DVD disk inside. I glance at my watch. I've still got plenty of time to prepare an appropriate welcome for Sierra.

I stuff the FedEx envelope and note into my briefcase, kick aside some clutter, and start for the door. I spot Sierra's mangled picture on the floor, stomp on it again, and pound out through the store. Keith and the other employees stare at me with fearful wide eyes as I pass.

I get to the door and zero in on Keith. "Make sure my office gets cleaned up!" I command. Then I storm out.

ELEVEN

I zoom through my Diamond Ridge Estates neighborhood, whip into my garage, hustle into the house and upstairs, taking them two at a time. I go to the hallway closet, grab some suitcases, carry them into the bedroom, and stuff Sierra's clothes into them. Then I heft the bulging containers out to the eco-friendly wheeled garbage cans in the garage, and toss the luggage beside them. I hurry back inside and up to the bedroom, rush into the connecting bathroom, strip, and get into the shower. I turn on the water to as hot as I can stand it and scrub hard to remove the slime of Sierra's deceit and the grime of my self-delusion.

Minutes later I'm back down in the living room, dressed and smelling good. I throw a log onto the fireplace, find some old Al Green hits, Sierra's favorite *The Best of Sam Cook*, some Teddy Pendergrass, and Lionel Ritchie, and set up the DVD unit and TV for when Sierra arrives. I double-check everything, pour myself a healthy glass of merlot, turn the lights down, sit on the couch, and wait.

Time passes. My mind drifts. I think of things—like Sierra riding Mr. X. The way she never looked at me when we . . . when we what? It was too laden with lies to be sincere lovemaking. It was too tame and dull to qualify as screwing. It was just bland coupling. And all those times she had her eyes closed she was probably thinking of *him*, yearning and wishing for *him* to be the one filling her instead of *me*.

The wind rustles the leaves on the trees outside the window. The wind chimes on the porch tinkle. Broad brushstrokes of the early evening gradually paint light purple over late afternoon's soft gold.

The smooth, deep-voiced DJ on the oldies radio station says, "And now brothers and sisters, a classic old school tune of heartbreak: the Chi-Lites singing *The Coldest Days of My Life*."

A car pulls into the driveway, and the garage door opens. I cut off the radio and start the CD music player. Al Green's smooth voice flows from the speakers, expressing shock, stun, and hurt about the discovery of his woman's cheating. I grab the remote, turn on the TV, re-check the DVD unit's settings, and get ready. All the doors and windows are closed, locked, and bolted. Once Sierra closes the garage there'll be no fast, easy way out.

"Hello!" Sierra calls, coming in through the kitchen. "I'm home."

I don't answer right away, letting the crackling log in the fireplace and the soothing music work their magic.

"Denmark! Are you here?" Sierra calls.

I finish the last of my merlot and relax. "I'm right here."

She steps into the living room, and I catch my breath. Sierra's a beautiful woman, but her Salina's "Encounter" has transformed her into someone who could've rivaled the beautiful Helen of Troy. Helen caused the men of Troy and Greece to slaughter each other in a ten-year war. Sierra could make them bow in immediate surrender.

"You look stunning," I say, forcing my lips into a smile.

Sierra giggles and twirls around. "I feel rejuvenated," she says. "Thanks for the wonderful gift."

I look deep into her eyes, searching for the Sierra I married, the woman I once loved to love, the one I'd have died for, the one whose face—if we'd ever had kids—would've been the heart-stopping beauty of my daughter and the noble strength of my son. But it was all an illusion. All I see now is a snickering snake. Every word falling from her lips is a lie. Every giggle is her point-ing at me and yelling: Sucker! Fool! Chump!

"This looks like you're expecting someone special?" she says, smiling and gesturing to the fireplace.

"I am," I say, patting my lap. "I've been waiting for you."

She comes over, sits crossways on my lap, and wraps her arms around my neck as we kiss. "And why have you been wait-ing on me?" she asks huskily.

I massage the back of her neck. All I'd have to do is grab and snap. "I want to give you your next surprise," I say. "C'mon and lie down on my lap, and I'll show it to you."

She doesn't hesitate, kicks off her shoes and stretches out, resting her head and neck right where I can reach them easily.

She reaches up for my face, tenderly holding my cheeks. "This is so perfect," she says. "It's like a dream."

"Yes. It certainly is."

She smiles large. "So what's your big surprise?"

"It's on the TV. I'll show you."

"Okay. What is it?"

"Hold your horses, Miss Impatient," I say. I reach smoothly down, grab the remote, and position it firmly in my grip. "It's a DVD recording. Just a small token of how much I appreciate you sharing yourself so freely."

"I can't wait," Sierra says excitedly, turning onto her side so she can get the best view.

I point the remote at the TV and press PLAY. Sierra shrieks: "Jesus! God! Jesus!"

She squirms, and I lock my arms around her. "No! No! Dear God! No!" she babbles.

"Shut up!" I roar.

She struggles frantically, but I've got her tight! The TV shows her down in front of Mr. X, swirling her tongue around the head of his missile. *"Yeah, baby,"* his garbled voice booms from the surround-sound speakers. *"That's the way I like it!"*

"Dear God! Please! Jesus! Help me, please God!"

She writhes, fights, and bucks. I lock her tight in my arms, squeezing until she can't move.

"Denmark, I'm sorry! Please! I'm . . ."

"Sorry! I'll teach you about . . ."

She bites my arm and rams her elbow into my balls. I scream and loosen my hold on Sierra as shock waves of agony hammer through my groin. She scrambles away on her hands and knees. I leap off the couch, grab her ankle, and drag her back. She kicks at my face but misses.

"Please, Denmark!" she pleads. "I'm sorry! *I'm sorry*!"

"Who is he?" I demand, coughing.

She madly thrashes her leg. "Let me go!"

"Tell me!"

"I don't love him."

"Of course you don't!" I blast. "You just *screw him*!"

She grabs a vase, smashes it against the coffee table, and stabs at my hand with its jagged edges. I let her go. She barely misses me, slicing into the carpet. She springs to her feet and sprints into the kitchen. I lunge after her but miss. She races for the door leading out to the garage. I hurl a chair, and it smashes into the door. Sierra ducks, dashes over to the island, and grabs a wicked-looking knife. She holds it like she means business. *That makes two of us!*

I move slowly to the left. "Tell me who he is!" I demand.

Sierra moves slowly around the island, keeping her eyes locked with mine and watching my every movement. "You've been cheating, too!" she accuses.

"What are you talking about?"

"Vondie!"

"*What?*"

Sierra slashes at me with the knife. I swerve out of the blade's path, then chase her around and around the island.

"You spent the weekend with her in Orlando!" she hollers.

"It was a business trip!"

"That's what you say!"

"Who is he?"

She throws the knife at me and rockets into the living room, heading for the phone over on the wooden stand. I snatch up the wrought-iron coffee table and heave it across the room. It lands on the phone and stand with a bomb-blast CRASH! Sierra spins away as glass, wood, and plastic splatter everywhere.

Her eyes snap over and onto me, her lower lip trembling as she wrings her hands. "Please, Denmark. It was a mistake."

"Loving you was the mistake! *Tell me who he is!*"

I start toward her. She backs away, looking frantically for a weapon. My chest heaves. Sierra backs up against the wall, sobbing and muttering apologies. Tears blur my vision. I love her. *Lying tramp!* I need her. *Sneaking slut!* She's my world. *Backstabbing whore!*

"Why, Sierra?" I ask, choking out the words. "Why did you do it?"

"I'm so sorry," she sobs. "I didn't mean to hurt you."

Her TV image says: *"No baby. You have to make me come first!"*

We glance at the TV, then at each other. She flies toward the front door.

"Get back here!" I shout, grabbing at the air.

She blurs into the night.

TWELVE

shuffle into the kitchen, grab a bottle of bourbon from the cabinet over the sink, get a glass, and plop down in the breakfast nook. I can't see. It's like I'm looking through a watery haze.

"No!" I shout, slamming my fist onto the table. *"No tears for her!"*

I pour myself a glass of booze and slug it down. Memories stampede through my mind. I down a second glass to slow them, but they thunder through. It's our wedding night, and Sierra's the most beautiful woman I've ever seen. I shudder as I slip inside her. We love each other into the next day, stopping only to get dressed and catch our plane to Toronto.

Third glass: I pull into the wide, circular driveway of our new house, cut off the car, and hurry to open Sierra's door. She's being a good sport, sitting quietly blindfolded while I get her ready.

I lead her to the front door and remove her blindfold. She blinks and looks around, bewildered. She smiles bright, steps back, and claps her hands over her mouth. I pull a key from my pocket, slip it into her palm, and close her fingers around it.

"Happy birthday, darling Sierra," I say.

Fourth glass: I wake up and find Sierra smiling and staring down at me in the early morning light of Colorado's White River National Forest.

"Hey, precious," she whispers, kissing my eyes.

I stroke her cheek and run my fingers through her hair. It's grown down to her shoulders. "You're beautiful," I say.

She smiles, unzips my sleeping bag, crawls in with me, and unzips my pants.

Guzzling from the bottle: I sit on the side of the bed, wipe Sierra's nose dry, and hold the teacup to her mouth.

"I hate colds," she says, taking a sip. Her voice is weak and scratchy.

I set the teacup on the nightstand, pull her into my arms, and rock her gently. "I know, baby. But don't worry. I'll take care of you."

She hugs me. "Denmark, I don't know what I'd do without you."

I push the bottle aside. It falls to the floor and shatters. I stagger over to the couch and fall face-first into the cushions where Sierra last sat. Traces of her sweet mustiness linger. I bury my face in the cushions, breathing deep to inhale her.

Memories assail my mind: "Do you, Denmark Vesey Wheeler, take this woman . . . Sierra, I love you . . . Be careful, sweetheart. I don't want to lose you . . . Before you, I was drifting . . ."

I roll onto my back. Tears trickle down the sides of my face. The fireplace log has burned out. The candles are melted blobs. Silence rampages through the house. I've got to get out of here! I've got to escape this grinding pain. I *must* endure. I *must* survive. But first I'm going to get plastered. I grab my keys. Moments later I stomp on the gas, and the Corvette tears into traffic.

THIRTEEN

park the Corvette near the front door of the Ebony Crystal jazz club, get out, and soak up the music that's seeping through the walls out into the night. The languid notes of the tenor saxophone float around me, massaging my ears with their soothing clarity.

I stroll into the dimly lit club and look up into the perpetually scowling face of a bald mountain of a man, standing with his bulging arms crossed and legs spread apart. He's a punishing machine, ready for action.

"Twenty-five dollars to get in plus a two-drink minimum," he rumbles.

I step up on him. "I wouldn't pay twenty-five dollars to flatten this dump."

He looks down at me, glares hard for a moment, then smiles. "Denmark! Where you been, brother?"

"Hey, Sutton, what's up?"

He grabs my hand with his meaty paw and pumps. "Man, I was almost starting to think you got hit by a bus or something."

I smile wryly. "That's not too far from the truth."

Sutton frowns in puzzlement, then shrugs. "It's good seeing you, thug."

"It can't be that good, not if you're about to charge me twenty-five dollars."

He gestures apologetically. "Hey, bro, what can I do? The price is the price." He leans close and whispers. "But since you're from the Brownfield District, I'll hook you up."

He steps aside and winks. I wink back, ease inside, look around, and inhale deep. The familiar sights, sounds, and scents are all here: expensive colognes, seductive perfumes, crisp money, faint traces of incense, a light haze of cigarette smoke, and finely dressed jazz-loving men and women, nursing their drinks of good high-quality liquor as they groove and sway to the beat.

For a moment it's five years ago and days before I'm on Continental Flight 5667, flying from Cleveland to Las Vegas. Vondie and I have been hanging out and having fun. We cruise down to the Ebony Crystal once a week to catch the latest, hottest jazz acts that club owner Reddy Bingham brings to town.

The Ebony Crystal was my escape. Problems were checked at the door. Time stopped. Conversations were low and easy. Liquor flowed like a quiet stream. And shredded hearts were healed by the ministers on stage who preached through their instruments.

"You've been gone awhile," someone says off to my side, his voice sounding like footsteps scraping across marbles.

I look quickly and see a stubby, chubby, shade-wearing coffee-skinned man. He's chomping on an unlit cigar. His hair is so unruly it almost looks like a style. He extends his hand, palm up, and I slap him five.

"What's up, Reddy?" I say.

He shifts the cigar from one side of his mouth to the other. "It's all about the jazz, baby. It's all about the jazz."

I nod slowly. "So it was, and always shall be."

He looks away from me to the stage. "Where you been, Denmark? Some good acts have come through here. Too bad you missed 'em."

Up until last year, Sierra and I paid frequent visits to the club. She wasn't into jazz like Vondie, but she always seemed to have a good time anyway. Then one night she invited her mother, brother, and sister to come with us. They were more stuck-up than regular bourgeois snobs, and they fidgeted, frowned, and grumbled through each set, later harassing Sierra about tolerating such lowbrow entertainment. Sierra afterward started finding excuses not to go. She started wishing I wouldn't. I refused to have problems between me and my wife, so I ditched the Ebony Crystal.

"That's my bad, Reddy," I answer. "I got busy living life, and got lost."

"It happens," he responds, bopping his head to a beat.

We stand silent for a few moments until Reddy says, "How's Sierra?"

I don't answer. Reddy turns and studies me over the top of his lowered shades. He purses his lips, nods sadly, then looks back at the stage. "Have a sit-down, brother. Take a load off. Listen to the message in the music."

"What's it saying, Reddy?"

He pats my shoulder. "Healing is a process, my man. Not a moment."

He steps off into the shadows, snapping his fingers. Reddy's always been insightful, but that's not why he read me so easily. I glimpsed myself in the Corvette's rearview mirror on the way here. My face was a war of emotions. I've got to get a grip. I've got to resurrect the street skills that once made it impossible for anyone to know what I was thinking or feeling until after I'd done my damage. I lost that ability with Sierra. It took months to open up to her, but once I did, I felt good and free. So I let my guard down and set myself up for tonight.

I spot an empty booth along a far wall and head for its

refuge. With every step, my anger surrenders to the club's grooving cool. This respite in the calm eye of my marital storm won't last long, but it's better than listening to the echoes of Sierra's lies. I slip quickly between tables and patrons who're mesmerized by the sax-playing sister on stage. She's telling her man through her music to come love her *now*.

I slide into the booth, sit back, and embrace the near solitude. The booth's in a dim, remote corner, but I can still see the stage pretty good. The sound's carrying nicely. And except for two jokers sitting nearby who're talking just a tad too loud, people are laid back and flowing with the tunes.

A slim, sexy, dark, so very dark woman glides in my direction. It's Salome Stevens. She's a flirty, vivacious, loves-to-party honey I've known from way back when I first started coming to the Ebony Crystal. We had a little something going for a few months but nixed it when she decided to give her marriage a second try.

I hated to see Salome go, but she was determined to make her marriage work. It was rough going. She'd sometimes call and cry on my shoulder, and I'd wonder why she was bothering to keep a husband who, according to her, was "more boring than watching paint dry."

"All Norman does is sit in that recliner and watch the Weather Channel," she'd complain.

I figured that if the sucker could live with somebody as fine as Salome and not be excited, he was technically dead. During their brief separation, when Salome and I hooked up, we had a ball. Salome's absence shocked Norman into his old self, and he came on strong. She still loved him enough to give it a second shot and went home. She's still there, so either something went right or she's resigned herself to living out the rest of her life sitting next to him as they marvel at televised tornadoes.

The two jokers nearby erupt with some hee-hawing laughter, distracting me from fine Salome. They settle down, and I check her out. She's dressed in the trademark black pants, gold blouse, and gold stiletto heels that are the uniform of the Ebony Crystal's servers, all female and all lovely.

Salome's carrying a tray with a glass on it and a brand-new bottle of something that looks good and strong. She strides boldly into the dimness where I'm sitting, keeping her eyes locked with mine as she sets the glass and bottle down in front of me.

"I've missed seeing you," she says.

"It's good seeing you also, Salome."

"Your timing's perfect. In another fifteen minutes my shift would've been over and I'd be on my way home."

Judging from her tone, going home doesn't sound like such a happy prospect.

"How's Norman?" I ask.

"Dry as sand and dull as toast. How's Sierra?"

I purse my lips and cut my eyes at the bottle. "What's the occasion? I didn't place an order."

Salome gestures with her head over to the bar. "It's a gift from Reddy. Enjoy."

"Tell him I said thanks."

She nods, scans the empty booth, and arches an eyebrow. "You avoided my question, and you're sitting here alone. Are you flying solo, or should I leave before your wife walks up and reaches the wrong conclusion?"

"It's solo, until further notice."

Her eyes soften. "I know that look, Denmark. What's the matter?" I look away toward the stage. Salome leans close and taps the bottle. "The answer's not in there, sugar. Believe me, I know."

"Have a nice night, Salome."

She sighs, turns away, then turns back. I look up at her. She places two fingers beneath my chin and leans over while lifting my face to meet hers.

She kisses me tenderly and smiles. "Cheer up, sweetie. It'll get better."

"Has it for you?"

She looks down and away. "It could be worse."

A husband who sits catatonic watching the Weather Channel, or a wife giving another guy a blow job? Salome's right. Things for her could be much worse.

"Take care," she says, gliding away and throwing much swing into her hips.

I'd watch longer, but I'm already committed to the booze in this bottle. I pour myself a healthy slug and gulp it down. I want this drunk to come quick. I want oblivion to enslave me. I pour another couple of glasses, holding the bottle tight as the booze burns a path of forgetfulness down my throat.

The sister playing the sax blows notes that swirl around me like a summer breeze. They smooth me into their flow, electrifying my senses as they ripple through my marrow.

"Stop lying!" blurts one of the loudmouths sitting nearby. "You might be dumb, but that's downright *stupid*."

Several people shoot irritated glances at them then refocus onto the sax-playing sister.

"I'm serious, man," answers his friend. "Single babes can't do squat for me. It's the married ones who got the best loving."

One couple gets up and moves. They're lucky it's the middle of the week, when they can find a table. From Thursday through Saturday, there's barely standing room in the Ebony Crystal.

The sister on stage blows tunes that wrap me in the warmth of her musical passion. Her background musicians add their magic harmonies, filling the club with sounds too beautiful for mere mortal ears.

"You're gonna get your silly self beat down," Bigmouth One loudly warns. "How'd you like it if somebody was stroking your woman on the sly?"

Bigmouth Two belts out a laugh that earns him more mean

stares and angrily hissed shushes. "I'm too smart to get sucker-played like that," he booms.

That fool's lucky he's not within reach and that I'm floating off into a nice high. He's like the snake in that video with Sierra. When I find him I'm going to hurt him, *bad*! I pour another drink and slug it down.

Reddy, who's sitting at the bar, calls a passing server I recognize as Nikki and whispers in her ear while gesturing at the two loud talkers. She nods, then eases over to their table and speaks softly to them. Bigmouth One scowls at her. Bigmouth Two waves her off. Reddy stands up and steps toward them, but they quiet down and he backs off.

The musicians blow out some notes that lift me high into a pristine stratosphere of freewheeling goodness, miles above the confusion of life, love, and loss. It's just enough to get me across the horizon of the next moment. With a few more shots of liquor I might make it into the next day.

The musicians wind down to a smooth, sultry end and are rewarded with steady applause and calls for more. They smile, bow, and wave, and the sax sister steps over to the mike.

"Ya'll are wonderful," she says, speaking low and cool. "Hang tight for a few minutes while we take a break and . . ."

"Don't worry, baby," someone shouts from the back. "We ain't going nowhere."

Light laughter ripples through the club, and the sister smiles. "Stay tuned. Stay cool. Stay put. When we come back, we'll be doing some selections from our new CD entitled *Finished at the Start*."

"You've got that right," I grumble, gulping down the rest of my drink.

There's more applause. The musicians file off stage, laughing and talking with each other as they head over to the bar. Ramsey Lewis's excellent music starts pumping through the club's sound system. Everyone settles back into some nice conversation. Servers hustle, taking new drink orders. People who waited through the stage performance hurry off to the bathrooms.

I sit back and relax deep into the booth's cushions. This is the escape I was hoping for. It's the . . .

"Man, I'm Prince Charming to every married woman in Cleveland," Bigmouth Two loudly asserts to his buddy. "When their husbands let them down, I'm there to pick them up." He winks and nudges him like they're sharing an inside joke. "And believe you me, I do a lot of picking up. It's all just a matter of time."

I and several others look over at them. Those jerks are swilling more booze, and they've run off anyone who was seated near them. I push away my glass and bottle, pull out my wallet, throw some money onto the table, and stand to leave.

"So much for the escape," I grumble.

But hold on. Reddy scowls, grabs a phone, and punches some numbers. He looks across the club for Sutton over at the door, but Sutton's not there.

"It's a matter of time before what?" asks Bigmouth One.

Two rolls his eyes in exasperation at his friend's ignorance. "Problems, man. Sooner or later one of those stupid suckers does something to piss off his wife. Once that happens, I'm there to help her through."

"Aren't you worried about getting caught?" Bigmouth One queries.

"Hell no!" Two boasts. "Look, man. You've got to understand women, especially the married ones. They don't want to be alone, and they'll put up with their man as long as he's not doing something stupid like beating on them. But just because they stay doesn't mean they're happy. That's where I come in."

Reddy whispers emphatically to Nikki, pointing toward the back office. She dashes off. He punches more buttons.

"So you're the married wives' happiness genie, is that it?" One inquires.

"Exactly!" Two laughs, nodding. "And my magic wand"—wink, grin, elbow nudge—"leaves them with a smile on their lips and a twinkle in their eyes."

"You're just a public servant doing a good deed."

"You know it, baby. I'm doing a *great* deed, and those horny homemakers love every inch of it."

"Man, I hope you got some good medical insurance," Bigmouth One advises.

Nikki emerges from the back and gets Reddy's attention. He angles toward her, and they meet halfway. I ease closer and lean against the wall, waiting to follow his lead. Nikki gestures at the back, talking fast and shaking her head. Reddy balls his fists, glares at the bigmouths, and continues toward them. I follow.

"And the best part," says Two, "is that I don't have to deal with any attitude, argument, and expectation. That crap I leave for the husbands."

Reddy walks up on the two bigmouths and clears his throat. "Say cats, ya'll need to keep it down. Okay?"

"How're you gonna tell us that?" demands Bigmouth One. "We're paying customers."

"Sure, you're right," Reddy responds. "But ya'll still need to tone it down. Others are complaining."

" 'Others' can blow me," Two chuckles, dismissing Reddy with a wrist flick. "It's a free country, and we paid our money. Get lost!"

The bigmouths laugh and slap each other five, then look at me, standing off to the side. Wife-tampering Bigmouth Two glares at me. "What're you looking at?" he challenges. "You don't like what I'm saying? I'll bang your woman too."

I explode and snatch Two from his chair, then hurl him across the room. He slams into a wall and crumples to the floor. He shakes his head, sees me flying toward him, and scrambles away. I pounce and smother him with an avalanche of punches, kicks, stomps, swats, and body blows.

"Get 'em off me!" he wails. "Get 'em off me!"

Shouting people grab at me. I fight them off. Two's face is a moonscape of welts, bumps, and cuts. More hands grab at me. Sutton and others drag me off. Bigmouth One flees the club. People clap and cheer. Men kick and punch as he races past.

"Damn!" Sutton exclaims. "You were fixing to send that fool to Emergency."

I shake myself free from his iron grip. "Get off me!" I growl.

Sutton lets go, lifts his hands in surrender, and backs off. "Take it easy, Denmark. I'm on your side."

"Where were you?" Reddy demands, his narrowed eyes fixed onto Sutton. "I called up front and in the back."

Sutton scowls. "I was out in the parking lot helping Salome with her car when Nikki came and got me."

Reddy's expression relaxes. "Oh, okay. Cool."

"Denmark, you should go," Sutton worriedly suggests. "His friend might call the police."

"Don't worry about this scum," Reddy counters, glancing at the whimpering waste on the floor. "He won't yap to the police once I tell him that I know four or five husbands who'd love to have a private talk with him in my storeroom."

"That's cold-blooded," observes Sutton. Then he grins and says, "I love it."

Reddy squeezes my shoulder. "You gonna be okay?"

"Yeah, I guess so."

He nods gravely. "Let it go, Denmark. Whatever it is, just let it go."

Not yet, Reddy. *Not until after I find out who's been screwing my wife.* We slap five and hug, and I leave.

FOURTEEN

'm half way to my Corvette when I hear a car's cranking engine, turning over and over, straining to start. Whoever it belongs to had better be careful before they drain the battery.

I keep striding across the well-lit parking lot but stop when a woman calls. "Excuse me!" she says loudly. "Could I get some help?"

She's standing directly beneath a light, and I start toward her. After a short distance I can see by the slim, fine figure that it's Salome Stevens. She's always looked good, but out here in the soft night, with the breeze making her rippling blouse cling to her proudly standing breasts, Salome's spectacular.

"What's the problem?" I ask, forcing a smile as I get close.

She frowns at her Chevy Malibu. "It's this stupid car battery. This is the second time it's left me stranded. Norman said it was good, but he's obviously *wrong*."

"Let me take a look," I say.

"Denmark, thank you so much!" she gushes. "Sutton was helping, then he was called inside." She peers at me oddly. "Are you okay? You seem . . . tense."

After bludgeoning Bigmouth Two, I'm relaxed and satisfied. "Pop the hood," I gently command Salome. She releases the hood latch, and I quickly find the problem. "You've got a bad cable connection."

"Is it serious?"

"Not in the least. I'll have you running in a heartbeat."

I drive my Corvette over to her car, get some tools, and tinker for a few minutes with her battery cables. "Okay. Try it now," I say loudly.

Salome in the driver's seat turns the ignition, and the Malibu's engine roars "Wonderful!" she exclaims.

Salome meets me as I close the hood and finish wiping my hands on a cloth. "After this, I'm doubly glad you came out tonight," she says.

I wink. "For someone as gorgeous as you, it was my pleasure."

Salome sighs. "It's so refreshing to know a man who still gives compliments." She looks hard at me, her eyes deep and inviting. "I hope Sierra knows what she has in you."

"Trust me," I growl. "She doesn't!"

She steps close until we're only inches apart. "Well, I do. And I wish I could better express my appreciation, but this'll have to do."

She wraps her arms around my neck, pulls me close, and gives me a sweet kiss. I pull Salome close and hold her tight as the marital restraints that governed me for five years burst loose. In all that time I played by the rules, devoting myself to Sierra, always putting her first. I believed in our love and that doing right would get right results. I'd actually started believing elders like my aunt Phyllis, who'd always said that "What goes around, comes around," guarding my actions so that the "Come around" would be good. *That stupidity is over!*

"How thankful are you?" I ask, massaging the small of Salome's back.

Her eyelids lower seductively. "How thankful should I be?"

"Follow me home and we'll discuss it."

She arches an eyebrow, plants her palms firmly flat against my chest, and pushes me slightly away. "Won't it get a little crowded with your wife there?"

"I told you that I'm flying solo. I'm home alone, *for good*!"

She relaxes and strokes my cheek, her eyes sad. "Oh baby, I'm sorry."

"I'm not! With her out of the picture I can give you what you need."

Salome smirks smugly. "And what is it you think I need?"

I kiss her with scorching passion, let her go, and briskly walk the few short steps to my Corvette, then look back at her. She's fanning herself.

"That was an appetizer," I say, opening the door. "The main course is at my house."

I start to get in, and Salome says, "It's a shame to eat alone."

"Then come join me?"

"Will it be quick?"

"No."

She checks her watch. "Drive ahead. I'll follow."

Forty minutes later, Salome parks in the space beside my Corvette in the garage and watches as the softly humming door closes.

I unlock the door leading into the house through the kitchen, and gesture to Salome. "Ladies first," I say.

"Why thank you, sir knight," she replies, laughing.

Hold up! I can't let Salome see where Sierra and I fought. I take gentle hold of her arm. "Let's go downstairs," I suggest. "The living room's not in the best shape right now."

Salome nods. "Okay. I'm a neat freak too, so I know how you feel."

I open the door and turn on the light, and Salome starts down the steps. "I'll be right there," I say, stepping off to fill an ice bucket.

"It's beautiful down here!" Salome happily observes.

"Thanks. It cost a bundle for the interior decorator."

"It was money well spent."

"The hell it was," I grumble.

I find us two glasses and a bottle of Courvoisier, then join Salome downstairs. She's standing at the CD player, sorting through my CD library. She starts some music playing while I fix our drinks over at the bar.

The speakers come alive with an old cut of Boyz II Men, singing their agonizingly appropriate "Although we've come to the end of our road."

I hand Salome her drink and hold my glass up to her for a toast. "To roads with new beginnings," I say, and we clink our glasses together.

I sip my drink. Salome throws hers back in a single gulp, grimacing as the booze drains down her throat. "I needed that," she says, suppressing a cough.

"What else do you need?" I ask, polishing off my drink.

She sets her glass down on the bar counter. "More than what I've been getting at home."

"What are you missing?"

"Everything, it seems."

I wrap Salome tight in my muscular arms and look deep into her eyes. "I can fix that too."

"What if I'm too far gone?" she coyly asks.

I pull her into me and kiss her with naked passion. She grips the back of my head and sighs. A hunger, deep, relentless, and fierce, seizes me, and I need Salome more than air. I crave her sweet secret place. The fire in my loins roars.

I kiss her neck and shoulders, open the top buttons of

her blouse, and kiss along the bulge of her breasts. "Denmark," she calls softly, panting. "What're you . . . doing? I'm . . . married."

I turn her back to me, pull her into my chest, and rasp into her ear. "That's right! You're married to a man who's blind to your beauty."

"But . . ."

I kiss her earlobe. "He's more focused on his TV than you."

I massage her breasts, caressing them, squeezing, rubbing my fingers over her nipples. She covers my hands with hers as I tell her more. "He can't satisfy your hunger, baby. He can't supply the power, strength, and *long—thick—hardness* you need!"

I kiss along her neck and hold her tight. "He doesn't care that you need strong arms to hold you," I say, licking her shoulder. "Arms like mine that'll squeeze you tight when your love comes down. Arms that won't let go till you've been thrilled and satisfied."

I kiss her neck, and she tilts her head to the side, giving me room. I slide my hand down her chest and stomach and onto her magic. She pulls my head toward her upturned face and kisses me. I slip my hands inside her blouse, push her bra up and out of the way, and massage her freed, firm breasts, rolling her nipples between my thumb and forefinger until they're deliciously swollen and hard.

She undoes my trousers and takes hold of me. She looks down, and her eyes widen. "My, my," she says, arching her eyebrow. "He's definitely excited."

"And all yours," I rumble, pulling her close.

She kisses me with explosive yearning, grinding softly against my aching bulge.

"You're so sexy!" I whisper. I grab her rear end and pull her into me. "You're so hot! You're so irresistible!"

"What else?" she breathlessly urges. "Tell me more!"

"You're beautiful, baby. You can break a man down. You can make him beg for your touch."

She lifts her arms high as I pull her blouse and bra off. I suck her breasts, going lower and lower down and onto my knees, kissing her chest, stomach, and belly button to the top of her open pants.

She steps back, yanks down her pants and panties, then stands waiting for me. I pull her forward by her hips, inhale deep her womanly fragrance, and kiss along the edges of her sweetness. She exhales in soft erratic blasts. And then, slowly and gently, I speak to her wonder.

"Yes!" she whispers hoarsely. "Like . . . *that!*"

Her thighs shake and tremble, and she digs her nails into my shoulders. The shakes subside, and she stutter-steps over to a barstool and sits down. I stand quickly, tear off my clothes, and hurry over to her. She scoots to the stool's edge, locking her gaze onto my crotch as I approach. Her passion calls my hardness like a magnet to steel. I pick her up, and she wraps her legs around my waist as I spin around and sit down on the barstool. Then I slowly lower her onto me. She closes her eyes as her hunger swallows mine.

"Mercy!" she gasps.

She's a warm, moist velvety garden. Faster we move, and trillions upon trillions of sparks and explosions fire through my nerves. We're famished lovers, straining, longing, and yearning for volcanic release.

I stand, kick the stool out of the way, and motion for Salome to stand in front of me. She grips the counter, glances back, then closes her eyes and exhales loud as we re-unite.

My forearms ache. My throat's dry. My eyes feel oversized for my sockets. It's been so long since I've had it like this. *It's been much too long!*

I grip her hips tight and give her my best. She answers back the same. Tiny bursts of light flash before me.

"Denmark!" Salome screams, scraping her nails across the counter.

Firestorms sweep across me. Powerful quakes ripple through me. My muscles seize. Sweat pours off my back, and my thighs tremble as five years of dammed-up desire explode in a scream of ecstasy.

FIFTEEN

Salome's gone, but the scent of her sex lingers. I stroll casually across the living room sipping from a glass of Courvoisier, sit down on the couch, stare into the burning fire, and smile.

"Sweet, sweet Salome," I say softly. "Thanks, baby. You were so good."

We rocked and rolled for another hour before she said, "I have to go. Norman works third shift, and I need to be home when he arrives."

We had plenty of time before her hubby got home by 6 a.m., but a woman's no means *no!* So I backed off and fixed us some coffee as Salome got dressed.

"Maybe he's working too hard," she said, suddenly the good wife concerned about her husband's well-being. "He's a decent man, but this situation's so frustrating."

Twenty minutes earlier, her frustrations had boiled down to keeping up with me as I stroked her so good, hard, and deep that she had her arms and legs wrapped around me, clutching tight.

"But that's the way they do things down at FedEx," she'd continued. "Maybe that's why they have such high productivity."

I froze. "Your husband works for FedEx?"

"Yes," she'd answered, pulling on her pants. "He's been there for three years now."

It was grasping and irrational to connect the events, but that didn't matter. A FedEx delivery guy had delivered the DVD that precipitated my disaster. Although I'd just gotten with Salome, now that I knew her hubby's employer, I'd get with her again to even things up.

I stopped making the coffee and bee-lined for Salome. She looked up from fastening the front of her pants. "Denmark . . . what is it?"

I glanced at the wall clock. "You don't have to leave just yet."

"But . . ."

Her words fell silent when I pulled off my trousers. I was iron stiff and poised for action. She stroked me, tentatively at first, then with urgency. Her eyes smoldered with molten lust. Two minutes later, she held the back of the couch in a death grip, grunting each time my pelvis slapped up against her butt cheeks as I expended my irrationality behind her in energy-charged thrusts.

And now she's gone. Should I be worried about her? After all, what if tonight's the night Norman decides to come home early? What if he called and she wasn't there? What if he suddenly rediscovers his passion for her?

Who cares? I'm not sweating him any more than Mr. X sweated me. He and Sierra have shown me that the law-of-the-urban-jungle that dominated inside the Brownfield District rules outside it as well. In there, and out here, every man's for himself, taking what he wants, scoring where he can, and only the suckers will lose. I've been a sucker for Sierra and Mr. X, and it's time to return the favor.

Harry and Gordon were the only two people I'd told about

taking Sierra to the Sapphire Spire. It must be one of them. *It has to be one of them!*

I gulp down the drink in my glass and pour myself another. Whichever one of them it is, they're going to pay . . . *with their wives!*

I've first got some fence mending to do with Inez. And then there's Alice—sweet, patient, ever-understanding Alice. She wants me to be the same kind of friend to her that I've been to Gordon. I'll do her one better. I'll be the kind of friend that her husband's been to *my wife*. I'll get her *and* Inez ready to give up their booty just like Harry *or* Gordon got Sierra to give up hers.

Harry's still at work with his night janitor crew and won't be leaving for a while. I grab the phone and dial. After four rings a scratchy, thick voice labors out a "Hello?"

Inez sounds terrible. "Hi, Inez," I say. "It's me, Denmark."

"Denmark," she groans. "I'm surprised that you're still talking to me."

"Of course I'm still talking to you," I deflect. "I just wanted to call and apologize for being so harsh this morning."

"Why are you apologizing?" She yawns and clears her throat. "I was the one who went off."

"But still, Inez, I could've been more supportive."

She coughs several times and exhales a heavy sigh. "My head is pounding."

You ought to lay off that cheap liquor, I think to myself. "Are you okay?" I ask.

"I guess so." There's a long pause and she says, "Denmark?"

"Yes."

"I don't remember all of what I said or did, but I know I was upset. Harry says I act like a mean drunk, so . . ."

"You weren't mean. Just a little frustrated, and that's understandable."

"Thanks for saying that. But still, if I was difficult with you, I'm sorry."

"Let's just forget it, okay? You were under a lot of stress. Anybody would be if they suspected that their spouse was cheating on them."

There's a long, painful silence, then a sniffle. "I mentioned that to you?" Inez asks.

"Yes, Inez, you did."

"I'm sorry, Denmark. I didn't mean to drag you into . . ."

"Don't be embarrassed," I soothe. "Just know that in the future, if you want to talk, I'm here for you."

"That's sweet of you, Denmark. Thanks. I'll remember that."

"I'm serious, Inez. Call whenever you want. You deserve to know the truth."

More silence, apprehensive and uncertain. "What truth are you talking about?"

Hook, line, and sinker, she takes the bait. "There's nothing in particular at the moment. I'm just saying that when I know something, you'll know it too."

"Denmark, why are you doing this?"

"I know it seems awful," I contritely admit. "But I just found out"—I pause for dramatic effect, then with choked voice say, "I just found out that Sierra's been cheating on me."

Inez gasps. "Oh, Denmark, that's terrible. You must be going crazy."

"I'm better now," I reply softly. "But that's why, Inez, I decided to give you a call. The idea of someone else going through this is . . ."

"I understand," she assures me. "And you're precious for thinking of me like that."

"I'd had my suspicions about Sierra but didn't want to believe what I was feeling. And then I couldn't avoid the truth."

"This is horrible. We should talk, maybe get together for lunch."

I smile. It's wonderful when a good plan comes together. "Are you sure? I don't want to be a bother."

"You're nothing of the sort. How soon do you want to get together?"

We make plans to meet on Friday. "I'd meet with you tomorrow, but my Thursday's absolutely packed," says Inez.

"That's okay. I appreciate your making room for me."

"It's no problem whatsoever," she says, her voice saturated with concern. "Is there anything I can do in the meantime?"

That depends upon what I find out about *your husband* and *my wife*! "Just keep being your wonderful self."

"I will. You do the same for me."

"Consider it done."

The warm connection I sense between me and Inez is confirmed when she says, "Denmark, don't hesitate to call me if you need anything. And I mean anything at all."

"Be careful," I playfully threaten. "I might take you up on your offer."

"Nothing would make me happier."

We say our tender good-byes and hang up. Now, if everything Harry says about Inez's big mouth is true, he'll know before morning that Sierra's been cheating on me because Inez will tell him. And if Harry's Mr. X, once he's certain that I know, he'll be on guard, especially after having sent that DVD.

If Mr. X wanted to get my attention, he's got it! And I'm going to make it plain to Harry and Gordon—whichever one of them it is—that I'm stopping at nothing until I find the sucker. I was blind before and didn't know to look. My eyes are open now, and I'm not leaving a stone unturned.

I pull Alice's new business card from my wallet. She's probably not in Sydney yet, but wherever she is, it's worth a try. I dial the 1-800 number on the card and wait.

"Horizon Airlines," answers an efficient-sounding woman. "How can I help you?"

"Hello. I'm trying to get in touch with Alice Wilhite. She's a flight attendant and was recently reassigned to . . ."

"Hold please."

And so I hold. And hold. And hold. The person comes back. "Ms. Wilhite's not available. Would you like her voice mail?"

"Yes, that would be great."

"I'll transfer you now. Thanks for calling Horizon Airlines."

Alice's mailbox activates, and I listen to her soft, alluring voice. Her recorded message ends, and I let a couple of seconds go by before speaking. "Alice, this is Denmark. I've thought about what you said. Please call me. I'm ready to be the friend you need me to be."

I hang up, look at the Courvoisier, and smile. "Yeah, baby. I'm going to be real friendly. I'm going to be the best friend you and Inez ever had."

SIXTEEN

Bonk! Bonk! Bonk! In my dream, someone's banging on my front door. There's another series of knocks, faster and more urgent.

"This is the police, Mr. Wheeler!" says a loud, gruff-sounding voice. "Open up!"

Another one hollers, "Denmark, come out or—*I swear to God!*—we'll be back here with a search warrant!"

That's Sierra's punk brother, Amos.

"Mr. Wheeler! If you're in there, you need to open up!"

"Why are you wasting time?" Amos demands. "Get in there and arrest that wife abusing son-of-a . . ."

My eyes snap open. The gruff, now angry, voice says, "Mr. Montague, either pipe down or go wait by the cruiser."

I sit up *quick*. My mushy brain bounces off the sides of my skull like a soggy tennis ball. Everything's blurry, slanted, and spinning. I blink my eyes to clear my vision. My head feels like it's stuffed with cotton. My pasty tongue is heavy and thick. A vise grip squeezes my temples. A geyser of sour boozy bile erupts in my stomach. Everything rushes back: serving Sierra breakfast in bed, watching her suck and screw Mr. X, the fight, the hurt, the pain, missing her, *still loving her*. Bonk! Bonk! Bonk!

"I'll be right there!" I yell.

I glance at my watch. It's 7:16 a.m. I look around the living room. I can't let the cops see this mess. My head is like a steel ball swinging wildly on a chain. My stomach somersaults. I dash for the bathroom toilet, fall to my knees, and dry heave into the bowl. I wretch as a giant fist closes hard around my stomach, squeezing gastric sewage up into my throat. An awful taste invades my mouth, and I stagger over to the medicine cabinet, grab the mouthwash, and gargle.

The living room's a disaster, but there's no time to make it pretty. The police and Amos's being outside prove that Sierra's already called in her backup. She and her family have probably lined up every Cleveland power broker and wheeler-dealer they could find to make sure I'm buried.

I spit out the mouthwash and rush to the front door. "Mr. Wheeler! Open the door now or . . ."

I yank open the door to trouble. Staring back at me are two cops, and standing behind them is Sierra's fathead brother, Amos Montague. He's a bald, five-foot ten-inch, nasal-voiced, light-skinned, beady-eyed, pear-shaped gasbag. His weird shape is emphasized by his narrowed eyes; lips that are pursed into a sour, angry bulge; and flared nostrils.

I look at him so coldly my sockets feel frosty. "What're you doing on my property, *Anus*?"

The first policeman bites his lower lip. His partner smirks.

"Laugh it up now!" Amos snaps back. "You've messed with the wrong family."

He glares. I keep my eyes locked with his while I address the first cop. "What's the problem, Officer?"

"We received a complaint of domestic disturbance."

I check his uniform and see that he's a local. The police chief, Dan Parker, is a close friend of mine, runs a tight organization, and is one of the reasons why my annual bonuses for the last three years have been huge. After Sierra and I moved into Diamond Ridge Estates, Dan and I met on the golf course and started talking. He shared his frustrations about policing on a shoestring budget. I suggested that he save money by having Speed Shift Auto Parts perform the maintenance on his police cruisers. Six months later we had the contract. I got a fat paycheck, Dan didn't have to lay off officers, and they all started getting discount parts and service on their personal vehicles.

"You received a complaint from whom?" I ask.

"Who do you think?" Amos snarls.

Both policemen give Amos withering looks that cow him into silence. The first cop looks back at me and says, "Your wife . . ."

"Soon-to-be *ex*-wife," I correct.

"And not a moment too soon," Amos grumbles.

Cop One ignores us both and says, "She placed the call. We'd like to take a look around."

This is a no-win moment, but I don't immediately step aside. "Is there a problem?" Cop One asks.

I force a nice-nasty smile onto my face. "No, Officer, none at all. But before you come in I'd like to get your names and badge numbers."

The first cop's eyes flash with anger. I'll cooperate, but he needs to understand that he's not dealing with some ignorant hood rat. Advanced education, breathing the rarefied air of Speed Shift management, hours spent on golf courses, and schmoozing at cocktail parties have taught me some things about real power. And what I've learned is that people with position, education, contacts, and most of all *money* get justice. People without those tools get *screwed*!

The cop writes down his name and badge number and that of his partner on his notepad, tears off the sheet of paper, and shoves it at me.

I glance at the sheet of paper: Officers Anderson and Novak. I step aside. I've flexed my homeowner's authority, but they still barge in like I'm the lowly gardener.

"What about me?" Amos snivels. "Sierra wanted me to get her some clothes and other personal items."

"Sorry, Mr. Montague," replies Officer Anderson. "This is a police matter."

"Wrong!" Amos snaps. "It's a personal matter." He points a rigid forefinger at Officer Anderson. "You'd better make sure that by the time we leave, this bum"—he jerks his thumb at me—"is good and arrested."

Officer Anderson glowers. "Sir, if you don't close your mouth, the only person who'll be arrested is *you*!"

Amos gasps. He's genuinely surprised that this mere underling of the law is upbraiding him, the vice president of marketing for the Mid-Cities Insurance Company. They're one of the top insurance firms in the Midwest. They're also being investigated for allegedly swindling thousands of policyholders out of their life savings and reneging on medical claims, some of which have resulted in patient deaths.

Officer Anderson gestures to his partner while glancing at me. "Keep an eye on this area."

Novak grunts and positions himself so that he can check out the house without losing sight of me. I should be insulted about being treated like a suspect, but I'm used to it. Everybody in the Brownfield District, from toddlers to grandparents, was assumed by the cops to be a current or future criminal suspect.

Jellied blob Amos is still fuming outside the open front door. "She never should've married gutter trash like you," he carps. "You were never one of us."

I step toward Amos, and he jumps back. He's still the same lame coward he was the day we met. "*Anus*, being like you would've been a setback for *me*," I retort.

He flips me the bird, and I chuckle. "I thought you stuck-up-black-bourgeois-private-school-Skip-Chip-Scooter types didn't go for vulgar gestures."

Amos smirks. "We don't. But I know that primitives like you prefer that language."

Officer Novak strides across the living room over to me and Amos at the door. "Mr. Montague, I'm going to have to ask you to step away from the house."

"My sister wants me to get some clothes for her!" protests Amos.

"It's okay, Officer," I say. "I've already got her clothes packed and ready for pickup."

Officer Novak purses his lips, considers for a moment, and nods. I punch a series of buttons on the wall-mounted keypad near the door.

The garage door opens, and I look at Amos. "Her suitcases are sitting by the garbage cans in the garage."

"What!"

"You heard me. I put her and her clothes out with the trash."

He slowly looks me up and down, sneering. "At least she's no longer sleeping with it."

He laughs and walks off. If the law wasn't around I'd fix it so that this fool had a permanent bottom's up view of his intestines. But there's no rush. Now that the façade has fallen off the face of my marriage, the Montague clan's sure to attack with the fullness of their fury. And just like today, Amos will be their point man. He'd better never be alone.

The bad blood between me, him, and the rest of the family has been boiling almost from the moment Sierra took me home to meet them. Amos; her older sister, Samantha; and her mother, Sabrina, were all perplexed and vexed that she had curbed her surgeon intern boyfriend for me, a no-name auto parts salesman she'd met on a trying-to-forget-the-bum trip to Las Vegas. Two months earlier, Sierra had busted her intern boyfriend by show- ing up unannounced at his apartment, wearing only her blue fox fur coat and some sexy lingerie. They were both surprised—him to see her with the door key he thought he'd lost, and her to see him probing a fellow female intern with his very stiff organ.

By the time our Vegas trip was over, Sierra and I both knew that we wanted to be together. I quickly introduced her to the only immediate family I had, my baby sister, Harriet; brother-in-law, Herbert; and my nephews, Herschel and Humphrey. Sierra delayed taking me around to see her people, stalling with excuses like "My family's eccentric," "They're challenging in their own adorable way," or "Let me first get them warmed up to the idea."

What they needed "warming up to" was the fact that I didn't come from one of Cleveland's old-moneyed families. I hadn't attended a private academy and wasn't on my way to the Ivy League. My civic aspirations were to keep the politicians off my back and the IRS out of my pocket. The only thing I knew about money was to get lots of it. I sometimes said "axe" instead of "ask," laughed hard at good jokes, and dreamed of riding coast-to-coast on a powerful Harley-Davidson motorcycle instead of raiding and dismembering companies.

Unlike the Montague clan, which—as they never tired of repeating—had descended from free colored people and produced generations of doctors, jurists, professors, and business wizards, I was a culturally deprived, grasping opportunist. They had a proud heritage, were tenaciously committed to its continuation, and refused to stand quietly by as Sierra married someone who'd had the bad judgment to be born poor.

The only one of them who treated me decently was Sierra's father, Theodoric, a brilliant high-powered business whiz with the Cleveland Chamber of Commerce. He was a somber man who always seemed to be glancing at his watch and the front door. Rather than overtly despising me, he was just profoundly indifferent. He was also gone for weeks at a time, jetting between Brussels, Nairobi, Singapore, and London as he worked to get overseas businesses to come and invest in Cleveland.

In Theodoric's absence, I battled the rest of the family, trying to win their respect with stories of my struggle to get me and Harriet a better life, my fight up Speed Shift's corporate ladder, and my accomplishments at Kent State. One night at a family dinner, Sierra's mother, Sabrina, made it crystal clear that she was thoroughly unimpressed.

I'd finished explaining how I'd once risked everything by refusing to fire my best employee, who'd lied on his application about a conviction. He'd been busted for marijuana possession, done two years, been released, gotten married, and bought a house. Yet, the regional director wanted him gone. I argued for a suspension. The R.D. threatened to fire *me*!

Then one day the R.D. stopped by the store with his daughter to take care of some quick business. She wandered outside too close to the street. Some fool hit her, tried to escape, and crashed into another car. Dazed but unhurt, the driver jumped from his car and bolted. I ran the sucker down, throttled him, and hauled him back to the store, where the police were waiting. The little girl survived, the R.D. was my new best friend, and I'd earned another promotion.

All Sabrina could say was, "There are better ways of getting promotions."

That was the end of me trying to impress the Montagues. So, like I told Amos the day before the wedding: "My name is Denmark Vesey Wheeler, and I'm descended from slaves who *took* their freedom. I am what I am, and if that's not good enough then you can *kiss my very black ass*!"

Now, Amos huffs and wheezes his way down the driveway, lugging the suitcases the short distance over to his long Mercedes parked behind the police cruiser. He stops halfway, sets the suitcases down, and mops his forehead with a handkerchief. What a loser. Those bags are heavy, but even a blow-toad like him should be able to carry them. But he's the same blubber lump who has his maid pre-knot his neckties, claiming that tying them himself overstresses his fingers.

I check out Officer Anderson snooping near the steps, his partner by the front door, and get that old Brownfield District feeling. Whenever the cops started moving with that light-stepped nervousness, their eyes darting from side to side, one hand resting on the butt of their weapon, the other hovering near their nightstick, we knew something funky was going down.

"I need to make a phone call?" I say, stepping smoothly but cautiously over to my cell phone on the fireplace mantle.

Officer Novak grunts his permission, keeping his eyes fixed on me until he's certain that I'm actually making a call.

I punch a pre-programmed number, and my lawyer friend Nelson Fox answers his home phone on the first ring. "Hello!"

I turn slightly away from the cops and lower my voice, but not so much that they'll get suspicious. "Nelson, it's me, Denmark! Sierra and I had a fight. She called the police and . . ."

"You've been arrested?"

I glance at Officer Anderson, inspecting the kitchen. "Not yet," I answer softly. "But I've got two cops in my house *right now*!"

"I'm on it!" Nelson declares.

We hang up, and I'm hugely relieved that over the years I've kept my contact with Nelson. I step over to the living room's bay window and see Amos pacing in the driveway. He spots me in the window and hurls a series of words that probably sets a new standard for verbal filth.

From behind me and striding into the living room, Officer Anderson says, "Mr. Wheeler, we're going to have to take you in."

I sigh and face him. "Why?"

He pulls out some handcuffs. "Everything I've seen corroborates your wife's statement."

"And *her* word is all it takes to arrest me?"

From over by the front door, his partner says, "Do we have a problem?"

Officer Anderson's hand slides up to the handle of his nightstick. "Mr. Wheeler, we can do this the easy way or the hard way. What'll it be?"

I raise my hands slowly in surrender.

"Good choice," he says.

He reads me my rights while his partner handcuffs me.

SEVENTEEN

Officer Novak handcuffs my wrists behind me. I wince at their tightness. "Is this really necessary?" I ask. "Haven't I been cooperating?"

He grips my right elbow and pulls me toward the door.

"Won't you at least let me set the burglar alarm and lock the . . ."

"Cut the chatter!" he orders.

We step outside, and Amos smiles victoriously. "Finally!" he says loudly. "That animal's getting what he deserves."

Officer Novak nudges me over to his partner, hurries to Amos, and shuts him down. The moment Officer Novak turns away, Amos says, "We'll see about that! By the time I'm through you'll be directing traffic in a sewer."

He stomps off to his Mercedes, opens the driver's door, and spews more venom. "I'll see *all* of you down at the station." Then he gets in and screeches off, the engine roaring.

Officer Anderson opens the back door of his police cruiser, palms the top of my head, and guides me down into the back-seat. Sitting with my wrists jammed behind me hurts, so I turn sideways to relieve the pressure. This cruiser's a rolling prison with its black interior, gunmetal gray heavy mesh wiring separating the front and backseats, warehouse of electronics gear up front, no door handles in the back, reinforced roof, and barred windows.

After all my capers I never even came close to seeing the inside of a cop car. It took blind love and betrayal in marriage to put me into this backseat, and that's something that nobody in the Brownfield District—*not even the cops!*—could do.

Officers Anderson and Novak confer for a moment, then get into their cruisers. Officer Anderson calls in a radio report, starts the car, and backs down the driveway into the street, following Officer Novak, who was parked behind him. At every stop along the way, drivers look over at the cruiser, see me in the back, and stare accusingly.

We stop at a light, and a young long-haired ruffian shakes his fist from his Confederate flag-flying pickup truck. "I hope they arrest all you worthless *niggers!*" he hollers.

The light turns green, the redneck drives off, and I'm stunned to see Burned-out Bobby standing on the corner. He gestures to his sign, which reads: "God Knows."

Officer Anderson drives through the intersection, and I twist around to look out the rear window. Burned-out Bobby's eyes follow the cruiser. He keeps gesturing to his sign, keeping it pointed at the cruiser, and doing something that I've never seen him do: *he's ignoring other passing cars.*

Twenty minutes later, Officer Anderson turns into the Police Department, parks, and gets out. After riding like a human pretzel, my legs, arms, and hands have fallen asleep, so he has to help me stand. Full blood circulation slowly returns to my tingling legs. I can barely walk.

Officer Anderson jostles me up the few steps into the station, catching me as I nearly fall through the door as it's held open by an exiting cop. Amos Montague's already inside, sitting beside a desk and talking excitedly while a hapless police officer struggles to transcribe his story.

Amos sees me and smiles with such profound malice that, even though I know of his dislike for me, is surprising. Now that Sierra and I are ending, he's savoring the victory. Samantha and Sabrina will surely join him, all of them celebrating the restoration of their family's dignity now that it's been freed from the cancer of *me*.

"Get those cuffs off of him!" a voice booms from across the room. It's Police Chief Dan Parker.

Dan's a six-foot, silver-haired, barrel-chested, twenty-seven-year police veteran, and he's not happy. His lantern jaw is set and his face is crimson as he storms toward me and Officer Anderson.

"Well!" he snaps at the startled cop. "Take the blasted things off!"

Officer Anderson quickly obeys, and I massage my raw wrists.

Dan looks me over. "You look like you've been spat from a blender."

"You should see my insides."

Amos stands to get a better look. The smile on his face gives way to wonder, worry, and anger. "Hey!" he blurts. "What's going on?"

"None of your business," answers Officer Anderson, who's been listening to him. He glances nervously at Chief Parker and tugs on Amos's sleeve. "Sit down, will you?"

Amos jerks his arm free and marches over, his eyes fixed on Dan. The cop at the desk tries to stop him but backs off when Dan gestures for him to stay put. Everyone in the station—cops, crooks, and law-abiding civilians—stops to watch the escalating confrontation.

"Are you in charge of this clown convention?" Amos demands.

"Yes, sir," Dan answers, polite but coldly official. "I'm Chief Dan Parker."

Amos points at me. "Why are you releasing him? He's responsible for . . ."

"Sir, his release has been cleared by the court. Everything's in order."

My eyes snap over to Dan. "Are you serious?"

He nods. "You've got one dynamite lawyer. I don't know what he did or said, but he just saved you from going to the slam."

Amos has been following the conversation, getting steadily irritated. "Enough!" he interrupts. "I want you to book this field-hand, throw him in jail, and lose the key!"

Dan gestures to his glass-enclosed office on the far side of the room. "Sir, perhaps you'd like to step into my office and . . ."

"What I'd like," Amos snaps, "is for you to punish this Neanderthal for terrorizing my sister." He looks around the station, painting everyone and everything with his disgust, then re-focuses onto Dan. "You should know that I'm *very* good friends with Mayor O'Hara. Once I leave here I'm going straight to her and . . ."

Dan steps toward Amos. "You're going straight to her to do what?" he demands.

Amos sneers. "I'll teach you buffoons about trouble," he says. He glares at me. "I'm going to bury *you*." He glares at Dan. "And *you* should get ready for early retirement."

Dan's head turns deep red, almost purple. He glances at two hulking officers moving gradually closer, then looks hard at Amos. "Sir, if you leave now I won't lock you up for making threats inside my police station."

Amos sucks his flabby gut in enough to, for a moment, almost have a chest. "You wouldn't dare! Why, I'll fix it so that you're so deep in hot . . ."

Dan nods at the two cops. They're on Amos in seconds, their

large hands gripping him like flesh manacles. He looks up into each of their scowling faces and gulps.

"Now see here!" he shouts, resisting pointlessly. "Let me go!"

Dan jerks his thumb at a hallway sign that reads Detention Area. "Get him out of here!" he orders.

Amos struggles to no avail, looking like a yellow marshmallow trying to overcome two pillars of human granite.

"This isn't over!" he threatens. "I'll sue! Do you hear me? I'll sue you and this whole lousy . . ."

Amos's protesting voice fades as he's dragged deeper into the police station's labyrinth.

Dan shakes his head and looks at me through surprised eyes. "*That's* your brother-in-law?"

"Unfortunately, yes."

"Jeez! And I thought I had problems with my in-laws."

I extend my hand to him, and we shake. "Thanks for coming to the rescue," I say.

"I'd have come sooner, but I was downtown at an Antiterrorism First Responders Task Force meeting. I was listening to the scanner on the way back, heard Anderson call in about you, and hurried as fast as I could."

"I'm just glad you returned sooner than later."

"I can't take all the credit. Your lawyer shook some trees. You're walking because of him." He claps me on the shoulder. "Why don't you go wait in my office? I'll be right there."

I stroll across the station into Dan's glass-enclosed office and sit down in one of the two chairs in front of his desk. His walls are covered with plaques, framed certificates and diplomas, and pictures of him at various stages of his career.

I look to see what's keeping Dan. He's talking with Officer Anderson, intermittently nodding and grimly shaking his head. I hope Nelson gets here soon.

Dan finally finishes with Officer Anderson and joins me in

his office, closing the glass door and taking his seat. "Sorry about the wait. I was just getting a quick update."

"Do I need to guess about what?"

Dan leans forward, arms crossed and elbows on his desk. "Denmark, I don't like to beat around the bush, so here it is. Your wife's pressing charges against you. If she pushes this you could end up spending some time in a very cramped space."

I glance at the clock on Dan's wall. It's 10:10 a.m. Approximately twenty-four hours ago, I was sitting in the Hog Jowls restaurant with the guys and feeling mostly good about my wife, life, and future. Now my wife's a soon-to-be ex, my life is ruined, and I want to flee the future.

Dan sits up tall and speaks in a friendly but official cop tone. "Do you want to tell me what happened?"

"It's complicated," I curtly answer.

Dan leans slightly forward. "C'mon, Denmark, Officer Anderson says your house looked like it had been ransacked by drunk wrestlers."

"Jerk."

"Yes, he can be," Dan chuckles. "But that doesn't answer my question."

I shrug and answer crisply. "Sierra and I had a squabble. End of story."

Dan grunts. "You sure you want to leave it at that? I'm only trying to help."

I consider Dan's appeal. If, as he says, Sierra "pushes this," I'll need him firmly on my side, so I say, "Dan, do you remember telling me about the detective who was staking out the same hotel where her husband and his mistress had been meeting?"

"Sure, I remember. Maggie threw a fit when she saw them. We're lucky she didn't blow a year-long undercover drug invest . . ."

Dan looks hard into my eyes. I stare back, unblinking. He says, "Sierra?"

I nod grimly.

He shakes his head. "I'm sorry to hear that."

I nod again. The relative quiet of Dan's office is ripped apart by yelling and shouting out in the station.

I turn quickly around and look out Dan's glass door. The desk officer at the front is trying to get in a word edgewise with an obviously irate Asian man, who's harassing him with a combination of words spoken in heavily accented English and his mother tongue.

The Asian man's speaking so fast that his English is hard to grasp, but I still manage to hear bits of what he's saying: "Bums . . . cheap . . . Americans . . . junk . . . quit!"

Dan jumps up from his chair and hurries out the door. "Denmark, hold on while I go put out this fire!"

The Asian man sees Dan, marches past the officer he's haranguing, and heads straight for Dan. They're on a collision course, Dan the snorting bull charging toward the fearless terrier of a man who's rushing to meet him.

"Jiao, what's the matter this time?" Dan asks, not bothering to hide his irritation.

Jiao points straight up. "Antennas on roof are cheap! You want me to fix so you have perfect two-way talk. *Get good stuff*!"

"I've told you before, Jiao. I'm on a tight . . ."

Jiao wheels around and heads for the door. "Call when you serious. Till then, I got plenty of work."

Dan throws up his arms in exasperation. "Okay! You win! Tell me what you need."

Jiao stops and turns slowly back to Dan, a big smile commanding his face. He pulls a folded sheet of paper from the left breast pocket of his shirt and hands it to Dan. "Buy stuff and I fix. Quality work guaranteed. Not like crooked Americans."

Dan scans the list and starts to protest, but Jiao's already out the door. Dan strolls back to the office, shaking his head.

"Who was *that*?" I ask.

Dan answers as he sits down. "That was Mr. Jiao Minh Xing, a.k.a. the Electronics Doctor."

I glance back at the exit, then focus onto Dan. "He's the one in those obnoxious TV commercials that ridicule American products and service."

"That's him," Dan sighs. "Our communications system needed upgrading. I'm on a tight budget. Jiao offered a good price. And even though he's a giant boil on my butt, he *really* knows his stuff."

That's no small endorsement, coming from Dan, who spent eight years in the Navy troubleshooting all types of communications systems. The police scanner sitting on the table behind him crackles as an officer reports that she's on the way to the scene of an accident.

"What did Sierra say in her complaint?" I ask.

Dan looks at me admonishingly. "C'mon, Denmark, you know I can't tell you that."

I sit back and slouch deep into my chair. I'm very tired, very empty, and I ache all over.

Dan crosses his arms over his chest and studies me. "Are you sure there's someone else?"

I nod wearily. "I've seen them together, so to speak."

Dan waits for me to explain where, when, and how I found out. I let him keep waiting.

"Here's a word of advice," he says, after several long seconds. "Stay away from her."

"Excuse me?"

"Do yourself a favor and stay away from your, ah, wife," Dan emphatically repeats. He sits up straight, plants his elbows on his desk, and clasps his hands. "The moment I found out what was going on, I checked to see if a restraining order had been issued against you. It has." He leans forward. "So I repeat: *stay away from her*! The judge who issued the order almost lost his daughter last year to an abusive husband and . . ."

"But I'm not like that. Just yesterday Sierra and I were . . ."

"*And you can rest assured*," Dan interrupts, "that the *last* person you want to challenge on this is Judge Milford Barker."

I ball my fists and take a deep breath. There's a knock on Dan's door, and we look over. It's a cop, and standing behind him is Nelson Fox. He's dressed in a sharp gray pin-striped suit with matching shoes, a dazzling tie, gold cuff links, and a diamond Rolex watch that costs more than most cars. Nelson's not a good-looking guy, but like he once told me: "The honeys can have cute, or they can have diamonds. With me they get the owner of the diamond mine."

Dan waves them in. The cop says, "Chief, this is . . ."

Nelson strides past the cop over to Dan, extending his hand as he gets close. "I'm Attorney Nelson Fox." He gestures to me. "I'm representing Mr. Wheeler and would like to secure his immediate release."

Dan smiles sardonically at Nelson's blustery performance. "Keep your shirt on, counselor. He's yours just as soon as we've finished here."

"Finished doing what? I've cleared everything through the court. And I'm aware of Judge Barker's restraining order and will advise my client accordingly."

"We still have to process him here," Dan insists, clipping his words.

"Has he been charged with a crime?"

"No. But a complaint's been made, and, as you mentioned, a restraining order's been issued. I'm sure you can appreciate us following through to ensure that everything's in order."

"Indeed."

"So if you don't mind," Dan says, gesturing to the cop at the door, "Officer Radcliff will assist you in filling out the necessary paperwork so that your client can be released."

Nelson nods, then looks at me and winks. He and Officer Radcliff leave, and Dan looks hard at me. "Denmark, it's an ugly business, knowing that your wife's been stepping out. It can drive a man crazy." He narrows his eyes slightly. "But it's not worth rotting in a cell. No matter how bad it gets, she's not worth *that*!"

He's right. I might as well save my energy going after Sierra, especially since I can clobber her in court. But Mr. X! He's a different story. No matter what it takes, it'll be worth the effort to find him. And when I do . . .

I lower my eyes. "You're right, Dan. Don't worry. I've no desire to be one of your guests."

He smiles. "Good man."

We stand and shake hands. "Thanks a million," I say. "I'm indebted to you."

"No problem."

I turn to leave, then stop and turn back to him. "By the way, do you have the number for that Electronics Doctor guy?"

"Yes, but are you sure?" Dan asks in a puzzled tone. "He's a temperamental little cuss and . . ."

"I thought you said he *really* knew his stuff."

"He's the best in his business, but . . ."

"Then he's my man."

"Okay," Dan says, shaking his head as he writes down the number. "If you don't mind him busting your balls, then go for it." He hands me the note. "But you must have one doozey of a problem."

I fold the paper and slip it into my pocket. "It's a blurry and garbled video," I say. "One I'm hoping the Electronics Doctor will help me clarify."

EIGHTEEN

Nelson and I step outside the police station, and he looks me over. "You look pretty banged up," he says.

"I feel banged up."

We share a brief chuckle and start across the parking lot to his dark blue, window-tinted, chrome-wheeled Lincoln Navigator SUV.

"I called your job," Nelson informs me. "I told them you had an emergency."

I nod. "Thanks."

Nelson slows his pace and studies me, his eyes filled with concern. "Seriously, Denmark, are you all right?"

"I'll be better once I'm home, showered, and rested."

We get into the SUV and hit the road. Nelson slips a Maxwell disk into the CD player and adjusts the sound to a nice level.

"Okay," he says. "You want to talk about it?"

"No."

"I'm not your friend right now, Denmark. As the legal representative who just arranged your release I need to know what's been happening."

I hesitate. It's hard enough admitting to myself that my house is in disarray, and even harder admitting it to another man. But the chaos battering my life is getting worse, so I take a deep breath and tell Nelson everything.

"Is that all?" he asks.

"Isn't that enough?"

He ponders for a moment, slowly shaking his head. "Whoever sent you that disk was cold-blooded. What are you going to do now?"

My blood surges. "I'm going to divorce Sierra. Find the wise guy at 'I Got Your Back, Inc.' And then . . ."

"And then . . . what?"

I ball my fists. "Find the bastard in the blur."

Nelson whips over and into a Bulky Burger fast food drive-thru line. "What do you want?" he asks, pulling up to the meal selections display.

"I'm not hungry."

He orders two Busting Bulky Burgers, two large fries, and two large cherry Cokes, then hands me one of the orders.

"Nelson, I told you that . . ."

"These cholesterol bombs are bad enough when they're hot," he interrupts. "Don't let yours get cold."

I sit back in resignation as he pulls into a parking space and cuts off the Navigator. He leaves Maxwell playing and gets down to chomping. I bite into my burger, and it's the best thing I've ever tasted. Two minutes later, it and the fries are gone.

"I guess you were hungry after all," Nelson observes.

"Thanks, man. Rage and near-incarceration are powerful appetite enhancers."

Nelson arches an eyebrow. "Let's talk about rage."

I sip my soda and look at him warily. "Where's this conversation going, Nelson?"

He wipes his mouth with a napkin and gives me a long, penetrating look. "It's not about this conversation but *you*."

"Stop stalling and say what's on your mind."

He cuts off Maxwell and launches in. "Don't be a sucker."

I laugh bitterly. "It's too late for that."

"I'm not talking about your wife's cheating on you. Don't be a sucker by helping whoever's trying to set you up."

"Set me up? How do you figure?"

Nelson studies me for a moment. "Think about it, man. Do you think it's an accident that somebody sent you a video of your wife Godzilla-banging some blurry-headed dude?"

"No. They obviously wanted me to find out."

"That's true word. But the question is: *why*?"

"You tell me!" I answer loudly. "I surely don't know!"

Nelson's unfazed by my outburst. "That's exactly right," he confirms. "You're completely in the dark about their motivation, except for one thing."

"What?"

"They wanted to hurt you, Denmark. And they wanted to do it in the worst possible way."

I mutter expletives.

"And," Nelson continues, "them giving their address as 'I Got Your Back, Inc.,' means they wanted to ensure that the crap rubbed into your nose was shoved deep."

"When I find out who it is, I'm going to pulverize the mother . . ."

"See! That's what I mean. Now you're talking like a sucker." Still cool and deliberate, Nelson runs it down. "Look, man, criminal law's my thing, so I've seen enough scams to smell something here. Somebody's out to get even by making you hurt yourself!"

"What! That's the most stupid . . ."

"Is it?" Nelson challenges. "Think about it, Denmark. Are you certain that somebody you jacked years ago isn't finally making their move? Are you sure that some employee you fired on the way to management superstardom hasn't chosen this moment to bring you down hard?"

I want to dismiss Nelson's suspicion, but I have to consider it. A cold, clammy awareness creeps into me. I can't count the number of people back in the Brownfield District that I scammed, jammed, hustled, and pounded. And I've sent more than my share of misfit, airhead, thieving, lazy jerk employees rolling to the curb. Nelson might have a point, except for one thing.

"Even if you're right," I say, "it doesn't diminish the fact that *it was Sierra in that video*!"

"I agree. Sierra's dirty, but the dude behind the blur could be the one who's using her to cut your emotional throat. Maybe snaking her pipes wasn't good enough . . ."

"Will you stop with the metaphors?"

Nelson smiles sheepishly. "Sorry, man. I'm just saying that they wanted to make sure you knew. That's why he special-delivered proof of Sierra's infidelity through the mail. But what if lover boy's not behind it? What if the person who shot the video *isn't the dude*?"

"Nelson, stop riddling and make it plain."

"Just work with me on this," he insists. "What if the guy in the video was just some clown starring in a movie he didn't know was being shot?"

"What! Are you suggesting that he might not have known about the DVD?"

Nelson nods emphatically. "He could just be some rotten bum who was as ignorant as you were."

"No one could be that ignorant," I grumble.

Nelson purses his lips, nods understandingly, and continues. "Denmark, lover boy surely deserves some payback for boning your wife, but what if the person who sent the video was a third party? What if they somehow learned of Sierra's mischief and decided that the best way to slap you down was to film her and make sure you knew?"

I roll my eyes. "This is the most ridiculous . . ."

"What if the dude in the video was also *in* on the planning, someone who'd been paid to get with Sierra so she could be filmed as part of the effort to destroy you?"

"It doesn't matter!" I retort loudly. "Whether he participated willingly or not, paid or free, it doesn't change the fact that *my wife* was there with *him*!"

"I agree!" Nelson replies just as loud. "And I'm sorry if this is pissing you off. But man, you've got to consider that your almost going to the slam might've been *exactly* what somebody wanted."

"Nelson, nobody would be crazy enough to go through all this . . ."

"What about your brother-in-law? Based on what you've told me, he'd be partying in the streets if you ever got locked up."

Amos definitely wants to see me put away. But although he's scum and profoundly dislikes me, even he wouldn't have exploited his beloved sister like this. Or would he? Is getting me out of the family important enough for him, or them, to stoop to this level? A heart-rending thought forms in my head: Would Sierra really be part of such a scheme? No! She knows I'd react just as I did and would never put herself in that kind of danger. If anything, hers would be the blurry head and upper torso, and not the guy she was with.

"And then there's another angle," Nelson suggests. I groan. He ignores me and continues. "What if everything I've said is wrong? What if the person behind all this is some chick you once laid who's now out for a little revenge?"

"Are you serious?" I chuckle. Vondie Hamilton crosses my mind, and my chuckle gets weak and hollow. "Are you suggesting that some babe from back in the day has been bird-dogging me all this time to get a little payback?"

Nelson's gaze drills into me. "What if she really liked you, but to you she was just some booty? Maybe she's spent years, waiting until you were deep in love before lowering the boom? She obviously knew that seeing your wife with another man would push you over the edge, so she shot the video and made sure you got it."

Nelson, unfortunately, once again has a point. Before Sierra, the honeys entering my world were always on temporary visas. When they started acting like they were permanent residents, they were deported faster than an eye-blink. Sometimes there was crying and drama, other times just a pout and sniffle. Either way, *they were gone*!

I always had a pair and a spare, and they knew two things for certain: one, I wasn't a one-woman man; and two, the moment they acted up, *they were fired*! I was out for a good time; desired the sweet look, smell, feel, and company of a woman; enjoyed pampering and spoiling them; and guaranteed that if they acted right, I'd sex them in a way that would have them clawing for the moon and calling my name in ancient Egyptian.

I think for a few more seconds, then look at Nelson. "You need to give the wild conspiracy theories a rest."

Nelson snorts, arches an eyebrow, and smirks condescendingly. "So they're just wild conspiracy theories, huh? Okay. Why didn't this person who's so interested in the truth expose the joker who's been getting with your wife?"

I look at Nelson and glare. He keeps his eyes locked with mine. "After all," he continues, "a person committed to the full truth would also tell you that part." Nelson lets that statement linger and adds, "Why should they care about you knowing the full extent of such a painful truth?" He leans toward me. "Why would anybody go through all this trouble to reveal a truth that's guaranteed to hurt? A friend would tell all. Somebody with something to hide, or an agenda, would tell just enough to leave a gaping wound."

I take a deep breath and force a chuckle. "Nelson, do you know how stupidly incredible this all sounds?"

"It's probably as stupidly incredible as watching your wife suck another man's . . ."

My eyes snap onto Nelson, and he stops. His outline is fiery red. My voice is low, even, and taut when I speak. "Be careful, Nelson."

He gulps. "Look, man, I didn't mean any disrespect. I'm just trying to . . ."

"Take me home."

"Not until I'm finished," Nelson courageously deflects. He swallows and forges ahead. "Denmark, somebody, somewhere, and for some reason, sent you that disk knowing it would set you off, and it did! You should thank Sierra for escaping. If she hadn't, you'd be dealing with something uglier than a restraining order."

Nelson's right. I came close—*too close*—to being the instrument of my own destruction.

"So, as your attorney," Nelson continues, "I'm strongly advising you to not be a sucker. I'm sorry Sierra cheated, but you don't need to go to jail for it."

He starts the Navigator, backs out of the parking space, and gets back on the road.

"So are you telling me that I'm just supposed to roll over and play dead?" I ask.

Nelson's eyes flash angrily. "I'm telling you to stay free!" He turns into Diamond Ridge Estates and cruises slowly through the neighborhood. "Sierra's proved that she's no good, Denmark," he says softly. "You loved her hard, but it was like loving a rattlesnake. At the end of the day, she was still dangerous and crawling on her belly!"

"She wasn't like that in the beginning."

Nelson shrugs. "She is at the end, and that's what matters."

He pulls into my driveway and parks but leaves the Navigator running. "Man, I know it's easier said than done, but try to forget her. Get busy. Get away."

I open the door and get out. "What I want is to end this marriage." We shake hands. "Thanks for everything, Nelson. I owe you."

He backs out the driveway. I wave 'bye and go inside. This place looks terrible. Nelson's right. Going after Sierra is a bad idea. If anything happens to her, the cops will come looking for me. So I'm staying far away. I'm going to get a grip, divorce Sierra, move on, and be happy—*just as soon as I've dealt with her and Mr. X*!

NINETEEN

The kitchen telephone rings, and I hurry to answer.

"Hello?"

"Where you been?" demands Harry.

I haven't thought about Harry or Gordon for a while and that's good. If I had, they might be in an intensive care unit.

"Are you there?" Harry asks.

"I'm here."

"Where you been, Denmark? I was worried."

"I've been busy."

"I can understand that." Harry pauses, then says, "I heard about you and Sierra. Sorry."

I grip the phone tight. "Who'd you hear it from?"

"Who else but Inez? Somebody made the mistake of trustin' her with a secret, and now it's spreadin' like a virus."

So Inez didn't tell Harry that she got the news from me. That's good. She doesn't want him to know that we've talked. She's also probably worried that that knowledge would make him suspicious. This is perfect. Harry's temper is the deterrent that'll keep Inez's flapping gums quiet about the source of her information. As long as she's quiet about that, I'll have room to work her mind until I can work her body. And *I know* she won't blab about *that*!

"I called earlier to see if you was home," Harry continues. "I was gonna stop by and see how you was doin'. When I couldn't get hold'a you I got worried."

A guilt screw turns inside me. Harry doesn't sound like someone who'd hurt me. But if he was trying, he'd work hard to avoid suspicion. He'd be my most loyal, true-blue friend when the whole time he could be the one *screwing my wife*!

Harry's distant voice penetrates my thoughts. "Denmark!" he calls loudly.

"I'm right here. There's no need to shout."

He huffs and repeats whatever he was saying. "Is it okay if I drop by later?"

I don't feel like having company. But this might be my chance to see what Harry does or doesn't know. If he's lying, something will give him away: a tone of voice, shifty eyes, nervous body language, *something*.

"I'm not going anywhere," I say.

"Okay. I'll see you later this evenin'. And Denmark . . ." He sighs sadly. "I'm really sorry about all this. It's gotta be a miserable feelin'."

The guilt screw turns again. "Thanks, Harry. I appreciate that."

We hang up. It's nice that Harry's concerned, but he'd better be clean. I shamble upstairs to the bedroom, lean against the doorway, and stare at the bed. How many times have I stood in this exact spot, watching Sierra sleep? How many times did we snuggle in this bed, watching old love stories on videotape? Her favorite was *An Officer and a Gentleman*; mine was *Casablanca*.

I want some sleep but can't do it here! There are too many

memories. I shamble back downstairs and onto the living room couch. Faint traces of Sierra's perfume linger. The memory hail-storm blows harder. All the times we sat here, holding each other and staring into the flames of a burning log in the fireplace. Other times when we were being silly, chasing each other around the couch.

The phone rings, and I answer with a snap. "What!"

After a tense moment, an uncertain voice says, "Denmark, ah, are you okay?"

It's Gordon. "That depends," I meanly reply. "Why?"

"Well, Josie, my makeup tech, was getting her hair done today and . . ."

"Was she down at Our Hair?"

"Why, yes! As a matter of fact, she was. How'd you know?"

"Just call it a lucky guess."

"Anyhow, Josie overheard someone mention your name. She remembered that you and I ran together in the 4 × 100 relay and told me about, ah, well, you and Sierra."

We endure an awkward silence until Gordon asks, "So is it true?"

"Is what true?" I snap. "Is it true that Sierra's been having an affair? That she and I are through? Is that what you're asking?"

Gordon makes a hasty retreat. "Ah, look, I'm sorry to have bothered you. Maybe we should talk later when . . ."

"*Yes!*" I shout. "It's all true!"

He groans. "Denmark, I'm so sorry. You don't deserve this."

Gordon sounds sincere, and I could almost believe him. But he could also be the one who's been sneaking around with Sierra.

"Do you feel like having company?" he asks.

"Whatever. Harry's passing through later, so I'll be here."

"Okay. I'll coordinate with H and be right over after I've taped the show."

We hang up and I stroll through the kitchen, out the back

door, and into the yard. The hammock is swaying gently in a soft breeze. I climb in and let its lulling movements escort me into sleep.

I wake to a jarring clap of thunder. The hammock's swinging in wild, wide arcs. It's dark, and the sky's full of angry, boiling clouds. I sit up and stretch. A raindrop splashes onto my cheek. It's followed by another, then another, then more that come faster and harder. I dash to the house, kick off my wet shoes at the door, and dart inside just before the deluge hits.

Bathtubs of rain wash down from the sky, gradually slackening into a soft steady shower. I'm mostly dry except for my tear-soaked cheeks. *I miss Sierra.* I miss her laugh and the graceful movement of her body. I miss the light in her eyes and the way she bites the corner of her lip when she's puzzling out an answer. I miss seeing her with the towel wrapped around her when she gets out of the shower, the way it swishes when she walks, emphasizing the sexy shake and roll of her behind. I miss the way her nostrils flare when she hears about injustice. I miss the way she lets her shoe dangle off her toes when she's talking on the phone. I miss her in my joints, in my blood, in every breath I take.

The doorbell rings. I grab some napkins, dry my eyes, blow my nose, toss them into the garbage, and hurry to the door. I peek out the front window and see Harry's Jeep Durango and Gordon's Lexus Vindicator sports car. I take a deep breath and steel myself. This is going to be uncomfortable, but I swear, if they start offering me pity or wanting to share feelings, *I'll throw them out!*

I open the door and there they are. Harry's typical Harry, wearing his flaming red *Janitor Squad* (with each letter written like a jagged slanted lightning bolt) tee shirt, jeans, work boots, and a baseball cap sitting back on his head so that the bill is pointing up. And then there's Gordon, with his perfectly matching charcoal suit and shoes, tan collarless dress shirt, diamond pinky rings, and a haircut that looks like he lifted it off the page of a men's fashion magazine.

"Can we come in, or are you gonna let us get drenched?" Harry asks, smiling a tad too hard.

I step aside. "Come on in."

Harry pulls a six-pack of beer out from a bag he's holding and shoves it into my chest. "Here!" he says, breezing past me. "Pop us a few, will you? I would'a chugged one on the way but forgot that the good stuff needs an opener."

Gordon follows, offering his most brilliant TV smile. I've seen Gordon in action enough to know that he uses that brilliant smile to blind people to the truth of what he's thinking, feeling, or doing. His using it now is ample reason to watch him closely.

"Hi, Denmark," he says, hugging me. "No matter what, I'm behind you one hundred percent."

"What I want to know is if you were the one *behind my wife*!" I think to myself. I close and lock the door, then head into the kitchen for a bottle opener. Harry stands in the middle of the living room, his arms akimbo and looking around.

"Nice clean-up job, Denmark," he says. "But I can tell that you and Sierra must'a had one whale of a fight."

"Harry, c'mon, man," Gordon urges. "Ease up on the brother."

"What's to ease up about?" Harry retorts. "Denmark knows he fought with Sierra, and so do we."

"It's okay, Gordon," I say, strolling back into the living room with three open beers.

I give them theirs, making direct eye contact with Gordon as I hand him his. He briefly holds my gaze, then purses his lips and looks away. What's he hiding? I need to get a grip, play this smart, and make sure they're relaxed. The more comfortable they feel, the more likely they are to make a mistake.

Harry raises his beer bottle in a toast. "May she get a case of incurable crabs," he says.

Gordon and I look from Harry to each other, then back at Harry. "You're certifiable," Gordon comments with a smirk.

Harry winks. "True that. But are ya'll gonna toast with me or not?"

Gordon and I lift our bottles and clink them together with Harry's.

"To her incurable crabs," Gordon laughs.

"Crabs that I hope will itch and bite like hell," I say.

We laugh and take long swigs of our beers.

"Denmark, I hope you don't mind my asking," Gordon says, "but how'd you find out that Sierra was messing around?"

I look at Gordon for a long moment. Is he trying to connect something I know with what he's been doing? Or is he trying to check the details of what I think with the accuracy of what he knows?

Starting from "I Got Your Back, Inc.," I tell him and Harry mostly everything, leaving out the gritty details of Sierra's sucking and stroking Mr. X. They sit stunned with slack jaws. Gordon appears to be genuinely appalled, but that could be a well-rehearsed act, something easily accomplished by someone accustomed to being in front of a TV camera.

Harry says, "Denmark, if you want me to, I can score some good embalming fluid to preserve the guy's balls when you get 'em."

We laugh, easing the tension in the room as we engage in some raunchy banter. Gordon is relaxed, sitting back on the couch with his legs fully extended and crossed, trading barbs and insults with Harry. Harry slouches deep in Sierra's favorite plush chair, one leg thrown over the chair's arm.

"Sierra would have a fit if she saw you sitting in that chair like that," I say.

"She would!" Harry exclaims, faking alarm. "Well, then, she'd really hate this."

He lifts his butt slightly, frowns, and grunts as a loud fart explodes from beneath him. He smiles contentedly, and his eyelids flutter. "Aaahhh," he growls. "Better out than in, that's what I say."

Gordon fans the air in front of him. "Man, you're disgusting."

Harry grins and takes a pull of his beer. I go get some air freshener. "Harry, I swear, it smells like a skunk crawled up inside you and died."

My two "friends" seem perfectly normal—but then, so did Sierra.

I smile. "Harry, before you leave, do me a favor."

"Name it."

"Make sure you fart in that chair again."

He and Gordon stare at me wide-eyed and laugh. "That's the spirit, brother!" Harry says loudly. "Don't let her get'cha down. A guy like you won't have trouble findin' a new babe." He snaps his fingers, and his face lights up like he's had a flash of insight. "Denmark, I'll bet'cha it's somebody you know." He stares hard at Gordon. "Them cop shows always say that it's somebody you know. If I ever thought Inez was steppin' out, I'd look first and hardest at the people I know."

Good old Harry. He's taken us straight to the heart of what I'm wondering about him and Gordon. I seize the rope he's thrown and pull!

"I hope it's not anybody I know," I say evenly. "It'll be worse for them."

"What'll be worse?" Gordon asks.

I look straight at him. "The pain I'm going to inflict!"

There's fear in Gordon's eyes. "So you're going to be your own judge, jury, and executioner?"

"He's already been tried and judged. Execution's all that remains."

"What about justice? Anybody could make a mistake."

"Mistake!" I repeat loudly. "Are you suggesting that the guy who's been screwing Sierra has been doing it by accident?"

Gordon answers with a shaky voice and troubled smile. "C'mon, Denmark, you know that's not what I mean. And why are you looking at me like that? You're making me nervous."

"We oughta be nervous," Harry observes, leaning toward Gordon. "Like I said, them cop shows says it's always somebody you know. So I wouldn't blame you, Denmark, if you're wondering about me and G."

I shift my attention back to Harry. He's good, real good. "Sierra's a fine woman, and we've been in your house," he continues, "so it's only natural that you'd be wondering about everybody, includin' guys you know."

Gordon glares at Harry. "Speak for yourself! I'm not submitting to being put on anybody's list of suspects. And Denmark"—he looks back at me and narrows his eyes—"I hope that's not what you're doing."

"What if I am?" I challenge.

His jaw hardens. "There's no need to get angry. I was only . . ."

"What if someone had been banging Alice?" I say, getting loud. "Wouldn't you consider all the possibilities, including friends?"

Gordon's nostrils flare. "Alice would never . . ."

"How do you know?" I challenge. "Can you guarantee that she'd never cheat on you?"

Gordon balls his fists, and I press harder, driving toward the heart of his fear, that place where married men cower beneath a truth that circles overhead, waiting to swoop low and pick clean the bones of their slain and humiliated male pride.

"What if Alice is sucking off some guy *right now*?" I snarl. "What if she's worshiping his bone, getting it good and hard while she's getting good and *wet*?"

Gordon springs to his feet. "Shut up!" he roars.

I stand quickly to meet him. Gordon's eyes mist. "If I didn't consider you a blood brother, I'd kick . . ."

"Life's short!" I bellow. "Opportunity is *now*!"

Harry springs up, hustles between me and Gordon, and jams his palms into our chests. "Whoa, fellas!" he commands, shoving us away from each other. "Ya'll get a grip!"

Harry had better get a grip. After that note from I Got Your Back, Inc., he and Gordon are on borrowed time with me.

"This whole thing is messed up," Harry continues. "Denmark, I'm feeling your vibe, man. As much as Inez pisses me off, if she ever got busy with somebody else, I'd kill the sucker dead."

The focused implacability in Harry's eyes and the menace in his voice leaves no doubt that he's sincere. *So am I!*

Harry looks from me to Gordon and back. "Look, you guys, I love seein' a good fight, but why don't ya'll wait until after we win our 4 × 100 fifteen-hundred-dollar cash prizes in a few weeks."

Gordon snorts. I glare. "After that," Harry continues, "I'll be happy to count my money while watching you two cats beat each other into oatmeal."

Gordon glances into Harry's bemused face. After a few seconds, his strained expression relaxes into a smirk. Harry smiles, but it's forced.

Gordon looks at me. "Denmark, I wasn't trying to pick a fight," he says softly, almost submissively. "I guess I was pressing you because I'm not certain of what I'd do if Alice ever, if she, I mean . . . sometimes she seems so distant."

He closes his eyes tight, shakes his head, and drops his chin to his chest. This is a side of Gordon the viewers in TV land would love to see. He's no longer the ramrod-straight, testosterone-oozing, booming-voiced camera addict who loves to hear his own voice. Right now he's just a sniveling caricature of his TV host persona.

I've learned something about these two in the last few minutes. I'm stronger than they'd have been if what happened to me had happened to them. If Alice ever cheated on Gordon, it would break him. If Inez ever cheated on Harry, he'd be doing time.

"Let's sit down," Harry suggests.

Gordon and I take our seats, but Harry heads into the kitchen. "I'm gettin' us another beer," he says. "If I'd known all this drama was gonna happen, I'd'a bought a twelve-pack."

"I sometimes wonder if Alice knows," says Gordon, settling into the couch.

"You wonder if she knows about what?" I ask.

He stares glumly into his lap. "There have been a couple of times over the last few months when she almost caught me . . ."

"Are you serious?" Harry asks, as he saunters back into the living room. "That wasn't just some newspaper gossip? You've been messing around again?" He hands us newly opened beers and keeps talking. "After all them other times, you're still cheatin' on somebody as fine as Alice?"

"They weren't serious!" Gordon defends angrily. "Just rolls in the hay. I'd never leave Alice."

Harry takes a long swig of beer, burps, and wipes his mouth with his forearm. Then he looks straight into Gordon's eyes. "How many times do you think you can make a woman as fine as Alice swallow this kinda crap? She ain't some airhead bimbo who'll forget after the commercial. She's a flesh'n blood woman, and gorgeous to boot. Why should she settle for gettin' cheated on when she could have somebody who'll keep his pole in his pants till it's time to give it to *her*?"

Gordon scowls. "Harry, I'm not sure I like the way you've been admiring my wife."

Harry shrugs. "No disrespect intended, but, too bad. Alice is a nice-lookin' woman, and I like nice stuff. Besides, how's my ad-mirin' her any worse than you slippin' the sausage to your guests and co-workers?"

Gordon glowers and thrusts a stiff middle finger at him.

"Careful," Harry warns. "The surgeons'll have a tough time gettin' that outa your sphincter." He takes another swig of beer and smiles at Gordon. "Don't worry about it, G. If Alice ain't confronted you yet, she probably don't know. But then again . . ."

"Then again what?"

"She might be keepin' it to herself. What if Alice, like Sierra, has been doin' some cheatin' of her own?"

"Wait!" I declare. "Sierra wasn't acting in response to something I did. There's a big difference."

"I hear you, Denmark," Harry agrees. "But the bottom line is that Sierra's definitely been cheatin', and G, you're worried that Alice might be."

Gordon deflates further. "Impossible. I know Alice too well. I'd have detected something different about her and . . ."

Harry waves Gordon into silence, then looks at me. "Denmark, did you know?"

I clench my jaw. "No."

"Case closed," Harry says, looking back at Gordon. "Think about it, G. Denmark's one'a the smartest cats we know, but Sierra scammed him clean." He finishes off his beer, then continues. "To find out if a woman's cheatin', you gotta be like a deer hunter: smart'n alert and with tons'a patience."

"And why is that?" I ask.

"Because deer'n women are the same: smart, quiet, and efficient about their business. Even experienced hunters have walked right past deer in the woods."

Gordon forces a chuckle. "You've been breathing too many cleaning chemicals."

Harry smiles smugly like he knows secrets that poor Gordon is too dim to handle. "Maybe you're right," he says. "But I bet'cha Denmark believes me."

He stares at me for a moment. Harry's bluntness could still

be his smoke screen to divert my attention away from something he's hiding. It might also be a bold gamble to lure me into discounting the guilt of someone who's being so open.

"A woman'll be strokin some other clown in that smart, quiet, stealthy way of theirs," Harry continues. "And the whole time their husband is struttin' around blind as a bat, thinkin' ain't nobody dared to even sniff *his* booty."

I scowl, and Gordon looks nervously from me to Harry and back. Harry grins sheepishly. "Sorry, Denmark. You know what I mean."

I nod and take a swig of beer. Harry keeps talking. "Men can't cheat as smooth'n good as women. We're like elephants. When we sneak we leave monster footprints. And even if the woman can't find the footprints, there's still the big piles of crap, the broken trees, and all that noise."

I clear my throat. "So Harry, according to your theory, I stand a pretty good chance of finding Sierra's lover."

He nods confidently. "Just follow the footprints and turds to the big, noisy, tree-toppling elephant."

"When you find him, then what?" Gordon asks.

It doesn't escape me that Gordon asks "when" rather "if." "He's in for a season of pain," I rumble.

Harry glances at his watch. "Hey, ya'll. I gotta go. I got a new night crew over at the Monroe health center, and l wanna check on 'em before they finish."

Gordon glances at his watch, and his eyes widen. "I need to leave also. I have an appointment."

"Yeah, right," Harry scoffs, rolling his eyes. Gordon glares.

"Denmark, will you be all right?" Harry asks, stopping at the door.

His expression is so sincere, his eyes so full of concern—how could it possibly be him? But the note about the Sapphire Spire; it has to be either Gordon or *him*.

"I'll be fine, H. Thanks for stopping by."

We shake hands and hug. Gordon and I do the same. "Are you sure you'll be okay?" he asks.

"I'm positive."

Harry strolls out the door down to his Jeep and waves. "Remember, Denmark," he laughs, "just follow the footprints and turds."

Gordon follows with "If you want to see a therapist, I know a good . . ."

"No! I'm not paying some quack to tell me what I can figure out *myself*."

Gordon raises his hands, palms up, in mock surrender. "Okay, okay. It was just a suggestion."

I wave as they back out the driveway. Moments later they're gone, and I'm pacing in my living room. Okay, what have I learned? All of Harry's in-your-face obviousness could be the camouflage hiding his treachery. And Gordon's doubtful questioning could be him asking about himself, but using me. He could also be asking about me for fear of me finding about *him*. The only thing I know for certain is this: I need to keep watching those two.

TWENTY

t's 8:40 a.m. on Friday when I pull into my regional director's parking space in front of the Henderson Village store and cut off the Corvette. I've just come from a meeting at downtown corporate. Another Speed Shift store was robbed early this morning. The boss was livid and earned me the hostile envy of my peers after berating them for not doing more to protect their stores.

"The rest of you better get on the ball like Denmark!" he'd railed. "Or I promise you, heads will *roll*!"

He'd wet himself if he knew that street thug Blinker Hughes was providing security for "my" stores. The best part about using Blinker's "services" is his connection to his undercover cop cousins, Stinker and Thinker. Those two hoodlums with badges have the perfect setup, routinely going outside the law to enforce the law. There's still bad blood between them and Mason Booker over the jailing of their brother and former partner, Tinker. It doesn't help that just before Mason left the police force he testified against Tinker, mysteriously got a hefty sum of cash, then retired and started up Second Shadow Enterprises.

But that's between them. Blinker's motivated these days to clean up his image since he's decided to run for city council. He recently asked me to see if Sierra's father, Theodoric, would endorse him. It would be a nice boost, since Theodoric's a power down at the Chamber of Commerce. He and I have always respected each other, but these new developments between me and Sierra might change that. I'll be lucky to get him to say hello, never mind endorsing a friend with a shady present and an even shadier past.

Before going inside I sit for a few more minutes, contemplating the lousy changes that have seized control of my world. Two short days ago, I was happy, in love, and living a life that was beyond any dream I'd ever had in the Brownfield District. But that video proved that the life I had wasn't real anyway.

I start to get my briefcase and drag myself into the store when I see Burned-out Bobby, slouch-stepping down to his corner. He's grim proof that things could always get worse. After the last few days, I'm not so sure that they won't.

Bobby gets to his corner, faces oncoming traffic, and holds up his sign. Every time someone passes by, he points at whatever message he's written on the front. One person shrugs. The next scowls and shakes her head. Another flips up his middle finger and yells an epithet.

What's he got written on that sign? I leave my briefcase on the Corvette's front passenger seat, pull a twenty-dollar bill from my wallet, get out, and stroll quickly over to Burned-out Bobby.

"Hey, Bobby," I say, walking up on him. "How're you doing this morning?"

"Better'n yesterday. Not as good as tomorrow."

I hand him the twenty and try to read the sign, but he turns quickly away so that the driver of an oncoming car has no trouble seeing it. The driver slows his car down, reads the sign, shakes his fist, and hits the gas. As he drives off Bobby turns back to me. The sign says: "Why not you?"

No wonder most of those people reacted negatively. We've all got problems, and Bobby's sign is the callous equivalent of saying, "So! Who cares?"

I re-read the sign and purse my lips. "What's this supposed to mean?" I ask, slightly irritated.

"You tell me."

I shake my head in frustration, whirl around, and step off. I don't have the time, energy, or desire to play around with riddles—*especially one coming from a burn-out like Bobby!*

I grab my briefcase from the Corvette and get into work. "Hello Denmark," someone greets me.

It's Mrs. Randall, in buying her daily car air freshener. My face creaks into a smile. "Hi, Mrs. Randall, how're you doing?"

"I'm just peachy. How was your anniversary?"

I clench my jaw. "Unforgettable."

She smiles large. "That's nice. It's so good to see young people celebrating marriage."

My smile's so brittle I can feel my teeth cracking. "And your wife has been positively glowing," Mrs. Randall continues. "Whatever you're doing, keep it up."

Sierra's *glowing?* My head is about to explode. If my soon-to-be ex is glowing, it's her lover who's generating the brightness. I bite my tongue and will myself into calmness. "When did you last see Sierra?" I ask.

"Come to think of it, I saw her the day before your anniversary. She and her boss are a real team."

"What do you mean? How often do you see them?"

Mrs. Randall ponders for a quick moment. "Well, come to think of it, I've been seeing them a lot lately. It's such a joy seeing black men and women in positions of power working so closely together. They seem to have a genuine understanding and respect for each other."

My insides shatter. Sierra couldn't have been with Brad the day before our anniversary. She said that the reason he assigned her full responsibility for coordinating the architect's conference was his being swamped with work. How is it that Brad's suddenly not so overwhelmed? How is it that he suddenly has time to work so closely with his good-looking sexy subordinate? *Sierra had to have been with Mr. X!*

Sierra's always admired Brad's brains, clout, and cultured upbringing, sometimes to the point of being annoying. I'd suspect Brad of being Mr. X if it weren't for one thing: Brad is *white*. The guy in that video with Sierra is black. So unless Mr. X's pigmentation has been altered to make him look black, it's not Brad. I've got to hurry and get with that Electronics Doctor guy and have him analyze that DVD.

"Well, I have to go now," says Mrs. Randall. "See you tomorrow."

"Bye, Mrs. Randall. You take care."

"And you too, Denmark. And tell Sierra to feed you more potatoes. Your cheeks look a little sunken."

"I'll be sure and do that."

She leaves, and I go back into my office. The night janitor crew did a great job cleaning up my mess. I'll have to commend them.

I sit down at my desk and start checking my phone voice messages and e-mails. It's amazing that so many have accumulated, but that's okay. The extra work will help me keep my mind off Sierra.

I check through all my voice messages and e-mails, answering, archiving, or deleting them as necessary.

One of the voice mails is a jittery apology from Yarborough Montague, Sierra's crack-head nephew. "Say, Denmark . . . I, I'm really sorry . . . about the other day. But if you could just la, loan me . . ."

I delete the message. Yarborough needs professional help. His family's pockets are deep enough for him to get the best counseling available. He'd better ask them instead of expecting me to enable his self-destruction.

I roll on through my e-mails, establishing some pretty good momentum until I see a message from *CKeller@Law.net*. It reads: "This is the law office of Attorney Charles Keller, who is representing Sierra Montague Wheeler in her petition for divorce. It's urgent that you call 330-644-2578 as soon as possible."

I check my office phone's voice mail. Sure enough, the message is also there. I'm obviously dealing with someone who will persist to get what Sierra wants. But I wouldn't have expected anything less. Sierra's got access to some of Cleveland's best and brightest people, who have resources to spare and a lifetime of expectation that, of course, they'll get their way—especially when it comes to dealing with "wrong side of the tracks" orphans like me.

I start to call the number but instead type Charles Keller's name into Google. I click on the right links, and there he is. He's a distinguished-looking black man, with a strong chin, a small Afro, and a smooth high forehead, dressed in a lawyerly black suit with white shirt and black striped tie. I stare into his eyes. He's a lion. Good! I prefer facing a warrior.

I snatch up the phone and dial the number, drumming my fingers on the desk through two short rings.

"Keller and Associates," answers a dainty, nasally male voice.

"Hello? My name's Denmark Wheeler. I received a couple of messages to call Charles Keller."

"Hmph!" snorts the phone fuzzy. "Hold on."

There's a click, then a beep. An oily smooth male voice says, "Mr. Wheeler?"

"This is he."

"Mr. Wheeler, my client's suing you for divorce on the grounds of adultery, assault and battery, mental distress, and sexual imposition."

I grip the edge of my desk. "She's lying!"

"That determination will be made by a judge and jury."

"You're bluffing!" I challenge. "There's not a court in the state that'll buy this crap!"

"Mr. Wheeler, I don't need every court in the state, just one in this city. And I *never* bluff. If necessary we'll take this to the fullest extent of the law. Unless . . ."

"Unless what?"

"You cooperate."

"Mister, if you're trying to rattle my cage, you'd better shake a little harder."

"If you don't want to end up in a cage, you'd better pay attention."

My mouth freezes shut. Sierra's pulled out the stops, and I've got to stay free. Right now that means listening so I can learn the mind and methods of Charles Keller.

"Okay," I say. "What does Sierra want?"

His tone pulses with victory. "It's not a matter of what we want, Mr. Wheeler, but rather how to best settle our differences. In any case, it's not appropriate to discuss the matter over the phone. Our preference is to set up a meeting."

"What kind of meeting?"

"We've arranged a mediation session. We'd like to talk . . ."

His frequent references to "we" and "our" magnifies the chasm separating Sierra and me. Once upon a time, my wife and I talked face to face for hours about everything. Now we're going to talk through hired guns who will indignantly suffer for "us" as though they'd been offended themselves.

". . . about the division of assets and other related matters," he finishes.

"Mr. Keller, with the evidence I've got, I don't need to mediate."

"We know of the video," he says, sounding bored. "And as

interesting as it might be in a case for divorce, it could also be used to show motivation if we press *criminal charges*."

Is this possible? Did I give up the thug life all those years ago just to have incarceration hunt me down anyway, *twice in the same week*?

"With mediation," Charles Keller continues, "there's a better chance we can reach an amicable solution."

I don't respond right away, and he adds, "Unless you'd prefer taking your chances with a judge and jury."

I grip the phone tight. "You know good and well that the judge and jury option is my worst possible choice. It might as well be a lynch mob."

He chuckles. "I see you know your American history."

"Yes, I do!" I snap. "And I can tell a *house nigger* when I hear one."

For several long seconds there's a great arctic silence. When Charles Keller speaks again his voice is taut and vibrating with anger. "Mr. Wheeler, I'm told that you're friends with one Mr. Bernard Hughes, a.k.a. Blinker. I'm also told that even though Mr. Hughes is running for City Council he's still quite the unsavory character. Anyone even slightly associated with him runs the risk of being tarred with the same brush."

Fear serpents slither up my back. Over the years, I've shared my sordid past with Sierra, telling her things that I'd otherwise have taken to the grave. She knows details about so much—all my strengths and hopes and, more importantly, my weaknesses and fears. And now I'm confronted with the greatest of my crimes: trusting her with that information.

I'm silent and fuming. Charles Keller adds, "Imagine how irate Mr. Hughes will be if his election prospects are jeopardized by questioning that's connected with a certain friend going through a divorce. What if the questioning of that 'friend' leads to revelations about Mr. Hughes and his unsavory dealings?

Hurting Mr. Hughes's image at such a critical point in the up-coming election would certainly mean that this friend would have his hands full, especially since I gather that Mr. Hughes doesn't mind resorting to violence."

He has no idea of how Blinker loves to resort to violence. He's recently boosted his personal terror quotient with the addition of his two pit bulls, Killa and Attila.

Charles Keller's got me checkmated and knows it, saying, "It's your move, Mr. Wheeler."

I keep my voice calm and even. "What's the time and location of the meeting?"

He chuckles and transfers me back to the male receptionist who answered when I called. I listen quietly as the receptionist, speaking for Charles Keller, who now speaks for Sierra, tells me where to go.

I hang up and sit for several minutes, thinking about how Blinker will react if my marital mess reaches out and involves him. There's nothing to think about. He'll be like a grizzly bear that's stepped on a rusty nail, howling with rage and in no mood for talk. I could hope that events won't go that far, but I'd be crazy to take such a gamble.

I grab the phone and dial. Someone answers on the first ring. "Speak!"

"I need to talk with Blinker, *now*!"

"Not till he knows who's callin'."

"It's Denmark Wheeler."

"Wait!"

A few seconds and then: "Zup?" Blinker's voice sounds like it's lurking at the bottom of a deep well.

"I've got a problem."

"Don't everybody? Run it down."

"I caught my wife screwing around. We had a fight. It got bad. She's pressing criminal charges and . . ."

"Raw deal, but why should I care?"

"I just got off the phone with her lawyer. They're threatening to press criminal charges if I don't cooperate."

"Get to the point, or talk to the tone."

"She's threatened to involve *you*."

"No she hasn't."

"But . . ."

"Handle it!"

"Listen Blink, I'm only saying that things might get . . ."

"You'n me is tight. But if I catch heat, won't none'a that matter."

My palms are slick with sweat. "I'll do my best."

Blinker chuckles. "Yeah, I know."

TWENTY-ONE

After I hang up with Blinker, I glance at my watch, then hurry off to meet Inez for lunch. A half hour later we're seated in a nice, quiet booth in the Olive Garden restaurant in Montrose, a suburb of Akron about forty minutes south of Cleveland.

Inez decided that it'd be best to meet here so there'd be less chance of one of Harry's many business partners, employees, suppliers, or customers spotting us. Her worry is a good sign. She might have a big mouth when it comes to broadcasting everyone else's business, but she knows how to stay quiet when it concerns *her.*

She shoves aside the last of her lasagna and hangs onto my every word as I finish telling her the bare essentials of what's been happening the past few days.

"I can't believe they sent that DVD to you on your anniversary," she says.

I nod gravely. She shakes her head. "That's awful. It's hard to imagine someone being so cruel and malicious."

"Believe me when I tell you that such people exist."

She purses her lips and looks down at the table for a moment, then back at me. "So I guess you're going to divorce Sierra."

"There's no guessing in it, Inez. It's *definitely* going to happen."

Her eyes fill with sadness. "After you saw that DVD, there's not much else you could do."

"I could stay in the marriage, but being stupid once is enough."

"I know what you mean," she replies. "I know Harry's cheating, but I can't prove it." She looks hard into my eyes. "Denmark, is he"—she swallows a lump—"is Harry cheating on me?"

I reach across the table, take her hand, and give it a gentle squeeze. "I can't say for sure. But I'll tell you this much: he's given a lot of thought to what it would take."

Confusion lines furrow along her forehead. "I'm not following you."

I share the details of Harry's theory about how men and women cheat. "He said men are noisy, clumsy elephants, leaving an obvious trail of discovery. Women are deer—smooth, silent, and stealthy."

Inez's eyes flash with anger. "There's only one reason for him to be talking about this: *he's got someone else!*" She clenches her jaw as tears fill her eyes. "How could he?" she sobs. "How could he do this to *me?*"

I rush over, slide into the booth beside her, and hug her. "I'm sorry, Inez. I didn't mean to upset you. You don't deserve this."

She slams her fist onto the table and sobs for a few moments, then downs the rest of her wine, and mine too. "I've had my chances," she recounts in a trembling voice. "I could've had other men. But I stayed faithful. Even when he broke my heart about not wanting children, I stayed faithful!"

I look deep into her eyes. "It's his loss, Inez. Harry will never find someone as good as you."

Her eyes tear up again. "What makes him think he can do this to me and get away with it?"

I shrug and shake my head in frustration. "I asked myself the same thing about Sierra." I pull her close. "Maybe we can help each other through this."

She smiles bravely. "Yes, Denmark, I'd like that. We'll be each other's support."

I place my forefinger under her chin and lift her face up to me. "How can Harry not appreciate you?" I ask. "If he saw what I'm seeing right now, he'd never look at another woman."

She tenderly strokes my cheek with her palm. "And how could Sierra have desired someone over you?"

I playfully tweak the tip of her nose. "Forget them. Our priority is to help each other any way we can."

Inez smiles softly. I smile back. "This is some rough business, Inez, so I don't want you to hesitate if you want to talk or need something."

"I won't. And you do the same."

"Never mind me. I'm adjusting to my new harsh reality, so . . ."

She firmly places two fingers over my mouth. "Denmark, whatever you need or whenever you want to talk, just call me."

I arch an eyebrow and smile, thinking to myself, "Don't worry, baby. As soon as I find out about Harry, you'll know *exactly* what I need."

TWENTY-TWO

'm heading back to the office after lunch with Inez. That turned out well. It's just a matter of time before I know the truth, and that'll determine whether or not I punish Harry through Inez.

"And it'll be literally *through* her," I chuckle.

I park, stride briskly back to my office, and close the door just as my phone rings. "Speed Shift Auto Parts: Denmark Wheeler speaking."

"I hope you're sitting down," says a female voice.

It's Desiree Easton, owner of Our Hair Salon and Beauty Boutique. "Hey, Desiree, what's up, homegirl?"

"Nothing with me, but there's plenty of action at your house."

I grip the phone tight. "Say what?"

"I drove past just now on my way into the salon and saw Sierra and a couple of men with trucks. They didn't look like they were making a delivery."

I'm flying out the door before Desiree's uttered her last word. The traffic is flowing, the lights are mostly green, and I'm thankful that the cops are pointing their radar guns elsewhere. I turn onto my street and see at my house a small U-Haul parked at the curb, and a large one parked in the driveway. I step on the gas, and the Corvette leaps forward. Seconds later I skid to a stop behind the curbed U-Haul.

I jump out of the car, race around to the open back of the mammoth truck parked in the driveway, and look inside. It's filled with *my furniture*! I tear off my tie and march into the house. I bump into a burly guy in the doorway. He's carrying my favorite portrait of Malcolm X.

"Put it back!" I order, my voice low and seething.

"Who are you?"

"I'm the owner of *this* house and *that* portrait!" I snatch the picture from him.

He tries to grab it back. I catch his hand and twist his wrist backward until he's kneeling and pleading in front of me. He starts to call out, and I whack him across his mouth. Blood spurts from his lower lip.

"Shut up!" I hiss.

"C'mon, man," he begs.

My eyes snap over to the kitchen when I hear Sierra speaking loudly. "Amos, I want to take the stove and refrigerator also. They're too expensive to just leave here."

I lean down and whisper into my prisoner's ear. "Who's got the keys to the trucks?"

He slips his shaky free hand into his pocket and pulls out a set. "These are spares. Amos has the originals," he confesses.

Hearing Amos's name, I tighten my grip. "Where's Amos?"

He points upstairs, grimacing as I add pressure. I take the keys from him and twist his wrist viciously, and he blubbers.

"Leave!" I order.

I shove him onto his side. He jumps to his feet and wobbles away. I stalk quietly into *my* house and across *my* bare living room toward the kitchen, slowing when I hear an unfamiliar male voice upstairs.

"This is one complex bed," he says. "My wife and I once had a canopy bed—nothing as top of the line as this—but it wasn't the assembly nightmare this thing must've been. I'll bet Sierra's husband had his hands full putting this together."

Amos laughs. "That loser couldn't arrange alphabet blocks. There's no way he put this bed together."

They laugh. From the kitchen Sierra says, "Amos, while you and Dillon are up there, make sure you get . . ."

She steps into the kitchen doorway, sees me, and shrieks. "What are you doing in *my* house?" I demand, stepping toward the kitchen.

I glance upstairs when Amos says: "Oh—my—God!"

He's standing at the top of the steps staring at me, his eyes bulging as his rotund gelatinous stomach shakes and quivers from his hyperventilating breaths.

"You'd better hope God's in a prayer-answering mood," I threaten.

Another man, Dillon, hurries over beside him. He's a heavily mustached, tall weed of a man. The lower part of his shining bald dome is encircled by a thick wreath of salt-and-pepper hair. I'm still glaring at them when a tomato splats onto my head. I look at Sierra, and two more tomatoes splat into my face. I start for her and am knocked back several steps as she starts hurling potatoes.

"Stay away from me!" she shouts.

A potato smashes into my forehead and another into my groin. Streaks of pain shoot through my lower abdomen. A honeydew melon slams into my chest, followed by a cantaloupe to my solar plexus, both of them partially knocking the wind out of me. I fall to one knee. Sierra scrambles out the back door. She races around the house, clambers up into the larger U-Haul, slams the door, and starts the truck. Then she roars down the street, almost running down a jogging neighbor. He screams and dives into thorn bushes as Sierra flies around the corner, knocks down a STOP sign, and rockets away.

I spin around from the window as Dillon races downstairs. He sees me and looks desperately left, right, then back upstairs. I've recovered from Sierra's fruit and vegetable barrage and hustle over to Dillon. He falls to his knees, wrings his hands, and points upstairs.

"It was Amos's idea! I only did it for the money! I've been unemployed and . . ."

I grab his collar and yank him close. "Shut up! Where's fat boy?"

Dillon stabs the air, pointing upstairs. "He's looking for a phone to call the cops."

We had four phones in the house: one in the bedroom, one in the kitchen, one in the living room, and one downstairs. The one in the living room was smashed on Wednesday night when Sierra and I fought. I moved the one from the bedroom downstairs to replace it. It made sense, since I couldn't bring myself to sleep in the bed. If Amos is looking for that phone, he's out of luck.

"Please," Dillon begs. "Don't hurt me. I've got kids. I . . ."

I shove him away. "Get out!"

Dillon streaks out of the house. I run up the stairs as Amos dashes into the master bedroom.

"No phone," he whimpers. "There's no phone!"

"It's downstairs, *Anus*!"

Amos spins around and starts backing slowly away. He holds his hands out in front of him, palms up and fingers wide apart as though he were literally pushing me back.

"I'll sue!" he threatens. "I'll sue!"

"Do you promise?"

Amos's lower jaw trembles like an invisible hand is jerking it around. "You're crazy!"

"No! I'm *pissed*!"

Amos throws up his fists to do battle. "All right!" he declares. "I'm not going down without a fight."

I tear off my shirt and undershirt and crack my knuckles. Amos looks me up and down, his eyes lingering on my tight, muscular stomach, the chiseled wall of my chest, and my bulging biceps. He gulps, runs across the room, and dives out of the nearest window. I hurry downstairs and outside and see Amos limping frantically toward the smaller U-Haul. He opens the door, lifts his flab inside, and zooms off in the wake of Sierra's fear.

Forty minutes later I'm pacing in my living room like a snorting bull as I wait for locksmith Linwood Powell to arrive. Linwood's got the contract to service "my" ten stores and said he'd be right over once he finishes his current job.

"I should be there within the hour," he said.

I've checked through the house to see what's missing. It's like a cavern in here. The only things remaining are the canopy bed upstairs, an old beanbag chair from my bachelor days, the appliances that Sierra intended to take, the Malcolm X portrait I snatched from the guy outside, and a tiny countertop TV in the kitchen. They even took the DVD player and surround-sound system that Sierra gave me at my surprise birthday party last year. It's a good thing I put that disk back in my briefcase. Having it fall into Sierra's hands would've deprived me of solid evidence against her.

This was too close for comfort. I was going to visit the Electronics Doctor after I got off from work, but I need to see him now! As soon as Linwood arrives, I'll show him what I want done, stop by and thank Desiree, then get into lower Cleveland and find the Electronics Doctor. After seeing him I'll pay my good friend and private eye Mason Booker a visit. Between myself, the Electronics Doctor, and Mason, I should be able to learn all I need to know about Sierra and Mr. X.

A horn blows out front. I open the door and see Linwood Powell getting out of his work van. He's a slender, average height, caramel-skinned, corn-row–wearing, earring-in-his-nose, free-spirited hip-hopper. He's also a magician on the computer, hacking into high-security government systems just for fun, and staying a bare half step ahead of the cyber police, so far. Linwood's biggest plus is a dynamic work ethic that's made him one of the most valued locksmiths in Cleveland.

"I got here as fast as I could," Linwood says, extending his hand as he approaches.

I shake his hand quickly and gesture for him to follow me inside. "I appreciate the fast response, Linwood. Let me show you what I want done."

"Wow!" he exclaims, stepping into the empty living room. "Were you guys hit by a gang of burglars?"

"No!" I snip. "Sierra no longer lives here, and I don't want to discuss why."

Linwood shrugs. "That's cool, man. Just tell me what'cha need."

I take Linwood through the house, showing him every lock and latch that I want changed.

"No problem," he says. "How soon do you need it done?"

"Close of business today would be great!"

Linwood frowns and scratches his chin. "Okay, man, but it'll be expensive."

"I'll pay it. Just get it done."

Linwood pulls out his cellular, calls his office manager, and tells her to adjust the schedules of his other two locksmiths to accommodate the change in his appointments. He hangs up and looks again around the living room. "Man, the first thing you should've done was changed the locks and alarm security code."

"Obviously," I grump, looking around the bare space.

Linwood shakes his head. "This is why I became a locksmith," he says. "After getting cleaned out by two girlfriends I said later for sleeping on the floor. These days my action's set up tougher than Fort Knox."

"Do the same here, Linwood."

Linwood looks around again. "From what I remember of that Christmas party ya'll had last year, this place had some really nice stuff."

I clench my jaw. Why can't Linwood just shut up and get to work?

"When did she do this?" he asks.

"I caught her just a little while ago."

He nods admiringly. "The next time I move, I'm calling Sierra. She knows her stuff."

"*Linwood*, how soon before you get started?" I snap.

He smiles sheepishly. "Sorry, man. I'll get right on it."

"Okay! I've got some business to handle so I've gotta go."

He nods. "No sweat. I'll switch everything over and lock it up."

We arrange for me to pick up the new keys, and I go get in my Corvette and zip off to Our Hair. After that, it's straight to the Electronics Doctor, then Mason Booker.

TWENTY-THREE

I pull up in front of Our Hair Salon and Beauty Boutique and start to get out of the Corvette when my cell phone rings. "Hello."

"Hello, Denmark."

It's Alice, Gordon's wife. I close the car door, sit back, and get comfortable. "Well, hello, Alice. How are you? And where are you?"

"I'm in Oslo, Norway, on vacation."

Oslo, Norway? That's *way* off the beaten path from Sydney, Australia, even by air! And she's on vacation, too? Alice clearly isn't spending her time wringing her hands about what Gordon might be doing. Come to think of it, she doesn't sound concerned about him at all.

"I'm a lot better than the last time we spoke," she says.

I can tell. Her speech is more energized, her tone lighter, and her voice stronger. "I'm glad, Alice. I felt so helpless that day at the restaurant when . . ."

"I got your message."

She's getting straight to the point. Good! Her impatience

will be my windfall, so I'm more than happy to take the assist. "Alice, we need to talk."

"And why is that?"

"I want to put things right between us."

"There's nothing wrong between you and me, Denmark. And if you're talking about Gordon, don't worry. I've already made up my mind concerning what to do about him."

This isn't going as planned. I need to think quickly and get her back on *my* program. "Look, Alice, I won't try to snow you with how awful I feel that for years Gordon's been . . ."

"I know what he's been doing!" she snaps. "And don't remind me of how many years it's been."

Whatever Alice is breathing, drinking, eating, or smoking in Oslo, it's put her on the offensive. "Does this have anything to do with Sierra's cheating on you?" she flatly asks.

My jaw drops. "Huh? When, I mean, how did you . . . ?"

"Gordon told me. After all, he is my husband." She laughs a laugh that sends creepy sensations corkscrewing through me.

Gordon's in big trouble. Alice sounds like she's finally decided that enough is enough. "Is that why you called me?" she asks, her tone hard and angry. "Are you finally seeing things from my perspective? It's an ugly vantage point, isn't it? It's tough looking through all that humiliation and hurt, wouldn't you say?"

I slump in my seat. I could remind Alice that I'm not the one who routinely cheats on her. Nor did I force her to stay in her marriage. But I understand her anger. "Alice, you must think I'm no better than Gordon. I was supposed to be your friend, but just stood by watching you agonize through your heartbreak. I still don't know what I could've done differently, but I realize now that doing nothing surely didn't help."

"Oh my God," Alice says in sad surprise. "Denmark, I'm so sorry. I have no right to be angry with you."

I purse my lips. "Yes, Alice, you do. I let you down, and I apologize."

"Please don't apologize. It wasn't your fault. There was nothing you could've done, and it was unfair of me to expect you to compromise yourself."

Her old sweeter self has momentarily conquered the toxic presence of the "new" self, and I'm saddened to think that the Alice I knew might someday be banished into silence.

"I'm sorry to hear about Sierra's cheating on you, Denmark. I guess I should've told you."

I stiffen and sit up tall and straight. "You should've told me what?" I ask, demanding.

She sighs. "I didn't have any proof. In fact, it was just a feeling. But Gordon's always been crazy about Sierra, and, well, that's been his pattern. Sooner or later, he tries taking to bed whoever pleases his eye."

I'll pulverize the worm! Gordon's certainly admired Sierra's brains and looks, but he always knew to keep himself in check. And now Alice, armed with a woman's powerful intuition, is saying that he was in full pursuit. Since she's told me her suspicions about Gordon, I tell her about mine concerning Mr. X, namely that either Gordon or Harry has to be him. I add that I intend to get solid verifying evidence.

"I hope you get what you need, Denmark," she says. "I'd do the same with Gordon, but there've been so many, I'd rather not know the details."

"I wish I could be like you, Alice, but I've got to know the guy's identity. I need to know who's responsible."

"Our spouses are responsible!" she asserts. "No one could've cheated with them without their help."

"True word," I agree. "And even though Sierra and Gordon have been cheating, what if it's been with each other?"

Alice sniffles. "Then you and I have a lot to discuss."

"We certainly do."

We listen to a long, sweet, and inviting silence. "It'll be good seeing you, Denmark. It sounds like we suddenly have a lot more in common."

"I agree. When will you be back in Cleveland?"

Alice explains her schedule. She'll be back the morning of the Greater Cleveland Sports Challenge's Victory Banquet. "I'll be checking into the Lake Shore Gardens Hotel," she informs me.

The Lake Shore Gardens is where they'll be holding the banquet that evening. It's also where Sierra's organizing that architect's conference with the help of Mrs. Randall. I'm either jinxed or lucky to have all this activity intersecting at the same place.

I almost ask Alice why she's checking into the Lake Shore Gardens instead of going home to her big, plush house. But she probably doesn't want to be around Gordon anymore than I want to be around Sierra so her choice is understandable.

"I want to see you," says Alice, "but I don't want you to miss getting your trophy and cash prize."

I don't want to miss it either, especially since we'll each be getting fifteen hundred dollars. That's money I can use, especially with this divorce looming. It'll take all my strength to make it through the banquet without crushing Gordon's windpipe.

"The banquet won't be until evening," I inform her, "so we'll have plenty of time to . . . talk."

After a brief pause Alice says, "I'll look forward to our . . . discussion."

TWENTY-FOUR

After hanging up with Alice, I sit in the Corvette for a few moments, relieved that everything's falling into place. "It's about time things started working out right," I grumble.

I get out of the Corvette and stride briskly into Our Hair Salon and Beauty Boutique.

"Come on in, Denmark," Desiree says, smiling. "I'll be right with you."

Her shop still looks, feels, and smells brand new, even though it's been two years since her grand opening. There are four workstations, each with a comfortable elevating chair. Along the far wall is a nice little setup for manicures and pedicures. At the front is a multi-racked display of hair-care products, cosmetics, nylon stockings, and small African sculptures for sale.

Hanging on the wall over Desiree's station are three pictures: one of a veiled and agonizingly beautiful Coretta Scott King at her husband's funeral, the second portraying a gorgeously strong Hattie McDaniel, and the third showing the simply dressed but quietly powerful and indomitable chief conductor of the Underground Railroad, Harriet Tubman. The sultry, sexy voice of the late songstress Billie Holiday sings out from ceiling speakers as she laments the pain of loving her cheating man.

Ellen, the hairstylist at the second station from Desiree, sees me, waves, and shakes her head. "How're you doing, Denmark?"

"I'm all right."

She smiles tenderly. "I'm sorry about what happened with Sierra. All I can say is that she's stupid."

Well, at least I don't have to pretend that nobody knows. But it's better for it to be out in the open. I can be real with them, and they don't have to walk on eggshells for me.

"She's super stupid," agrees Leticia, the manicurist, looking up from the hand of her client. I look her way, and she greets me with batting eyes and an "I'm yours!" smile.

"Don't worry, Denmark," Leticia assures me. "You're too much man for somebody not to snatch you up"—she snaps her fingers—"like *that*!"

"Thanks, Leticia. I owe you and Ellen hugs for being so sweet."

Ellen grins and gestures to me. "Give me my sugar *now*."

I saunter over to her, opening my arms on the way. Ellen's an attractive full-figured woman and presses all her womanly curves into me as she holds on tight and feels just right.

"Mmm, baby," she says softly. "Where have you been all my life?"

"Married for the last five years of them, but that's ending soon."

She gives me a final squeeze. "Tell your lawyer to hurry up. I'd love to dump my couch-potato boyfriend and get busy with a hunk like you."

I kiss her cheek. "And what would you do with me?"

"Tell your lawyer to hurry up, and you'll find out," she giggles.

Karen, the massage therapist, steps out from the massage room. "Well, well," she says, taking quick measure of me. "Where have you been hiding?"

I wink. "It's my bad, Karen. I've been foolishly depriving myself of your beauty."

She laughs, gets some lotion off a shelf, and gets back to her client, winking at me as she closes the door.

Tall, statuesque, and thick-boned LeeAnne, the hairstylist at station three, looks me up and down with obvious appreciation. "Hey handsome," she greets. "You're still looking fit and trim."

"It's all for you, baby."

She smiles and puckers her glossy, beckoning lips. This feels good. It's been ages since I've indulged in some snappy flirting, and my old self is having a ball. And it's nice that everyone's being so bold. As long as Sierra and I were together, Desiree's crew held back. Now that I'm free, they're being more direct—and it's great!

I stroll across the shop to take a seat and notice several women checking me out in that smooth way honeys do when they're looking without looking. I'm checking them out too. These stunning sisters are a rich panorama of colors from dark ebony, light chocolate, and golden brown to burnished bronze, autumn red, and morning yellow. They're all heart-stopping beautiful whether clipped, curled, weaved, washed, rinsed, rolled, finger-waved, fluffed, poofed, or straightened.

I'm basking in the light of these lovely descendants from the royal houses of Africa. Their strength, love, and endurance are making my heart beat faster and harder and sending sparks of desire shooting along my neural pathways. In my five-year effort not to flirt, I've missed their company, their wit and wisdom, and their passion, intelligence, and power.

I sit down a few chairs away from a fine, leggy sister who's sitting beneath a hair dryer. She must've known I was stopping by today and decided to wear her sexiest short skirt. She looks at me from the corner of her eye without turning her head or losing her focus on the article she's reading.

Her magazine "falls" to the floor. She starts to get it, but I gesture for her to let me. It's conveniently fallen where I'm guaranteed a close-up view of her smooth strong thighs and elegant ankles.

I stand and hand her the magazine, and she smiles. "Thank you."

"You're welcome," I say, speaking close to her ear. "My name is Denmark. What's yours?"

"June."

"That's nice," I say, extending my hand to her. "I think that June just became my favorite month. I'm pleased to meet you."

"It's good meeting you also," she says.

Desiree walks past and taps me on the shoulder. "Stop your sweet-talking and follow me up to my office."

"I'm right behind you," I answer, watching as Desiree starts up the stairs. I'll follow her just as soon as I make this June connection. I lean close to her ear. "Here's the deal," I begin. "I think you're sharp, captivating, and alluring, and I'd like to get to know you. Would you consider going out for drinks or coffee with me?"

"Aren't you married?" she asks, glancing at the light spot on my finger where my ring used to be.

I bring it close so she can see it better. "I'm entering my second bachelorhood."

"What do you mean?"

"As in, my marriage is over and I'm available."

June listens closely. Then she lifts her left hand that she's been shielding, so I can see her wedding ring. "I'm flattered," she says, "but I'm happily married and . . ."

"Are you happily satisfied?" I interrupt.

She blinks in surprise, like it's never crossed her mind that happiness and satisfaction should go together. "Whether I am or not, I'm *still* married."

I lower my voice. "Look baby, I don't want to cause problems, distribute drama, or break up your marriage. You're a stunningly attractive woman who I can tell has a lot on the ball, and I just wanted to be in your gorgeous presence no matter how short the duration."

She smiles. "And how do you know so much about me so fast?"

I lean close and smile back. "Beauty and excellence are their own best advertisements."

"My husband's a good man," she lamely offers.

"I'm sure he is," I concede. "But you don't want to turn down this offer to go out with me."

"And why don't I?" she challenges.

I look deep into her eyes. "Because I'm prepared to shower you with adoration and worship the ground upon which you stand."

She blushes and squeezes her thighs together. I tenderly kiss the top of her hand. "You don't have to answer right now. Just think about it. When I'm through talking with Desiree, we'll exchange numbers and take it from there."

I wink at June and hurry upstairs into Desiree's office. She's sitting on a love seat with her shoes off and her feet tucked beneath her, smoking a cigarette. "So did you stop them?" she asks.

"Yes and no. Sierra pretty much cleaned me out. But thanks for the warning."

She waves me off. "Denmark, you don't ever have to thank me for anything. I still owe you for thumping Odin Meers back in Brownfield." She smiles devilishly. "But you know I could've handled him by myself."

"Whatever you say," I agree, smirking.

She gets up and pads over to the mini bar. I follow and sit on a bar stool. "You want a glass of Hennessy?" she asks.

"No thanks. So how long have you known about Sierra's cheating?"

Desiree answers matter-of-factly, "Four or five months."

"Say what!" I blurt.

"I wanted to tell you," she calmly explains, "but you were so head-over-heels in love, I couldn't bring myself to bursting your bubble."

I cross my arms. "Desiree, I need you to be straight with me. What do you know about this guy Sierra's been sleeping with?"

"I wish there was something to tell," she answers, taking a drag off her cigarette and sitting down on the bar stool next to me. "But Sierra and I aren't all that close, so I don't know a thing."

"That's news to me," I say. "Whenever I saw the two of you together you seemed pretty chummy."

"Chummy!" Desiree laughs. "Denmark, you and I are both ex–street soldiers, so let's be real. Sierra looks at me like I'm an escaped circus act. She doesn't respect me."

"How long have you felt this way about Sierra?"

"From the moment we met."

"Then why'd you befriend her?"

Desiree laughs. "I wanted to see just how stupid she was."

"Where'd you get the idea that she was stupid?"

Desiree's eyes meander up and down my body. "She didn't know how to treat a fine good-looking man like you."

I allow my eyes the pleasure of slowly mapping the surface of her body. "I believe that I will have that drink," I say.

She smiles and fixes it for me, stirring it with her forefinger just before she hands it to me.

"Now I've got a question for you," she says, sticking her stirring finger into her mouth and slowly pulling it out as she sucks off the booze.

"Ask away."

"Why didn't you ever cheat on Sierra?"

I shrug. "It never crossed my mind. Like you said, I loved her."

Desiree laughs. "Denmark, you're sweet, handsome, and a definite hard-body, but you can't help being a man."

"And you say all that to say *what*?"

"C'mon, sugar," she chuckles. "Don't try to out-slick the slicker. You're protecting your pride. With the stingy crumbs Sierra was throwing your way, I can't believe that you never thought about it."

"I just hope that you never go through something like this," I say.

"Are you referring to my piece of marriage with Brice?" she says, rolling her eyes and chuckling. "He thinks I don't know he's fooling around when he's out touring with that band, but the joke's on him. I could've busted him with my eyes closed."

She takes a drag off her cigarette. "Believe you me," she continues, "that fool's just a tax writeoff. As soon as he and those musical misfits start making enough money for a decent alimony check, I'm divorcing his sad butt. Hmph!"

She exhales twin curls of smoke from her nostrils. "Sure, I loved him in the beginning. He was"—she shrugs—"interesting. But hey, even the most streetwise among us make mistakes. Take you, for instance, marrying that materialistic ice princess."

"She wasn't always that way."

Desiree's eyes darken with mischief. "She said that she's way different when she's with her lover man."

I slam my glass down hard on the bar's counter, sloshing out some of the liquor. "Desiree, you know something. Tell me who he is!"

"Sierra didn't say."

"If she told you about their lovemaking she had to have mentioned his name."

"Not necessarily. Sierra may be a bourgeois two-faced tramp, but she's not crazy. She kept that secret to herself."

"I'm not playing, Desiree. I want to know!"

"If I tell you, what's in it for me?"

I walk slowly up on Desiree. Her eyes flicker momentarily, but she stands her ground. I slip my arms around her waist and pull her into me. "What's in it for you is something you can't handle," I say.

She smiles. "So says you."

I give her a solid kiss, tasting the fullness of her tongue and lips. I pull away, and her eyes are glazed. She presses her abdomen up against me.

"Oh my," she says softly. "I knew Sierra was stupid, but not *this* stupid."

"If you tell me what I want to know, I'll show you just how stupid she was."

Desiree pats my cheek. "Denmark, honest baby doll, she didn't say."

There's no lying in her eyes, so I say, "All right, if you say so, I believe you."

"Does this mean I don't get to find out?" she asks, pouting.

I study Desiree's face. She's another man's wife, but *so what*. It's not my fault that Brice is a has-been and doesn't know it. If Desiree's willing to let me send her yodeling into the stratosphere, I might as well soar with her. But I don't have enough time this afternoon, so I'll instead leave her with a taste of my goodness.

I kiss her with electric, unrestrained passion. She relaxes so much that I almost have to hold her up.

"Thanks for calling me about Sierra's raid on my house," I say. "And this," I kiss her softly around her neck and eyelids, and the tip of her nose, "is a sample of my"—I whisper into her ear—"*deep, deep* gratitude."

"You're naughty," she says coyly.

I wink. "And you hope I stay that way."

"Go finish your day," she orders, laughing.

I stroke Desiree's cheek and head back down into the shop. June's up and prepared to leave, but she's digging around in her purse "looking" for something. She sees me and "finds" it. I say 'bye to all of Desiree's crew and leave. June follows at a safe, respectable distance.

I escort her down to the far end of the parking lot where her Cadillac Escalade SUV is sitting. "Thanks for waiting," I say.

"You're welcome. I almost started to leave. What were you two doing up there?"

"Hugging, kissing, and plotting to have an affair."

She studies me for a moment, then laughs. "So you're not only confident but crazy, too; is that it?"

"I'm crazy like a fox."

She smiles and unlocks her vehicle's door with her keyless control. I hold her door open and help her into the SUV.

"So are you a gentleman, too?" she asks.

"Yes, I'm *very* gentle."

She gets into the vehicle and looks at me, her expression full of apology. "Look, Denmark, you're a nice, attractive man, but I just don't do this sort of thing."

I shrug, confused. "You don't do what—talk to people in the parking lot?"

She smiles wryly. "You know what I mean."

I get serious. "June, all I know is that right now, I'm supremely irritated that your husband saw you first. So maybe you're right to not let me show you what happens when a man like me focuses on a sweet, smart, sassy, sexy woman like you, doing things for and to her that'll make her *never* want to go home."

She stares hard back at me for a long moment. "I believe you would."

I take her hand, softly kiss the center of her palm, then look up into her eyes. "Tell me what you need, June. Just say the word and I'll do what you want, the way you want, for as long as you want."

She exhales softly through slightly parted lips, then grabs out a pen and notepad from her purse. She writes her cell phone number on a sheet and shoves into my hand.

"Don't mess up and not call," she warns. "I don't give second chances."

"I don't need them."

Her eyes flash excitedly as she starts the SUV. "Don't make me wait."

"That ended the moment we said hello."

She smiles and shakes her head, either in admiration or in amazement. "You're certainly a man who won't take no for an answer."

I close her door and step away as she backs out of the parking space. She waves as she drives off, passing me as I stride over to my Corvette.

TWENTY-FIVE

On my way into lower Cleveland I call Mason Booker's Second Shadow Enterprises. It's embarrassing, asking Mason to nose into my private life, especially for something like this.

"Second Shadow Enterprises," Mason answers in his smooth Southern accent. "We're a private contractor ready to serve your surveillance needs."

"Hey, Mason. It's me, Denmark."

"Well, the moon must be turning blue," he laughs. "How'zit going, Denmark?"

I almost start to answer that everything's fine, but stop. "Things could be better."

He's instantly serious. "Okay. Clue me in."

"I'd rather do it in person. Can you make some time for me today?"

"I'd make time for you on any day. When can you stop by?"

I'm relieved and give him an estimate of when I'll be there after I've stopped by to see Jiao Minh Xing, the Electronics Doctor. We hang up, and thirty-five minutes later I'm in lower Cleveland, rolling slowly down Henley Avenue, passing bar after bar as I look for Jiao's shop.

Two drunks are fighting out in front of Rockin' Rodney's. In the trash-strewn alley next to Jackson's Joint a man and a woman are groping each other like two lusting octopi. Bald-headed, shade-wearing, muscleman-tee–shirted, gun-toting gang bangers, most of them gabbing on cell phones, cluster outside of Dusky Pleasures. And the bright red, purple, and green neon flashing letters over Babes, Booze'n Billiards advertises: "Tonight Only— Come See Marilyn's Mammoth Mountains!"

The light at an intersection turns red. I stop and double-check the address for the Electronics Doctor. "Eleven-eleven Henley Avenue is what he said," I mutter.

I also check the time. It's 5:20 p.m. The Electronics Doctor closes at 6 p.m. on Fridays, so I've got to hurry. The light turns green, and I roll through the intersection. An olive-skinned woman wearing bright red thigh-high boots, painfully tight white short-shorts, and a bright red halter that's barely halting her nipples calls to me from a corner. "Hey, sweet daddy, you want a date?"

She ought to fire the cross-eyed stylist who gave her that Old English sheepdog hair weave. I chuckle and keep rolling. It's been a while since I've been in this kind of setting, and I don't know whether to feel sad or glad about feeling so comfortable so quickly. Maybe Sierra's family was right. Maybe I'd never have fit into their world no matter how hard I tried.

I keep rolling and finally see the Electronics Doctor. I pull up in front, park, and go inside. A weak buzzer whines when I open the door, but it's barely noticeable over the blaring country-western music. At least it's Charlie Pride, one of the few, and certainly one of the most famous, black country-western singers.

I stroll to the counter and look around. This place is a junk-yard for TV sets, video players and cameras, computer monitors, and anything else that beams an image or used to. Boxes of parts and accessories clutter the floor. Stacks of used and battered videotape cassettes crowd the small, narrow counter, its space further diminished and made unusable by the buckled vomit-green linoleum.

I search the chaotic counter, see a handbell, and pound it. "Wait!" someone yells from the back.

"How long?" I shout.

There's no answer.

"How long?" I shout again.

"Till I finished!"

I look around at some obsolete arcade video machines. Sierra and I used to go to the mall arcade and spend hours playing each other. At first, she couldn't see the point. After a while, she was trouncing me at my best games.

"What's problem?" someone yells from behind.

I turn around quickly and see Jiao Minh Xing. He's fixing his shirt and trousers and finger-combing his tousled shiny black hair. He fumbles beneath the counter, and the music's volume decreases.

"People piss me off," he complains. "Always interrupt when I taking a dump."

I ignore Jiao's disgusting comment and get to the point. "I'm Denmark Wheeler. Chief Dan Parker recommended that I . . ."

"Yeah, yeah, what's problem? Talk fast. I had long day and no feel like baloney."

I pull the DVD disk from my inner jacket pocket. "There's a blurry image of my, ah, a man on this disk and I'd like for you to clear . . ."

He snatches it from my hand, shoves aside a pile of magazines, and slips the disk into a DVD player.

"Hey!" I protest. "You can't watch that here."

The monitor sitting on a shelf above it bursts into life, showing Sierra on her knees in front of Mr. X.

"Wow!" Jiao exclaims. "She got talent."

"Let's skip the commentary, okay?"

Jiao glances at me, grins, and stares back at the monitor. "Hmm," he says. "Look like combination digitized distortion, satellite suppression splicing, and SELF scrambling."

"SELF?"

"Super Extra Low Frequency."

I lean close to the monitor screen with Jiao, both of us staring side by side as Sierra thrills Mr. X.

"How can you tell?" I ask.

Jiao points, touching the screen. "See outer edges of head blur?"

"Yeah, I see it."

"Spectral wobble. Solar coronal effect." He leans closer and talks to himself again. "Barely visible."

I look at Jiao, the monitor, the DVD player, and I wonder how he's seeing anything on this junky equipment. Jiao notices me casting doubtful glances.

"No be fooled by appearances," he cautions. "Good equipment. I build myself."

"You build your own stuff?"

He ignores the question. "This maybe satellite overlay with VTM hyper-spanning intermix flux."

"What's a . . ."

"Or reverse feed microwave bandwidth decelerator."

I shake my head. "What are you talking about?"

There's a crash at the front door. Jiao and I whirl around and see a tall, formidable black woman storming in. "I'm gone wring your neck, you cheating little bastard!" she hollers.

Her face looks like it's been stomped by horses, but her body could inspire myths about Amazon warrior women. Her dark skin contrasts nicely in a strange sort of way with the bright, blonde braids draping her shoulders.

Sweat boulders roll down Jiao's forehead. He wrings his

hands and mutters in Vietnamese. The woman stomps over to the counter, shoves me aside, and snatches Jiao by his collar.

"Sharonda Jefferson!" the woman shouts, shaking Jiao like a rag doll. "Are you sleeping with her?"

"No baby! Jiao give loving only to *you*!"

She slings him from side to side. "That ain't what I been hearing. I heard that you've been loving Sharonda large, and with *my credit card*!"

"Please baby. Let Jiao explain. I . . ."

She whacks him upside his head and throws him up against the counter. Jiao slams into the DVD player and monitor, knocking them off the counter. They crash onto the floor, and my insides shrivel. I try to see the extent of the damage but have to duck a wild looping punch thrown by this mad woman. Jiao barely gets out of the way before she knocks a hole into a wooden display.

"Start talking!" she demands, struggling to pull her fist free. "Explain them roses my cousin saw you buying for Sharonda Jefferson while ya'll was in that florist shop on Tanglewood and Frisser."

Jiao falls to his knees and clasps his hands in front of him like he's praying. "For you, baby! Roses for you! Shar, Shar . . ."

"Sharonda fool!"

Jiao nods emphatically. "She help Jiao pick out. She say she know what colors you like. Jiao was going to give you tonight."

The woman's face softens ever so slightly. "Huh? You bought some roses for me?"

"Swear to Buddha, ah, I mean your God, baby. Jiao no need nobody but *you*!"

She grabs his collar, yanks him to his feet, and shakes him again. "Where are they?"

Jiao points beneath the counter. The woman tosses him aside and pulls out a sky-blue box wrapped with a bright red ribbon tied into a large heart-shaped bow. She tears open the box, sees the roses, and smiles.

"Oh Jiao!" she cries, suddenly sounding like a spring debutante. "They're beautiful."

She grabs trembling Jiao, lifts him from his feet, and squeezes him until his eyes bulge.

"Careful . . . baby," he gasps. "You know how easy I . . ."

She plants her mouth over his and shoves her tongue down his throat for a slobbering tongue-to-tonsils kiss.

Jiao pulls his head back and sucks in a breath. "Be gentle, baby. I . . ."

She laughs and tosses Jiao onto a box of videotape cassettes that sends them clattering onto the floor. She grabs the roses off the counter, snatches a handful of Jiao's shirt, yanks him to his feet, and pulls him close until they're nose to nose.

"I'm going to the apartment," she says in a soft sexy growl. "You close up at 6, which means you'd better be with me by 6:05. You got it?"

Jiao gulps. "Okay, baby. Jiao come quick. Love only *you*!"

She snorts, tosses her hair, and pounds out from behind the counter. I'm in the way again, and she shoves me aside. I stagger back into an open cabinet of video games. Several fall, clonking me on the head. The Amazon thunders out, slamming the door shut. Jiao and I glance at each other.

"That's some woman," I say, rubbing my head.

"She ten women," Jiao mutters glumly, "and they all trying to kill me." He snaps his fingers. "You go now. I close up. Daisy really pissed if I not on time."

"Daisy?" I repeat, smirking.

Jiao glares, looks over at his DVD unit and monitor on the floor, and spews a cloud of English-Vietnamese expletives.

"Fourth time this month she break stuff," he complains. "Someday I find new babe"—he glances at his watch—"but not today."

I look around the clutter and gasp. Lying on the floor near the destroyed electronics equipment is my DVD disk, broken into several jagged pieces.

I grab them up. "Look what you and that maniac did!" I accuse. "Now I'll never know who's behind the blur."

Jiao dismisses me with an impatient wave. "Stop busting Jiao's balls. You still get to know who poking woman."

"Impossible!" I declare, waving the shattered disk pieces under his nose. "Even you can't reconstruct *this*!"

Jiao narrows his eyes. "No need to with copy."

"What copy?"

He points to a small computer-looking device beneath the counter. "Signal image capture processor. Daisy all the time destroying stuff, so I build. Get automatic copy from primary unit."

He flips up a screen and presses a green button. Sierra fills the screen. She's on her knees in front of Mr. X, diligently pursuing her task. And the image is more brilliant and clear than the original.

I look at Jiao and smile. "You're the real deal."

He ignores me and focuses hard on the screen. "Guy who did this knows his stuff," he says. "*Really* knows."

"Obviously," I grump. "Can you figure it out?"

"Of course!" Jiao snaps indignantly.

"How soon?"

Jiao shrugs. "Work at home. Best equipment there."

"But this is really important. If you could just tell me . . ."

"You no harass Jiao. I make you copy. You go choke chicken till I finished."

I clench my jaw. "Look! I've got a divorce hearing coming up pretty soon and . . ."

"Yeah, yeah," Jiao interrupts. "No bust my balls. You leave. I go keep Daisy happy. Jiao live longer."

I couldn't care less about Jiao's domestic difficulties, but what can I do? "Just tell me this much," I say. "How clear do you think you can get the image?"

Jiao smiles. "When I finished, you see lint hairs in lover-boy's bellybutton."

TWENTY-SIX

Mason Booker's Second Shadow Enterprises is located in a seen-its-better-days business block, sitting between two expanding industrial parks that have steadily crowded out homeowners, schools, and green space. His office is in a narrow two-story building in a row of buildings, a pawn shop to his right and a tattoo parlor on the left.

I get out of the Corvette and march up to the front door of Second Shadow Enterprises. The door's locked, so I press the intercom button. Mason's melodious Southern-accented voice comes through the speaker like a cat's claw scratching tin.

"Can ah help you?"

"Mason, it's me, Denmark Wheeler."

Mason buzzes the door open. "Come on in," invites his scratchy disembodied voice.

I slip inside and wait until the door's heavy lock clicks solidly shut. "I'm back here in my office," Mason announces.

I ease my way around the two other workstations of Mason's co-investigators. His enclosed office is in a rear corner. His door's open, and his radio's turned up loud. I step into the doorway, and he looks up from some paperwork, snapping his fingers and smiling.

At an even six feet, Mason's a ruggedly handsome man with medium chocolate skin, a nicely trimmed five-o'-clock-shadow beard, a wide-nostril nose, a squared mouth, high cheekbones, large penetrating dark brown eyes, and an all-around tight haircut. He's not heavily muscled but definitely well-toned, a necessity for his line of work.

"Man, ah love myself some George Benson," he comments.

I nod and purse my lips. Benson's singing words that match my dismal reality: "*We're lost inside this lonely game we play.*"

Mason gestures for me to sit in one of the simply styled, thick-cushioned chairs in front of his desk. He turns off his radio and closes the folder of whatever case he's working on. Then he sits back in his chipped and creaky wooden swivel chair, drumming his desktop with the fingers of his right hand while gripping the chair's armrest with his left.

"It's good to see you, Denmark," he says. "It's been a while."

"It's good seeing you too. You're in a good mood."

"Ah oughta be," he answers buoyantly. "Business is booming. May the world keep producing embezzlers, swindlers, liars, and cheats."

I laugh grimly. "I don't think you'll be facing a shortage anytime soon."

"That's bad for society but good for me. So Denmark, what kin ah do for you?"

"I need some work done. And I need it quick!"

"No problem. Tell me the employee's name, and ah'll get right on it."

"It's not an employee, Mason. It's personal. It's for . . . *me.*"

The smile drops from Mason's face. He sits up straight, plants his forearms flat on the desk, and interlaces his fingers. "Ah'm listening," he says, his tone instantly all business.

I look down into my lap. Mason once remarked at a company picnic I'd invited him to attend that if he ever got married, he wanted his relationship to be like the one I had with Sierra. A nanosecond later he added, "But marriage is a long shot for me."

"Why?" I'd asked.

He snorted with disdain. "Who needs the aggravation?"

"Sorry, Mason, but you're wrong!" I corrected. "Aggravation was when I had to constantly duck, dodge, and outmaneuver all the baggage-dragging, poison-attitude drama queens, gold-diggers, neurotics, and fatally attracted psychos of the dating world."

Mason clapped me on the shoulder and smiled. "That's great, Denmark. Count yourself a blessed man amidst a sea of sad married schmucks."

"What do you mean?"

He chuckled. "Seventy percent of mah cases are wives'n husbands who suspect that their honey-buns are doing the fat-nasty with somebody else. The sad part is that *they're mostly right!*"

I was incredulous. "Are you for real?"

Mason laughed. "But believe it or not, ah'm a fan of marriage. The more we have of 'em, the better. It's good for the economy. Jewelers, bridal shops, and caterers get 'em at the start. Me and the lawyers get 'em at the end."

There's a millstone of embarrassment hanging from my neck as I prepare to admit to Mason that I'm one of those spouses he's getting at the end. I'm one of his seventy percent, just another statistically failed sad married schmuck.

There's no face-saving way of telling Mason, so I just say it. "My wife's been cheating, and I want you to identify her lover."

Mason purses his lips, lowers his eyes, and shakes his head sadly. "Ah'm sorry to hear that, Denmark."

"Not as sorry as I am to tell you."

Mason shrugs. "Okay. When ah find 'em should ah cut off his balls, or do you wanna do it?"

I answer with a wry smirk to match his. "Let me do it. He's been plowing my field, so it's only right that I mangle his tools."

We laugh the kind of laughter that's desperate to deflate the uncomfortable tension filling the office. It doesn't help, so Mason presses ahead. I'm grateful. The best way to end this awkward meeting is to hurry and end it.

He picks up a pen and taps it on a yellow legal pad. "Okay. You probably want this information sooner than later, so it'll help if you can gimme some clues."

I pull the "I Got Your Back, Inc.," FedEx envelope from my briefcase and toss it onto his desk. "You can start with this."

He briefly examines the envelope, then looks at me, his eyebrows arched into twin question marks. Mason has some old-fashioned notions about men competing fairly and with honor. I tell him everything, getting more encouraged as his jaw hardens and lips tighten.

"What's that you say?" Mason asks. "The guy's upper body and head was a blur?"

"Yes. And his voice was garbled, so there'd be no chance of recognizing him that way either."

"Man, this cat definitely meant to mock you. First with that address and then making sure you knew he was, uh . . ." Mason's unfinished statement hangs in the air for a moment and he moves on. "So where's the DVD?"

"*Why?*" I bark.

Mason flinches. The disk is an obvious piece of evidence that could expedite his search, but I don't want him seeing my wife naked, especially while she's *screwing another man*.

"It's been destroyed," I answer calmly. "Freak accident."

"That's too bad. It could've taken us a long way toward establishing identity."

If Mason runs into serious difficulties I *might, maybe, possibly, perhaps* let him view the copy Jiao made for me. But it shouldn't come to that. I've got enough information that'll help get him started.

"Don't worry about it," Mason assures me. "Ah'll find 'em."

"I have a couple of names you can check into *immediately*."

Mason prepares to write. "Anytime you're ready."

I take a deep breath. Memories of all the laughter I've shared with Harry and Gordon, and the fun—running the 4 × 100, lifting each other during down times, celebrating with each other during successes, and so many other moments—those recollections block my words. Uttering their names will forever change our relationship, but things have already changed.

"Harry Bancroft and Gordon Wilhite," I say.

Mason stops writing and looks up. "These names sound familiar," he comments. "Is this the same 'Getting Down with Cleveland' Gordon Wilhite who's also on your 4 × 100 team?"

"They both are."

Mason shakes his head, perplexed. "Ah guess you just can't tell about some folks."

"I guess not."

Mason purses his lips. "So why do you suspect 'em?"

"On the day of my anniversary I was going to take Sierra to the Sapphire Spire restaurant for dinner. I told them about my plans and *no one else*!"

Mason nods grimly, his eyes filling with comprehension. "And since 'I Got Your Back, Inc.,' mentioned the name of the restaurant, you're thinking that it has to be one of them."

I clench my jaw and nod.

"I recollect that these guys are married."

"That's right," I confirm.

"This'll be a piece of cake," Mason observes.

"How do you figure?"

He smiles slyly. "I've tailed enough cheating spouses to know that their stepping out takes a lot of time, energy, and skill. But that's only if they're worried about getting caught."

"What do you mean?"

Mason shrugs. "Some people don't care. They're either too stupid or unconcerned and don't bother hiding their action. But most of 'em aren't like that. They'll go through all kinds'a changes to keep it a secret."

"Would that include doing something like having their image blurred and voice garbled on a video?"

"Yep, that's why I wanted to double-check about 'em being married. Single guys messing around on their girlfriends are careful," Mason chuckles. "Well, they *think* they're careful, but this guy's downright paranoid. He's got something to hide, something beyond not wanting you to know who he is."

I frown. "But if he was so worried, why make a video? Why send it to me?"

Mason lifts his hands in a palms-up "who knows" gesture. "Maybe he likes playing cat and mouse. Maybe this was an act of revenge . . ."

Icy fingers grip my spine. Nelson's wild conspiracy theories suddenly don't sound so wild or theoretical.

"Maybe," Mason continues, "he figured that by blurring the picture and garbling the voice there was nothing to lose."

"I swear, I'm going to punish this fool," I rumble. "He made sure *he* couldn't be identified but left Sierra wide open."

Mason looks at me intensely. "You're still in love with your wife, aren't you?"

Long moments pass as I stare hard back at him. "How much is this going to cost me?"

"Forget the cost. This'll be gratis. Ah'll do it myself."

"What's the catch?"

"There's no catch. You're a friend, and this guy's broken the rules."

"What rules?"

"The rules every man oughta respect to his dying breath: Don't mess with a brother's money. Don't mess with his car. And for *damn sure* don't mess with his *woman*!"

I smile. Mason's more old-fashioned than I thought. And I'm more certain than ever that I'll soon know the truth about Harry and Gordon.

Mason glances at the list. "This shouldn't take too long."

"How soon can you start?"

Mason grins and says, "Ah already have."

TWENTY-SEVEN

I get in the Corvette and turn off my cell phone to make sure that I'm not disturbed for a while. I start the car and tune its satellite radio to 96.3 and get the "Quiet Storm" show from Howard University in Washington, D.C. Patti LaBelle's voice beams down from the sky, strokes my cheek, and promises that one day everything will be all right. I turn into traffic, settle back, and cruise.

Night has covered the sky in a velvety dark blue. Billions of shining stars pulse like bursts of glitter. A warm breeze blows through the Corvette's open windows, and I feel better than I have in days. Now that I've seen the Electronics Doctor and Mason Booker, I'll soon know the identity of Mr. X. And tomorrow morning's 10:30 a.m. appointment with Hilda Vaughan is the first step in legally ejecting Sierra from my life.

I soon pull into my driveway and park beside locksmith Linwood Powell's work van. He steps out the house, locks the door, and sees me.

"It's all done!" he announces as I get out of the Corvette.

"That's great," I say, walking toward him. "I appreciate the effort."

He stows his tools and closes the van's rear double doors. "It's no biggie," he says. "One'a my guys finished early on a job in Shaker Heights, so I had him come help."

He hands me my new keys. "There you go, Denmark. You've got all new locks and latches to keep you safe and secure."

It's too bad Linwood can't install some locks and latches onto my heart, but I'll do that job myself. The next time a woman gets into my heart . . . what am I talking about? *There'll be no next time!* Just like before I met Sierra, they'll get *only* what I want them to have, and know *only* what I want them to know.

Nice, clean, and simple—that's how I want it. No entanglements, no expectations, and no drama. We'll hook up, get down, have fun, and be done. I don't want them to love me; worry or wonder about me; or feel sad, bad, or glad for me. All they've got to do is be fine, smell good, and be willing. I'll do to them all the things I spent five years wishing I could do to Sierra, stroking them strong and slow, deep and gentle, in wide and tight grinding circles, in and out, long and hard, sexing them so good they'll cry to the constellations for mercy.

"All right, man," says Linwood. "I'm gone."

We shake hands. "Thanks, Linwood. You take it easy."

"That's how I roll," he replies.

He sidles over to his work van, gets in, and backs out of the driveway, bopping his head to the deep based *whumphs*! of Z-Chosen-1, Cleveland's new chart-topping rapper. I chuckle at Linwood's youthful hip-hop exuberance, but it's a short laugh.

I was once like him, carefree and flipping off the world. The lion I was then would never have been trapped into my predicament. I invited Sierra into the most fragile part of my heart and trusted her to protect it. She knew my thoughts, my moods, my ways . . . everything.

I stick the key into the new lock, and it opens smoothly. I go inside, close and lock the door, turn on the light, and stare into my hollow, empty cave. I turn off the light, go sit on the steps, and lean forward, elbows on my knees, and stare down at the carpet. Tears trickle to the tip of my nose and drop. I promised myself that there'd be no more tears for Sierra. But knowing she's been with another man, knowing he's expertly familiar with her every curve, that he's kissed her most sensitive places, that he's joined her in ways she'd forbidden to me, that she'd wanted him more than she wanted me . . . *it hurts so bad*.

"Why, Sierra?" I rasp. "Why couldn't you want just *me*?"

The telephone rings, and I hurry and answer. I check the caller I.D., don't recognize the number, and start to ignore the racket. But this could be Jiao or Mason with quick good news. "Hello?"

"I've got evidence about you and Vondie," Sierra asserts. "That alone is grounds for divorce."

I swallow a groan. "Your so-called evidence is useless, since *nothing* happened between me and Vondie!"

"So now you're going to play stupid, is that it?"

"No, Sierra. Playing stupid was when I believed that loving and cherishing you would keep you happy and loving *only* me!"

"I did love *only* you, until you stepped outside the marriage!"

"You're a liar!" I explode. "I never cheated on you!"

"Yes—you—did!" she fires back. "Deny it all you want. I've got a witness."

"All you've got is speculation. I've got a video showing that for all of your prissy holiness, you're just a sanctified slut!"

She cusses. I cuss back. She slams the phone down. My head hurts. Sierra knows that I *never* cheated on her. And I'm wondering who's been filling her head with that lie. This shows just how desperate she's become. I need to stop her, and quick.

The phone rings again. I check the caller I.D. It's from the

Stouffer's Towers Hotel downtown. I hesitate but answer anyway, wondering what business the Stouffer's has with me. "Hello?"

"Denmark!" shouts store manager Keith Billings, slurring. There's a lot of loud talking, laughter, and music in the background. "You won't believe it!" he says.

"I won't believe what?"

"It's Nadine!" he blares. "She's pregnant! I'm gonna be a father!"

Keith's already been a father, *four times*! But since this is a brand-new baby, maybe it counts as a brand-new experience.

"Keith, that's great!" I say, pumping joy into my tone. "When are you passing out the cigars?"

"I'm doing it now! I couldn't get you on your cellular, so I'm glad I caught you at home. Come on down and join us."

"Who are us? And where am I going?"

"Some family, friends, and co-workers," Keith answers. "The moment Nadine told me, I decided to celebrate."

"I'm glad," I reply, laughing.

"So are you coming?"

It's Friday night. I should be having my own party. I should be down at the Ebony Crystal, jamming to the music until Salome gets off work. I should call Desiree and shed light on her curiosity: *"Mmm . . . I knew Sierra was stupid, but not this stupid."* I should do something—*anything!*—besides sit in this house.

"Where's the party?" I ask.

called June just before I left the house on my way to Keith's and Nadine's pregnancy party.

"I'm surprised you called," June had said.

"There's more to come."

"Is that right?"

"Absolutely, and we'll be right too, once we get together."

She laughed. "You're a fast mover."

"Not normally. But you're so overpowering I can't help myself."

After a brief pause, she said: "And how exactly do I overpower you?"

I told her. By the time we hung up, she was pressing me to tell her when she could expect my next call.

I stride down a large hallway in the Stouffer's Towers Hotel and through the heavy double doors of the Sky Sweep room and step into an audio storm of laughter, talking, and upcoming rap sensation Akon's like-it or lump-it lyrics. The room is packed with ebony and a few ivory bodies, and crackling with human energy. Whirling ceiling projectors beam bright yellow, robust red, piercing blue, and cool purple light at spinning silver balls, painting the room and everyone with a kaleidoscope of brilliant luminous sparkles. On the dance floor, brothers and sisters are twisting, dipping, sliding, and hyper-stepping in obedience to the creative power of their African genes.

"My people, my people," I chuckle. "We sure love to party."

"Denmark!" someone shouts off to my right. "You're here!"

I look toward the voice but can't see through all the gyrating bodies. After a few seconds, I spot Keith weaving his way through the crowd. He's dragging Nadine behind him. She's small, shapely, and petite, with big soulful eyes, an angular jaw line, and braided hair that falls onto her shoulders like a shimmering curtain of cords.

Every few steps someone hollers, "Congratulations!"

Nadine graciously accepts the well-wishes but seems mostly embarrassed by all the fuss. Keith wobbles up to me and sways from side to side. "Heeey!" he greets me, exhaling a blast of his alcohol-reeking breath. "Man, I'm glad"—belch, hiccup—"you could come."

"I wouldn't have missed it for the world," I reply, turning slightly away from Keith's grinning face.

Nadine keeps him steady, frowning at him and looking apologetically at me. "I'm sorry about this, Denmark," she says. "He goes crazy like this every time we get pregnant."

"That's right," Keith slurs. "We're preg-nant, and I'm happier than a, uh, I'm happier than a . . ." He frowns and looks at me. "What am I happier than?"

"You're the happiest man in the world," I answer, laughing.

He beams a wide, toothy smile. "That's right! I'm"—hiccup—"the happiest man"—hiccup—"in the world!"

They look at each other with so much love and affection that I feel like a voyeur. I kiss Nadine's cheek and shake Keith's hand. "Congratulations to both of you."

"Thanks," Nadine replies.

They melt back into the dancers, and I spot a bar on the far side of the room. I ease around the human swarm and see Vondie Hamilton. She's sitting on a bar stool with her perfect legs crossed, showing much thigh and revealing enough gap at the top of her short skirt to send a brother's imagination into overdrive.

This might be a good thing. If I can get Vondie to testify that nothing happened between us in Orlando, it'll kill Sierra's allegations of infidelity. For her reward, I'll give Vondie some of the best loving she's ever had, even better than when we were together. But I've first got to deal with the loser whispering in her ear. Her expression says that he might as well save his breath.

I make my way to the far side of the bar, keeping out of Vondie's eyesight as she sips on a straw sticking out of a huge glass of something that looks very red and very good.

"What'll it be?" asks the bartender.

"Give me a vodka and orange juice on the rocks."

Vondie's rocking gently to the music, barely paying attention to the dude. She shakes her head no to whatever he just said, and he frowns. He keeps whispering into her ear, and she shakes her head no again.

"Here you go," says the bartender.

I pay him and turn back to Vondie. The dude traces his finger along her shoulder. She flinches away from him and glares. I grab my drink and stride over to them, getting there in time to hear Vondie say, "So don't ask me again!"

"C'mon, baby," he presses. "It's just a phone number."

"It's a phone number she's not giving, so *stop asking!*" I command.

Vondie spins around and sees me. Her eyes flash wide with happiness then relax with relief.

"Who invited you?" the dude demands to know, puffing up for battle.

I take a sip of my drink and study him for a quick moment. "I invited myself! And I'll still be here when the paramedics carry you away."

His eyes narrow. I set my drink on the bar counter. Several people who're sitting close by slither out of harm's way.

"Make your move!" I challenge. "It's *your* pain, so I won't mind."

He glances from me to Vondie then grumbles off into the crowd. The people who moved out the way mutter their relief, sit back down, and continue swilling their drinks.

Vondie watches the dude leave then turns to me. "Thanks. He was plucking my *last* nerve."

"Glad to help," I say, sitting on the bar stool beside her. "Besides, I needed to get him out the way so I could sit here."

We laugh and look out at the mass of people. "This is quite a gathering," I observe.

Vondie nods. "It sure is."

We enjoy the music for a few moments, then Vondie says, "Denmark, I apologize for Lennox's behavior at the restaurant the other day. I don't know what got into him."

"What got into *you*?" I gently counter. "It seemed like you were egging him on."

Vondie smiles sheepishly. "Well, maybe I was. He's such a pompous bore. I knew you'd take him down a notch, so I guess I pushed a little."

We laugh, and I hold my glass up to Vondie for a toast. "Still friends?"

She clinks her glass against mine. "Yes, we're still friends."

We listen to a little more music, and I give Vondie the once-over. "You look great," I say.

"Why, thank you," Vondie answers, blushing. "You're candy for the eyes also."

She raises her drink, and we clink our glasses together again. "To good-looking people like us," she says.

We laugh and sip our drinks. "So, Vondie, how do you know Keith?" I ask.

"He worked for me in procurement when he started with the company. He met Nadine when he made an inventory analysis of the Sunbury Hills store, where she was assistant manager. He harassed me for a transfer to floor sales staff so he could be near her all the time. Four months later they were married, and"—she gestures at the gathering with a wide sweep of her arm—"here we are."

"Are you serious? He voluntarily took a demotion to floor sales staff?"

"Not just a demotion, but a pay cut," Vondie emphasizes. "You *know* that had to be love."

"No doubt," I grouse, watching Keith and Nadine sway through a slow dance. Poor Nadine looks like she's the only reason her booze-bombed hubby is still standing. "They're a great couple," I observe.

"Yes, they are," Vondie agrees.

"You want another?" asks the bartender, glancing at my near-empty glass.

I polish off the rest of my drink and hand him the glass. "Yes. Make it the same as before."

"You got it."

He fixes my drink and slides it over to me. I take a long sip as the DJ puts on an old cut by Lauryn Hill from her album *The Miseducation of Lauryn Hill.*

Vondie smiles and bops her head to the beat. "Baby girl could rock," says Vondie, looking hard at me, "just like you and I were at one time."

Vondie finishes her drink and calls the bartender over. "Fix me another strawberry daiquiri," she orders, thrusting the empty glass toward him. "And go heavy on the alcohol."

The bartender puts on his best smile. "Maybe you should

slow down, pretty lady. You don't want to wind up later tonight with your face in . . ."

"Did I ask you to be my father?" she snaps. "Just fix my drink before I decide you're not worth the tip I was going to leave."

The bartender clamps his mouth shut and does as he's told. Vondie glances indignantly at me. "Why are you looking at me like that?" she demands. "Haven't you heard? We're here to celebrate the beginning of new life, for Nadine and Keith, their baby, me, and even *you*."

She laughs, and my skin crawls. "Okay, Vondie. I'm getting the same vibe I had at the restaurant the other day. What's your beef?"

She answers with a casual dismissive wave. "Oh, Denmark, don't mind me. I'm just having fun." I look hard at her for a long moment. She frowns and tenderly touches my forearm. "What's the matter?" she asks. "You seem bothered."

Vondie's eyes are pools of sincerity, so I relax. "Stop tripping," I scoff. "You know that letting things bother me isn't my style."

She smiles and strokes my forearm. "Now that's the confident Denmark I remember."

I glance at her hand moving slowly back and forth along my arm. Her touch feels good. I glance at her legs, my gaze moving up her thighs to the gap at the top of her skirt.

Vondie jerks her hand away. "Sorry about the physical contact," she apologizes. "I know you're happily married, so . . ."

"It's cool. Don't worry about it."

She looks at me quizzically, then offers me a tentative smile. "Are you sure?"

"I'm certain." I lean close and say, "I'd forgotten how nice it was being touched by you."

Vondie smiles coyly and slowly wraps her lips around the

daiquiri straw, exaggerating their pucker as she sucks. I finish the rest of my drink and order another. There's no point in Vondie being in a good mood all by herself. And since she's being so friendly, I might as well make my move.

"Say Vondie, I wonder if you'd do me a favor."

She pulls the straw from her mouth, licks the tip of it, and pouts. "I'm insulted that you have to wonder."

The bartender slides me my drink, and I take a swallow. It feels good going down, and I feel a nice buzz coming on.

"Just tell me what you need," Vondie says, stroking my forearm again. "I'll help in any way I can."

It's been hard explaining my mess to other people, but compared to telling Vondie they were a cakewalk. Their hearts weren't broken like hers when I chopped our relationship after falling in love with Sierra. But I can't let regret paralyze my tongue, especially since Sierra's prepared to slander me in court.

"Here's the deal," I begin. "Sierra and I, well, we're getting . . ." The words logjam in my throat.

"Just say it," Vondie gently urges. "It'll be okay."

Her reassurance gives me strength. It's too bad that I wasted five years giving my best to Sierra when the better woman was right here in front of me the whole time. "Sierra and I are getting divorced," I say quickly, shoving out the words.

Vondie covers her mouth with her hands, muffling a gasp. "Oh, Denmark, I'm so sorry."

I purse my lips. "Thanks."

We gaze at our drinks for several awkward moments. "Do you mind if I ask why?" she asks.

"She's been having an affair."

Vondie takes my hand. "You must be feeling horrible."

"Horrible was two days ago. Right now I'm just numb."

"Oh sweetie, tell me how can I help?"

I answer with controlled calmness so that I don't appear too anxious or desperate. "Sierra's accusing me of adultery," I explain slowly. "She's saying that I cheated with you on that business trip to Orlando."

"Me!" Vondie blurts, frowning. "She's crazy. We've never even come close . . ."

"You know that, and I know that. But her liar-for-hire lawyer intends to prove otherwise."

Vondie glowers. "You must be angry enough to chew nails."

"Big, hard, rusty nails," I confirm.

Vondie smiles understandingly and squeezes my hand. "What did you need me to do?"

I stare hard into her eyes. "Vondie, I need you to testify on my behalf. If you tell the court that nothing ever happened between us, Sierra's scheme won't stand a chance."

Vondie nods, but her eyes are worried. "Denmark, I want to help; believe me I do. But are you sure that I won't hurt your case more than help it?"

"Hurt it? How could you possibly hurt it?"

She shrugs. "I don't know. It just seems like you're in a pretty tight spot, and I'd hate to say or do something to make matters worse."

Right now the "spot" I'm in is more annoying than tight. If Blinker gets dragged into this mess, messing up his chances in the election, it'll be tight to the point of strangulation. He might even put Stinker and Thinker on my case with the legitimate power of the police backing them up.

"I'm on the ropes," I say, "but your testimony would stop Sierra in her tracks."

"My goodness," Vondie says, blushing. "You're making me feel so important."

I take Vondie's hand and stare deep into her eyes. "That's because you are, baby. More than you know."

Her eyes swim with warmth and affection, and I kiss the back of her hand. "So will you help me?"

"Are things really that bad?"

"They're worse than ever."

She leans forward and pats my cheek. "Well, in that case—no, Denmark. I will *not* help you."

The stunned look on my face must be raw, genuine, and complete. It must be all that and more for Vondie to be laughing so hard and loud. "You should see yourself," she cackles, holding her stomach. "You look so, so . . ."

Some people sitting nearby see her cutting up, and they shrug. Others succumb to the contagion of her comedy and start chuckling, their expressions amused but confused about what's so funny.

"I've waited for years," she chortles. "And now, oh my God, you should see your face."

"Shut up!" I snap.

"Aw, don't be like that," Vondie taunts. "Maybe if you'd contacted me before I talked with Sierra's lawyer . . ."

"What! You've talked with him?"

Vondie nods slowly, thoroughly enjoying herself. "He called asking if I'd testify for your little wife."

"What did you say?" I demand, struggling to keep my voice low.

Vondie sips her drink then answers. "I told him *yes*! I'd love to help destroy you."

There's no humor in Vondie's eyes, voice, or expression. "How does it feel?" she hisses, leaning close. "It's like an acid eating out your insides, isn't it?"

"Get away from me," I rumble, staring at my drink.

"It's like a billion tiny bombs going off inside your heart, isn't it?"

I grab Vondie and jerk her close. "Shut up!"

"Or what?" she challenges, tears spilling from her eyes. "What will you do that was worse than what you did to me five years ago?"

The agony in Vondie's voice hits me with the awful cruelty of my past actions toward her. She wasn't the one I chose to marry, but she also didn't deserve the mean boot I gave her. Vondie had her faults, but she was nice, smart, and fun, and probably she would've stuck by me. Then a prettier face came along, and just like that she was history.

The heat on the back of my neck from peoples' disapproving stares grows hotter, and I release Vondie. She sits back on her bar stool, orders another drink, and glares at me. I get up and stalk off into the dance crowd.

"Does this mean we can't be friends?" Vondie baits.

I hurry, putting steps between me and her before she pushes me too far. "Like they say in the movies," Vondie hollers, "I'll see you in court!"

TWENTY-NINE

smooth-step into the dancers; see a curvy, built woman dancing with some high-yellow, wavy-haired pretty-boy; and cut in.

"Hey!" protests Romeo.

The woman laughs and starts dancing with me. She turns and shakes her big round butt like a killer earthquake's rippling through her African cheeks. The DJ scratches and mixes some old Sly and the Family Stone with Fifty Cents' newest, switches to DMX, doubles back to an old Bone, Thugs'N Harmony classic, then throws on some rump-shaking tunes from Beyonce. The music is pumping, I'm warming up, and the booze and rage has got me flying high.

My partner's former Romeo taps me hard on the shoulder. "Hey, man!" he shouts. "This is my spot!"

I keep dancing, riding high then low on my partner's quivering, joggling butt. I feel like giving it a quick, solid *spank*.

"Hey!" shouts Romeo, tapping me again. "I said . . ."

I slam my palm into his chest. He staggers back into a knot of people. Women complain. Men shout and swat. Romeo crawls for safety.

The DJ hollers into the microphone. "Are ya'll having a good time?"

"Yeah!" we thunder.

"I said is everybody having a good time?"

"Yeah!"

"Then put your hands in the air like you don't care and say paaar-*taaay*!"

"Paaar-*tay*!"

"I said paaar-*tay*!"

"Paaar-*tay*!"

"Now get down!"

The hammering hip-hop beat is suddenly overridden by James Brown's powerful, gravel-scratched voice, booming his old classic "Poppa's Got a Brand New Bag."

"Dance, brothers and sisters!" the DJ shouts. "Give up that funk to the Godfather of Soul!"

The floor goes wild, and we're partying back. The dimmed floor lights go off, leaving the room bathed in a myriad of colors, bouncing off the spinning silver balls. I've lost my big booty partner, but she's quickly replaced by a long, slim sister who's dancing with her hips thrust forward like she's saying, "Come and get it, daddy!"

I go to "get it!" when sister girl is bumped out the way by . . . *Desiree Easton*? Sister girl narrows her eyes at Desiree, who's already shaking, sliding, and spinning with me.

"Step off!" Desiree commands the woman.

Sister girl looks at me and I shrug. She rolls her eyes and dismisses me and Desiree with an exaggerated "Up yours!" Z-snapping of her fingers. Then she shimmies off to shake her yummy elsewhere. Desiree's dressed in silver high heels, black leather pants, and a black leather jacket that's opened down to the third button, generously revealing her beautiful cleavage. Her soft, shining hair is feathered as it sweeps from front to back to just below her earlobes.

We blend into each other's rhythm, connect with the beat, and control our piece of the floor, laying down moves that earn the nodding respect of lesser dancers.

"Hey, cutie!" shouts Desiree. "I thought I recognized you."

I laugh. "You get around. What're you doing here?"

"I do Nadine's hair."

"Is there anybody in this city whose hair you don't do?"

"Just my white brothers and sisters, but give me some time and I'll be doing them too."

We laugh and get into the music, moving with each other like we're sharing the same body.

"Are you here with any of the crew from the salon?" I ask loudly.

Desiree shakes her head no. "No, baby. I'm flying solo tonight."

"Brice is special edition stupid for letting you party alone."

"Forget him. He got home and started acting foolish, so I left for the night."

"You're out for the *whole* night?"

Desiree laughs, lifts her arms high, shakes her hips, and gives herself over to the power of the beat. "That's right!" she says. "When Keith invited me to this party I went ahead and got myself a room."

Desiree's raised arms have lifted her ample breasts, squeezing them together and making larger and more enticing the soft brown bulge of her jiggling cleavage.

"You two must've had one serious blowout," I say.

"We sure did, babe. But—I—don't—*care*!"

"That's cold-blooded," I admonish, smirking. "You know Brice probably wanted some booty."

"He knows where the Vaseline is."

Desiree laughs, dips low, and moves her hips in slow, wide, sensual circles. The DJ slaps on a got-to-move tune from Snoop Dogg, and the crowd answers with a roar of approval. I spin

Desiree around. She stops with her back to me, grabs her knees, and wiggles her booty around in ways that dare me not to stare. I thrust my hips forward and try to follow the whirling movements of her gyrating butt. She straightens up and spins around, shaking her shoulders and making her cleavage ripple and bounce.

"You'd better stop moving like that," I warn loudly. "Brice wouldn't like it."

"Brice can kiss my butt."

I take a long glance down into the lush valley of her bouncing breasts. "You'd better stop looking at me like that," Desiree warns. "Sierra wouldn't like it."

"She can lick my balls."

Desiree laughs and moves so smooth and sexy that every man dancing near us is gawking at her.

I waggle my finger admonishingly at her. "Look at all the trouble you're causing."

"And I'm going to cause a lot more," she laughs, shaking her booty harder.

"Desiree, you're one fine hot sister," I say, speaking into her ear.

"I know," she giggles. "And you're one fine hot brother."

I take firm hold of her hips and pull her pelvis toward mine. "We ought to do something about all this heat."

She laughs and pulls my head close. "Denmark, you're not ready for *this*!" she says, grinding against me.

"You're just afraid that I'll turn you out and leave you begging."

"Negro, please," she laughs.

"Is that a challenge or a request?"

"You're a smart man. Guess."

I take Desiree's hand and lead her off the dance floor, out into the hallway, and down to the elevators.

THIRTY

Desiree and I are kissing and pulling at each other as I kick the door of her room closed. She rips open the top buttons of my shirt, then kisses my neck and shoulders. I pull her black leather jacket off. All she has on beneath it is a sexy black lace bra. My heart slams against my chest.

I reach for Desiree, but she quickly steps away. "Just watch," she says, speaking low and husky.

She reaches behind her, undoes the clasp of her bra, and slowly pulls down the straps, revealing second by second and inch by inch her wonderful Ethiopian beauty. And finally her breasts are free and beckoning. I answer their call, then stand tall, circle my arms around her, and pull her close.

"You're gorgeous," I say softly, looking down into her eyes.

We kiss, and her moist, willing lips open to invite my tongue to come share space with hers. I undo Desiree's black leather pants and pull them down slowly, kneeling in front of her and helping her step out of them. Then I gently pull down her black lace panties, kissing every inch of her as I roll them past her beautiful hips and off past her soft, smooth feet.

Her toenails are painted deep red. An elegant gold bracelet circles her right ankle, just below a tattoo of Cupid preparing to shoot an arrow. I caress and kiss her feet, leaving blooming flowers of passion up her calves and along her thighs until I'm standing again and facing her.

She brushes her lips across mine. "Let's take a shower," she whispers, softly biting my earlobe.

We walk hand in hand into the bathroom and keep holding hands as I turn on the water and adjust the temperature. We get into the tub and kiss, holding each other tight beneath the warm splashing water. I lather up the soap sponge, then cover her with suds, moving the sponge smoothly across her soap-slicked body. I kiss her neck, suck her earlobes and turn her so that her back is to me, wrap my arms around her, and pull her into my chest. Her hands cover mine as I soap her breasts, our hands sliding together over their magnificent roundness.

The water rinses away the soapsuds as I turn Desiree toward me and kiss her with the hunger that I had to suppress for so long with Sierra. The shower's warm water sprinkles over us like millions of tiny massaging fingers. Desiree reaches down between us and gives me a gentle squeeze.

"My goodness!" she exclaims. "You must have cement in your blood."

"You're crazy!" I laugh, lifting my face into the spraying water.

Desiree soaps up the sponge and washes me as I washed her, then we playfully splash water into each other's faces as we rinse. I cut off the shower, step out the tub, and extend my hand to Desiree. She steps out behind me and stands regally as I dry her off. Like a queen being tended by her male servant, she lifts her arms, moves her head, and turns slowly so that I can wipe every part. I dry her back and rear cheeks, kneeling down to kiss her royal African behind.

"Now I'll have to think of something else," she says, looking back at me and smiling.

"What do you mean?"

"For if you ever make me mad."

"I don't understand."

"You're already kissing my butt," she giggles. "If you ever make me mad, I'll have to think of something else to say."

We laugh, and I plant a few more playful kisses on her ebony moons. She steps off for the bedroom as I hurry and dry off.

"Do you give massages?" she asks, stopping and looking back at me.

"I give outstanding massages."

She points at a small suitcase. "There's some lotion in there," she says, getting into bed.

I rummage through the bag, find some cherry blossom–scented lotion, and pour a generous portion into my palm. Desiree's lying flat on her back, looking like a perfect living sculpture. The majestic rise and fall of her chest and the downward slope of her firm, flat stomach makes my throat dry. Waves of sexiness rise from her, *calling* me, *urging* me, *demanding* that I hurry and love her good and thorough! But I'm going to take my time. I'm going to pleasure her slow and good while savoring the heat of my boiling blood and the pleading in my loins.

I step smoothly over to Desiree and, starting at her feet, spread the lotion along her body, moving up her legs, her stomach, her breasts, her shoulders and neck. I pour some more lotion into my palm and slowly rub it into her skin, moving my hands in firm, caressing circles. Her breathing deepens. I massage down to the rich region of her inner thighs. She opens her legs a little more, and the intoxicating scent of her pleasure wafts up into my nose.

I kiss her body as I rub in the lotion, licking along, around, and below her breasts, eventually getting into bed beside her. I move over Desiree, gently lift her left leg into the crook of my elbow, and learn the secrets of her joy.

.

Desiree nudges me awake, ruining some of the most satisfying sleep I've had in days. And it was that *good after-lovemaking kind of sleep*, which is some of the best snoozing in the world.

"C'mon Denmark, wake up," she gently but firmly urges.

"What's the matter?" I ask, speaking through a dry, raspy throat.

"Nothing's the matter. I just want you to get up."

"Why?"

She gets out of bed and turns on a light. I blink my eyes quickly to adjust them to the sudden glare.

Desiree answers with a steely sweetness. "Never mind why. All you need to know is that I want you to get up and leave."

I prop myself up on one elbow and rub my eyes awake. "What happened to Desiree the sex tigress who a little while ago was trying to hump my bones loose?"

Desiree puts on a thick bright white robe, ties its belt tight, sits down beside me on the bed, and pats my cheek. "She's still here, baby doll. But do you remember how I said I was flying solo tonight?"

I nod. Desiree's smiling, but she's serious. "That goes for you, too. We've had our fun, but it's time for you to leave."

I look deep into her eyes. She definitely wants me gone, but it sure would be nice to hit that booty one last time for the road.

"What's the rush?" I ask, trying to loosen the knot in the robe's belt.

She slaps my hand away. "Why the sudden change of attitude?" I persist, easing my hands back over to the loosened knot. She glances down at my slowly working hands then looks back at me.

"There's nothing sudden about my change of attitude," she

says. "I needed to get away from Brice so I could clear my head. It's been nice being with you, and you were definitely good. But you're blocking my flow so you've got to go."

"You don't want me to leave," I counter. "You woke me up so you could get some more goodness."

She rolls her eyes. "You really think you're all that?"

"Never mind what I think. It's what you think that matters. And you're thinking that you're still hungry for some sexing."

"What I think is that you need to get up and . . ."

I take her hand and slide it over and onto her new best friend, who's stirring awake between my legs. Her eyelids lower seductively as her fingers slowly circle around her buddy, renewing their bond of friendship. I keep loosening her belt until her robe's open enough for me to see the full outline of her breasts. I lean forward and lick her nipple.

"Denmark, what did I say?" Desiree demands softly.

"Are you sure you want me to leave right now?" I ask, licking her nipple again and again.

"Yes, baby," she says, breathing hard. "I want you to leave . . . right now."

I kiss my way from her breasts down to her stomach and along her inner thighs. "You want me to leave this very minute?"

She opens her legs slightly. "Yes, I want you to . . ."

I kiss closer in toward her sweetness. "Will you help me?"

She opens her legs wider. "Help . . . you do what?"

My tongue explains. She sighs deeply, pulls the covers off me, pushes me onto my back, and straddles me.

"You're distracting me from my solitude," she says huskily, looking down at me.

"I'm sorry."

"No, you're not."

I smirk and shrug. She slaps me softly, closes her eyes, and has her way.

THIRTY-ONE

drive home, floating on the afterglow of Desiree's sweet loving. I'd feel sorry for Brice—but forget *him*. He's the source of Desiree's hostility, so too bad. She's his wife, but if he can't satisfy her he'll just have to deal with the fact that *I will*!

I pull into my garage, press the button to close the door, park, and get out. I saunter into the kitchen from the garage, flip on the light, and close the door behind me. The lock closes with a nice solid *click*! Thank you, locksmith Linwood Powell. I get a beer from the fridge, pop it open, take a swig, and glance at my watch. It's almost 2:35 a.m. I need to hit the sack.

I stroll to the doorway and flip on a light to head upstairs—and my heart leaps into my throat. Blinker Hughes is sitting on the steps. Sitting on either side of him are his lean and lethal-looking pit bulls, Killa and Attila. Leaning against the wall beside the three of them is a very large, very muscular, very dangerous-looking man.

"His bugged-out eyes must mean we surprised 'em," chuckles Muscleman.

Blinker smiles wickedly. "Yeah, seems like it," he agrees, his voice deep and menacing.

My surprise turns to anger. "What're you doing in my house?" I demand to know, staring hard at Blinker.

The dogs growl and bare their teeth. Blinker's smile melts. Muscleman stands tall. Blinker grabs his arm. "Hold up, Troy."

"He'd better show some respect," Troy threatens.

"Or you'll do what?" I challenge, keeping my eye on the canines. If they move a muscle, I've got a bat in the closet next to me that'll send them to Jupiter.

Troy's eyes narrow. He's built like a wall, and putting him down won't be easy. But Blinker knows that when it's over, Troy will be scattered in pieces.

Blinker looks from Troy to me. "Give 'em a break, Denmark. Troy's from Minneapolis and don't know about the Brownfield District like *we* do."

Blinker's reminder that he battled through the same mean streets I did resurrects chilling memories. And what I remember is that while I spent nearly every day back then dreaming, scheming, and planning my escape from that hell-hole, Blinker loved it. He lived for it, and he was nurtured and strengthened by it. He wanted to rule its abundant miseries. The more there was of its havoc and suffering, the more he adored that urban desert. He's risen from being its loving disciple to reign as its grasping tyrant, and now he wants to be elected its benign dictator.

Blinker stands and ambles over to me. "Let's talk," he orders. The dogs fidget, and Blinker points a rigid finger at them. "Stay!"

They whine their displeasure but keep still. Blinker starts past me, heading into the kitchen. His caramel skin, close-cut hair, smooth-shaven face, wide almond eyes, and angular jaw give him the look of a ruggedly handsome movie action hero. His gleaming black boots, thighs bulging against his faded blue jeans, and biceps straining against the sleeves of his waist-length black leather jacket make him look even more powerful. If Blinker had chosen another path in life, his six foot three inches of power could've dominated the body-building world. But he's ruling the world he wants, and the buff body that would've bulged from magazine covers is just another one of his weapons.

Troy stays put like the other two well-trained pooches and flips me the bird. I chuckle, pucker my lips at him, and join Blinker in the kitchen, but he's not there. The door leading out onto the wooden deck is open. Blinker's reclining on a thickly padded lounger and smoking a cigarette. I step out with him and close the door behind me.

"Take a seat," he directs, gesturing to a deck chair directly opposite him.

I ignore the command and half-sit on the deck's wooden rail. "How'd you get into my house?" I demand to know. "I just had new locks put on the doors and windows."

Blinker chuckles, takes a drag of his cigarette, and blows smoke rings. He's right. It's pointless asking *him* that question. Alarms and locks are deterrents for regular people. For Blinker they're not even a nuisance. But I'm still going to give locksmith Linwood Powell a thorough fussing out about his *not so good* work!

"So tell me what's going on," says Blinker. "How's you not handlin' *your* woman suddenly *my* problem?"

"It's not your problem!" I insist too quickly. "It won't even be an issue if I can work things out."

Blinker cuts his eyes at me. "I thought you said she's been slammin' another dude."

"She has been."

"Then there ain't nothin' to work out. Unless you talkin' about her funeral arrangements."

"Wait a minute, Blinker. I don't want you . . ."

"You think I came out here to talk about what you want?" he interrupts, crushing the cigarette out on the lounger's arm rest.

214 FREDDIE LEE JOHNSON III

His glacial eyes sweep over me. "I told you to never talk about me, didn't I? But'cha did, and now I gotta decide how pissed off I need to be."

He shakes his head in disgust. "What happened to you, Denmark? What made you think a babe would do right and watch your back till death did ya'll part?"

I lower my eyes. "It was love," I mumble.

"Say what?"

"Love made me think it."

Blinker snorts his disgust. "Love has gave you something new to think about, ain't it?"

He unzips his jacket, stands, and stretches. The light beaming from the kitchen window shines onto the pistol in his shoulder holster. He starts for the door and stops beside me. "Am I gone have'ta fix this?"

"No, Blink. *I'll* handle it."

He studies me and lights another cigarette. "All right, outa respect for the old days I'm'a hang back and let'cha do your thing."

"You're going to hang back for how long?"

He takes a drag of his cigarette and blows a jet of smoke that barely misses my face. "You've always been a smart brother, Denmark. Be smart now." He goes in the house and calls for Troy and the pit bulls, and they leave.

THIRTY-TWO

Blinker's cryptic visit ruined an otherwise good night. I've got to steer Sierra and her lawyer away from him, but it's going to take some good legal help. That's where Hilda Vaughan comes in. Her law office isn't located in an imposing, severe modern building like where Nelson's downtown suite is located. Hers is a house in a nice, quaint historic neighborhood just on the edge of the city. It's also conveniently in the same general route that I take to get to work.

When I pass by Henderson Village, Burned-out Bobby's on "his" corner, gesturing at passing vehicles and pointing to his latest sign, which reads: "Got problems? Look up!"

Given his living conditions, Bobby ought to take his own advice. Better yet, he ought to get a job. But forget him. I've got to stay focused and on task to arrest my situation before it spirals any further out of control.

I stride briskly up Hilda's front walk, admiring the surroundings as I go. Rosebushes line the smooth walkway. There's a nice-sized backyard with the greenest, most brilliant emerald grass

I've ever seen. In the thick old trees surrounding the house, squirrels chase each other, zipping and leaping from branch to branch.

I go up the steps and see the shingle hanging just to the right of the front door. The first line reads "Hilda Vaughan, Attorney at Law." A second line reads "P3/6."

"It must be some licensing designation or registration number," I muse aloud.

The mystery of the shingle can wait. What I need to know right now is if Hilda can punish Sierra through the law the way Sierra's been punishing me through the heart. I knock on the door several times.

"Just a moment," a woman loudly answers. I glance at my watch. It's 10:30 a.m. exactly. The door opens.

"Good morning," says a smiling dark princess. "You must be Denmark Wheeler."

If the earth, sun, moon, and stars had gotten together and said, "Brothers, let's get busy and fashion from the shimmering night an African angel who'll make men forget their woes, subdue their aggression, and intoxicate them with sweet desire," it would be this woman before my eyes.

She's beautifully dark, with smooth, luxuriant skin. Her long black satiny hair flows down the sides and back of her head, framing her gorgeous oval face like a masterpiece. She's about five feet, five inches, maybe six, with a slim willowy body that curves in all the right places with just enough protruding emphasis so that everything's in balanced proportion. She has big slightly round eyes, like a Somali woman's, soothing and wise, hinting at a deep capacity for love. And her lips—they're full but not large, slightly moist, and beckoning.

"Hello?" she says playfully, waving her hand back and forth. "You are Denmark Wheeler, aren't you?"

I shake myself out of my gawk and try to answer coolly. "Yeah, I'm him. You must be Hilda Vaughan."

"That's correct," she says, opening the door. She extends her hand, and we shake. "I'm pleased to meet you."

"Likewise."

"Come on in," she says, gesturing me inside. "Just give me a second. I'll be right back."

She leaves me standing in the doorway and hurries into a back room. She's dressed in a jogging warmup suit and wearing only white cotton socks on her feet. As fine as she is, I'm not feeling good about this.

The house's interior is as immaculate as the exterior. The shiny hardwood floors, soft tan walls, high ceilings, and African artwork spread tastefully throughout give the room a gentle but sturdy feel. Huge bookshelves line one wall. I stroll over to see what's in Hilda's library. Even if she turns out to be a good lawyer, knowing what she reads will tell me who she is as a person.

I check through her selections and see a title that immediately boosts her currency with me: *Slave Rebellions in North America*. I pull it off the shelf and flip to the section pertaining to Denmark Vesey: "*. . . and so came the day of his execution. Vesey and his co-conspirators were hanged for daring to take their freedom. Betrayal by one of his own cost him his life . . .*"

"There they are!" Hilda says loudly, from a back room. "Lucille always puts my shoes where I can't find them."

"Is Lucille a relative?"

She laughs. "No, she's my assistant, but she might as well be a relative. Why?"

She comes from the back room wearing running shoes on her feet and wrestling her thick long hair through a rubber band.

"When I called to make my appointment, I know you said she was your secretary, but she sounded to me more like your elder aunt."

She gets the last of her shiny strands through the rubber band, and her hair hangs in a loose ponytail. "I do a lot of volunteering down at a hospice," Hilda informs me. "Lucille was a patient there. The doctors had given her only a few months to live. We got to be friends. She beat the odds but was all alone. I needed the help, so I offered her a job."

All I can do is blink. Coming from the Brownfield District and spending years in corporate America hasn't prepared me for such stories of kindness. But I'm glad I asked. It gives me some insight into Hilda. On the other hand, I hope she's not so kind that she can't do what's required to legally dismember Sierra.

"Okay!" she says, grabbing a waist belt wallet and strapping it on. "I'm ready to go."

"Go where?"

"I hope you don't mind. I got up late and missed my morning run. We can talk at the track before I do my workout. I promise to be one hundred percent attentive."

I purse my lips to swallow my irritation. She's jaw-dropping good-looking, no doubt about it, but bump this. She's too flighty for what I need. I'm going to chew off Nelson's ear for recommending this flake.

If this is any indicator of how Hilda practices law, I might as well mail Sierra my scalp and get it over with.

So when Hilda says, "Do you mind if I drive?" why do I answer with "No problem"?

She gestures me out, locks the door, bounds down the steps, and stops upon seeing my Corvette. "That's the only true American sports car," she says.

I walk up beside her. "Yeah, it's a gem."

"The closest I ever came to owning a Corvette was my '72 Chevelle SS."

My head snaps around to her. "Are you saying that *you* owned a 1972 Chevelle Super Sport?"

Her expression tightens. "Do I detect a sexist tone in your voice?"

I clear my throat and answer in a more gender-neutral fashion. "No. It's just that among the muscle cars, the Chevy SS was tops."

She goes back to admiring the Corvette. "Mine had a 396 engine, positraction rear end, slick stick shifter, and roller-bearing cam. I loved that car, except that I had to keep on adjusting the timing belt."

I blink at Hilda. She arches an eyebrow and smirks. "That's right. I worked on my own car."

This woman's got some grit. Sierra sometimes has difficulty sticking her key in the ignition of her Lexus. But Hilda's running down engine, transmission, and power train specifications like she's studying for a mechanic's exam.

"I'd have kept it, but I had to get through law school," she continues.

"I don't follow you."

"There are a lot of SS enthusiasts out there. I was putting myself through law school and running out of money. Selling my car brought me the cash I needed to finish. I hated to do it, but poverty and failure weren't options."

"Where did you grow up?" I ask.

"Cincinnati. My parents were regular middle-class people, nothing spectacular or flashy, just good solid folks."

"I grew up in the Brownfield District."

Her eyes widen. "And you lived to tell about it? I'm impressed."

"So am I."

We laugh and walk side by side to her Ford Explorer SUV. "How do you like this vehicle?" I ask.

"I love it. Lucille wanted me to buy a minivan, but I told her no way."

"What don't you like about minivans?"

She unlocks the doors with her keyless entry. "Hmmm, let me see. What is it that I don't like about minivans?" She looks at me, smiling slyly, and says, "Everything."

We laugh, get into the Explorer, and back out her driveway. We just might have some things to discuss after all.

THIRTY-THREE

Hilda and I sit on a park bench facing Lake Erie, just a few yards from the beach that's sloping down to the water. I'd heard that eco-sensitive redevelopers were trying to clean up and beautify the lakefront after years of Cleveland's wanton waste and pollution, but this is fantastic.

Behind us is Olympiad Place, an attractive outdoor complex with an oval competition track, basketball courts, tennis courts, skateboard obstacle course, and three volleyball sandpits. Yuppie parents jog by, pushing their infants in tricycle strollers. A man off in the distance tosses a Frisbee to his energetic golden retriever.

Hilda's sitting back against the bench, deeply inhaling the fresh aquatic air. She looks relaxed, but her intense expression suggests that she's fully alert and focused.

She takes a deep breath, then looks at me. "And you're certain that the sender was I Got Your Back, Inc.?" she asks.

"I'm positive."

She sighs and shakes her head sadly. "There's no end."

"Excuse me?"

"There no end to how low human beings will stoop to hurt each other."

I grunt my agreement and watch the waves roll ashore. "Have you thought about trying to reconcile?" Hilda asks.

I look at her. "Are you serious?"

"Yes, I am," she blandly answers, returning my gaze. "I understand that Sierra's probably the last person you . . ."

"Forget reconciliation," I interrupt. "The marriage is over, plain and simple."

"First hear me out," Hilda admonishes. "Along with being a lawyer I'm a counselor. I know that you're deeply hurt and angry, but that's why I asked the question. Emotionally driven decisions seldom turn out right. If you're going to be my client, I have to ensure that you've considered all the alternatives."

"Hilda, I watched a video of my wife blowing and screwing another man. What's there to think about?"

"Are you still in love with her?"

I clench my jaw and return my gaze to the lake. Hilda keeps looking at me, her eyes heating up the side of my face. "Denmark?"

I quickly face her. "Have you been listening to me? Somebody named 'I Got Your Back, Inc.' sent me a DVD showing my wife having sex with *another man*! They put a note with it urging me to have a great conversation about the video. Trust me, Hilda. I have *not* been having a great time or a great conversation."

Hilda's unperturbed. "I understand, but are you still in love with her?"

I blink at her in disbelief. What part of this doesn't she get? "Hilda, have you ever loved someone so much that they became the air you breathed? Have you ever been prepared to give everything to make someone happy? Have you ever been so connected to someone that when they hurt, you hurt; when they laughed, you laughed; and if they were angry with you, your world crumbled?"

"Denmark," she calmly responds, "are you *in* love with your wife?"

I turn back to the lake. "If you don't want to take my case, just tell me. I'll see if Nelson's got another recommend . . ."

"The first thing that needs to happen is for you and your wife to talk."

"Say what?"

Hilda gently taps my shoulder, and I turn toward her. "You and your wife need to talk," she repeats.

Images from the DVD flash before me. *No baby, you have to make me come first.* "No." I glance at my watch. "Just drop me off back at your office and I'll be on my way."

"You owe it to yourself, the life you shared, and the love and time you invested into your relationship to know—*really know*—that it's over."

"And what makes you think I don't know that already?"

Hilda speaks softly. "You still haven't answered my question."

I grimace inwardly. "Will you take my case or not?"

"That depends on whether or not you'll agree to speak with your wife."

"Why is that so important to you?"

"What's important to me is that you not do something you'll end up regretting for the rest of your life." She looks out at the lake and keeps talking. There's an odd tone in her voice, like she's speaking more to herself than me. "True love is so precious and rare, Denmark. It's far too precious to casually throw away."

"There's nothing casual about this, and I'm not the one who threw it away. My wife's a cheating slut who . . ."

"Will one day regret losing the man who loved her with all his heart."

I glare at Hilda. She holds my gaze until I look away. I'm

not angry with her but at myself for letting her see the destruction that Sierra's caused in me. Hilda better get a good glimpse at this display of my emotions. It's the last she'll ever see of them.

"If you're already convinced that Sierra's lost me, why are you insisting that we talk?" I ask.

"Because *you're* not convinced."

"Is that right?" I scoff. "Tell me, Hilda, was mind reading something you learned in law school, or is this genetic?"

"Are you still in love with your wife?"

I stare once more, hard and unblinking, into Hilda's eyes. Once more, she holds her ground. "No, Hilda," I answer tightly. "I no longer love my wife."

"Then having a conversation with her before we proceed shouldn't present a risk."

"Since that *is* the case, what's the point of having the conversation?"

"First of all, it's procedural. You want this over with quickly, so I recommend dissolution. It's faster and cheaper, and it shouldn't get as messy as a full-blown divorce."

"Fine. Whatever will work fastest and best is all right with me."

"Dissolutions require both parties to discuss the terms of separation until they agree."

"Agree on what?"

"The division of assets, support, and . . ."

"We don't have any children, so there's no child support issue."

"That'll make things easier, but there's still the question of alimony."

"*What*? How's a judge going to look at the evidence and require me . . ."

"She could end up paying you."

I swallow the rest of my protest. "Go on," I say.

"Some couples can amicably iron out the details one on one with each other while their lawyers give occasional technical guidance."

"Kind of like a do-it-yourself divorce?"

Hilda nods grimly. I shake my head. No wonder people like Mason Booker are so cynical. "*I'm a fan of marriage*," he said. "*It's good for the economy.*"

"And like I said before," Hilda continues, "dissolutions are usually cheaper and less complicated. That allows for faster processing."

"This all sounds good," I say, sitting back and stretching. "It also sounds like you're taking my case. Are you?"

"Before I answer, you need to understand that if I do, I'm going to win for you. I'll push as hard as I need to, and I'll stand firm until we get the desired result. I don't believe in half-stepping, and I will protect your interests with all the skills and resources at my disposal."

This is sounding more like what I want to hear. I might've found myself a lawyer after all.

"I can keep it soft and clean or play it hard and messy," Hilda continues. "That's another reason why I insist that you talk to your wife. I don't want to get halfway through this process only to have you suddenly discover that you love your wife after all."

Hilda's words vibrate with a lethality that's comforting. She's talking herself into a job. "I tell you these things," she continues, "so that you'll see the sense of talking with your wife before we begin."

"Why?" I ask, smiling and feeling more encouraged. "Am I supposed to warn her that Hurricane Hilda's on the way?"

"No!" Hilda snips, her expression hard and her tone deadly serious. "I don't want you losing heart when I start putting your soon-to-be ex through a sawmill. My time and resources are too valuable to be expended on ventures and people who don't know what they want or won't follow through."

I sit up tall and speak deliberately so there's no misunderstanding. "Hilda, I can assure you that I will not lose heart."

Hilda's eyes narrow, and she leans slightly toward me. "No, Denmark, you can't assure me of that."

"What're you talking about?" I indignantly challenge. "I just told you that I no longer love my wife."

Hilda gets up and starts stretching for her run. She's amazingly limber, bending, twisting, and turning her lithesome body with an ease that makes my warm-ups look stiff and arthritic. She finishes, strips off her lightweight warm-up top, hands it to me, and stands with her arms akimbo. She's wearing a light blue half tee shirt that hangs just below the pleasing bulge of her full breasts, exposing her narrow waist and hard flat stomach. She's a lioness prepared for the hunt.

"Denmark, what I'm talking about is that you still haven't answered my question."

I take a deep, frustrated breath. "I just told you . . ."

"Yes, I know. You don't love your wife, but I'm asking are you *in* love with her."

"Honestly, Hilda, what difference does it make?" I ask, exasperated.

"Think about it. I'll be back shortly."

Hilda jogs off to the track. I clench my jaw and turn back to Lake Erie. She's a typical lawyer—splitting hairs, manipulating language, and turning something simple into a Byzantine nightmare. Whether I'm in love or not, the bottom line is that I want out of this marriage. As long as Hilda gets paid her fee, what does she care? She's acting like a marriage counselor, not a lawyer. She's nothing like Nelson. He'd get the facts, unleash his destruction, and go on vacation. But maybe there's an advantage to having a lawyer who'll take things personally. I'll get more of her attention instead of being just one of her stable of clients. Hilda doesn't strike me as someone who runs a legal assembly line, but someone who really believes in justice. She can believe in whatever she wants just so long as she wins.

I turn around and watch her. She's got a nice running form and long, flowing strides, with all of her body parts moving in sync. There's no wasted motion with her.

The breeze from Lake Erie picks up, and I turn toward it, close my eyes, and inhale deep. Sierra loves Lake Erie, especially at sunrise. Sometimes we'll drive the ninety minutes to a lovely park just across the state line in Presque Isle, Pennsylvania, and watch as the sun slowly arcs its way into the early morning sky. The wind will blow Sierra's hair over her head, and she'll hug me tight. I'll pull her into me and stroke her hair as she lays her head on my chest. At those moments there's no one else I'd rather be with or . . .

"Are you *in* love with her?" the wind whispers.

"*No, baby, you have to make me come first.*"

Hell no—I'm not in love with Sierra! Then why am I having this conversation? It's Hilda and all of her legalistic double-talk. I turn around to see her running on the track, and I'm stunned. She's flying! And the way she's moving, so swift, smooth, and effortless, every time her feet hit the track I half expect to see lightning explode from beneath her shoes.

She rockets around the track for another two laps, then slows into a half-sprint and a jog. Finally she walks off toward me. She's breathing hard, but it's not labored. Her hands are on her strong hips, and her head is held high, her nostrils flared as she takes great breaths, each inhalation and exhalation causing her beautiful chest to rise and fall in a smooth rhythm.

I grab her water bottle and hand it to her. "Well," she says, huffing smoothly. "Do you see the difference between loving someone and being *in* love with her?"

I ignore the slight condescension in Hilda's tone and answer her. "Yes, Hilda. I do."

"So are you still in love with . . ."

"No!" I snip. "I am not *in* love with my, ah, with Sierra so will you *please* stop asking."

Hilda eyes me with heavy suspicion. "Okay, whatever you say."

"Thanks. Will you take my case or not?"

"Will you talk with your wife?"

I clench my jaw. I'll say this much for Hilda, she's no pushover and clearly possesses the spine to work an issue until she gets what she wants. And that's exactly why I want her.

"Yes, Hilda," I answer, suppressing a sigh of resignation. "I'll talk with my . . . I'll talk with Sierra."

She extends her hand. "You just hired yourself a lawyer."

We shake, and I get down to business. "Sierra's lawyer has already scheduled a meeting. Can you arrange for it to cover this territory?"

She takes a mighty swig of her water. "Consider it done."

I give her the time and place details that Charles Keller's phone fuzzy passed on to me for next week's meeting. "What's the meeting's purpose?" Hilda asks.

"Her lawyer said it was to begin the process of mediation. But to be honest, it sounded more like a summons for me to hear their dictated terms."

"Does he intend to have Sierra there?"

"Not that I'm aware."

Hilda uses her towel to wipe dry the sweat oozing from her pores, her motions and matter-of-fact acceptance of her body's power and processes underscoring her raw and powerful beauty. She's so different from Sierra, who would've needed three showers; a facial; massage, hair, manicure, and pedicure appointments; shopping spree; vacation; and therapy to recover from the trauma of excreting a drop of sweat.

"Is there anything else I need to know right now?" Hilda asks.

Blinker's face flashes before me. So does Sierra's family, along with the certainty of their high-priced attempts to impale me. "Yes," I answer. "But I'd rather discuss those details in your office."

Hilda nods. "Okay."

She starts stretching again as part of her cool-down. She bends over, grabs her toes, and amazingly touches her nose to her knees. The tight curvature of her rear end defies being ignored, and my eyes are too weak to resist. Until I notice her looking at me.

I quickly cut my eyes away. "Are you competing in the Greater Cleveland Corporate Sports Challenge?" I ask.

Hilda straightens up and mercifully pretends that she didn't see me ogling. "Isn't that Cleveland's version of a corporate Olympics?"

"Yes. You might call it that."

She shrugs. "I've thought about competing but never bothered. Why do you ask?"

I smile and explain.

THIRTY-FOUR

Recalling one of his last battles with first wife Clarisse, Harry once said: "Ain't nothin' like a divorce to show you who your spouse *really* is."

I glance at my desk calendar. It's 9:12 a.m. on Wednesday, and one week to the day since I watched Sierra with Mr. X on that video from "I Got Your Back, Inc." Five lousy minutes was all it took for that piece of plastic to obliterate a life that seemed so good, so sweet, and so right.

In just a few minutes I'm going to get up and go downtown for this meeting Hilda insists that I have with Sierra. I'll be there well before it starts, but that'll give me time to get myself together and confer one last time with Hilda.

Sierra, mostly through her lawyer, Charles Keller, has repeatedly warned me that I'd better cooperate. The house, stocks, mutual funds, IRAs, retirement property we bought down on the eastern shore of Virginia, the bulging 401Ks, the vacation cottage in the Austrian Alps, the 28% share ownership in *Run Sucker*, an up-and-coming racehorse, and anything else connected with money has been the focus of their barrages. It's been my focus also, since a lot of what's in dispute, she and I—WE—acquired together.

But along with what she's legitimately entitled to get, Sierra also wants my shirt. Having grown up in wealth, plenty, and opulence, then lived as an adult in more of the same, she's determined to ensure not only that her life continues the luxurious journey but that my back be the highway upon which she travels.

It's amazing that so much has happened in one short week. Seven days. One hundred sixty-eight hours. It's like some cosmic magician waved a wand over me and said, "Poof!" It's been raining crap ever since. But thanks to Hilda, some of it's fallen onto Sierra, and my soon-to-be ex hasn't appreciated it—not one little bit.

While I was meeting with Hilda yesterday, Tuesday, at her office, she stepped out to the bathroom and my cell phone rang. I answered without first looking to see who was calling, and I was immediately sorry.

"Hello?"

"Hello," Sierra said. "I don't care what happens at this meeting, I'm not changing my position."

"Why start now? You've only got the one."

Sierra chuckled. "That was just with you."

I gritted my teeth, inhaled deep, and tried to remain calm. "It's my lawyer who wanted this meeting. I'd be happy never seeing, hearing from, or thinking about you again."

Sierra gasped and sputtered. "Denmark, so help me God— *I'm going to . . .*"

I laughed. "Is this the same God whom you were praising and worshiping while married to me and banging your boyfriend?"

There was a long silence, but not one of malice or anger. I sensed from Sierra a profound sorrow and . . . regret. "I'm going to ask His forgiveness," she said.

"You might as well," I mocked. "You won't find it on this side of town."

"Look!" she snapped, her holy moment over. "If you don't want this meeting, why allow the obstruction?"

"Hilda thinks it's a necessary step in the process."

"The outcome's going to be the same."

Hilda strolled back into the room, saw my somber face, and said, "Who's *that*?"

"Sierra," I mumbled.

She came over, snatched the phone from my hand, and hung up. "Hey!" I said. "What're you . . ."

She stabbed a rigid forefinger at me, ordering me into silence. I sat back and listened. "If she calls to threaten or harass you again, I want to know about it," Hilda firmly stated.

"No problem," I replied.

"This madness is wrenching enough without all the fireworks."

It made sense. But if that was Hilda's concern, I couldn't understand why she was still so determined for me to talk with Sierra.

"Consider this," Hilda explained. "You've mentioned that every time you two talk, it turns into an argument. That's normal, given the circumstances. But something else might be at work. Beneath the hostility there could still exist love, enough to salvage the relationship and begin the process of healing."

"That's crazy! I'd never . . ."

"Didn't your elders teach you that you should never say '*never*'? People don't expend all the emotion you and Sierra are investing into your arguments if what they're arguing about doesn't matter. What would be the point? Generally speaking, when couples argue, either they truly hate each other, or one of them has been deeply hurt by the person they've loved, still love, and still might want to love. You and Sierra need to know which is what."

"It still sounds like you're trying to save my marriage," I grumped.

Hilda fired back quickly. "Only *you* can save your marriage. I just want you to be certain that ending it is the right thing to do. If you decide it is, I'll be more than happy to do my job, take my fee, and remodel my kitchen."

I didn't know whether to be offended, relieved, or just plain old puzzled. Hilda didn't give me time to figure it out.

"It's time for lunch, and I'm hungry," she announced, looking at her watch. "Could you go for some pizza and beer?"

I could, and we did. Twenty minutes later I'd parked the Corvette in the Pizza Hut parking lot and we'd placed our order. From the moment the server walked off to the last drop in our quart of beer, Hilda had me cracking up as she told a series of "Why did the chicken cross the road?" jokes that were so lame and corny I had to laugh. My attempts to dazzle her with some vaguely remembered childhood "Knock, knock," humor proved too feeble, so I willingly, and laughingly, conceded that she was the worst joke teller I'd ever heard.

We were walking across the parking lot to the Corvette when Hilda said, "That car is a portrait of power."

And words left my mouth that never had, and never would've, been heard by Sierra, who viewed sports cars as extravagant toys for misguided male egos. "Would you like to drive?" I asked, looking at Hilda.

Her hand sprang out, palm up and open. "I thought you'd never ask," she answered, grinning.

I tossed her the keys, and we got in. Hilda jetted back to her office, shifting gears, taking corners, and maneuvering through traffic with the road generalship of a NASCAR driver. I sat back and enjoyed the ride, smiling inwardly that Hilda's performance on the road was as impressive as it had been on the running track.

Harry had scoffed and Gordon had chuckled when I told

them she'd agreed to be the fourth person on our 4 × 100 relay team. Hilda made them true believers by smoking them during timed trials. I barely edged out a victory against her, expending more effort and energy than I cared to admit. Harry started calling her "Rocket." Gordon mainly ogled. She and I started working out together down at her favorite track near the beach at Lake Erie, wind sprinting, practicing handoffs, or just jogging and talking.

Hours after we'd gone our separate ways that day, it struck me that I hadn't been the least bit worried about letting Hilda, whom I still didn't know too well, drive my four-wheeled baby. Maybe it was the way she'd handled Sierra during that phone call. She had charged into harm's way to protect me then, and it seemed sensible to think she'd be just as protective of me in my car.

Having a protector was a new, weird sensation. In the Brownfield District I'd always been the guardian enforcer, routinely taking the fight to the enemy. Now I had Hilda as my intrepid warrior princess, keeping the barbarians from the gate, and it felt good, *real good*.

My desk phone rings, jostling me into the present. I take a quick moment to yawn, then answer. "Speed Shift Auto Parts. Denmark Wheeler speaking."

"Zup!" replies a canyon-deep baritone voice.

I sit up straight. "Hey, Blink. What's going on?"

"Has anybody called you yet?"

Ice crystals form along my spine. Has he engineered a hit against Sierra? I'm furious with her, but not enough to celebrate Blinker's harming her. "Has anybody called me about . . . what?" I ask tentatively.

"The Speed Shift store over on Haynes Avenue just got took down."

I sit back relieved. Sierra's safe. It pisses me off that it matters. It pisses me off even more that Hilda might be right about needing to talk with my soon-to-be ex-wife.

"You're pretty calm for somebody's who got a store less than three miles from that robbery," comments Blinker.

He's right! Haynes Avenue runs along the edge of "my" territory. If the thieves hit that Speed Shift location, their next target might be . . .

"When did it happen?" I ask.

"About five minutes ago."

"Five minutes!" I blurt. "How'd you find out so . . ."

"One of my boys was coming out the liquor store next to it when they hit. He ducked behind some cars and saw the whole thing."

Blinker stops and lets the silence swell. He's going someplace with this information and wants me to follow, and I oblige him. "Is your guy going to help the cops' investigation?" I ask.

"Hell no," Blinker calmly answers. "You're paying me to watch only *your* stores, for now."

I press the phone hard against my ear. "What're you saying, Blinker? Give it to me straight."

"Man, don't play me. You told your old lady about our little arrangement, didn't you?"

I grimace inwardly. "Yes."

"Sucker," he sneers. "If the heat comes, and it better not, I'm'a have'ta put some distance between you'n me."

"Blinker, don't do this. My stores will be left wide open."

"What'chew better be worrying about is making your bosses understand why you had a street crew doing your security. You know how it'll go down," he says. "Once it's known that I was doing your security, one'a them suits is gone suggest that you'n me set up them robberies so your boys would look bad while you sat fat."

I groan. "How much worse can this get?"

"You'd better hope it don't get much worse," Blinker warns,

adding, "Denmark, before I lose this election or go back to the slam, I'll deal with your old lady. And since you're her husband, they'll come looking for *you*, not me!"

I grip the phone tight. "Blinker, listen to me. I . . ."

He hangs up, and I fume. I've got to resolve this chaos—and fast. But I need information. I need Jiao and Mason to tell me something—*anything*—that'll put Sierra in check.

I pull the business card for the Electronics Doctor from my wallet and dial quickly. There's no answer at the store, so I dial Jiao Minh Xing's home workshop number. I wait through four agonizingly long rings before he answers.

"*What?*" Jiao hollers. "Talk quick! I'm in emergency."

"Jiao, this is Denmark Wheeler," I say hurriedly. "I'm calling to see if you've made any progress on . . ."

"Not yet! Keep choking chicken. Jiao gotta go!"

"Jiao!" a husky female voice calls from the background. "C'mon and put some more of your Zen in my den."

"Uh-oh," Jiao groans. He mutters in his native Vietnamese.

"Look!" I snap. "Can't you estimate how long it'll take to before . . ."

"You check later!" Jiao interrupts. "Have update then . . . if Jiao still living."

"Gimme some more honey, you little love machine," Daisy commands.

Jiao yelps, and the phone clatters onto the floor. This *sucks*! Jiao's taking too long, and with the way things are going, his delay is going to cost me more than what I stand to lose in a crumbling marriage. I've got to put some pressure on him and Mason to get me answers. It'll have to be later. Right now I've got to get to this meeting.

THIRTY-FIVE

On my way out of the store, I see Mrs. Randall. We wave to each other. "How are you today, Mrs. Randall?" I greet, slowing down to shake her hand.

"I'm doing just fine. And you?"

"I guess I'll make it."

She frowns slightly. "Come now, Denmark, life's too grand to just be making it."

I glance at my watch and ease toward the door. "Okay, Mrs. Randall, whatever you say. You take care."

"You also, and tell Sierra I said hello. She and her boss have been really working hard. Their conference is certain to be a hit."

I stop so fast, my feet could leave skid marks. "Are you still seeing them a lot?"

"Often enough," Mrs. Randall confirms. She gathers up her bag with its single car air freshener and heads for the door. "Anyway, tell her I said hello, and you have a nice day."

Millions of thoughts stampede through my mind as I watch her leave. I'm going to have to get Mrs. Randall to give me a detailed description of Sierra's "boss." Or maybe I should have

Mason Booker do it. After all, he's the expert. I'll decide later. I've got to get to this meeting.

I get in the Corvette, and as I get into traffic the cell phone rings. "Hello?"

"Hi, Denmark, it's me, Hilda."

I smile big. "What a pleasant surprise," I say. "I'm just on my way downtown to meet you."

"Well, then, I'm glad I caught you before you got too far."

I tense up. "Is everything all right?" I ask.

"Sure. I was just wondering if you'd stop by to get me. I know it's a little out of the way, but . . ."

"It's no problem, and it'll be my pleasure."

"Thanks. Hold on a sec, will you?"

Hilda speaks loudly to Lucille. "Go ahead and take the Explorer. I've got a ride."

She exchanges a few more words with Lucille and then turns her attention back to me. "So I'll see you in a little while?"

"I'm on the way."

A little while later, I park in Hilda's driveway and knock on her door. "I'll be right there," she calls from inside.

I glance at her shingle and wonder again at the P3/6 inscription. "Okay," Hilda says, opening the door. "I'm ready."

I gesture to the shingle. "What's that deal with your shingle?"

She locks the door and smiles. "It's a gift from Lucille from when she first came to work for me. It's from chapter three, verse six in the book of Proverbs: 'In all your ways acknowledge Him and He shall make your paths straight.' "

"That's cute."

Hilda's smile tightens. "She wanted me to always remember that the law should be used for justice and mercy, not revenge or greed."

I almost say something about revenge and greed coming as natural to lawyers as ducks swimming in water until I remember that Hilda's a lawyer. I also remember that my pursuit of Mr. X is to *get even*.

I gesture to the Corvette. "Shall we?"

We get in the car and get going. On the way downtown Hilda describes once more the procedures of what'll happen.

"The meeting will be run by a moderator appointed by the court," she explains. "This person's a magistrate, not a judge, but they've got the power of the court behind them, so listen close and follow instructions."

Once there I park and start to get out when Hilda grabs my arm. I turn and meet her gaze. "Are you ready?" she asks.

I nod. "With you here to back me up, of course I'm ready."

"Okay then. Let's do this."

THIRTY-SIX

Hilda and I stroll briskly down the ornately decorated hallway of the law firm of Savage, Pahlunder, & Crooke. Sierra's family connections have come in handy on this occasion. Most divorce cases take months, but the famed Montague clout has pushed ours way ahead of schedule, and that's fine with me. Charles Keller wanted us to meet in his office, but Hilda insisted upon a neutral site and pulled some strings of her own, and we have a space all to ourselves. She strides confidently through a doorway with a sign over it reading Quisling Conference Room.

A handsomely attractive, well-tanned, stylishly dressed but stern-looking woman with blazing-white hair sits at the center of a long shining mahogany table. High-backed chairs with thick deep burgundy cushions surround the table. Three high-tech–looking telephones are evenly spaced across the table, with one at each end and one in the center. Portraits of the firm's elder statesmen and stateswomen hang on the walls, their eyes seeming to follow us as we enter. The thick carpet is the same deep burgundy color as the chairs. And the room smells of freshly cut flowers.

"There are people I know in the Brownfield District who'd like to live in here," I whisper to Hilda.

She giggles, gets serious, and greets the woman. "Good morning, magistrate."

"Good morning, Ms. Vaughan. You're looking well."

Hilda thanks her and introduces me. We're instructed to take our seats at one end of the table, which we quickly do. Hilda gets her notes in order, and we chat for a few moments until Sierra and Charles Keller glide through the door.

My heart skips a beat. Sierra looks ravishing. Part of me misses her and hopes that I'll let bygones be bygone and we can pick up from where we left off. But where we left off was me living in a dreamland and her in the shadows, screwing Mr. X. So *no*! There'll be no forgiving, no forgetting, and absolutely *no going back*!

Charles Keller's definitely a lion, of the alley cat variety. He's the classic little man overcompensating for his height by projecting attitude and ego. He greets the magistrate and introduces Sierra just as Hilda did with me, and they take their seats at the end of the table opposite us.

The magistrate clears her throat and explains the rules. We're to keep things civil, or the meeting will be adjourned and the offending party will be cited with contempt. She asks if we understand, we do, and she directs us to begin.

Silence—long, sad, and swirling with the lightning, winds, and thunder of emotion—goes marauding through the room. The magistrate glances from left to right. Charles Keller sticks out his chin. Hilda sits calmly in her chair, arms crossed over her chest and waiting. I glower at Sierra. She reflects it back.

I sit up tall and speak. "I never cheated on you, Sierra."

Her eyes narrow. "Yes, Denmark, you did."

"Did Vondie tell you this? If so, you need to know that she's only trying to get back at me for . . ."

"I didn't need Vondie," Sierra interrupts. "I put it together myself the night I called the hotel in Orlando and you weren't there."

"What phone call?" I ask, getting loud. The magistrate clears her throat. I continue, speaking more softly. "There was no message."

"Why would I leave a message when I knew what you were doing?"

I shake my head, completely baffled. "I don't know what you're talking about."

"How dare you, Denmark, how dare you sit there pretending to be ignorant?" she asks, her eyes flashing.

"If you're referring to your affair, then *yes*. I was totally ignorant. I was ignorant of you lying every time you said you loved me. I ignorantly believed you could be trusted. I ignorantly thought that if I loved you hard and good enough, you'd be true to me like I was to you."

I clench my jaw hard, gritting my teeth to keep my emotions in check. "I did, Sierra," I say through a tight throat. "I loved you with everything I had." Large tears fall from her eyes. "And now," I continue, "I despise you in the same way."

"Don't test me, Mr. Wheeler," warns the magistrate.

"You brought it on yourself," Sierra asserts. "You slept with Vondie."

I ball my fists, but maintain control. "What—are—you—*talking about*?"

Charles Keller hands Sierra some tissues and pats her back with tender "There, there, now" taps. She dabs her eyes and nose dry, then focuses on me. "Okay, Denmark. Let me explain so you can stop this juvenile game of 'don't remember.' "

I scoot close to the table so I can hear every word. Sierra says, "Before you left for Orlando you'd told me that on your first day down there you, Vondie, and Porter Grant would be in meetings all day, then come straight back to the hotel."

"And that's exactly what happened."

"Let her finish," the magistrate admonishes.

She's as interested in hearing the story as I am. Sierra nods at her. "I waited until late in the day to call you so I wouldn't disturb you conducting business. Porter had your cell phone. He said he'd borrowed it to call his wife . . ."

"She was pregnant," I clarify.

The magistrate scowls. Sierra continues. "Yes, she was. Porter was worried and wanted to check on her. He went to find an area with better phone reception. When he came back, you and Vondie were gone." Her voice trembles, and fresh tears waterfall down her cheeks. "He waited and waited, finally got tired, and went to bed."

She's sobbing now. "Denmark. I called your room several times and no one answered. So don't tell me you didn't cheat. Even Vondie admits . . ."

I groan, and fall back against my chair. It all makes sense now. Sierra had been uncharacteristically cold when I'd talked with her later that evening. She was snippy, anxious to get off the phone, and generally unpleasant. Upon my return from Orlando I asked her what had been the problem. She deferred, hedged, and evaded. Then everything returned to normal and I concluded that her odd behavior had been the by-product of a bad day.

"Stop the dramatics," Sierra commands. "Just be a man and admit . . ."

I bolt upright. "Don't lecture me about manhood! You think you're so smart and clever. Well let me enlighten you about what *really* happened."

"Keep it calm," Hilda gently advises, leaning close.

I explain it all. The conversation Vondie and I had after Porter left. Her going up to her room, *alone*! The woman who'd bought me the Florida Hurricane. My telling the bartender where Porter could find me. Me hurrying down to the beach, where I spent hours enjoying the wind and waves, and wishing that my wife—*my one and only*—had been there with me.

"I don't believe you!" Sierra loudly retorts.

"This meeting is about to be adjourned," the magistrate threatens.

I will every decibel of anger from my voice. "Well, then, maybe you'll believe Vondie, especially since you recruited her to lie for you."

"What! Why I never . . ."

I look at the magistrate. "Magistrate, may I use the phone?"

She blinks, surprised. "What's this? Why?"

I summon all the pleading I can muster. "Magistrate, please trust me. This phone call will clear things up."

She purses her lips, thinks it over for a moment, then nods. "All right, Mr. Wheeler, this is highly unusual, but I'll allow . . ."

"Your honor, I must protest," bellows Charles Keller. "The purpose of this meeting was to . . ."

"Mr. Keller, don't lecture me about procedures and protocol. Be quiet."

His majesty scowls but shuts up. I grab the phone nearest me and Hilda, punch the speaker option, and dial. The speakers on the other two phones sitting near the magistrate, and at the other end with Sierra and Charles Keller, activate.

A voice answers from the phones. "Speed Shift Procurement: Vondie Hamilton speaking."

Sierra's eyes widen. She and Charles Keller exchange glances. I lean close to the phone in front of me and Hilda. "Vondie, it's me, Denmark Wheeler."

Her vocal demeanor plummets from cordial professionalism to rabid hostility. "What do *you* want?"

"How much are you getting paid to lie about what happened in Orlando?"

She answers with a slow, sinister chuckle that underscores

the great pleasure she's deriving from my predicament. "Not a cent, but I'd do it for free anyway."

And just in case Sierra, Charles Keller, and the magistrate are still in doubt, I say: "Vondie, you know we never, ever slept together."

"You're right," she answers laughing. "I know that, but your little wife doesn't. I'm going to enjoy watching you squirm and suffer just like I did when . . ."

I hang up. The magistrate's grim. Charles Keller's scratching his head. Hilda looks like she wants to hug me. And Sierra's staring wide-eyed.

"Sierra," I begin softly, "Vondie and I never slept together. It's just as I told you."

She bawls. I stare at the tabletop and shake my head. The magistrate calls a recess.

THIRTY-SEVEN

Twenty minutes later, we're all back at the table. "Denmark," Sierra says. "I'm sorry. I truly thought that you and Vondie . . ."

"Is that why you cheated on me?"

She lowers her eyes. Charles Keller bristles. The magistrate looks from me back to Sierra, her face full of interest in the soap opera.

"What did you get from your lover that you weren't getting from me?" I demand. A little voice in the back of my mind urgently asks: *Are you sure you want to know this?* I press on anyway. "Tell me, Sierra. What was it?"

Sierra looks up, wipes her eyes, and answers with one simple word: "Freedom."

"Say what?"

"I was never totally free with you," Sierra explains. "I always felt like I had to be more perfect and pure than other women you'd known. You imprisoned me on a pedestal. You were constantly judging me."

I grip the edge of the table. "Sierra, what are you talking about? When did all this happen?"

"It was in the first few weeks we'd known each other. We went to your apartment after a late movie . . ."

"We'd gone to see *Gladiator* with Russell Crowe."

She nods and smiles softly. "You loved the fighting and the glory of Rome."

I smile back. "You loved him."

"Ahem," coughs the magistrate.

Sierra glances at her and keeps talking. "We started . . ."

"I remember. We were on the couch."

"It was the first time that we'd ever really gotten physical and . . ."

"You're right," I interrupt, glancing at Hilda. "Things got . . . serious."

"I wanted to do something special for you but . . ."

I stare past her as the memory vividly replays itself. "Then you stopped and gave me the weirdest look."

"It was because of the disgust and disappointment on your face. I couldn't understand. We'd talked about what we liked best when making love. I could tell that you'd be a superb lover . . ."

The magistrate looks me up and down and arches an eyebrow. Sierra continues, saying, "And I thought you'd enjoyed oral . . ."

Hilda coughs. Charles Keller fidgets. Sierra blushes but keeps talking. "Anyway, when I saw your expression, I felt dirty and ashamed. You looked so disgusted. It was like I'd let you down for destroying your perfect image of me."

"Sierra, I was . . . surprised. Maybe it was naïve, but I was caught off guard, seeing that someone like you was so ready to do what a common street hoochie would . . ." I shake my head in frustration. "And compared to all the losers I'd known you were perfect."

"No! I was normal. I was glad that you considered me special, but I still had drives, needs, and a desire to explore."

I massage my pounding forehead. "And you're saying that I shut you down?"

She nods. That's why our lovemaking was always so plain, why Sierra always seemed to be holding back, why she was so liberated with Mr. X.

"I thought I could adjust," Sierra explains. "But I was always so afraid. Then I got angry for not being able to fully express myself with you."

I stare hard into her eyes. "But you didn't feel that way with your lover?"

"Denmark, he's not the man you are, but he lets me be me."

"And that's why you cheated, because he lets you be you?"

Sierra scowls. "You make it sound so trivial—but yes, that's why. But I didn't do anything until after your incident with Vondie."

"There was *no* incident!" I emphasize, snapping.

Sierra's shoulders droop. "I know that now. But at the time, with everything that was going on, he came along and . . ."

Sierra looks down and away. Charles Keller's looking glum. Hilda's biting her lower lip. The magistrate wearily shakes her head like she's heard this kind of story one too many times.

"Who is he?" I ask, staring at Sierra.

"What difference does it make?"

"Just tell me who he is!" I demand.

"No!"

"You're still sleeping with him, *aren't you*?"

"That's none of your business."

I ball my fists. Hilda grips my forearm. "Sierra, tell me or I'll . . ."

"Or you'll do what, Mr. Wheeler?" the magistrate forcefully asks.

My gaze meets hers, and I get the message. I'm about to talk myself into a small locked space with bars and bad company.

The tension eases. Long seconds pass into a minute. The

magistrate looks left and right at each delegation. "Does either party have anything more they'd like to say to each other?"

Sierra looks at me. "Denmark, this has all been a big misunderstanding, and I hope you'll find it in your heart . . ."

"No!" I snap. "What I saw on that DVD was crystal clear. And what you've said here today is simple to digest. You were resentful of me, thought I had an affair with Vondie, and used it as an excuse to free yourself." I stand and lean forward, fists on the table. "Consider yourself freed, flushed, and forgotten!"

I storm out of the conference room with Hilda fast following.

•

Moments later, I'm in the bathroom and quickly pacing back and forth as I try to calm down. I glimpse myself in the mirror, stop, and stare at the reflection. *"Avenge me!"* it demands.

I exhale with a snort and charge out into the hallway. Hilda's waiting for me. "Are you all right?" she asks.

"I will be once I'm finished."

She frowns, confused. Movement off to our side draws our attention, and we freeze. It's the Montague clan, passing by us as they head for the elevators. There's sniffling Sierra and her mother, Sabrina, who's glaring; her sister, Samantha, who's scowling; pear-shaped blubber-lump Amos, who's snarling (and flips me the bird on the sly); and her tall, stately father, Theodoric, looking worn, weary, and slightly irritated.

Sabrina and Samantha put their arms around Sierra and escort her down the hallway, whispering words of comfort while every few steps throwing nasty glances back at me.

Amos watches them pass, then turns on me. "Now that this little charade is over, you're going to feel the full force of . . ."

"Amos, go get the Cadillac and wait out front," Theodoric orders.

Amos, suddenly reduced to his seven-year-old self, says, "But Dad, I just want to tell this . . ."

"Get the car!"

Amos pouts, and his flab sags. But he does as he's told and shuffles down the hallway, muttering and grumbling. Theodoric steps confidently and briskly over to me and Hilda. She edges close to me. "Denmark, who is he?" she asks softly.

"That's Theodoric Montague, Sierra's father. Don't worry. I've never had a beef with him."

"You've also never divorced his daughter."

I glance at Hilda. She's got a point. Either way, I'm standing my ground. Once Theodoric's close he nods curtly at me and extends his hand to Hilda, and they shake.

"Ms. Vaughan, I'm Theodoric Montague, vice president of international business ventures with the Cleveland Chamber of Commerce. You've had an impressive career. The pro bono work you do for the homeless is much appreciated. Keep up the stellar work."

Hilda does free legal work for the homeless? She's truly impressive. Burned-out Bobby could probably use her help.

She's slightly rattled by Theodoric's knowing so much about her, but I've told her that, unlike the rest of Sierra's condescending clan, Theodoric's the genuine article, a brilliantly suave class act. Now she's seeing for herself.

"Why, thank you, Mr. Montague," she says. "Hearing that from a civic leader like you means a lot."

He smiles and looks at me, and his lips straighten into a serious line. "Denmark, I'd like a word in private, if you please."

Hilda stiffens. "With all due respect, Mr. Montague, I don't think the two of you should be discussing . . ."

I give Hilda's arm a reassuring squeeze. "It's okay," I say, staring into Theodoric's eyes. "There's mutual respect between us."

"Indeed there is," Theodoric confirms.

Hilda hesitates, then nods. "I'll wait for you down in the lobby."

She walks off, and Theodoric and I stand facing each other.

He's intense and steadfast. I'm resolute and prepared. "So," Theodoric begins, "I suppose there's no chance of reconciliation between you and my daughter?"

"Not a snowball's chance in hell," I calmly reply.

He nods with grave resignation. "I'm sorry things have turned out this way."

"So am I."

He clenches his jaw. "Denmark, Sierra's my daughter. No matter what's happened, *I will not* stand by and see her hurt."

"I don't want to hurt Sierra. I just want to end this quickly and fairly."

He purses his lips and looks down for a moment to ponder then back at me. "She's a good woman. You know this."

"I'm sure she will be, for *someone else!*"

His eyes flash and narrow, then he sighs. "Perhaps we'll meet again under more pleasant circumstances."

"Yes, perhaps."

He steps off, then steps back. "By the way, has my grandson, Yarborough, tried contacting you?"

"He's called asking for money, but I turned him down. Why?"

He clenches his jaw. "He's been missing. The police suspect foul play . . ."

They're probably right. The hyper-violent world of crack addicts significantly shortens their life spans.

". . . and we're asking anyone who knows him if they might have information on his whereabouts," Theodoric finishes.

"Sorry," I shrug. "I haven't seen him."

Theodoric nods and leaves.

THIRTY-EIGHT

Hilda meets me in the lobby, and we get into the Corvette and drive back to her office. "Is there anything I should know about your talk with Mr. Montague?" she asks.

I give her the brief essentials, then we finish the trip in silence. I turn into her driveway, shift the Corvette into park, and wait for her to get out. "Would you like to come inside and talk?" she asks.

"No."

She purses her lips. "Denmark, I know you're upset and want to lash out, but you need to reconsider. You've still got much life to live and plenty of opportunities to love."

I shift the car into reverse. "I need to go."

"Will you at least call me later and let me know how you're doing?"

"Sure. Whatever."

She studies me for a long moment and gets out. I back out quickly and leave. I need to go for a run. I need to generate buckets of sweat, work my muscles until they burn, and pound out every remaining emotion that's within me.

My cell phone rings, and I check the caller ID display. It's the Speed Shift store at Henderson Village. Alarms blare inside me. Please don't let this be Keith calling about a robbery.

I answer quickly. "Hello!"

"Hey, Denmark," Keith calmly replies. "Sorry to bother you, but we've got a couple of representatives from some ad firm here talking about making a commercial."

That's right! I completely forgot to tell Keith about Speed Shift's hiring Forrester & Company to shoot this commercial. At first it was to tout Henderson Village as an example of the company's commitment to help revitalize an area that had been economically depressed. Now management wants to use the commercial to counter the mounting negative publicity from those robberies.

Keith's capable of handling those reps, but I want to make sure this goes right. It shouldn't take too long. They probably just want some ideas of how to proceed for when they start filming.

I work my way through traffic. A little while later I pass Burned-out Bobby as I turn into the Speed Shift parking lot. He's manning his corner like a soldier dutifully standing guard. When Bobby sees me, his eyes light up and he gestures to his sign: "Know God. Know Peace. No God. No Peace."

What a crock. If dingy, homeless Burned-out Bobby represents how God treats his friends, no thanks. I park, hurry inside, and meet the two ad reps. The woman is dressed in a conservative but attractive dark blue business suit, matching pumps, white blouse, silver earrings, and bracelets, with her hair cut close and styled sharp. Her male partner artistic consultant looks like a Heavy Metal refugee with his spiked hairdo, tattoos, ripped jeans, and chest web of rattling chains.

Keith introduces us, rolls his eyes, and gladly returns to waiting on customers. I give the reps a quick tour, then they saunter off on their own, nodding and muttering to each other. They're

totally oblivious to all the odd stares they're getting, but the com-
motion is short lived, and they soon leave. I follow them out the
door and meet Mason Booker coming in.

My throat constricts, and I struggle to swallow. I thought I'd
be ready to confront the awful truth. I thought I could muster
the courage. I thought it would be as simple as letting things be
as they would be. I desperately want to know who Sierra's been
screwing. I need to see who Mr. X is so I can judge what kind
of man he is compared with me. But Mason's light step, soft
whistling, and gentle smile aren't the signs of someone who's
bearing bad news.

"Hey, Denmark," he says, extending his hand. "Ah was in
the area and decided to stop by. Got a minute?"

"For you, I've got two minutes," I say warily, shaking his
hand.

He smiles, looks hard into my eyes, and correctly senses my
anxiety. "It's nothing bad," he gently informs me. "Ah just wanna
run something past you."

I gesture to the back of the store. "Let's talk in my office."

We head to the back and up the few steps into my office. I
close the door and turn quickly to Mason. He's leaning against
the wall with his arms crossed. His news may not be bad, but I
brace myself anyway.

"So how's the investigation going?" I ask, getting to the
point.

"A lot better than when ah first started," Mason responds.
"This guy's slick, but he ain't slick enough. Ah'm hot on his trail,
and ah'm gonna get 'em, you can rest assured of *that*."

If I had the energy, I'd hug Mason. He's been a rare bright
spot in this mess, and I'll have to reward him handsomely when
this is all behind me. But first things *first*!

"How long do you think it'll be?" I ask.

Mason shrugs. "Probably sooner than later, but that's what
ah wanted to discuss with you."

I sit up tall, my energy renewed and my mind alert. "Go on. I'm listening."

"Denmark, you know ah don't pull no punches. This is bound to get ugly before ah'm done, and ah wanna make sure you know that."

"It got ugly the moment I found out."

He clenches his jaw. "So then you don't mind if ah do whatever it takes to find this SOB?"

I stand and look straight and hard into Mason's eyes. "What would you do if it were *your* wife?"

He nods with grim understanding, shakes my hand, and leaves.

THIRTY-NINE

I t's the final race of the Greater Cleveland Community Sports Challenge. It's the money race, the one where the winning 4 × 100 relay team gets the glory, and each team member gets paid! For the last few days since that meeting with Sierra, my insides have been boiling with angry energy. I'm going to channel that energy into a performance that'll help me smoke the opposition in this race. That's what I've been doing during my workouts with Hilda.

A few days ago, I met her on the beach at dawn. Harry and Gordon were supposed to join us, but Gordon had a breakfast meeting with prospective guest Dr. Valencia Burton, who'd just returned from her heroics in Sudan. Harry wanted to keep re-modeling the barbecue joint he'd just purchased from Skinny Bumpers so he could meet his target opening date. So it was just me and Hilda.

I got to the beach at Lake Erie just as the sun burst over the horizon. The wind was brisk. Waves lapped lazily ashore. And the steady breeze carried the invigorating scents of aquatic life and distant places. I watched as a seagull glided effortlessly on wind currents, dipped every few seconds from side to side, caught a new current, and floated steadily upward. A huge fish leaped out of the lake, flipped onto its side, and landed back in the water with a loud splash.

From behind me, Hilda said, "Good morning!"

I spun around and had to catch my breath. She was beautiful, standing there in the new day's light and soaking up the morning like it was her nourishment. Her eyes were closed, her face lifted toward the sun, and her arms outstretched.

She opened her eyes wide, inhaled deep, then focused on me. "So!" she exclaimed. "What do you think of this fantastic morning God's given us?"

I shrugged, ambled closer, and joined Hilda as she stretched. "I guess it's cute; nothing special, but definitely cute."

She stood straight, and looked hard at me. "You don't have much faith, do you?"

"I've got faith in *myself*! If God expects the same, He needs to earn it."

Hilda pursed her lips. "Denmark, He's not some cosmic clown who needs to impress you." She shook her head and said, "Describe everything you've done this morning."

"I got up, got dressed, and came down here."

"And in doing all of that, what happened?"

"What do you mean?"

She exhaled a huff like an exasperated teacher trying to reason with a determinedly dim student. "Did you feel the morning chill?"

"Yes."

"Did you see and hear the waves?"

"Yes," I answered, getting irritated.

"Did you see the sky fill with the sun's brightness?"

"Yes! What's this got to do with anything?"

Hilda stepped toward me. "Are you mentally sound?"

"Of course I am."

"And are you physically healthy?"

"You can see that for yourself."

"And did you just draw a breath?"

"C'mon, Hilda, why don't you just get to the point?" I snapped.

She sighed. "I'm happy and sad for you, Denmark."

"Why?" I asked, annoyed at the pity in her tone.

"I'm happy that God showed Himself to you this morning, and sad that you chose not to see Him."

Then she turned and jogged away. I caught up with her, and she broke into a full-striding run, staying ahead of the wind and leaving me behind. Angry energy pumped into my legs, and I surged past Hilda. Three hundred yards later I was resting and waiting for her at our designated finish line.

It's time to tap into that angry energy now. The 4 × 100 teams are all lined up in each of the track's eight lanes. Everyone's poised, primed, and ready. A pistol fires, and Harry blasts out of the starting blocks. He powers into the lead and hands off to Gordon. Gordon drops the baton. Runners blow past. He recovers, churns down the track, and hands off to Hilda. Runners blitz toward their anchormen, who wait anxiously with me. Hilda runs them down like a lioness chasing goats. She hands off to me. I blitz across the finish line in first place.

We're jubilant. I pick Hilda up, spin her around, and set her down in time for Harry to grab us both and squeeze us into a mighty group hug. "You two are the best!" he joyously yells.

Gordon finishes signing autographs for a flock of his fans and hurries to join us. It's like old times, and I feel good—until I remember: *one of these bastards is screwing my wife!*

Twenty minutes later, the glad-handing and back-slapping is coming to an end. The official city representative, Deputy Mayor Vicente Valdez, gives his parting words.

"Now remember, everyone," he booms into the microphone, "the victory banquet will be next Saturday evening, exactly one week from today, in the Perry Ballroom at the beautiful Lake Shore Gardens Hotel."

A cheer erupts from the crowd. Deputy Mayor Valdez gestures for quiet and continues. "At that time we'll celebrate these marvelous athletes by handing out trophies and cash prizes. See you there!"

The crowd answers with another cheer. News crews pack up. The congested bleachers thin out. The sexily muscled captain of the first-place tug-of-war team jogs over. "Hey, you all," she calls. "A bunch of us are going out for some food and drinks. How about joining us?"

"I'm for it!" Gordon quickly answers.

"Count me in!" Harry enthusiastically agrees. "We ain't gotta wait till next week to have a victory banquet."

I look at Hilda. I'd planned on following her down to the beach to join Lucille at a family reunion.

"What about Harry and Gordon?" Hilda had asked. "They're part of the team. Won't they want to do something afterward?"

I still haven't told her of my suspicions regarding them, nor of Harry's suspicions regarding Gordon. We may be a 4 × 100 relay team, but we're less and less a crew.

"They're married," I'd responded. "Their wives will help them celebrate."

And maybe they would, if Alice was back in the country, and Inez wasn't so ready to break Harry's neck. But Alice won't be back until Saturday, when she and I are scheduled to "talk." And I've kept Inez off balance, feeding her just enough misinformation to drive her nuts as she wonders about Harry's alleged infidelity.

Hilda arched an eyebrow and shrugged. "Okay," she'd said cautiously. "You've known them longer than I have, so if it's okay with you it's okay with me."

We beg off the invitation but urge Harry and Gordon to have a good time. Gordon, already eyeing the tug-of-war captain, waves a quick good-bye and scampers off to join her. Harry's telling his new best friends (and potential customers) about his rib shacks.

Hilda and I start for the parking lot and our separate vehicles. I would've ridden with her but had to be at the track several hours early to man a booth for Speed Shift Auto Parts, one of the Sports Challenge's sponsors.

We're talking and laughing when I look up and see Mason Booker standing between my Corvette and his black-on-black Cadillac CTS. I gasp and stop cold.

"Do you know him?" Hilda asks, eyeing Mason warily.

I nod. "He's a friend."

"He doesn't look happy to see you. And you," she looks at me, "don't look too thrilled to see him."

"We've got business," I state flatly.

I step off briskly for Mason. Hilda calls after me, but I'm focused on Mason. His jaw is set, and his lips are pressed into a taut thin line. He's wearing dark shades and shoes, and a dark suit, shirt, and tie. He stands tall and grim.

I take a few more long strides, and we're face to face. "Nice race," says Mason with a slight drawl. "Congratulations."

"Thanks. Do you have something for me?"

He clenches his jaw. "You ain't gonna like it."

·

Powerful streams of cool air blast out the dash vents of Mason's Cadillac, but I'm burning up. Mason pulls a large brown business envelope from his door's side pocket. "Ah've got photos of the guys who've been with your wife," he says.

Time slows. The world slants sideways. Everything fades to gray. Mason's talking. Nothing's coming out. He gestures at me in slow motion. Worry lines etch his forehead. "Denmark?" he shouts. "Are you okay? Ah said that ah've got . . ."

"I heard you!" I snap, shaking my head clear. "Are you telling me that she's been sleeping with *more than one?*"

"Two, to be exact," he confirms, sighing. "Ah'm sorry, man. Ah was gonna try and break it to you easy, but this info stinks no matter how you get it."

His hand trembles as he hands me the envelope. I stare at it for an eternal moment. Just like the night when Sierra and I fought, memories whiz through my brain, every touch we ever shared, every word we ever spoke, every smile we exchanged, every tender moment we cherished.

"It's all in there, Denmark: pictures, phone records, hotel receipts . . ."

I grab the envelope, tear it open, and pull out the proof. Reality smashes me in the nose. Life's steel-toed boot kicks me in the balls. I can't tear my eyes from the pictures: Sierra and Harry, hugging in a parking lot; Sierra and Gordon, kissing in a rainstorm; Sierra and Harry, staring lovingly into each others' eyes at a restaurant; Sierra and Gordon holding hands in a park; Sierra and Harry in a cab, sitting close and snuggly; Sierra and Gordon, kissing in front of an open window; Sierra smiling softly as Harry runs his fingers through her hair.

I scan the phone records. Call after call after call. The same numbers, over and over, Harry and Sierra, Sierra and Harry, Gordon and Sierra, Sierra and Gordon.

And the hotel receipts—the Hilton, Marriot, Lake Shore Gardens, Aristocrat, Wyndham Heights, Blakemore, Stouffer's Towers, the Chester, the Ascot, and more. Room service, adult movie orders, in-room cash bars . . .

The evidence falls from my hands into a heap on the floor. Mason, speaking softly and tentatively, says, "Denmark . . ."

"Leave—me—alone!"

He gulps, opens his door, and gets out.

FORTY

t's 9:51 on Sunday morning. I'm still dressed in the sports clothing I wore during the 4 × 100 relay, and I'm driving back from
Chicago. How did I get to Chicago? Why'd I even come here? I
can't remember how long I've been, or what I've seen along the
way. Mason's evidence left me shocked, numb, and vacant. I sat
for a long time in his car. I sat for a long time in mine. But I don't
know when I got on the road or why I came in this direction. All
I know is that everyone I've trusted over the past five years has
stabbed me in the back!

My cell phone beeps. The display indicates that five messages have been added to my voice mailbox. When did I get five
messages?

I grab the phone and start checking them. One is from Alice.
She'll be arriving in Cleveland this coming Saturday morning,
but she still wants to meet with me before the victory banquet on
Saturday evening.

"I'm looking forward to our . . . talk," she says.

I'm looking forward to it also. After seeing what Mason collected, I've got plenty to say, and I'm going to put my message to

her, over and *over*! Gordon will hear her thrilled screams of understanding from miles away.

Next is Harry's message, asking to camp out at my house for a few days. "Inez is goin' crazy!" he nervously complains. "I don't know what's got into her."

What's gotten into her is the information I've been feeding her. It's been just enough to further poison her suspicions. When she sees the pictures Mason took she'll be ready for the next thing that gets into her: *me*!

One message is from Gordon. "That Hilda's a greyhound. Keep her happy so she'll run with us again next year."

There'll be no next year. And speaking of Hilda, the other messages are from her: "Denmark, where are you? It's getting late." "Denmark, what did that man say to you?"

I punch her numbers and wait. Hilda's answering machine activates, and I leave a message. "Hilda, I'm sorry about yesterday. If you feel like talking, I've got something to show you that'll fully explain. Later."

I hang up. The phone rings. I answer fast. "Hello!"

"I'm going to recommend your case to another attorney," Hilda declares. "His name is Belton Goodrich. He's competent and . . ."

"Hilda, wait! I . . ."

"He'll do a good job for you."

"Hilda, just hear me out. I . . ."

"I waited for you at Lucille's family reunion for hours, worrying that something had happened to you when you met with that man after the race. I called repeatedly, and you ignored me. I can't work with someone who doesn't respect me enough to return my phone calls, Denmark, so . . ."

"Hilda, please! *I'm truly sorry*. But I've got something that will help you understand. I promise!"

There's a slight thaw in a brief subzero silence. "I'm attend-

ing a church program with Lucille this afternoon. I'll be back by
five P.M. Be here on time, or don't come at all."

I start to assure her that I'll be there with minutes to spare,
but she's hung up.

Hilda sits beside me on her couch, staring wide-eyed at the pho-
tographs. "Oh my God," she says softly, her voice laden with
shocked disbelief.

She looks at me. Her eyes are filled with utter, profound sadness. "Denmark, I'm so sorry." She looks back at the pictures, receipts, and phone records, trying to make sense of it all. "This is
simply awful." She takes my hand. "And they were your friends."

I glare at the evidence. "She was my wife."

Hilda rubs my back in slow massaging circles. "With all this
documentation, we shouldn't have any trouble getting an agree-
able settlement."

"That's not good enough," I rumble.

Hilda's brow knots in confusion. "What are you saying?
With what's here, all your wife's lawyer can do is ask what terms
you prefer."

"I want more." I swallow hard, choking down the stew of
emotions bubbling in my throat. "They took more than material
possessions. They took my life. They robbed me of everything
that meant anything to me." I get up and start pacing. "They've
got to feel pain. I want them to choke on it!"

"Denmark, calm down . . ."

"Every second of every day for the rest of their miserable
lives," I fume, balling and unballing my fists. "I want them to feel
what they've given me."

"Denmark, I told you that I won't use the law as a weapon."

"I'm not asking you to!" I snap loudly. "Besides, this is beyond the law. The law is too weak and corrupt to give me what I
need."

Hilda stands and blocks my path. "And what is it you need?" she demands to know.

"I need justice!" I boom. "I want them to suffer!"

She plants a firm palm in the center of my chest. "You're lying!" she accuses. "You're not looking for justice but for revenge. The only person who'll get hurt is you."

"They're going to hurt more!"

"Please don't do this!"

I grab her firmly by the shoulders. "Why are you protecting *them*?" I blast. "You're getting paid. Just do your damn job!"

Seconds drag by as an ugly, pained silence invades the room. Hilda's eyes narrow, and she shakes herself loose from my grip. "Is that what you think?" she asks, her voice trembling. "Do you think you're just another client to me? I thought we were friends."

My insides wilt. "Hilda, I can't let them get away with this. *I can't just let them walk.*"

She sits back down and exhales a deep soul-wounded sigh. "Denmark, just listen for a moment. I was still in law school," Hilda begins. "His name was Addison Marker, and we were going to be married. Then *she* showed up."

Hilda sounds remorseful. But when she said "she" her voice pulsed with a surge of anger. "Felicity Beal was her name," Hilda continues. "She knew Addison and I were engaged, but she took him anyway."

"Nobody could've taken your fiancé or my wife without their consent," I interject.

Hilda cuts angry eyes at me, and I shut up. "I hated them," she explains, "especially Felicity. She'd always had everything and could've had any man she wanted, but she went after mine."

I sit down beside her and speak softly. "Then you understand why I've got to do this."

Hilda's eyes bore into me. "Oh yes, I refused to let Felicity have Addison, and I wanted her to know my pain."

She sobs softly but keeps talking. I try to hug her, but she pushes me away. "No, Denmark," she admonishes. "I need you to listen. I took out a school loan and hired a high-priced call girl to seduce Addison. She did and gave me the audio recording of them together. Months later, he and Felicity moved into an apartment and had a housewarming party. I showed up unannounced with the help of a girlfriend of mine."

She balls her hands tight together in her lap. "I played the tape. People were horrified. Addison was busted, Felicity was shattered, and I got even."

I suppress a smile of relief and merely say, "And that's all I want."

She places her hand tenderly over mine. "The call girl had AIDS."

My jaw drops.

"Addison passed it on to Felicity. He's dead. She's dying."

I swallow a lump. "She's the one you're always visiting at that hospice?"

She nods, takes my face into both her palms, and pulls me close. "I live every day with what I did, Denmark. I've prayed to be freed of the guilt, but it stays. Don't do this to yourself, or to them."

I gently pull Hilda's hands away from my face, hold them with tender tightness, and speak softly but emphatically. "Hilda, can't you understand? If I don't do something about this I'll be living with *that* every day."

She shakes her head with slow, profound sadness. "You don't have the capacity to reap what you're about to sow."

I'm in the Corvette and peeling out of her driveway when she rushes outside and calls after me.

FORTY-ONE

t's Wednesday, and three weeks to the day since I first saw Sierra on that DVD with Mr. X. Twenty-one days. Five hundred four hours. And now, just like Harry and Gordon have changed my world, it's time to change theirs, starting with Harry.

I'm in Suite 1622 of the Aristocrat Hotel, sipping a glass of Scotch on the rocks and looking out a large window facing serene Lake Erie. When I made the reservation on Monday, I told the clerk that I specifically wanted this suite. Yes, it has an exquisite view of the lake. Yes, it's in a secluded wing of the building. Yes, it's on the most expensive floor. And *yes*, the room has a minibar stocked with the best beer, wine, and small shot bottles of hard liquor. It also has a satellite TV with twenty-four-hour adult movies and lickety-split, round-the-clock room service.

But none of that's why I wanted this space. According to the receipts Mason gathered, Suite 1622 of *this* hotel is where Harry and Sierra met most often. So his favorite spot for doing Sierra is my preferred spot to *sex Inez*.

The timing is perfect. Yesterday morning, Tuesday, Harry called ecstatic that his son Claude had finally contacted him. Best of all, Claude said he was attending classes down at the University of Cincinnati. Harry immediately called Inez and notified his employees and business partners that he was heading south for two days to love and hug his son, then fuss him out for having kept his old man in suspense. He won't be back until Saturday, the day of the victory banquet, which leaves Inez in Cleveland, alone, angry, and wondering.

She's ripe for the picking. After speaking with her almost every day for the past few weeks, dropping hints about getting closer to the truth concerning Harry and his phantom girlfriend, I let Inez live in silence through Monday and most of Tuesday. She imagined things about Harry's infidelity that were more destructive than anything I could've conjured. We finally talked late Tuesday night. Inez was hoping for the best but starving to hear the worst, and I didn't disappoint.

"I'm not sure you're ready for this," I'd said. "Maybe we should wait."

"No!" Inez had demanded. "Whatever it is, just give it to me."

I stalled with an excuse she reluctantly bought, then told Inez when and where to meet me. "Why down at the Aristocrat?" she wanted to know.

"Sierra's lawyer got the court to order me out of the house until we get things settled about who'll get it."

"That's too bad."

"Not as bad as what I have to show you."

Inez's anxiety poured like syrup through the phone. Her angst added to Harry's shock will make sumptuous nectar.

There's a knock on the door. I don't answer right away. Every second of Inez's suspense works for me in wearing her down. There's another knock. I sip my Scotch and watch as a speedboat off in the distance knifes through Lake Erie's aqua-blue waters. There's a third knock, faster and more emphatic, maybe even desperate.

I chuckle, finish off the Scotch, and answer the door. And, surprise, surprise, it's Inez. She's always been attractive, but she's a traffic-stopper today. Her hair hangs simply and straight down just past her earlobes. She's wearing a salmon jacket and matching mid–thigh-length skirt, an off-white blouse, and a sharp pair of salmon-colored Fendi open-toed shoes. Her gold bracelet, earrings, necklace, ankle bracelet, and toe rings add nice adorning touches.

She smiles nervously. "Hi, Denmark; I came as soon as I got off work at the Port Authority."

"Thanks, Inez. Come on in."

I step aside and watch her swish by. "Would you like a drink?" I ask, closing the door.

"I'm so nervous right now that if you don't fix it I'll do it myself."

I smile softly. "I understand, Inez. Believe me, I do."

I gesture for her to sit down on the couch in the suite's living room. The TV's on and tuned into Gordon's hit afternoon show, *Getting Down with Cleveland.* He's crowing about the upcoming Sports Challenge victory banquet, softly needling his network bosses about not doing a special live broadcast of the event. Gordon's real grouse is that he wants a live broadcast of *him* getting his award.

I chuckle softly. On Saturday, while Gordon's preparing to cruise down to the Lake Shore Gardens to thrill his worshipers, I'll already be there *thrilling his wife.*

"Gordon's show has come a long way," Inez comments.

I grunt my agreement. "Will Scotch on the rocks be okay?"

"Just Scotch. I don't like my liquor watered down."

I fix the drinks, hand Inez hers, and sit down in the plush, comfy chair angled off to the side of the couch. The moment my butt hits the cushion, Inez sets her empty glass down on the lamp table beside her.

She crosses and uncrosses her thick, shapely legs and nervously preens, patting her hair.

"Would you like another drink?" I ask.

She glances at her empty glass, shakes her head no, then says, "On second thought, yes."

I fix it and sit down. Inez stares morosely into her glass. "Are you okay?" I ask.

She looks up and smiles bravely. "Yes, it's just . . . all this waiting."

I nod understandingly. "I know, Inez. Part of you wants to know; most of you doesn't."

"Please, Denmark," she says, barely above a whisper, "just tell me."

I tear a page from Gordon's book and sadden my expression as I point hesitantly over at the bed. "Over there, in the brown envelope."

Inez turns quickly toward the bed and stares for a long moment. I know what she's thinking. The moment she sees what's in that envelope, nothing will be the same. But if she doesn't look, she'll never know the worst. Maybe she and Harry could heal their marriage. But if she opens that envelope, it's over.

She hurries over to the bed, grabs the envelope, and pulls out the photos of Harry and Sierra, exhaling a low, steady groan as she looks. I sip my drink and calmly watch as piece by piece she falls apart.

"I, I need a, a drink," Inez stammers.

I move to get it, but Inez helps herself, hurrying over to the minibar and throwing back a first then second shot of booze. She lumbers over and into a chair at the dinette table, slams down the glass, rests her arms and head on the table, and sobs.

"Not me," she laments. "This wasn't supposed to happen to me."

What Harry did to me was bad. But seeing what he's done to Inez, he deserves whatever he gets. It's time to help her, help me get some payback.

I finish my drink, pad over to Inez, and stand just behind her as she cries. "What more could I have done?" she groans. "I tried so hard. God help me, I tried."

I gently squeeze her shoulder, lean close, and speak softly. "Don't blame yourself, Inez. It's not your fault that Harry's scum."

She whirls around and whacks me across the jaw. "Men!" she shouts. "You're all scum!"

I stagger backward falling across the couch and onto the floor. I push myself up but am slammed to the floor when Inez lands on my back, swatting and punching.

"No good dirty rotten bastard!" she rails, her arms flailing like super rotating windmills. "Nobody cheats on *me*!"

I cover my head with my arms and twist and turn, trying to throw her off. Inez grabs the heavy brass-based table lamp. I spin out the way a split second before she slams it down where my head was. She loses her balance and topples to the floor. I jump to my feet and brace myself for another assault, but it's not coming. Inez is face down, flat on the floor, sobbing uncontrollably.

I glance at myself in the wall mirror. My right cheek's throbbing. My left forearm looks like it's been mauled. And my lower back feels like it's been mule kicked.

Inez moves, and I jump, startled. She slowly pushes herself up, shambles over to the minibar, and downs three small shot bottles of hard stuff. She grimaces as she swallows the last of the third bottle, drops it onto the floor, and looks at me.

"Take me," she says softly, stepping toward me.

"Inez, hitting women isn't my bag," I warn. "But if you jump me again, I'm doing you like I would a man."

She steps closer, her eyes narrowing. "I—said—*take me*! Make love to me *now*!"

She keeps coming and starts undressing, pulling off a piece of clothing with each step. Then she stops, standing before me in just her panties. She licks her fingers, circles them around her nipples until they're erect, then slides her hand down her stomach and onto her preciousness, massaging herself.

"It's calling you, Denmark," she says huskily.

My big head's still throbbing from Inez's whack, but my little head's throbbing with excited expectation. Inez eases closer, and I relax my guard. Step by step she comes until she's only inches from me. Her exhaling breath reeks of alcohol. My little head convinces me that it's eau de perfume. She staggers to the right, and I catch her. She grabs my shoulders, pulls herself steady, then gently rubs my right cheek.

"You poor thing . . . I'm sorry," she slurs. "Did I . . . do that?"

"Yes!" I answer tautly.

She reaches down, and I flinch, instantly worried that my balls are goners. "Stop being so nervous," she giggles. "I'm only . . . trying to help."

She unzips my pants and lightly runs her fingers back and forth along my hardening length.

"Oh, baby," she says, staring hungrily down at me. "How'd you get all this in such a tight place?"

Electric insanity arcs through my groin. She pulls my head down for an alcohol-soaked kiss, her soft lips and snaking tongue stirring up gale force winds of desire in me. Somehow, some way, she comes out of her panties, lifts a leg, and joins with me. I grab her cheeks and pull her in tight. She wraps her legs around my waist, and we rock, sway, and moan. Then she stops, grabs my face in both her palms, and looks straight into my eyes. Hers are awash in tears.

A bolt of fear shoots through me. I'm not looking at drunk,

lusting Inez but at someone else. She's afraid, desperate, and star-ing up from deep inside where she's imprisoned and begging for rescue. Boozing Inez slams the door in her face.

"Screw me, baby," she urges, moving slowly up and down. "Do it so we can get even!"

I smile inwardly, set Inez down, take her by the hand, and lead her quickly over to the bed. She gets in and onto her back as I strip.

"Hurry!" she orders.

I toss aside my underwear, get into bed, and obey her com-mand. She closes her eyes and exhales in stuttering gasps. She hooks her ankles behind my thighs, I grab big handfuls of her butt, and we grind out our frustrations. Frenzied minutes whisk by until Inez suddenly pushes me off and rolls onto her stomach.

"Like this!" she demands, lifting her butt slightly.

I get behind her and gently find my way, then tend to the deepest parts of her garden. She grabs fistfuls of sheet and buries her face in the pillow, muffling her moans. The bed hits the wall with rapid, steady machine-gun thumps. Rivers of sweat roll down my back. Inez's firm, round butt shoves back at me as I thrust into her. She screams into the pillow. I bite my lip and taste blood. We shake, tremble, and hang on as our roaring tidal wave of passion blasts ashore.

I roll off Inez and onto my back, my chest heaving as I inhale great gulps of air. I reach for her, but she's over at the minibar, guzzling another shot bottle of booze and a beer. She tosses them aside, then looks at me with renewed hunger.

"I want . . . some more!" she mumbles.

I prop myself up on an elbow, smile, and pat the bed. "Then come and get it."

FORTY-TWO

It's 1:22 early Thursday morning, and I've knocked several times on locksmith Linwood Powell's front door. No one answers, and I knock again, pounding.

"All right, all right!" he grumps loudly as he stomps closer. "Chill out! I'm coming!"

He scratches around behind the door, most likely looking through the peephole. I bend down, look back, and wave. "Denmark?" he says, surprised. "Is that you?"

I lean close. "Yes, it's me. Open up!"

"Okay, man. Hold on. This'll take a minute."

It sounds like he's opening a vault to a Swiss bank. After just about a minute of clanks, clicks, slides, rattles, and jiggles, he opens the door. "What's up, man?" he asks, rubbing sleep from his eyes. "You're out late for a weeknight."

"Linwood, I need your computer hacking expertise."

"Right now, at this time of night?"

"You owe me for that lousy lock job you did."

He frowns. "Hey, man. I resent that. My work's guaranteed to . . ."

I shove past him. He chuckles resignedly. "Well, please do come in."

"Linwood, who is it?" a female voice calls from a back room.

"Uh, go back to sleep, baby. It's just a friend needing some money."

"What kind of friend stops by this late to borrow money?" she demands to know, coming out dressed in an oversized tee shirt.

She looks me up and down, sees that I'm fully male, rolls her eyes, and trundles back to bed. I glance at the door and do a double-take. It's covered in locks, bolts, chain restrictors, and any other entrance preventive device.

Linwood shrugs and grins. "It's like I told you," he whispers. "I ain't getting cleaned out by any more girlfriends."

"Whatever. Look, I need you to do something for me."

I explain, and Linwood's eyes light up with mischief. Moments later we're in his junky computer room. I stand over his shoulder and watch amazed as his fingers fly across the keyboard.

He makes a final keystroke, grunts with satisfaction, and turns to me. "Where do you want it to come from?" he asks. "I can send ghost e-mail from the Department of Defense, NASA, the CIA . . ."

"Are you for real?" I ask, incredulous. "You're into the CIA?"

He laughs smugly. "It's the government, Denmark. They've got every door closed but the front one."

It's too good to pass up. "Set it up so I can ghost it from the CIA," I say.

Linwood hits a few more keys and then gets up out the way. "It's all yours, my man."

He watches as I sit down and start typing. I stop and turn to him. "Linwood, if you don't mind, I'd like to send this in private."

He frowns, nods, and sidles out, grumbling about being disturbed at all hours to have his computer commandeered. I pull a small digital camera from my jacket pocket and download into the computer the picture of a passed-out Inez, her head lying in my lap and her lips right next to my semi-hard pole. Once the picture's fully loaded and attached, I type out the message: "Harry, here's your wife, Inez, sleeping soundly after another man has sexed her long, hard, and *well*."

I sign it "Your tax dollars at work" and hit the send button.

FORTY-THREE

t's 9:17 on Saturday morning, the day of the victory banquet. It's been two days since I got with Inez, and only a few hours are left before I "talk" with Alice.

I've just finished a three-mile run and am ready for a shower but want to fix some coffee for after I get out. I wrap a towel around my waist, set up the coffee maker in the kitchen, and start back upstairs when the phone rings.

"Who's this calling so early?" I grumble, going to answer. I pick it up. "Hello?"

"Ah, Den, Denmark, it's, it's me," stammers crack-head Yarborough.

I roll my eyes. "What's up, Yarborough?"

"Nothing . . . I mean, you know, same old, same old. Yeah, ah, hey man, I was wondering if you could loan . . ."

It's a short conversation. He begs for cash. I tell him no. He gets pissed and cusses me out. I hang up.

Several minutes later I'm cleaned up, in my robe, sipping coffee, and reading the morning paper when the phone rings again. This time I check the caller ID, see that it's June, and smile. We've been talking two, three, sometimes four times a day. She says it's a relieving outlet because her husband, Zachary, spends his days on the phone, helping people resolve their computer problems.

"By the time he gets home, he's not in the mood to talk to *me*," June told me a few days ago.

And so we talk. I don't know how she's keeping her conversations secret with a husband, two kids, friends, co-workers, and anyone else who might eavesdrop, but that's her issue. I'll talk as often as she wants for as long as she wants. Making love to her mind is the bridge leading to the sexing of her body.

I let the phone ring a few more times, then pick up. "Hello?"

"Well, good morning," says June.

"Hold on. Give me a second while it fills me up."

"Give you a second for what to fill you up?"

"The happiness I get from hearing your voice."

We laugh. June's is light, uninhibited, and genuine, like she hasn't laughed like this for a long time. "What were you doing?" she asks.

"Sitting here thinking about you, and hoping desperately that you'd call."

"Oh, Denmark," she says, breathless. "You're so sweet."

"You make it easy."

Several tender seconds of silence pass before she says, "I'm on the turnpike right now."

"Are you taking a trip?"

"No. I just decided to drive around for a while so I could talk to you freely."

"Are the kids with you?"

"No. Zach's at home watching them. We're going to the zoo later."

That Zach's a good man. After June and I are over, I'll have to write him a thank-you note.

"What're you wearing?" June asks.

"I've got on just a robe. Except for that, I'm butt naked."

"Mmm, that sounds enticing."

"You ought to come see for yourself."

"Baby, I want to. Believe me, I do! Please don't get impatient."

I speak softly but firmly. "June, understand one thing: I could *never* be impatient with you. However long it takes for us to be together, it'll be worth the wait."

On the other hand, if I haven't stroked her booty by next weekend, June will be waiting by herself.

FORTY-FOUR

I haven't talked with Inez since Wednesday, when she plummeted into her oblivious, drunken sleep. I moved fast to finish my business with Linwood Powell. He lives just a few blocks from the Aristocrat, so I was able to get to his house and be back in time to get some sleep, and later sex Inez into the stars again and again.

Now I'm down at the Lake Shore Gardens Hotel, and it's time to do Alice. I sprinkle rose petals onto the bed, tune the entertainment unit radio to a channel playing round-the-clock soul love ballads, adjust the lights down low, put the champagne in an ice bucket, and light candles all around the suite.

The phone rings. Like clockwork, I chuckle to myself as I go to answer. "Hello?"

"I've just landed, and I'm hurrying through the airport to catch a cab," says Alice.

"You must be exhausted after traveling between so many continents."

"I've actually been visiting with friends in D.C. for the last couple of days, so I'm wide awake and full of energy."

"And you're going to need every ounce of it," I think to myself.

Alice called Thursday afternoon to give me her arrival details. She didn't mention anything about being in Washington, but no matter. We had a good conversation. By the time it was over, she'd agreed that it made no sense for her to get a room at the Lake Shore Gardens when she could just stay with me in *mine*. Our exchange was natural, adult, and refreshingly straightforward. We both knew what was going on, and neither of us tried to pretend that nothing would happen.

"So what room are you in?" Alice asks.

"I'm in Suite 2701."

And there's a reason for that, sweet Alice. Mason's information showed that your lousy husband, a.k.a. my rotten-to-the-core former friend, preferred this suite when he was with my wife. So, just as I did with Harry (he'll be rolling in from Cincinnati any time now. He'll be pumped after seeing Claude. If he wants to stay pumped he'd better wait to open that e-mail until *after* the banquet), I'll repay Gordon in the same room where he backstabbed me while front-jabbing my wife.

"My goodness," says Alice, impressed. "I've heard about those suites at the Lake Shore Gardens. Did you have to take out a loan?"

I laugh. "I'm winning an award. Why not splurge? And besides . . ."

I pause, letting the silence swell until Alice says, "And besides *what*?"

"I want this to be a memorable occasion."

Her voice vibrates with the energy of expectation. "I've been thinking a lot about this moment."

"So have I."

She sighs. "You know, Denmark, I've been feeling so good about our meeting. I can't remember when I felt this way. I almost wish that . . ."

She lets it hang until I say, "You almost wish that *what*?"

She precedes her answer with a soft, delicate laugh. "I'll tell you when I see you."

"There's a key waiting for you at the front desk."

"My, my, aren't we efficient."

"When you get here, just come in."

A little while later, I'm on the phone with June again. I glance at the clock and smile. Alice should be here any minute. In the meantime, I'll talk to June, getting her prepped for when I finally show her all the good loving she's been missing.

"Stop teasing," she says. "You didn't even give me a second thought."

I dump truckloads of sincerity into my voice. "I'm serious, baby. The instant I saw you, my mind went blank. I was in a twilight zone of joy. Every nerve, cell, and molecule in me was ready to obey you."

One day soon, while her hoops-shooting husband is out sinking baskets, I'll be scoring with June. When he comes home too tired to tend to her needs, she won't mind, since she'll have already been satisfied by *me*. That ignorant sucker will be lucky if she wants to come home at all.

"You're so silly," she blushingly giggles.

"There's nothing silly about my feelings for you, or . . ."

"Or what?" she asks, her tone serious, focused, and hopeful.

"How much I want to be with you."

She sighs. "I want to be with you too, Denmark."

She tells me just how badly and I sit back and smile, wondering which of Cleveland's hotels will be best for her to prove her point.

Nearly ten minutes have passed since I hung up with June when Alice enters. She finds me sitting in a large, big-cushioned blue chair. I'm dressed only in slippers; tight, stylish crotch-hugging shorts; and a tee shirt that might as well have been painted on over my rippling muscles.

She closes the door, stops, and looks at me. I stand smoothly and quickly. "Hello, Alice."

She smiles. "Hello, Denmark."

We spend a moment just looking at and appreciating each other. Alice is heart-stopping lovely. She was already in shape, but she's slimmer, and it's working. Her Horizon Airlines uniform accentuates her smooth curves. Her hair's longer, shining, and styled in elegant simplicity. Her eyes are smoldering with desire. Her legs are toned and slender. Her breasts bulge nicely against the light cloth of her jacket. And her rich but understated perfume almost turns my knees to water.

"You look radiant," I say.

She glances down at my crotch. "And you look delicious."

I arch an eyebrow. Alice is starting early. Okay. I'm down with that plan. I glide swiftly across the room, keeping my eyes locked with hers. She drops her purse and kicks aside her small roller-wheeled suitcase. Her eyes flash as I get closer. I'm short steps away, and she opens her arms. I take her into mine, and we kiss. It's so good, so sweet, so tender, and powered by new passions unrestrained. And then we just stand, holding each other. She lays her head on my shoulder. I turn my face into her thick hair and inhale its freshness.

"I've thought about this forever," Alice says, holding me tight.

"I should've been with you all along."

She looks up at me. "Do you mean that?"

I kiss her. "Yes, baby. I do."

We hold each other a little longer. Alice pushes her pelvis firmly up against me. My crotch rebel extends a greeting. Alice notices and pushes harder. Our breathing deepens. My mouth is dry and wet all at once. She feels so good, soft, and delicate in my arms.

"I could stay like this," she says just above the whisper.

"And I'd protect you and never let you go."

She looks up at me, strokes my cheek, and smiles. "I should take a shower." She steps back and starts undressing, keeping her gaze fixed with mine. "Are you watching?"

I swallow the boulder in my throat. "Oh yeah, baby. I'm totally focused."

And then she's there, a breathtaking diamond descendant of Africa's rich ebony abundance. "I'll be out shortly," she says huskily, stepping past me. "And then we can . . . talk."

Twenty minutes later, Alice has finished her shower, and I'm standing behind her, holding her tight as we gaze out the room's huge window at Cleveland's subdued but sublime skyline. She's dressed in one of the hotel's monogrammed bathrobes, and I'm bare-chested, wearing only my stylish shorts and slippers. We've drunk champagne and kissed and hugged a little more. Now we're letting the moment carry us where it will.

She leans her head back onto my chest, and I kiss her cheek. She reaches behind and strokes the back of my head. "This is so beautiful," she says. "It's nice to get reacquainted with this feeling."

I pull her into me. "It's my privilege to help you remember," I whisper.

Alice turns toward me and pulls my face down to her, and we kiss. Then she steps back and undoes her robe. I slip my hands inside, pull her close, and kiss along her shoulders, her neck, her face, and her lips. Her breathing deepens. I pull the robe down from her shoulders and off her body. She massages my expanding hardness.

I take her hand and lead her over to the rose-petal–covered bed. She gets in. I pull off my shorts, toss them aside, and join her. Her breasts are delicious, and I linger on each nipple, tasting, licking, and working each one like it's the *only* one. Alice exhales a deep, soft sigh.

I kiss down her body along the center of her smooth stomach, moving from left to right, hip to hip, going lower. The sweet fragrance of her precious femininity wafts into my nostrils. I kiss closer to the source, and Alice trembles.

"How could she not love you?" she whispers. "How could she not?"

I move back up along her body and kiss her tenderly, our tongues moving slowly over and around each other. I'm painfully hard. I kiss the center of her palm, lick in between and suck each of her fingers, then massage her delicate treasure.

"Denmark!" she calls with soft urgency.

"I know, baby. I know."

I kiss back down her body, lingering near and around her sweet places. She closes her eyes tight and sucks in air through her teeth. I kiss along her inner thighs, down her calves, along her beautiful feet, then back up to her passion. I lift Alice's legs so that they're resting in the joints where my biceps meet my forearms. Then I look deep into her eyes as I slowly, gradually, and tenderly join with her. She gasps, arches her back, then relaxes and enjoys.

Being with Alice has been the most sensual experience of my life. Everything was so smooth and gentle. We each knew what the other wanted, how much, and in what ways. Egos didn't intrude. I was on top, then she was. I spoke face to face with her luscious, then she spoke face to face with my rebel. We whispered to each other, laughed softly, knew each other, kissed, touched, and rode winds of pleasure until we tumbled into a gentle waterfall. Then we held each other until precious sleep came, our breaths merging into a perfect rhythm.

I'm just waking up as I lie on my back in the comfortable king-sized bed. I stretch and take a deep breath. Alice's disarming perfume lingers strongly in the sheets and pillows. My wrists feel funny. I look up at them and . . . *what the hell is this?*

FORTY-FIVE

My wrists are handcuffed to the bed's heavy brass frame. I jerk and pull, but it's no use.

"I hope they're not too tight," says Alice.

I look over and see her sitting calmly in the big-cushioned blue chair. She's fully dressed and has her bags packed beside her.

"Alice, what's this all about?" I demand to know. "What kind of game is this?"

She laughs. "Now isn't that ironic? Imagine *you*—of all people—accusing someone of playing games."

I jerk and pull, and grunt and strain against the cuffs. "Okay, Alice. Jokes are jokes, but this isn't funny. *Let me go!*"

She sits back and folds her hands into her lap, looking like a portrait of contentment. "If you like this part, watch this."

She points the TV remote at the entertainment unit she's moved to the foot of the bed and turns on the television. The screen fills with Gordon moving back and forth through an adoring crowd, randomly interviewing people, joking, laughing, and being at his talk-show-host best.

He stops abruptly, looks into the camera, and gives his trademark "You're the one!" finger point. "Stay tuned, Cleveland," he says, smiling brightly. "We'll be right back after the commercial break as we broadcast *Getting Down with Cleveland* live from the beautiful Lake Shore Gardens Hotel."

Alice mutes the sound. "He harassed the network to do this live broadcast until they finally agreed."

"Alice! Why . . ."

"I know, Denmark. You want to know what this is all about." She gets up, pushes the chair closer to the bed, sits down, and leans slightly forward, looking straight into my eyes. "I'm going to tell you a story."

I pull with all my might against the handcuffs. The left side of the bed groans. Alice calmly reaches inside her purse and pulls out a nine-millimeter pistol. "Be still," she quietly orders.

I lie stiffer than a log. She smiles. "That's better. Now listen closely." She sits back, crosses her legs, and holds the pistol loosely as it rests in her lap. "Once upon a time, there was a fool named Denmark and a woman named Alice. She was married to a lying, cheating son-of-a . . ."

She bites her lower lip as her eyes fill with tears and she chokes down a sob. "Alice loved Denmark. It wasn't erotic love, but the kind one has for a true friend. She thought he'd never hurt or deceive her, especially since he knew about all the humiliation she'd endured . . ."

Her expression twists with agony, and she sobs. My head falls back onto the pillow, and my heart sinks. I look up at her. "Alice, please, I'm . . ."

"Shut up!" she shouts. She shoves the pistol at me, her arm straight and rigid and her finger tight on the trigger. "Don't apologize. Apologies can't undo the hurt."

My mouth freezes shut. I'm drenched in sweat. Alice wipes her nose and eyes with a tissue, sits back, and continues. "Alice wanted Denmark to be the same kind of friend to her that he was to her slime of a husband. But Denmark was loyal to the slime."

She looks distractedly at the TV. "Did you know that Gordon's doing a live call-in show today? Anything you want to discuss, just call in and talk to Mr. Glory."

"Alice . . ."

She springs out of the chair and shoves the pistol into my mouth. "I—told—you—to *shut up*!"

I relax every muscle and wilt. Alice smiles devilishly, slowly pulls the pistol from my mouth, and sits back in her chair. "Anyway," she says, resting the pistol back in her lap, "Alice enjoyed being away from her rotting marriage, and made enough money to hire two private detectives, one to watch her slime husband and the other to watch Denmark's worthless wife."

My lips tremble. Alice casually points the pistol. I swallow my words. "Alice had seen Denmark's wife at Cleveland-Hopkins airport with a man who looked to be more than a friend. Alice thought maybe he was her brother or a cousin, but then they hugged and kissed. Denmark's wife was cheating."

I scream inwardly. Alice presses on. "The private detective Alice hired proved that Denmark's wife *was* cheating. Alice felt closer to Denmark, since they were experiencing the same misfortune. She was going to tell him, but she wanted to get more convincing evidence so he'd believe. Poor Denmark loved his wife so much, he'd be hard to persuade."

Tears wash down Alice's cheeks. I feel like the lumpy clods falling from a horse's rear end.

"While Alice was away," she continues, "her slime husband called and told her about poor Denmark watching his wife with another man on a DVD. Alice wanted to comfort Denmark. But then something strange happened. Denmark called saying he wanted to be Alice's good best friend."

Alice pauses and looks at me, her eyes full of accusation and hatred, then moves on with her story, speaking in a shaky voice.

"Alice was thrilled. But then she started thinking. Denmark had only told Gordon and Harry about the Sapphire Spire restaurant. She guessed that since Denmark had told only those two people about his anniversary plans, maybe Denmark figured that Sierra's lover was one of them.

"Alice didn't want to believe the worst. But then she and Denmark actually talked. He was more affectionate than ever. Alice grew more suspicious. Maybe Denmark figured that Alice's slime husband had been with Sierra. But what Denmark didn't know was that Alice's slime husband had *never been with Sierra.* The other private eye proved that Alice's slime husband was definitely cheating, but *not with Denmark's wife.*"

She leans slightly forward in the chair. "Denmark wanted to get inside Alice to even things with her slime husband, who'd been a true friend to Denmark after all. Alice was devastated. She couldn't believe that Denmark would use her for revenge, but what else could she think?"

I stare at the ceiling. Alice picks up the cordless telephone and dials. "Look at the TV," she orders me.

I lift my head and obey. Alice says, "I've just dialed the special number Gordon told me to call if I ever needed to get through to him at the station."

She turns up the TV's volume as she waits for an answer. While she's waiting, she finishes the story. "Once Alice knew that Denmark was using her, she knew that he was no different than her slime husband. Denmark broke her heart."

I look at her and blink my eyes clear. "Alice, I'm sorry."

"Alice decided to avenge herself against her slime husband by first screwing his so-called friend Denmark. She'd then avenge herself against Denmark for scheming to use her like a Styrofoam cup."

Someone finally answers Alice's call. "Hello," she says. "This is Alice Wilhite, Gordon's wife."

She frowns when she says "wife," like she's swallowing bile. She verifies who she is, then says, "I'd like to speak with him, please. Oh yes. I figured it would be a nice surprise for one of the callers to be his wife."

Seconds pass. Gordon's conducting his talk show with ballet precision and excitement. Someone alerts him that he's got a special call. He faces the camera, his face aglow with exuberance. Gordon's happier than I've ever seen him. And I realize something: he's really good at this gig.

"Well, what do you know, audience," he booms into his handheld mike. "My wife's on the line."

The audience claps and cheers. Alice covers the phone and looks at me. "He told me that there'll be heavy press coverage on this. If all goes well, the network might give him national exposure." She grins. "It's not going to go well."

Gordon stares earnestly into the camera. The many happy faces of the studio audience stare with him. Everyone's having a good time.

"Alice," Gordon says into the mike. "Honey, are you there?"

"Yes, I am. Can you hear me?"

Gordon gestures to the crowd. They answer with claps and approving hoots. He looks back into the camera. "What a wonderful surprise. Say hello to the audience."

Alice gives them a warm greeting. Gordon rouses them to cheer for his beloved wife. "Honey, we're all really happy to hear from you. Where are you?"

Alice covers the phone and winks at me. "Here we go." She looks back at the TV and says, "I'm upstairs in Suite 2701 at the Lake Shore Gardens Hotel, where you're broadcasting from."

Gordon's momentarily puzzled by Alice's news but answers with a beaming smile. He turns to the audience. "Did you hear that, audience? My wife's in the hotel with us!"

Claps and cheers. Gordon turns back to the camera. "Well,

sweetheart, since you're here, come on down and join me so the audience can see the beautiful woman who for twelve years has made me the happiest man in the world."

More claps and cheers. They're louder and more energetic. Everyone loves it that local celebrity Gordon is so affectionate and committed to his wife.

"I'll be right down," says Alice. "But I thought you'd first like to know that Suite 2701 isn't my room. It belongs to Denmark Vesey Wheeler, your friend." She enjoys a quick laugh. "I've been up here with him for hours—*having sex*! This is a family show, so I won't get vulgar, but I've got to tell you, he's got some skills. And he's *very* well hung."

Gordon face is stone. A hush swoops over the audience. Peoples' eyes are bulging, and their mouths are hanging open.

Alice smiles a smile so wickedly mean that my blood runs cold. "I'd like your bosses to know that all those stories about you sexing your female guests and co-workers are true," she says. "The station will probably be fighting a series of sexual harassment lawsuits pretty soon. Ladies, there's no time like the present."

The microphone falls from Gordon's hand. He staggers a few steps to the side, trips, and falls to his knees. The cameras that he's loved to love faithfully follow his collapse.

Alice laughs. "Denmark thought you were cheating with his wife," she informs the world. "He hatched a little plan to get some Old Testament eye-for-an-eye, wife-for-a-wife justice by cheating with me. Inez Bancroft secretly told me that she'd been talking with Denmark, too. My guess is that our Denmark's also pulled a fast one on Harry."

Gordon's chin drops to his chest. "Isn't it ironic," Alice needles. "Sierra was the one person you never went after."

Gordon's former adoring audience skewers him with disapproving glares. An ugly murmur ripples through the crowd.

Several people get up and walk out. They're quickly followed by others.

Alice glances at her watch, then back at the TV. "By the way, Gordon, you should be getting a visitor right about . . . *now*."

A man walks into view of the camera and stands over Gordon. "Are you Gordon Wilhite?"

Gordon looks up at him, his eyes wide, wet, and disbelieving. The man hands Gordon an official-looking envelope. "You're being served," he says, then spins around and marches away.

"That's right," Alice confirms. "You've been served with divorce papers. Just sign them, Gordon. I'm only irritated right now. You don't want to get me mad."

She stands and grabs her purse. "You people in the press. If you want to interview the man who betrayed Gordon, he's handcuffed to the bed in Suite 2701. Hurry to the front desk and get the special key for the elevator. He'll be here waiting."

FORTY-SIX

Alice gathers up her belongings and heads for the door. "C'mon, Alice, don't do this," I plead.

She looks back at me. "Don't do what—be cruel like you've been with me?"

She steps off, then stops and stares back at me. "On the other hand, I don't want to leave you with the impression that I'm as despicably disgusting as you and Gordon."

She unlocks one of the handcuffs, slips the pistol back into her purse, gets her luggage, and places the handcuff key on a table just out of my reach. "Goodbye, Denmark. Don't try contacting me. I never want to see or hear from you again."

"Alice, wait! Don't leave me like this. Look, I was wrong. I'm sorry. Please forgive me."

She smiles, but her eyes are crying. "I've already forgiven you. Now I'm going to forget you."

In one fluid motion, she wheels around and leaves, slamming the door behind her. It takes every straining muscle and shred of willpower I've got to reach the table where the handcuff keys are. It's a fumbling, frustrating effort, but I finally get them and unlock the remaining handcuff. My arm feels like a thick tube of lead.

I scramble and get dressed. The press might be here any moment. On TV, Gordon's bawling. Only a few people remain in the audience, looking at him with puzzled expressions of sympathy and disgust. The camera sweeps across their faces, and I gasp. *Hilda!*

It instantly makes sense. Gordon kept his live broadcast a secret but asked if I'd be available today. I told him that I'd be busy until this evening's victory banquet. He couldn't ask Harry, since he was out of town. The only other member of the 4 × 100 relay team left to invite for his big moment was Hilda.

The phone rings. I ignore it, grab anything else belonging to me, and get out. I sprint down the hallway toward the elevators. When I'm halfway there, the bell rings, and a flock of reporters tumbles out. They look left, right, and at me.

One of them, seeing the alarm on my face, points and yells, "That's him!"

I sprint in the other direction, find the stair exit, blast through the door, and fly down the steps, taking three, four, five at a time, and leaping down whole flights. The relentless mob's voices echo through the stairwell.

I burst through the lobby door, quickly get myself together, and as calmly and quickly as possible speed-walk toward the Lake Shore Gardens' exit. The lobby is packed with people, and I'm suddenly glad that this hotel's a favorite spot for conventions, conferences, receptions, parties, and other big events.

I'm almost at the exit when someone loudly calls my name. "Denmark! How good it is to see you."

I cringe. It's one-air-freshener-a-day Mrs. Randall. "Hello, Mrs. Randall. Good-bye, Mrs. Randall."

She grabs my arm. "Now, what kind of greeting is that to give to an elder?" she admonishes. "I'm sure your parents raised you better."

I'm about to tear my arm from her when her eyes light up. "Well, what a surprise!" she says delightedly, looking past me. "It's your wife and her boss."

My eyes snap over to where Mrs. Randall's looking. I can barely see through all the passing people.

"Yoo-hoo! Sierra!" Mrs. Randall calls, waving and gesturing. "Look who I've found!"

Sierra looks through the crisscrossing mass of people and sees me. Her eyes bulge. I glimpse Sierra's "boss" right as he glimpses me and *runs*! A toxic swirl of rage, frustration, and hatred explodes in my chest.

I'm after him. He dips, ducks, and dodges his way through the crowds. I'm closing in on him. From the back he looks familiar, but it can't be. *It simply cannot be!*

Sierra's "boss" bursts through the exit doors and hurtles into the traffic of a busy main street, dodging and sidestepping cars. Angry drivers pound their horns. I'm gaining on him. A delivery truck's horn blares. The driver slams on brakes and swerves. I leap out of the way, hit the sidewalk hard, and roll to a scraping, scratching stop. I sit up quickly. Sierra's "boss" runs for his life off into the distance.

FORTY-SEVEN

I storm into Jiao Minh Xing's shop, hustle to the counter, and pound the bell. Jiao's the only one who can now confirm or crush my suspicions about whomever it was I was chasing at the Lake Shore Gardens. If only there hadn't been so many people. If only I'd been able to get a longer, clearer look at him. But there was so much going on, so many distractions; all of those people; me trying to outrun those reporters; Mrs. Randall's excited chatter; the shock of seeing Sierra; the stun of suddenly being so close to the possibility of pummeling her lover!

I pound the bell again, this time longer and harder. "Is anybody here?" I yell.

"Keep shirt on!" Jiao hollers. "It's tough taking leak with one hand."

I wait, pacing back and forth, until Jiao finally comes out. He's limping, has his left arm in a cast, and is wearing a neck brace. He sees me and smiles, revealing a big gap where one of his front teeth used to be.

"What happened to you?" I ask.

"Daisy excited when Jiao propose marriage. Give Jiao plenty good booty."

I roll my eyes. "I'm happy for you. Look, I need to know . . ."

"Jiao just thinking about you," he interrupts. "Disk ninety-seven percent clear. I keep working until . . ."

"You've got ninety-seven-percent clarity?" I say loudly. "Why didn't you call me?"

Jiao grimaces and covers his right ear with his good right hand. "No holler!" he hollers, grimacing harder. "Last night's cheap booze still got head pounding."

I slam my fist onto the counter. Jiao flinches. "Show it to me," I growl.

He mutters in his native Vietnamese, cussing me out, I'm sure. He gestures with his good right hand for me to come behind the counter and follow him into the back. It's a bigger electronic junkyard than the chaotic front. He motions me over to a clearing in the clutter, where there sits an impressive looking super-high-tech DVD player and monitor.

"You wait," Jiao says. "Go get disk. Be back in a second."

Jiao returns quickly, followed by Daisy, who's glaring at me.

"What's going on?" I ask, glancing at Daisy. Her eyes are narrowed and her nostrils flared.

"Daisy for protection," Jiao confidently answers, thrusting out his chin. The movement's too much for his sore neck, and he winces. He recovers and scowls at me. "Last guy who bring in disk of cheating woman get pissed and try to kill Jiao."

"Hmph!" snorts Daisy. "And my baby was only trying to help him."

Jiao nods in agreement. "Jiao no take chances this time."

"That fool should be finished with his physical therapy in another year or so," Daisy obliquely warns. Jiao sneers a "Take that!" smile at me.

"Look, you two," I say, struggling to maintain calm. "All I want is to see the disk, and I'll be on my way."

Jiao and Daisy exchange a loving glance. "Go ahead, snookum-wookum," Daisy gently encourages. "I've got your back."

I stiffen as Daisy's words send a bolt of bad memory zapping through me. Jiao beams a gap-toothed smile at Daisy. "You Jiao's sexy African love goddess."

She tweaks the tip of his nose. "And you're my potent Asian sweet daddy."

She grabs a handful of his straight, shining black hair; jerks his head back; and nearly swallows his head. Jiao cries out in pain, but it's muffled by Daisy's slobbering kiss.

"Hey!" I shout.

Their kiss ends with a POP! as they both look up at me, startled. "Who're you hollering at?" Daisy demands.

"I'll make you a deal," I say quickly. "I've reserved Room 2701 over at the Lake Shore Gardens Hotel for myself, but I can't use it."

"That's on top floor," Jiao comments.

Daisy glares at him. "How do you know where it is?"

Jiao quickly explains about the service contract he recently signed with the hotel. She snatches him by the collar. "You'd best not be lying. You know I'm'a go over there and ask."

Jiao groans in pain. "Swear to hip-hop and fried chicken, baby! Jiao no lie."

Daisy narrows one eye in suspicion and looks back at me. Jiao's hanging from her grip like a limp fish. "What about this room?" she asks.

"It's the Royal Cleveland Suite. It's plush, romantic, paid for, and yours if you show me the disk—*now*!"

A sunburst of smile covers her face. "Really, our own little love nest for the night?"

"Square business," I answer. "But first . . ." I point emphatically at the DVD player and monitor.

She slings Jiao toward the unit and smacks him up'side his

head. Jiao yelps in agony. "Show 'em the video!" Daisy gruffly orders. "Then get ready for your African love goddess to sex you into a pretzel."

Jiao shudders and looks like he wants to flee, but he quickly obeys. He turns on the monitor and hits the PLAY button. I rush forward and shove him aside.

Daisy says, "Don't be pushing my . . ."

"Shut up!" I bellow.

She does, sensing correctly that I'm about to go off in a way that she won't survive. I stare unblinking and slack-jawed at the screen. My legs turn to rubber and my insides crumble as Sierra's image says, *"No baby. You have to make me come first,"* to her excited lover . . . *Mason Booker*!

FORTY-EIGHT

stagger back into a cabinet full of electronic junk, and it topples over, landing with a loud crash followed by clangs and bangs as its contents fall out.

"No!" I wheeze. "Not him. *It can't be him!*"

But there they are, Sierra and Mason, on the DVD monitor and going at it with abandon. Sierra's totally free, surrendering herself to her howling urges. Mason vigorously answers back, humping and grinding harder and faster at her command.

How could he be Mr. X? Only Harry and Gordon knew about the Sapphire Spire. And the pictures, phone records, and hotel receipts were all solid evidence. But there's Sierra and Mason on the DVD monitor, giving each other their best.

Jiao and Daisy watch me like bemused researchers observing a lab rat reacting to a super hallucinogen. "You ain't gonna renege on that room, are you?" Daisy wants to know.

I creak to my feet and tell them in mutters how they can get permission to use the room. I shamble from Jiao's back room and out to my car. I'm floating. The world's spinning. I've got to stay focused. I've got to concentrate. *I've got to find Mason Booker.*

I slam on the brakes and the Corvette screeches to a stop. I jump out of the car, fly to the front door of Mason's house, and pound. "Mason! Open up, you maggot!"

I pound harder, channeling all my fury into each whack. "Come out! I know you've been with Sierra!"

I run around the house, looking for signs of his being home. He doesn't have a garage, so it'd be easy enough to see his car, but there's no car here. His newspaper is still on the front step. Every window is dark.

A next-door neighbor pulls back the corner of a curtain and looks out. I back slowly away from Mason's house to my car but keep searching for any signs of life. I've got to go. The last thing I need is getting rousted by cops investigating a strange man who's yelling and banging outside a neighbor's home. I back away to the Corvette, look again, and take off.

Minutes later I whip into a parking space in front of Second Shadow Enterprises. I get out and pound, yell, and threaten at the front door. This is pointless. It's Saturday. Even if Mason was working a case, he'd be in the field. Now that I know about him and Sierra, he also knows that his home and office will be the first two places I'll look. So they're the last two places he'll be.

I'm incredibly weary and lean against his office door to keep from collapsing.

"*Once upon a time, there was a fool named Denmark,*" Alice's voice whispers.

"This isn't over," I growl. "I'll find you, Mason. No matter what it takes, I'm going to hunt you down!"

I shamble back to the Corvette, start the car, and turn on the radio. I need music, lots and lots of loud music to distract me from the guilt spreading through me like a cancer. The DJ news-caster says: *And now for some local news. Cleveland's been busy, folks. This afternoon, another Speed Shift Auto Parts store was robbed, continuing a string of violence against that beleaguered retailer. Once again, the thugs got away with the loot. And police have arrested Cleveland native Inez Bancroft for attempted manslaughter. She was taken into custody after police found her husband unconscious from a massive trauma to the head . . ."*

FORTY-NINE

I sit next to Harry in his hospital room and rest my head on the bed's raised metal side railings. The dimly lit room is bathed in the soft glow of red and green from the digital numbers of monitoring equipment. Harry's bed is partially inclined. He's sleeping flat on his back, one arm hanging out of the railing, the other lying on his stomach. His head is heavily bandaged and his cheeks are slightly sunken, but his face is relaxed and strangely peaceful. An IV sticks out of the top of his right hand, held in place by transparent tape. A weird clothespin device covers the top of his middle finger, its wires snaking up past his head to a monitor.

"Please, Harry," I whisper. "Wake up."

The radio news reporter I heard on the way to the hospital told a sketchy story of Inez and Harry arguing: "*Inez Bancroft alleges that the victim flew into a rage and attacked her soon after he'd returned home from Cincinnati, where he'd been visiting relatives. The trauma allegedly occurred as she struggled to defend herself . . .*"

I lay my hand across Harry's huge motionless bear paw and give it a gentle squeeze. "I'm sorry, Harry. I'm so sorry."

"The doctor says he's in a coma," says a woman from the doorway.

I turn toward her. Our eyes meet. "Hilda, what're you doing here?"

"I've only known Harry from practicing for the race, but he's my friend . . . *just like he thought you were.*"

Her words are a speeding cannonball to my solar plexus. "All right, Hilda, we all know I'm a heel, but . . ."

"Attending Gordon's show was quite an experience for me. At first I thought the phone call from his wife was a joke. But when I heard the news about Harry and Inez, my lawyer's instincts told me to investigate."

She casts sorrowful eyes onto Harry. "His wife would be here, but she's in jail."

"Hilda, please. Just let me ex . . ."

"Did you know that Harry's listed you, after his wife and son, as the next person to contact in cases of emergency?"

"Hilda . . ."

She looks back at me, her eyes brimming with tears. "The admissions specialist said that Harry's going to need a lawyer. Mid-Cities Insurance won't cover his injuries."

That's the outfit Amos Montague works for. That company's still under investigation for swindling thousands of policyholders out of their life savings and reneging on medical claims. It's so fitting that Sierra's sorry brother works for them.

Hilda's voice trembles. "Since Harry's in a coma, I guess I'll have to help him find a lawyer."

I slouch deep into the chair. "Hilda, I know what you must be thinking, but . . ."

"No, Denmark, you can't possibly know what I'm thinking. As a matter of fact, it's best that you don't know."

She walks calmly into the room, stands on the other side of Harry's bed, and peers down at him. "They fear that he might have brain damage—if he wakes up at all." She slips a small cross into Harry's meaty paw and folds his fingers around it.

I nod approvingly. "He's going to need all the luck he can get."

Hilda's eyes snap angrily onto me. "The cross of Christ isn't a lucky charm, Denmark! It's the doorway to a second chance."

We sit on either side of Harry's bed, staring glumly at him. Minutes pass into an hour. Hilda's expression is full of pain as though she were the one suffering.

She stirs and glances at me. "So tell me, Denmark. Was it worth it?"

I lower my eyes. "Hilda, I wish there was something I could say to help you understand. I was so angry. It was so unfair. I just wanted the person responsible to feel what I . . ."

Hilda wipes her cheek. I imagine myself running desperately after a train, yelling to Hilda standing on the caboose as it pulls away faster and faster.

"Hilda, I didn't mean to hurt anyone, especially *you*."

"That's what I tell Felicity every time I see her. But you know what? She's still going to die."

A merciful quiet descends upon the room, and we gaze on my precious friend Harry. More minutes pass. A nurse briefly checks on Harry, shooting me sharp, accusatory glances every few seconds, then she leaves.

"Denmark, please leave the room," says Hilda.

"Huh? But . . . why?"

"I'm going to pray for Harry. Your lack of faith will interfere."

I'd protest, but I'm just too tired. I step heavily to the door and look back. "Hilda, before you condemn me, please try and understand my point of view. I had my reasons."

"I'll be sure and explain that to Harry. Now please leave."

FIFTY

The disasters I've caused are spiraling out of control, and the disappointment in Hilda's voice will haunt me for days.

I pull into my garage, cut off the Corvette, and sit, savoring the peace in this moment of solitude. It's barely begun to close when a jet-black, chrome-wheeled Hummer SUV pulls in beside me. I try to see who it is, but the heavily tinted windows are too dark. The driver's-side door opens, and Blinker steps out. He's followed by his pit bulls, Killa and Attila. One walks to his left, the other to his right.

"What now?" I grumble.

I get out of the Corvette and go to meet him. He takes a final drag of his cigarette and flicks the butt onto the floor. The front and rear passenger doors on the far right side of the Hummer open and shut together. I try to see who's getting out, but the bulky vehicle blocks my view.

"Blinker, what's this all about?" I ask. "I don't have time to . . ."

Blinker points at the garage door overhead. "You'd best close this."

"First tell me what's going on."

"Close the door!" he snaps.

I glance at Killa and Attila, hurry over to the wall control, and press the button. The Hummer's back hatch lifts up as the garage door comes down.

"You remember my cousins Stinker and Thinker, don'tcha?" Blinker casually asks.

My stomach somersaults. Individually, Stinker and Thinker are one hundred times more dangerous than Blinker's ever been. Together they qualify as a threat to national security.

Blinker chuckles grimly. "I can tell by your face that you're rememberin' 'em pretty good."

Something falls from the rear of the Hummer onto the floor like a sack of rice, followed by a loud "Oomph!"

"Get up!" someone harshly commands.

Something else hits the floor, followed by a solid punch and a muffled cry of pain. Blinker lights up another cigarette and grins. Average-height, scarred-cheek, dreadlock-wearing, thick-necked Stinker and lanky, bow-legged, cleft-chinned Thinker step out from behind the Hummer. Staggering before them are two pathetic bums. Along with having their mouths covered by duct tape, they're handcuffed, whimpering, and suffering from welts, bruises, scratches, and cuts.

One prisoner smells like fermenting garbage. He's wide-eyed, twitching, trying to scratch, and covered in layers of filth and grime. The other prisoner's clothes are shredded, and he has one eye swollen shut. He's sweating profusely and groaning.

Stinker and Thinker shove the dregs to the floor and deliver swift kicks into their sides. The prisoners groan and whimper. Blinker's eyes narrow. Killa and Attila growl. I'm shaking with fury as I look down on the depleted forms of Yarborough Montague and *Mason Booker*.

FIFTY-ONE

rush Mason Booker but am snatched back by Blinker and Thinker. "Let me go! He's been sleeping with *my wife*."

"Him!" says Blinker, surprised. "He's the one?"

"I saw them on a DVD."

"That's cold-blooded," Stinker observes. He swats the back of Mason's head. "Cousin Blink, order one of them dogs to chew off his balls."

Mason's eyes bulge, and he worms and squirms to get away. Stinker kicks him like a rolled-up carpet back to where he was. My energy drains. After the last few days of nonstop high-intensity emotional drama, I'm exhausted.

"So along with his capers, this sucker's been banging your woman," says Blinker.

"What capers?" I ask, catching my breath and wiping sweat from my brow. "All I know is that he's been with *my wife*!"

Stinker grabs a handful of Yarborough's wildly growing hair and jerks him up onto his knees. "Him and this clown's part of the crew that's been hitting Speed Shift stores."

"*What?*" I shout.

"They took down the wrong one today," Blinker adds. "That store was in *my* territory. Soon as they hit it, my street soldiers was on their case."

Re-energized, I break loose from Blinker and Thinker and snatch Yarborough by his collar. "It was you?" I demand to know. "You've been robbing the stores?"

"Him and two others," says Stinker.

"We got his partners stashed," Thinker shares. "This fool's the key."

"He's the key to what?" I ask loudly. I rip the duct tape from Yarborough's mouth. He screams in pain. "Talk to me!" I blast.

"Pa, please," Yarborough drivels, "just get me a hit. I, I'll tell you everything . . ."

Blinker shoves me aside and whacks Yarborough across the mouth. "Talk, *punk*!" he commands.

Blinker snaps his fingers, and Killa and Attila charge forward, snarling and snapping. Yarborough shrieks and curls into a fetal position.

"Now that's what I call scaring the piss outa somebody," Stinker chuckles.

He gestures to a yellow puddle spreading out beneath Yarborough. "Back off!" Blinker commands. The dogs quiet down and back away.

"It was him!" Yarborough gibbers, gesturing with his head at Mason. "He, he was my contact! He gave me the alarm codes. I wasn't trying to hurt anybody. I, I needed the *money*!"

"To feed that habit," Stinker observes. "When cousin Blink found out, he called us."

"As a future city councilman, I've got to keep things legal," Blinker smirks. He glances at Mason. "The most important part was learning that *he* was involved."

Thinker nudges Mason with the tip of his steel-toed boot. "From what we could gather from, ah, questioning this douche-bag"—he grins and winks—"he used his position as a Speed

Shift security contractor to get his hands on store alarm and safe codes." He glances at Yarborough. "Then he passed them on to this cum bubble."

"How come we didn't think of pulling a scam like this?" Stinker asks, looking at Thinker.

They share a laugh, get instantly serious, and glare at Mason. "We've been waiting a long time for this," Thinker rumbles.

Stinker kneels down, grabs blubbering Mason's lower jaw, and squeezes so hard that his cheeks collapse inward. "You set up our brother Tinker."

"And now you're going down!" finishes Blinker.

I walk slowly up to Mason. His eyes grow bigger with each step I take. Stinker backs away, clearing my path. Mason's trembling like a naked man in an arctic blizzard. Blinker, Thinker, and Stinker form a semicircle of power behind me. Yarborough mutters in his piss puddle.

I grab Mason's collar and yank him up to me. He screams a cry that, even muffled by duct tape, pulses with terror. He hangs limp from my grip, babbling and pleading. I rip the tape away from his mouth, and he moans.

I snatch him close. "WHY?" I growl. Mason sobs and mumbles. I shake him furiously. "Tell—me—*why?*"

"It was for . . . her," Mason sniffles. "Ah did it for Sierra. Ah love her."

I let Mason go. He crumples to the floor. Stinker and Thinker chuckle and say, "Love? Is that all?"

"Shut up!" Blinker orders. "Ain't you two fools ever cared about somebody besides yourselves?"

Stinker and Thinker glance at each other and shake their heads no. Blinker rolls his eyes.

"Ah loved her the moment ah saw her," Mason sniffles, sitting up slowly.

"When was that?" I demand to know. "You'd never seen Sierra before the company picnic I invited you . . ."

The words suspend. That's right! It was the company picnic I'd invited Mason to attend. The same event at which he stated that marriage would never be in his future. The event at which he said: "Seventy percent of mah cases are wives'n husbands who suspect that their honey-buns are doing the fat-nasty with somebody else!"

Mason explains further. He struck up a conversation with Sierra at the picnic. The mutual attraction was instant. From their conversation and what I'd told him, he had a good idea of how wonderful she was. He spent weeks following her, watching and studying her, learning everything about her down to the most finite details. He "accidentally" ran into her at public places. They went out to lunch once, twice, three times and more.

She talked about me, her life, and our marriage. She shared the details of her frustrations and anxieties, and he was a willing, compassionate sounding board. He absorbed every drop of information, storing and considering everything for future use. With every contact, look, and thought of her, his love grew deeper. He was at first satisfied just to have her physically. But the day came when that wasn't good enough.

"Ah wanted her for *myself*," he sniffles, staring at the floor. "Ah had to have her always."

To get her, he'd destroy my marriage. He made the DVD, wrote a note that led me to suspect Harry and Gordon, and salted the wound by sending it from "I Got Your Back, Inc."

"How'd you know about the Sapphire Spire?" I ask. "I'd told only Harry and Gordon about my plans to take Sierra there."

"Sierra told me that your anniversary was coming up. She said you'd probably do something special to impress her. She said you were always doing something to hide your shame about growing up poor in the Brownfield District."

I whack Mason across his jaw. He howls. Blood splatters

onto the Hummer. "Don't be bleedin' on my ride," Blinker rumbles.

"Forget the Brownfield District!" I shout, shaking Mason furiously. "How'd you find out about the Sapphire Spire?"

Mason talks through his sobs. "Ah started calling around to the best clubs and restaurants, pretended to be you double-checking a reservation, and kept at it until ah hit gold. Then ah called Harry and Gordon, said ah was one of Sierra's old friends who'd be meeting ya'll in Vegas, and expressed how great it was that you were also taking her to the Sapphire Spire—and they confirmed it in their responses."

I think back to the day I asked Harry and Gordon if they'd told anybody. They'd both said no, which was technically true. If Mason called them, pretending to be someone who already knew, then they would've concluded correctly that the leak had originated with me, not them.

"Keep talking!" I order, shaking Mason.

"Sierra said that Harry and Gordon were the only two people you really trusted," he snivels. "I wrote the note so that you'd think it came from one or both of them."

Blinker, Stinker, and Thinker listen quietly, hanging onto every word. Yarborough begs for a hit of any drug and is shouted into silence. The dogs yawn and lie down.

"Explain the blurred video," I say. "Explain the pictures of Harry and Gordon with Sierra. Explain why you got mixed up with this wretch!" I demand, gesturing to Yarborough.

Mason looks up at me, his eyes wet, red, and swollen. "Ah needed to get you out of Sierra's life. Ah knew that seeing her with another man would set you off, make you reject her, and ah'd have her all to mah'self. If that didn't work, ah knew that you discovering that she'd been with your best friends would do the same, and ah'd still have her all to mah'self."

"How'd you get the photos?"

"They were from meetings Sierra had with Harry and Gordon last year when they were planning your surprise birthday party."

"But . . . the holding hands, the kissing, and . . ."

"Computer manipulation," Mason answers, just a bit too proudly.

I snatch him up again by his collar. "Don't gloat, sucker!"

He sobs. "Ah used the computer to make it look that way."

I shove him back to the floor. "What about him?" I demand to know, hooking my thumb at Yarborough. "Why help him?"

Mason scowls at muttering Yarborough. "The crack-head was bound to get caught. He'd implicate me, but ah'd turn the spotlight onto you and your thug street security."

Blinker glowers.

"The combination of you two being family, you being in Speed Shift senior management with access to store alarm codes, and a street thug doing your security would add up to your arrest and conviction," Mason details. "You'd all go away for a long time, and ah'd have Sierra to myself."

Blinker rushes Mason but is caught by Stinker and Thinker. "You were trying to set me up like you did Tinker!" he hollers. "I'm gone bleed you!"

"Save it, cousin," Thinker advises. "You're running for office. Stink and I will handle this clown."

"Go ahead!" Mason insanely challenges, sobbing. "Ah've lost the only woman ah ever loved, so nothing matters." He folds into himself, sobbing and repeating over and over, "Ah've lost Sierra, so nothing matters."

FIFTY-TWO

I t's Sunday, visitor's day at the Cleveland city jail and the first day I've been allowed to see Inez. I'm sitting on one side of a glass-walled booth, waiting for the guards to bring her in. The door opens. Inez shuffles in. She's wearing a bright orange pajama-type outfit, looking like a flamboyant hospital orderly. Her face is ashen and plain. Her hair looks like a battered squirrel's nest. Her hands are cuffed, her feet are shackled, and the neon-blue slippers she's wearing seem no thicker than rice paper.

She sees me, and her eyes ignite. "Denmark, you bastard!" she hollers. "It was you, wasn't it? Harry knew because of you?"

She charges the glass, falls from her shackles, and lands hard on her side. Two guards, one male, one female, close in quickly, drawing their batons. She kicks the woman in the chin, bloody-ing her mouth and sending her reeling. She drives both her fists into the male guard's balls. He falls to his knees, eyes wide, clutching his crotch, gasping and coughing.

Inez hops to her feet, hobbles fast toward me, and throws herself shoulder first against the glass. "I trusted you!" she blasts. "Why'd you do it? *Why?*"

She grabs a chair and slams it against the safety glass, but it barely cracks. She hurls the chair, and the glass creaks and groans as jagged fissures split from top to bottom.

Guards pour into the room and pounce on Inez. She fights them like a rabid wolf. "I'll get you, Denmark. So help me *I'll— get—you!*"

She disappears beneath a cloud of whacking batons and punches.

Visiting Inez was a debacle. I drive out to my and Hilda's favorite park to clear my head. Maybe a long, uninterrupted moment of calm will help me see where I didn't have a choice. But who am I kidding? Inez wouldn't be in jail if it weren't for me. Harry wouldn't be lying comatose in a hospital if it weren't for me. Gordon's career wouldn't be sliding into the toilet if it weren't for me. And sweet Alice would never have drunk so freely from the cup of revenge if it weren't for me.

I've got to try and make things right. I get into the Corvette and hurry over to the home of my friend and lawyer, Nelson Fox. He likes to sleep in late on Sundays but answers the door anyway. He listens patiently as I explain the devastation that's been occurring the last few days. Once I'm through, Nelson sits across from me at his kitchen table, his expression inscrutable as he sips every few seconds from a cup of coffee.

"So will you do it?" I ask him.

"Of course I'll represent Inez Bancroft," he quickly answers. He gets up, pours himself another cup of coffee from the automatic brewer, then leans back against his counter. "Who's going to cover my fees?"

"I will."

"Good. It might take some doing, but I'll get her out of there."

I sit back and sigh with relief. "Thanks, Nelson. I truly owe you one."

"Just cover my fees—then never cross my path again."

I sit up stiffly, energized by the sharpness in Nelson's tone. "What's got your back up?"

He takes my cup of unfinished coffee, pours it down the drain, and fixes his hard, angry eyes onto me. "Every day I talk to young people about staying out of trouble, counsel parolees to ditch their no-good former thug friends, rack my brains to keep brothers and sisters out of jail—and now this."

"And now this *what*?" I ask, demanding.

"You and all this chaos you've caused!" Nelson fires back. "I told you to leave Sierra alone. What she did was low, but you still don't have her back. And unless I'm as talented as we hope I am, one of our black sisters will do time after being manipulated by *you*."

"Nelson, I feel rotten about this. Why do you think I'm here?"

"You're here to get me to do the work of clearing your conscience."

I spring to my feet. "I'm trying to right a terrible wrong."

"You're too late. If I got Inez sprung in the next five minutes, she'd never be the same. She has a record. She's emotionally and psychologically scarred. Her marriage is over. Her employment prospects are nil. And she's wearing the shackles that your namesake and ancestor fought to the death against."

I look down and shake my head. "Nelson, what would you have me do?"

He huffs to his front door and whips it open. "Get out!"

FIFTY-THREE

Today's Wednesday, and I'm hibernating in my office, pursuing my new pastime: staring at my computer's screen saver. It's been four weeks to the day since I first saw Sierra on that DVD, happily smothering Mason Booker with her delights. Twenty-eight days. Six hundred seventy-two hours. And lives are in ruins.

I heard through the grapevine that even after spending wads of her parents' money for every kind of jackleg, syndrome-inventing therapist she could find, Sierra's started drinking anyway. She passed out at the wheel, crashed into a parked school bus, and nearly totaled her Lexus. Mercifully, no kids were on the bus, and she got out with only scratches. She was charged with reckless endangerment and nearly found herself behind bars . . . until the famed Montague clout stepped in and saved her.

The moment I heard, I rushed over to the house to see if Sierra was okay. I wasn't hoping to start a process of getting back together, but I was genuinely concerned. We'd both made mistakes, hurt each other, and mutually strangled our marriage. But

I'd once truly loved Sierra and didn't want to see her come to harm.

Her sister, Samantha, answered the door. She was unusually cordial and encouraged me to go see Sierra out by the pool. I wondered about her smirk but squashed her from my mind. There were larger matters to contend with than hassling through her games. Then I stepped out on the pool patio and understood. Sierra was lying on a double lounger, snuggled up against another man. She saw me and sprang upright, her expression seized by surprise.

"I guess you're all right," I said, then spun around to leave.

"Who's that?" I heard the guy ask.

She told him, and he replied loud enough for me to hear, "Just so long as he knows you've got a *new man!*"

I stopped, turned slowly around, and glared at him. "Denmark, don't start anything," Sierra nervously warned. "This isn't the Brownfield District!"

Her new hero's eyes widened with fright, and he fidgeted. His obvious fear was pleasing to my eyes, and it took everything I had to keep from using the chump as a pool-cleaning tool. But I swallowed my anger and hurried out.

Just as I reached the front door, Samantha, standing at the top of the steps and smiling slyly, said, "Have a nice day."

I looked calmly up at her and felt something oddly different. It wasn't anger, bitterness, or even irritation. It was more like . . . sorrow, not so much for what she'd just done to me but done to *herself!*

"Be sure and duck low," I advised her. "That boomerang you just threw is going to leave a nasty knot."

She responded with a puzzled frown. I left wondering about all the boomerangs that would one day come flying back at me, starting with the one from Inez.

Nelson finally cooled off enough to tell me that he's doing his best to get her released on bail, but the judge adamantly refuses.

Nelson's glumly conceding more and more that Inez will probably do time until her trial. With the ugly mood of the courts concerning domestic violence, she might be doing time after that.

Gordon's been fired and his talk show scrapped. Plus he's being bankrupted by lawyer's fees, defending himself from all variety of sexual harassment allegations. Worse yet, he's got the Feds on his case about taxes. And the TV that was once his loyal mistress is now the powerful, all-invading eye that constantly hounds and harasses him so that he can't even take out his garbage without being swarmed by a mob of media storm troopers.

And Alice—her voice mail response to my message said: "Denmark, I knew you'd call. If you're serious about finding me, take a flight to anywhere. When the airplane gets high enough, jump without a parachute. I'll be on the ground, celebrating as you *splat*!"

My desk phone rings. "Speed Shift Auto Parts: Denmark Wheeler speaking."

"Hello, Mr. Wheeler. I'm Dr. Giselle Hoskins, Harry Bancroft's speech therapist."

I sit up straight and tall. *Please* don't let there be anything else wrong. "Yes, Dr. Hoskins. What can I do for you?"

She laughs softly. "Harry's been giving me quite a time. He insisted that I call you so he can show off his progress."

I smile. "That's great! Go ahead and put him on."

She lowers her voice. "He'll be out of the bathroom in a moment. I wanted to first warn you that his speech is still a little slow, so be careful to respond as normal."

I grip the phone tight. "Tell me the truth, doctor. Will he fully recover?"

"Mr. Wheeler, at this rate Harry will be speaking better than you or me. He's getting a second chance."

I slump back in my chair and exhale relief. I also think of the cross Hilda slipped into Harry's hand that day at the hospital. "I can't tell you how glad I am to hear . . ."

"Okay! Here he is."

She turns the phone over to Harry. "Den-mark?"

"I'm here, Harry. How are you?"

"I . . . I'm . . . fine!"

"The doctor says you're making great progress."

"I . . . I told . . . her . . . this was . . . no-thing."

I smile and wipe my eyes dry. In all the years I've known him, Harry's always chopped off words ending in "g." But he just now placed a "g" at the end of "nothing."

"Den-mark?" Harry calls.

"Yes, H."

"The insur-ance says . . . they won't pay . . . for my . . ."

"Don't worry about it," I interrupt. "H, I promise you, Mid-Cities Insurance is going to do the right thing. *I swear it*!"

I don't have the slightest idea of how I'm going to get them to do it, but I will. I think Hilda's still working to find a solution, but she's not talking to me, so I don't know how much progress she's made.

I've tried over and over to contact Amos Montague, but I've been repeatedly stonewalled by his corporate lackeys. I know that as the vice president of marketing for the Mid-Cities Insurance Company, Amos possesses enough influence to help Harry. But he'd be helping a friend of mine, which means he'd be helping me, and that's where everything breaks down. Either way, Harry's going to be looked after, even if I have to pay for his expenses *myself*!

I can feel him smiling through the phone. "Thanks . . . Denmark. I . . . told them they were . . . wrong about . . . you."

"Who're you talking about, H?"

"There were . . . some re-porters . . . saying things . . . about . . . you and Inez."

My throat's drier than sandpaper. I try to speak but can only cough. "Harry, when all this is over, you and I have to discuss . . ."

"I told them . . . that if . . . they were right . . . you wouldn't . . . be trying to help me . . . would you?"

"No, Harry," I lie. "I guess not."

"Den-mark . . . that's why," he struggles for a moment then finishes with, "you're the . . . only one . . . I trust."

I choke down a sob. "And I trust you, Harry. You're a great, good guy, and I want you to call me if you need anything at all."

"Do you mean . . . that?"

My stomach tightens. Maybe he knows about me and Inez after all and is about to launch his own vengeance scenario. "Yes, Harry," I hesitantly answer. "I mean it with all my heart."

He chuckles. "Good! How about . . . getting me . . . some *ribs*!"

It's 4:12 p.m., eighteen minutes before I'm out of here and time for me to call Hilda. For the past few days, I've waited till this time to call her. It's when she's least likely to be busy. I dial, wait, and as usual get her voice mailbox.

I repeat the message I've been leaving. It's the message I'm going to keep leaving until I have a chance to sit down face to face with Hilda and explain.

"Hilda, it's me, Denmark. I've been going back to that park along the shoreline of Lake Erie, thinking of all the things you said and . . . I understand now. You were right, and I was wrong. I miss talking with you, Hilda. I miss . . . well, you take care."

And like I've been doing for the last few days, I hang up and get ready to leave. There's shouting and screaming out on the retail floor. This can't be another *robbery*!

"You can't go in there!" shouts store manager Keith Billings.

Something crashes against my office door. I rush to open it and see Keith sprawled on the floor and shaking his head clear. Standing over him is the spitting image of Harry, just younger and thinner. I can tell from the pictures Harry's always proudly shown that it's his son, Claude. He's average height but has his old man's bear-paw hands, horizon-to-horizon shoulders, and powerful legs that look like they could kick mountains into space.

For an instant I'm happy to see him, but he's not happy to see me. His eyes are narrowed, his jaw set, his hands balled into fists, and his chest heaving as he exhales angry snorts.

"I've been down to county lockup to see my stepmom," Claude growls, stepping toward me. "She told me what you did."

"Claude, listen. It was a mistake. I never meant for . . ."

"No!" he snaps, cutting me off. "You listen."

He walks up on me, getting in my face. My Brownfield District reflexes command me to drop him and stomp him, but I inwardly shout them down.

"It's because of you that my dad's in rehab playing the banjo with his lips," Claude accuses.

"Claude, the therapist says that Harry's making a stunning recovery. He'll be back to normal in . . ."

"You'd better watch your back," he shouts, his voice quaking with emotion. "Day and night, twenty-four-seven, you'd better *watch—your—back*!"

He wheels around and pounds out the store, shoving aside an entering customer as he leaves.

FIFTY-FOUR

'm glad this day is over. All I want to do is go home, pour a glass of wine, sit down in the new lounger I recently bought, and lose my thoughts while staring at a burning log in the fireplace.

I leave the store, toss my briefcase onto the Corvette's front passenger seat, and start to get in until I hear a strong but elderly voice calling me. "Mr. Wheeler! Please wait!"

I turn toward the voice and see a plump older woman hurrying up the sidewalk. I close and lock the Corvette's door and walk briskly toward her so she doesn't have to labor so hard getting to me. She's dressed in a flower print dress circa 1985, has her beautiful silver hair pulled back into a bun, and is wearing a pair of thick, black-rimmed cat-eyed glasses that on someone else would look goofy, but on her they look elegant. She's also carrying a rather large thin, flat package wrapped in gift paper.

"I'm Denmark Wheeler," I inform her, getting close. "Is there something I can do for you?"

She smiles and fans herself to cool down while catching her breath. "I was afraid that . . . I'd missed you," she huffs softly.

A shudder bolts through me. I hope this isn't more fallout from all that's been happening. This sucks. How long will it take before the shock waves of what I've done finally dissipate? I've got a miserable feeling that it won't be any time soon.

The beautiful older woman extends her hand. I take it gently, and we shake. "My name is Lucille Herndon," she says.

Lucille? I wonder if this could be the same woman who works for . . .

"I work for Hilda Vaughan," she continues. "I stopped by to thank you and . . ."

I hug her tight. "It's a thrill to finally meet you!" I say. "How's Hilda? Has she gotten my calls?"

Lucille's surprised by my sudden exuberance, and she blushes. "Well, yes, I'm glad to meet you also. Hilda's doing fine, but I don't know about any calls. Please, I don't have much time."

I collect myself and pay attention. "Mr. Wheeler, I just wanted to thank you personally for the kindness you've always shown to my husband, Robert."

"Robert? I don't know anybody named . . ."

"People on the street call him Burned-out Bobby."

I stagger back a step. I'd never have connected Burned-out Bobby with this elegant, dignified heir of Africa's matriarchal excellence. And now that she's mentioned him, I realize that it's been a while since I've seen Burned-out Bobby.

"Mr. Wheeler, are you okay?" Lucille asks, arching one of her eyebrows in concern.

"I, I'm fine. What's that you were saying about Burned-out, ah, I mean, Robert?"

"I wanted to thank you for the kindness you've always shown him."

"But how did you know that I even knew . . ."

"Hilda does pro bono work for the homeless, and she's been helping me look for Robert. He'd been missing for so long but was recently picked up by the police. Hilda ran across his case and put the pieces together, and he's back with people who love him, getting good help. He's often mentioned your name and your kindness."

I shake my head, totally confused. Lucille clears things up. "Some years ago, Robert took our grandson ice fishing. He misjudged the conditions, the ice cracked, and"—she wipes away tears forming in her eyes—"our grandbaby drowned. Robert couldn't live with himself and withdrew. One day I woke up and he was . . . gone."

She glances at her watch. "I've really got to go," she hurriedly says. She pats the large, thin, flat, gift-wrapped package. "Robert wanted you to have this."

"Wait!" I insist. "Where's Bobby now? Is he okay?"

She smiles softly. "He's doing fine. I did some Internet research and discovered a foundation that helps people like Robert. He's getting some of the best counseling and therapy possible at the Cleveland Clinic."

She glances at her watch again. "I really must go. I eat dinner with Robert every day. We have so much catching up to do."

She hands me the package. "Thank you, Mr. Wheeler. And God bless you."

She turns and hurries down to a Ford Explorer that I recognize as belonging to Hilda. She gets in, starts the vehicle, and zips to the parking lot exit, waving at me as she passes. She waits for an opening in the traffic, then takes off.

I stand speechless, watching until the Explorer disappears into the distance. Then I look at the package. What could Bobby possibly have of value to give me? I open the package. It's a simple cardboard sign with a simple message: "God forgives."

I'm finally home. It's gotten so that I really enjoy coming home. It's sane, safe, and my oasis from life's rigors. But that's what I thought when Sierra was here, so maybe I'm still delusional.

I cut off the car, close the garage door, and sit for a few moments in the Corvette before going into the house. The guilt of what I've done and all the people I've hurt weighs me down like an anvil. The reflection that once daily stared back at me from my morning mirror, urging me to take my revenge, is annoyingly silent. Now that people have been hurt and lives turned upside down, I'm left to bear the burden alone.

I go in the house, toss my briefcase onto the kitchen counter, and start a fire in the living room fireplace. I loosen my tie, get my glass of merlot, kick off my shoes, and park my butt in my new lounger. The log crackles. The wind chimes out on the deck tinkle. And I settle into the chair, grateful for the nothingness that rules the moment.

There's a knock on the door. I stay put. Maybe whoever it is will go away. They knock again, and again. I stay put. The knocks continue. This person clearly means for me to answer the door.

I grumble an expletive, creak to my feet, and slouch over to the door. I look to see who it is and nearly drop my glass of wine. It's *Amos Montague*!

"What the hell could he want?" I grouse.

I wait a few moments, pondering whether or not to answer the door for this toad. He knocks again. "Denmark, are you there?" he calls.

Something's different in Amos's tone. There's no sneering, smug, dismissive condescension. It almost sounded like he said my name with . . . respect.

I open the door. "What do you want?" I ask.

"Can I speak with you for a moment?"

"No!"

"Denmark, please. I know things haven't always been good between us, but . . ."

I slam the door and walk away until I hear Amos sobbing. "Please, Denmark," he blubbers. "I don't know where else to go."

"I've got some suggestions," I grumble.

This is a moment I've lived for. I don't know who or what caused this, but they have my gratitude. I've yearned to see this arrogant, high-brow sack of crap reduced to groveling. But I suddenly remember what I said to Samantha about boomerangs. I've already got some whoppers coming my way, and I don't need to add another. So I turn, open the door, and let him inside.

"All right, Amos," I say, closing the door. "What is it? And make it quick."

He snorts and sniffles, wiping his snotty nose with his sleeve. "My, oh my, how the mighty have fallen," I think to myself.

"It's about Yarborough," Amos says, clearing his throat. "They're sending him to jail."

"So! That's what happens to people who commit armed robbery."

His eyes fill with tears. "I can't let that happen, Denmark. He's my son. He won't survive in there. He's not cut out for . . ."

"Do you think anybody else's son is cut out for it?" I counter loudly. "But that probably never mattered until it was *your* son. I'll bet you never even thought about other people's sons who get sent up because their families aren't wealthy or connected enough to *buy* their justice."

I get in Amos's face. "You know what happens to those people's sons?" I growl. "They do their time, even the ones who are innocent. Yarborough's not! He's a crack-head, a thief, and an armed thug, and he's going down!"

Amos grips my arms in desperation. "Please help me!"

"Get off me!" I snap loudly, shoving him away.

He staggers backward and nearly falls onto his rump, but regains his balance. "I've been everywhere," Amos sobs. "Everybody says their hands are tied, that the evidence is too strong, or it's too risky."

His face twists into an expression of anger. His eyes are

glassy and wild, looking at but not seeing me. "They're treating us like common, low-down *ghetto trash!*" he blasts.

His eyes widen with shocked embarrassment as he suddenly remembers whom he's talking to and the place of my "common, low-down" origins.

I shake my head and chuckle bitterly. "I've got news for you, fat boy. They were already treating you like that. The only difference is that *now you know it!*"

"Denmark, please; you know that Blinker guy who's running for City Council. You grew up with him and those cop cousins of his who arrested Yarborough. Won't you speak with them?"

I'll say this much for Amos. He's been doing his homework. "Speak with them and say what?" I demand to know. "Should I tell them that even though you wouldn't invite them to sit down at the same table with you for coffee, you want them to put their careers and necks on the line to save your guilty-as-hell son?"

Amos bawls. I feel like thrashing him for every sneering comment made to me, every smirk when I made an etiquette misstep, every rolling-eyed yawn when I tried to fit in, reinforcing that I'd forever be an unwelcome stranger in his land.

He mutters about loving Yarborough more than himself, failing him as a father, and cursing the system that seems so slanted. I'm tempted to ask him how the allegedly hyper-intelligent "free colored people" of the Montague line managed to miss that detail over the past three centuries. But a more pressing thought intrudes.

Amos is the vice president of marketing for Mid-Cities Insurance Company, the robber barons who are screwing Harry on his medical coverage. This might be a productive encounter after all.

"How badly do you want my help?" I ask.

Amos' eyes widen with hope, and he wrings his hands. "I'll do anything! Just name it!"

I give him the name of Harry Bancroft. Then I explain the needs and that I expect total compliance from Mid-Cities on every test, tool, drug, therapy, device, and anything else Harry will need during his full recovery, for as long as he'll need it.

Amos agrees to everything, including giving me a guarantee that Theodoric Montague will soon be the newest, most ardent supporter of hood politician Blinker Hughes.

FIFTY-FIVE

It's Friday morning, and it's been just over a week since Amos Montague paid me a visit. I'm standing at the kitchen counter, sipping a cup of coffee and reading the morning paper. I'd prefer to sit and read, but I haven't yet replaced the kitchen dinette set that Sierra took during her daylight raid.

A lot has happened since Amos darkened my door. Tinker Hughes is free. Theodoric Montague is Blinker's biggest backer. And Harry's getting all the support he'll ever need from those crooks at Mid-Cities Insurance. If he has the slightest problem, Amos knows that I'll make a phone call that'll have his beloved crack-head son spending the next ten years being some hulking, tattooed convict's girlfriend.

I'm glad this is the last workday of the week. I'd wanted to take off on Monday, catch an airplane, and fly—well, anywhere, just as long as it took me away from the memories, pain, and shame. But I had to be here for those people from Forrester & Company who've been shooting this commercial. That flakey spike-haired artistic consultant has been a giant pain in the neck, whining and having tantrums. This should be the last day we have to deal with that pansy, so I, and the rest of the Henderson Village crew, will grin and bear it.

I glance at the newspaper and re-read one of today's lead articles:

One Cleared, One Caught

. . . in a vindication of the innocence he had maintained all along, former Cleveland police officer Tecumseh "Tinker" Hughes was released when another former officer, Mason Booker, owner-operator of Second Shadow Enterprises, made an unusual and unexpected sworn statement clearing Mr. Hughes of all wrongdoing. Mr. Booker, who years before had given key testimony resulting in the conviction of Mr. Hughes, was immediately arrested and is scheduled for arraignment . . .

Mason's sudden desire to come clean was inspired by a lot of pounding from Stinker and Thinker, who gleefully promised more of the same if he didn't confess. He agreed, and they walloped him anyway. He was a shambling wreck by the time they finished. The latest blow came when he was charged with being an accomplice in the Speed Shift robberies, committing perjury against Tinker Hughes, and taking bribes as a cop—which was how he got the money to start up Second Shadow Enterprises. I keep reading the article:

. . . Tecumseh Hughes had been serving a ten- to twenty-five-year sentence for theft of police evidence, obstruction of justice, and peddling illegal narcotics. He will work as a liaison for the new Chamber of Commerce president, Theodoric Montague. Mr. Montague has come out in strong support of Brownfield District candidate Bernard "Blinker" Hughes, who is running for City Council and is considered an overall favorite to win.

When told that Tecumseh Hughes was a cousin of the candidate, and asked if there was any connection, Mr. Montague deferred, stressing that he hoped to capitalize upon the former police officer's training and knowledge of the penal system to develop strategies for keeping young people free and productive . . .

Mason Booker's been a cunning, ruthless adversary, but he's finally paying for what he did to Tinker—and to *me*! Blinker did as I asked and ordered his inside contacts to make Mason's life miserable, but not kill him. Stinker and Thinker passed the word to their prison guard friends that there's lots of money for anyone who doesn't notice whenever Mason gets beat down.

This should be a total victory for me, but it feels instead like a defeat. Mason might be spending his days caged like an animal, but I'm spending mine caged by the hatred that ruled my heart. He might be afraid to close his eyes at night and sleep, but I'm lying awake, wondering how Sierra and I went so wrong. He might be physically harassed 24/7, but I'm constantly harassed by guilt.

And then there's Hilda. She sent me a polite but frigid e-mail, informing me that she'd turned my case over to a colleague whom she highly recommended. I didn't protest. That would've caused her more anxiety, and the last thing I want to do now is cause Hilda (or anyone else) pain. I even called Blinker, suggesting that he have his enforcers go easy on Mason. He laughed and hung up. So it's beyond me now. Blinker, Stinker, Thinker, and most of all *Tinker* have their own agendas for dealing with Mason. Hilda was right: *I don't have the capacity to reap what I've sown.*

I finish my coffee, rinse out the cup, grab my keys and briefcase, and start for the garage until my eyes sweep over Burned-out Bobby's cardboard sign, hanging on a nearby living room wall. It's been encased in a sturdy but beautiful hardwood frame. The clerk at the picture shop gave me an odd look when I showed him what I wanted framed. Then he shrugged and took my money.

I re-read the sign's message and wonder if it could be true for me. Faces flash before me: Harry, Gordon, Inez, Alice, and *Hilda*. There's also Salome Stevens, Desiree Easton, and June. What was I doing? What was I thinking?

In my rampage to punish the one who'd hurt me, I inflicted needless pain on so many innocent others. I went off on a mad spin, churning up anything and everyone who crossed my path. Everyone became my enemy. Even when it didn't make sense for me to deliver harm, I did it anyway. I knew that the men whose wives I was sleeping with wouldn't appreciate it. That was the point in going after Inez and Alice. I told myself that I wasn't doing anything worse than what had been inflicted upon me through my wife.

That excuse collapses when I consider Salome, Desiree, and June. Neither they nor their husbands hurt me. So I guess this means that I'm more despicable than Mason Booker. He at least loved Sierra and wanted to make a life with her. I was on a self-centered punitive flesh hunt, thirsting for emotional blood any way I could get it. And no matter how long I massage the reasons, invent excuses, or duck the glare of responsibility, it will never alter one riveting fact: *I was wrong!*

I glance again at Burned-out Bobby's sign, consider taking it down, decide against it, then quickly leave.

The day's finally over. The commercial is shot. And it's time to go. I call Hilda, leave her my usual message, then head out to the beach. I pull into a space near where we would meet for our workouts, and my cell phone rings. I check the display. It's June. This has got to stop.

I *will not* start another chain reaction of disaster, especially one involving small children. June's kids possess the modern rare gift of having both parents living under the same roof. If she wants to gamble with her family's stability, she'll have to do it without me. It might already be too late. My intrusion into her life might've already caused irreparable damage. Whether it has or hasn't, no matter how much or little, I'm out!

So I answer the phone. "Hello?"

"Hey, baby," June warmly greets. "Where have you been? I've missed hearing your voice."

"I've been busy."

"You've been too busy to call me?"

"That's right, especially for that."

She gasps. "Denmark, are you all right? You sound really . . ."

"June, your husband Zach's a good man, right?"

She answers in a slightly embarrassed and remorseful voice. "Well, yes, he is. But what does that have to do with you and me?"

"Everything and nothing."

"He doesn't suspect anything, so why . . ."

"Be a good woman and love him back."

"What! How dare you . . ."

I hang up, turn the cell phone off, and hurry out to the beach. I take off my shoes and socks, dig my bare toes deep into the warm sand, and look out across Lake Erie's gently rolling waters. The late afternoon–early evening sky is clothed in wispy gray and light purple. A seagull swoops low and whizzes along the water, skimming the waves so close it looks like it's walking the surface. Clouds drift by, keeping their counsel, and condemnation, to themselves.

There have been so many lives ruined, and so much needless pain. "And it won't go away," I whisper.

An hour goes by, then two. A squirrel skitters down from a tree toward the water, thinks better of it, and skitters back up to safety.

"You're very persistent, aren't you?"

Relief, joy, and fear shoot through me all at once. I turn slowly around to Hilda. She's beautiful, dressed in a soft pink, backless sundress, her upper arms encircled by spiraling silver bracelets, and her hair blowing with soft majesty in the wind.

I fight to keep the strength in my legs while summoning my voice. Mercifully, it obeys. "It's good seeing you, Hilda."

I want to tell her more. I want to tell her that she was right a thousand times over, and that I'm so very sorry. I want to tell her that I never meant to hurt her. I want to tell her that I need a friend.

She walks toward the beach, slips off her sandals, and lets the incoming waves wash up on her feet. I follow a few steps behind, absorbing the sweetness of her presence but keeping my distance so she won't feel crowded.

She walks up the beach just beyond the water's reach and looks toward the horizon. I walk up almost beside her. Minutes pass, and the sun bows in surrender as night slowly stretches its commanding hand across the sky.

"Why have you been calling me?" she finally says.

I look at her, still facing the horizon. "Hilda, I wanted you to know that, from the bottom of my heart, I'm sorry. It might sound hollow, but . . . I didn't mean to hurt anyone. And I'm sorry I disappointed you." I lower my eyes, take a deep breath, and look back up at her. "Please believe me."

She looks at me, her expression soft and peaceful. "I will, if you forgive me."

"Huh? But . . . you haven't done anything . . ."

"Yes, Denmark, I did. Felicity died this morning. Before she passed, she squeezed my hand and said, 'I forgive you.' Right then I realized something. Christ spared and forgave me by grace and mercy even though I was undeserving. So He challenged me to explain how I could deny you the same when it had been given to me so freely."

She turns back to the lake. "So yes, Denmark, I forgive you."

I close my eyes and take a deep cleansing breath. Hilda turns back to the lake. She sits down, pulls her knees up to her chest, and rests her chin on them. Her sandals dangle loosely from her hand. I sit down beside her, not close enough to touch, but closer than before.

"Nothing turned out like I thought it would," I say softly.

She purses her lips and nods. "That's usually the case with revenge."

I exhale a sigh. "Everything's gone, Hilda. And there's nothing I can do to right the wrongs."

"I understand," she says, still gazing at the lake. "We have to press on, Denmark. We can't deconstruct the painful past. The only thing left is to build a better future."

She smiles and takes a deep breath. "Are your eyes open?"

"Yes, Hilda. They are."

"What do you see out there?"

A wave rolls ashore. A gull soars on an updraft. The brisk but gentle wind caresses my face. I glance at Hilda and see a single small cross dangling from her bracelet. I look back out at the lake and say, "I think I see a second chance."

ABOUT THE AUTHOR

FREDDIE LEE JOHNSON III grew up in the Washington, D.C., metro area. He attended Bowie State College, earning a bachelor of science degree in history and teacher education before going on to serve in the United States Marine Corps as a communications-electronics officer and infantry officer with the reserves. He later received master's and doctor's degrees in history at Kent State University. He now lives in Holland, Michigan, and teaches history at Hope College.